THE SOONER THE BETTER

THE SOONER
THE BETTER

Lynda Page

headline

First published in 2007 by
HEADLINE PUBLISHING GROUP

2

Cataloguing in Publication Data is
available from the British Library

978 0 7553 2832 1

Typeset in Stempel by Palimpsest Book Production Limited,
Grangemouth, Stirlingshire

Printed and bound in Great Britain by Antony Rowe Ltd

Headline's policy is to use papers that are natural, renewable and
recyclable products and made from wood grown in sustainable
forests. The logging and manufacturing processes are expected
to conform to the environmental regulations of the country of origin.

HEADLINE PUBLISHING GROUP
A division of Hachette Livre UK Ltd
338 Euston Road
London NW1 3BH

www.headline.co.uk
www.hodderheadline.com

For Diane Allen and all her wonderful staff at
Magna Large Print Books, especially
the exceptional Area Sales Manager, Mark Merrill.

They are a group of very special people,
totally dedicated to bringing the written word
to the visually impaired. I feel so very privileged
to be an honorary member of the 'Magna family'.

CHAPTER ONE

Lives can be shattered in many different ways.

Isabel Jenkins' own life was very cruelly devastated by Lawrence Clayton on July the twenty-third, 1961, at twelve-forty-three.

Izzie had been sitting in the works canteen at the time, sipping a cup of tea while she waited for Lawrence to join her so they could have their lunch together. Her heart had leapt on spotting him weaving his way through the tables towards her and, as usual, in order to quash the gossip over their relationship at work, on arrival he had made a great show of looking around for an empty seat before loudly asking Izzie if she would mind if he joined her.

They had chatted generally throughout their meal until he had pushed his empty plate away and stunned her completely by asking: 'Are you doing anything three weeks on Saturday at three o'clock, Izzie?'

She shook her head. 'I haven't anything planned that I know of. Why?' Then a thought suddenly struck her. After her long wait, fifteen years in total, Lawrence was finally going to ask her to marry him, three weeks on Saturday at three o'clock. She just knew it! The canteen was hardly the place she had thought he'd choose to propose to her, but did it really matter? Excitement flooded her as she held her breath, waiting for him to ask her the question she had been so desperate to hear all these years.

'Well, it's just that if you've nothing better to do, maybe you'd like to come to my wedding?'

This was a very strange proposal, she thought. A beam of utter delight and excitement bathed her face. 'Lawrence, I would love to.'

He looked pleased. 'Oh, that's great. Janet will be pleased to meet you. I've mentioned to her what a good friend you've been to me, helping me with Mother.'

She frowned, bemused. 'Janet?'

'Yes, Janet Spender, my fiancee. The invitation is for the reception afterwards, too. We've not planned a big do because we need all our money to put towards moving to Canada. Oh, I'm so excited about my new job, and life over there sounds so much better, especially for families. Janet wants at least three so she says. We leave to start our new lives a week after the wedding. I'm telling my boss this afternoon. I expect they'll be sorry to lose me.' He scraped back his chair and stood up. 'Well, better get back to work. See you, Izzie.'

Paralysed by shock, unaware that she was spilling the cup of tea she was clutching down her white blouse, Izzie couldn't at first grasp what Lawrence had just told her. He had never so much as hinted in any way that he'd been seeking employment elsewhere, let alone abroad, but far more importantly, he had strongly intimated on many occasions during the past fifteen years they'd been courting – or so she had firmly believed, all that time she had totally and unconditionally loved him – that it was she herself he would make his wife once he was free from the tie to his domineering crippled mother, who had finally, not without a determined struggle, breathed her last two months previously. Since then Izzie had been under the impression – she now realised mistakenly – that Lawrence was only waiting for a decent amount of time to pass before he approached Isabel herself to discuss plans for setting a date.

Izzie had had no idea, not an inkling, that Lawrence was even acquainted with the very pretty Janet, a twenty-three-year-old local government secretary who'd moved into Izzie's street two years previously. But he must have been, and for a considerable period, to be planning his imminent marriage to her. As the man who was breaking her heart was relaying to her all his future plans with another woman, Izzie just managed to keep the fixed smile on her face and express her best wishes for his and Janet's future happiness. Privately, she felt as if her whole being was crumbling, shattering into fragments, acute physical pain gripping her stomach as she foresaw her life ahead without Lawrence.

During his declaration, he had made not a single reference to her own relationship with him nor any comment on her readily apparent shock at the revelation. On finishing his announcement, he hurriedly downed the dregs of his coffee then launched his tall, thin frame off his chair, saying he'd work to see to urgently. She sat staring after him, bewildered and confused, until a colleague jerked her out of her stupor with a warning she would be late back at her desk if she didn't get a move on.

Three weeks later, witnessing the man she had believed she'd spend the rest of her life with declaring his undying love for another woman, was the worst loss she had so far suffered in her life, far more emotionally and physically painful than the loss of both her beloved parents while she was still a teenager, and a few years later the companionship of her best friend Freda who'd moved to Birmingham on her marriage to a squaddie stationed at the Army base in Rothley during his National Service. Izzie had not wanted to attend at all but had forced herself in an effort to stem the gossip over Lawrence's rejection of her. Outwardly she signalled to everyone that she fully approved of this union while secretly she was totally devastated. The tears she had shed during the ceremony were not of happiness for the bride and groom but from sheer misery.

Three months later, despite all her efforts, she was still having extreme difficulty in coming to terms with what had happened, only managing to function on a daily basis with a supreme effort on her part. Privately she believed she'd never recover from this and death was the only thing that would release her from her suffering.

CHAPTER TWO

Sitting at the dining table in the back room of a three-bedroomed palisade terrace house on Harrow Road off the Narborough Road, a busy thoroughfare a short distance from the town centre, Izzie was pushing a well-cooked pork chop around her plate. From the kitchen the disgruntled voice of her sister-in-law, Patricia, was filtering through to her. From the level of it, Izzie was left in no doubt that Pat intended her to overhear just what she was saying.

'It's not that I don't muckle along well enough with Izzie, Arnold, but you promised me when we married that her living with us was only temporary, until she got married herself. That was twelve years ago! Now Lawrence ain't on the scene, it don't look like it's going to happen in the foreseeable future, does it? Well, at all really, 'cos, let's face it, Arnold, your sister's not exactly the catch of the century, is she? I know that's not her fault, yer can't help what yer born with, can yer? But it's not like men are flocking after her, and quite apart from her shortcomings in the looks department, at her age the chance of someone else coming along is pretty slim. Well, unless a widower or divorcée is desperate for a mother for his kids. Our girls will soon be at the age . . . well, they are now really . . . when they'll want a bedroom each and that ain't gonna happen when their spinster aunt is occupying the only other spare. Now you can't say I ain't been patient, Arnold, so what yer gonna do about it?'

As Pat had stated the two women got along together well enough though mostly that was down to Izzie's own easy-going nature. She tolerated Pat's high-handed ways in order to keep harmony between them. She had always been aware, though, that her own residence in the house was a source of irritation to her sister-in-law. Now, however, she felt like an unwelcome intruder in her own home as well as stung by Pat's frank assessment of her looks and desirability.

Izzie heard her brother give a fed-up sigh before he responded to his wife. 'She's got as much right to be living here as we have, Pat. This was our parents' home.'

'But it's not your parents' house any longer. It's your name that's been on the rent book for the last seventeen years.'

'Oh, for God's sake, she's me sister! I'm not chucking me own sister out on the street just to please you.'

'Oh, so yer sister is more important than yer wife?'

'Don't be stupid, Pat. This set up ain't ideal, I grant yer, but until Izzie's ready to leave then we're stuck with it. You know fine well she's not in any position to afford a half-decent place of her own on her wages. And anyway, it's not like she's any trouble, is she?'

'I never said she was but I married you, not you and yer sister.' Pat gave a despondent sigh. 'I've got visions of us all in our old age, sitting round the fire in our bath chairs together.'

'Well, at least that means we won't be stuck just looking at each other,' Arnold quipped, then hurriedly added, 'I didn't mean 'ote by that so don't get the hump.' His tone of voice turned coaxing. 'Look, Pat, this ain't so bad, is it? With our Izzie living here, at least you get a hand with the housework, and she's good at teking the girls off our hands to give us some time to ourselves. You'd miss having all that on tap if she moved into a place of her own. Now, am I getting me dinner or I'll miss the start of the darts match?'

Back in the dining room, Izzie's eight-year-old niece Suzanne, who possessed the alabaster skin of a natural ash blonde but wasn't quite the angel her face declared her to be, was looking at her solemnly.

'I don't mind sharing me bedroom with our Sally, Aunty Izzie.'

'*I* mind sharing with *her*,' her seven-year-old sister piped up, flashing Suzy a disparaging look. 'She makes me tidy up all the time, and she never makes the bed like Mam thinks she does 'cos it's me that always does it so we don't get our pocket money stopped.'

Glaring at her menacingly, Suzy shot back, 'I give yer a black jack out of me poke of sweets as payment.'

The tight carrot curls sprouting from Sally's head bounced like springs as she shook her head from side to side, her pretty face, with its splattering of freckles over her snub nose, screwed up knowingly. 'Only 'cos you don't like black jacks, our Suzy.' She fixed her startlingly blue eyes on her aunt, looking worried. 'You ain't leaving, Aunty Izzie, are yer? I don't want yer to. I'd miss yer. Who'd knit me dolly her clothes, or do jigsaws with me, or take us to the park on a Sunday afternoon while me mam and dad have their rest?'

Izzie stared distractedly at both her much-loved nieces. She didn't want to leave either. This was the only home she had ever known, its familiar four walls having seen her through every phase of her life so far from the minute she'd been born, one bitter-cold winter's night in 1920 in her parents' ancient brass bed. The snow had been so deep a neighbour had had to help with the delivery. Mercifully there had been no complications as the doctor hadn't been able to get through until after she'd struggled her way into the outside world. In time, in the privacy of her own bedroom, Izzie had mourned the loss of her parents and then the departure of her best friend for pastures new; there, too, she had spent hour upon hour envisaging her future as Lawrence's wife and all that it entailed. And recently it'd become her only sanctuary, the place where she could let the façade drop and allow herself to wallow in misery over the loss of him and their future together.

Isabel gave a deep sigh. It wasn't right, though, was it, that at thirty-five years old she should still be living with her brother and his family? The harsh-sounding label 'spinster of the parish' could legitimately be attached to her. As unkind as Pat's words were, Izzie knew they held more than a hint of truth. She had long ago stopped resenting Mother Nature for passing her by when she'd been dishing out the type of attractive features that turned men's heads, and accepted what she'd been given. Her face was round, cheeks sporting the rosy glow usually featured in farmers' wives. She had small hazel eyes with well-defined dark eyebrows sitting above a broad nose and generous mouth. Her thatch of dark brown unruly curls seemed to possess a mind of their own. She had no choice but to keep them in a short manageable bob unless she wanted to resemble an overgrown bush. On a much taller woman her figure might have been arresting, but at five foot four and size 16 she felt small and dumpy. She'd tried dieting and seeking out flattering clothes, but when she endeavoured to dress in the latest tight-waisted fashions she looked ridiculous. All things considered, Pat was probably right. Husband material for the likes of her would not be easy to find.

A momentary sadness filled Izzie's eyes. She had never harboured great ambitions for herself. Never hankered after becoming a famous actress, ballerina, or marrying a million-aire. All she had ever wanted for herself was a good man to love who loved her back. That and a houseful of children, with enough money coming in to care for them properly. She didn't think that such an unreasonable aspiration in the big scheme of things, but as matters stood it seemed it was going to remain unfulfilled.

Even if she wanted to depart this house for a place of her own, her brother was right: on her wages as a clerk in the post room of Jones and Shipman Engineering she'd be hard pressed to fund the equivalent lifestyle. At present she had a roof over her head, three square meals a day, and a little money spare each week for personal items and leisure pursuits such as taking her nieces to a Saturday matinee and treating them to an ice cream. She had always been careful too to add a few shillings weekly to her Post Office savings which over the years had built up to a nice nest egg of four hundred pounds. She had planned to discuss the best use of that with Lawrence on their marriage. But one thing that hadn't been mentioned in Pat's tirade and her brother's response was that her own weekly housekeeping contri-bution paid for extras they wouldn't otherwise be able to afford, so it wasn't only her help with the housework and babysitting lzzie would be missed for if she left.

Despite the inner turmoil their mother's words had caused her, she smiled tenderly at the young girls. 'Well, I'll have to leave someday, same as you both will when you get married.'

'I ain't never getting married,' scoffed Suzy, pulling a disgusted face. 'I hate boys. They're nasty and they smell!'

lzzie laughed. 'You'll change your mind when you get older, my darling.'

'I won't,' said Suzy resolutely. 'When I'm older I'm going to live in a castle in the country with servants looking after me and me children. And I ain't having no man moaning at me 'cos his dinner ain't ready, like me dad does me mam.'

'But you ain't getting married to Uncle Lawrence no more, Aunty lzzie, so you won't be leaving to get married,' put in Sally. 'Why ain't you and Uncle Lawrence getting married no more?'

Isabel swallowed hard, wincing as a surge of raw pain shot through her. She was constantly reminded by conversations such as this of all she had lost.

'Well . . . er . . . we never really had definite plans to get married, sweetie. Me and Uncle Lawrence were only good friends, that's all.'

The child seemed confused. 'But I've heard Mam telling Gran lots of times that she couldn't wait for the old dragon to kick the bucket so you and Uncle Lawrence could get on with sorting yer wedding date out. I ain't stupid, I know our mam was talking about Uncle Lawrence's 'cos Suzy calls our mam "the old dragon" too when she's had a go at us,' she added matter-of-factly.

Izzie stared at her blankly. Children should never be under-estimated, it seemed. Especially her nieces. 'Well, I shouldn't let your mother hear what you call her behind her back, either of you,' she said sternly.

'Why not?' Sally asked seriously. 'She's called me a dozy cow lots of times when she's mad with me.'

'And me a daft bugger and a brainless clot,' piped up Suzy. She fixed her eyes on her aunt. 'I've heard her call you . . .'

But Izzie was not going to find out what her sister-in-law nicknamed her behind her back at that moment in time as Suzy was stopped short by her father entering the room. Putting down his plate of food on the table, he settled his large frame in his carver chair, looking at his daughters enquiringly. 'What's wrong with yer dinners?' he demanded.

'N'ote, Dad,' they said in unison, hastily beginning to shovel food into their mouths.

He then looked at Izzie questioningly. 'Not hungry?'

She'd lost her appetite three months ago and it still hadn't returned. She'd eaten just enough to function without the risk of falling ill, and there was also the fact that if she didn't tackle what Pat had prepared then she would take offence and not hold back in showing her displeasure.

Before she could answer Pat herself arrived and, noticing the untouched food on Izzie's plate, snapped at her: 'Summat wrong with it?'

Despite what had just transpired and how upset she was feeling, Izzie smiled at her warmly. 'No, Pat. It looks delicious. I was waiting for you and Arnold to join us.'

'Oh, well, we're here now so tuck in.' Sitting down at her own place at the table Pat fixed her eyes on her daughters. 'And how many times do I have to tell you gels to stop slouching or you'll be round-shouldered and have a hump on yer back when you're older? *Then* you'll be sorry for not doing as I tell yer.'

Both girls, and Izzie, immediately sat ramrod-straight.

As she ate, despite joining in with the conversation when it was expected of her, Izzie's mind was far from any thought of food. She acknowledged that she could no longer justify living with her brother and his wife. She wasn't waiting any longer for her intended's mother to set him free. She no longer had an intended nor was there the least possibility of a substitute lurking in the background. And, in fairness, her sister-in-law had waited long enough to become sole mistress of her own home. Later on, in the privacy of her bedroom, Isabel would start giving the problem some serious thought.

With the evening meal cleared and no other household chores

needing her attention, Izzie was about to make her way upstairs but was stopped by the arrival of Pat's mother who came barging through the back door.

A thick-set, square-faced woman of sixty-seven, Edna Peel harboured a deep-seated grudge against life for taking her husband away from her through an accident at work not long after their only child had been born. Despite loving her daughter and struggling to do her best to raise her on a paltry income from her job in a local greengrocer's, on Pat's marriage Edna had grown increasingly resentful. Pat had got what Edna herself had been denied, a husband to help her shoulder life's burdens. It had never occurred to Edna that a replacement for her dead spouse might have presented itself several times over if she had just showed her fellow human beings a softer side to her nature. But unfortunately for her she was far too set in her ways now, and if anything her cantankerousness was getting worse instead of improving.

Stamping her zipper-booted feet on the mat just inside the back door as she unbuttoned her shabby black winter coat, she grumbled, 'Them kids playing football in the street have no respect for their elders. When their ball just missed knocking me hat off, I saw them all giggling. It's the parents I blame. No discipline these days. If I'd been disrespectful in any way to my elders when I was a child, me dad would have knocked the living daylights out of me.'

As she untied her apron, Izzie looked at the new arrival in surprise. 'Oh, but I've always found them a good bunch of kids, Mrs Peel. I'm surprised to hear they never apologised to you for the accident.'

'Accident be damned! That big lad aimed the ball at me on purpose. He's taken umbrage with me for clipping his ear that time he almost rode me over in his cart a few years back. Anyway, "Sorry, missus" with a smirk on yer face doesn't constitute a proper apology,' she snapped. 'If I could have got hold of that ball I'd have confiscated it and let them see how they liked *that*.'

Just then Pat appeared in the doorway. 'I thought I heard voices. Hello, Mother.'

Izzie had never been in any doubt that Pat found her mother's company as trying as she did and was therefore taken aback to note that for once Pat actually looked pleased by Edna's arrival tonight, something Izzie had never witnessed before in all the time she had known the pair.

'Why don't you go through for a warm by the fire?' Pat was saying to her. She addressed Izzie then. 'You don't mind keeping Mam company while I mash us all a pot of tea, do you?'

Her sister-in-law was looking at her as though to say, Well, it's not like you have anything more important to do with your spare time, such as getting yourself ready for a date with a man. Keeping my mother amused while I'm occupied is no skin off your nose, is it? Izzie wondered if Pat would so willingly commandeer her time if she had known that Izzie had been intending to put it to good use, working out a plan to leave this house. Instead she said graciously, 'No, of course I don't. Let me hang your coat up for you, Mrs Peel.'

If there was one thing that got Suzy and Sally performing a disappearing act, it was the prospect of having to spend time in their dour grandmother's company. Even worse was having to give her the expected kiss on her whiskered lips, her breath foul-smelling from the several daily doses of California Figs she took to keep her bowels regular. As soon as Edna's voice alerted them to her arrival, Sally slapped shut her Famous Five mystery novel even though she was at the most exciting part where the culprit was about to be revealed, something she had been desperate to know since she'd started the book. Suzy – midway through her favourite cut-out section in *Bunty*, a cute ballerina with several tutus – dropped the scissors and both girls made a double quick escape to their bedroom.

Settling herself in Arnold's armchair as she felt entitled to do as the matriarch of this family, Edna commanded Izzie: 'Give the gels a shout and tell 'em I'm here so they can come and give me a kiss.' She then looked with disapproval at the personal belongings they had abandoned in their haste to escape her. 'Our Pat's far too easy on them gels. She'd never have dreamed of leaving a mess like this behind her for me to clear up. She knew what she'd get in response.'

It would never occur to Edna that her grandchildren much preferred a ticking off from their mother, or even a clout around the ear, to having to endure her company if they could avoid it. 'They were both tired tonight, Mrs Peel, and I told them I'd clear up after them,' said Izzie by way of excusing them as she gathered together the abandoned items, piling them neatly on the table for her to take up to them later.

The older woman pulled a tight face. 'Well, if you want to be responsible for making the pair of them lazy, then that's your choice. You'll only realise what an idiot yer've been when the pair of them have you fetching and carrying everything for them at the snap of their fingers.' And she added disapprovingly, 'Which already seems to be the case.'

Wondering how long it would be before she could make her own escape, Izzie settled herself down on the shabby brown and cream moquette-covered settee which had been second-hand when Pat had insisted Arnold bought it, along with several other items, just before their marriage. She had flatly refused to move in unless the old-fashioned furniture that had belonged to his parents was disposed of, even though that furniture was of far better quality, the horsehair sofa far more comfortable than its replacement, and without even asking Izzie what her feelings were on the matter.

Settling her eyes on Izzie fixedly, Edna asked her, 'So what now, then?'

She frowned quizzically. 'Sorry, Mrs Peel?'

'For you, what now?' Adjusting the black felt hat that covered sparse grey hair scraped back in a tight bun, the fake cherries that had once adorned it long gone, she then leaned over to pull up the hem of her well-worn black dress to straighten one wrinkled beige wool stocking before leaning back in her chair, a knowing look on her face. 'Well, yer've had plenty of time to get over the fact that man you was associating yerself with had no intention whatsoever of marrying you. Mind you, I could have told yer that years ago. He wasn't a bad-looking chap – it were obvious to me he wouldn't have settled for someone like you. He was just after someone to

13

help with the burden of his mother's care until she popped her clogs and left him free to find a good-looker. He must have been romancing that pretty young secretary behind your back for a long time, the signs must have been staring you in the face, but they do say there's no fool like an old fool, don't they? Still, I'm sure you won't be so easily taken in again by a man's patter.'

During the last three months, Izzie had had plenty of time to come to the extremely painful conclusion that Lawrence's intentions towards her had never been honourable. Their 'romance' had been largely conducted in her own imaginings.

She had thought nothing of it at first when the tall, good-looking, newly qualified draftsman had asked her permission to sit beside her in the works canteen one lunchtime. She had been twenty at the time, resigned to the fact that she was not conventionally pretty. Regardless of the fact that she had never had a boyfriend, she still lived in hope that there was a man somewhere who would find her attractive. She'd been well aware that the man joining her was unlikely to be that type but it still did not stop Izzie herself from secretly fancying him. How their polite conversation progressed from the abysmal weather they were suffering to her sympathising with him over the burdens he was facing while caring for his widowed crippled mother she was never able to fathom, but before they parted to return to their own departments, Isabel had accepted an invitation to have tea with Lawrence and his mother the following Sunday afternoon.

In her naivety, Izzie assumed it was a date. Consumed with feverish excitement, she had dressed very carefully and on arriving at the address he had given her, desperately hoping her highly nervous state wasn't showing, had been overwhelmed to be enthusiastically received by Lawrence himself. It became immediately apparent to Izzie that Sybil Clayton was a very difficult woman. She knew exactly how to prick her son's conscience with her own disability and never missed an opportunity to do so. Izzie therefore accepted without question Lawrence's word when he told her that to go out of an evening leaving his mother on her own was not an option for him. She was well and truly smitten with him by now and just being in his company thrilled her beyond words. If that meant his mother was present also, then so be it. If it also meant Izzie read to her, helped her with her jigsaws, held wool while she wound it for her knitting, stayed with her alone twice or sometimes three times a week to give Lawrence chance to spend a few hours with his friends, then so be it too. She had accepted that he wanted them to keep their relationship to themselves for fear of gossip at work getting back to his mother, and the problems this would cause. When Lawrence continually told Izzie over the years that she would make a wonderful wife, she had assumed he had meant she would make a wonderful wife for him. When he frequently told her of his plan to sell this house and buy a family home with a garden for children to play in, once the inevitable happened, from the way he would look at her, hold and caress her hands, plus the way he kissed her goodnight on her departure, she had believed they would one day share that house and family.

At the time Izzie met the Claytons, no one witnessing Sybil Clayton's fragility or listening to her constant complaints over her poor health, her martyrdom to crippling pain, would have predicted she would last for another fifteen years. When she finally gave up her battle for existence, Izzie readily accepted that Lawrence was coping with his loss by clearing out his mother's home and attending to repairs on it ready for its sale. Despite being sad at her demise, Izzie was guiltily relieved that the old woman could no longer blight their lives. All they had to do now was observe a decent period of mourning and then she and Lawrence would be free to start their new life together. Or so she'd believed.

Three months later the memory left her feeling foolish and humiliated.

'Well, we all make mistakes, Mrs Peel,' she said softly.

'Mistakes have to be paid for. Fifteen years' hard labour in your case, ducky. From what you've let slip over the years it seems to me that Mrs Clayton was a selfish besom, but she weren't dottled enough in her brain not to seize her chance and treat you as an unpaid lackey. Worse still, you let her. Anyway, I don't need to ask what plans yer making for yerself now.'

'You don't?'

'Well, it's obvious. You'll be wanting a place of yer own.' Izzie was far too polite to point out to Edna that her living arrangements were no one else's business. But regardless of whether Izzie wanted to respond or not, Edna wasn't going to allow her the luxury of choice. 'Must be hard on yer, taking a back seat to my daughter, her being mistress of this house as she's married to yer elder brother. Every woman likes to be in charge of her own kitchen, don't she, whether she's married or not? And it must be wearing for you having those two little perishers constantly taking advantage of yer as you obviously let them do.' She flashed a glance at her grandchildren's abandoned possessions. 'You'll be after a nice little furnished flat for yerself.' Then she sucked in her cheeks. 'Mind you, it's all well and good wanting something, but affording it is another thing. You can't be getting that much as a post room clerk . . . you'll be hard pressed to fund a nice furnished flat *and* afford all the bills and incidentals, so it's a bedsitter you'll have to settle for. Yer gonna find that cramped after living all yer life in a house, even though you've shared it with others.' She paused, then clapped her hands together as a thought struck her. 'Well, I be damned if I ain't got the answer to your problem.'

Izzie frowned. 'You have?'

'You can move in with me. You can have Pat's old room.'

Izzie's jaw dropped open. Spending time in Edna's company when she visited was purgatory enough; the idea of living under the same roof as her filled Izzie with absolute dread. She blustered, 'Oh, but . . . but . . . I couldn't impose on . . .'

'Nonsense,' the older woman interjected. 'It's the ideal solution. We'll be company for each other. I'll get the room aired out and you can move in at the weekend. We'll discuss the money side after yer settled in. Oi, Pat, come in here a minute. We've some news to tell yer!'

Before her mother had said the last word Pat was in the room, looking at them both expectantly. 'Oh, and what news is that then?'

Struck speechless by the hole she found herself in, her mind whirling desperately for a way out, Izzie automatically turned to acknowledge Pat's arrival in the room. What she saw in her sister-in-law's eyes had her jaw dropping again. It was the glint of triumph. Immediately Izzie knew that Pat didn't need to be told this news. She already knew it. Izzie suddenly saw it all. This whole situation had been engineered between Pat and her mother. A two-act play in essence. The conversation overheard between her brother and Pat had been the opening act, and the one just now, between Edna and Izzie herself, the finale. Was Pat so desperate to have her sister-in-law's residence in this house terminated that she was willing to foist her off on her own mother, the woman who she herself was always glad to see the back of whenever their paths crossed? Pat herself certainly wouldn't under any circumstances move back in with her should the situation ever arise or agree to have her live with her, something she had made very plain to her mother from the outset of her marriage to Arnold, just in case her thoughts should veer in that direction.

It was very apparent that Izzie was not going to be allowed any chance at all to avoid her removal from this house to Edna's, as Pat was already busy making plans for it.

'I'll get the gels to call in the corner shop on their way home from school tomorrow for some empty boxes for you to pack your stuff in,' she was saying to Izzie. 'We'll all help carry it round on Saturday. I'll get some paint, too, and as soon as you've gone I'll get Arnold to give your room a freshen up so our Suzy can move in. Be good for the gels to have their own rooms. Might stop 'em squabbling so much. Well, I can live in hope at any rate. Now, in honour of the occasion I'm going to break open a packet of Garibaldi biscuits to have with our tea.'

As she hurried from the room, a feeling of doom descended on Izzie.

*   *   *

17

When Arnold was informed of his sister's impending departure he was too relieved that he would no longer have his wife's griping to contend with to spare any thought at all for whether Izzie was happy with her move to Edna Peel's.

CHAPTER THREE

None too gently, Marjorie Evans replaced the telephone receiver in its cradle, rose from behind her desk and marched over to the Xerox machine where Izzie was in the process of copying a memorandum of next year's bank holidays several hundred times to be distributed around the workforce on the factory floor. An ex-Post Office employee, strict but fair, forty-five-year-old Marjorie prided herself on running an efficient post room. Nothing upset her more than when a complaint was made against her domain, no matter how minor.

Arriving by Izzie, face tight under her blonde perm, she said, 'Isabel, stop what you're doing for a moment. I need a word.' As soon as she had Izzie's attention she launched in. 'I couldn't wish for a better assistant than you, Isabel. In all the five years I've headed this department you've never given me cause to complain about your work, you're the most conscientious person I have, but this morning I've had two telephone calls from departments complaining about other post being mixed in with theirs. They've had to divert their own staff to deliver it to the correct department.'

Izzie's face dropped. She was mortified. 'Oh! I'm so sorry, Mrs Evans. I'll apologise to the managers of those departments and promise it won't happen again.'

Looking suitably satisfied with this response, Marjorie made to depart but hesitated for a moment before turning back to look at Izzie in concern. 'I have noticed you haven't been yourself for a while now, two or three months in fact. You're not a forceful person by any stretch of the imagination but now you've really gone into your shell, so to speak. This morning when you arrived for work you had such a miserable look on your face that my first thought was a close family member had died, then I realised you wouldn't have turned up for work if that was the case. I think you know me well enough by now to understand that unless my help is specifically asked for, I don't make a habit of prying into other people's private lives. What goes on outside of work is their business, so long as it doesn't affect their work. But judging by your unusual reserve of late, along with the complaints I've received this morning, something is not right with you, Isabel. Because it's bad enough to affect your work, I feel it my duty as your superior to ask if I can offer my assistance in any way?'

The only confidante Izzie had ever felt comfortable with, and trusted enough to unburden herself of her innermost secrets and problems, had been her best friend Freda. Since her marriage and departure, Izzie had coped with life's ups and downs by herself. She got on well enough with Marjorie, felt herself very lucky to have a pleasant-natured woman as her superior compared to some of the tartars that worked here, but allowing her work colleague into her private life was something she didn't feel comfortable with. Besides, Izzie was aware that the reason for this show of concern was an attempt to safeguard Marjorie's department's standards before a far more serious mistake was made.

How she deeply wished, though, that Marjorie could do something to ease her plight. But unless she could miraculously take away the pain of Lawrence's desertion and urgently do something about Izzie's new living arrangements, there was no point in confiding in her. The only one who could deal with these problems was Isabel herself. What she must do now, though, was somehow push her private affairs to the back of her mind during working hours as any more mistakes could result in her finding herself looking for another job.

'I appreciate your offer, Mrs Evans, but it's nothing, really. I've just been feeling a bit under the weather, that's all. I didn't realise my work was being affected. I am sorry for that and promise I'll make sure it doesn't happen again.'

Marjorie had always felt herself fortunate to have inherited Izzie as her chief clerk. She was reliable and conscientious and did not take up any time other than on work-related issues, leaving Marjorie free to concentrate her efforts on running the department and keeping an alert eye on the post room junior who, despite showing great future promise, needed constant training and attention and advice, plus constant support in the personal problems she brought upon herself, mainly through her disastrous choice of boyfriends, and didn't seem to take the hint about not bringing her problems into the workplace. Plus there was the fact that Marjorie had her own fair share of family upsets instigated by three very pretty teenage daughters, football-mad husband with a tendency to be very vocal after a few pints on a Saturday night, and an extended family to cope with. She was therefore relieved that her offer to take yet more on board wasn't going to be taken up.

Marjorie glanced up at the clock on the wall. 'It's just on your lunchtime, Isabel, so get yourself off now and finish doing that copying when you get back.' She made to depart for her own desk when a question she'd always wanted to ask flashed into her mind.

'Isabel, I've often wondered why you didn't apply for my job yourself when it became vacant on Mr Holt's retirement. I mean, you were the obvious prime candidate, having worked here from school and knowing all the ins and outs of operating this post room. You must have realised you would stand a good chance of getting it?'

Izzie hadn't applied because at the time she had been under the impression that she was on the verge of becoming a married woman and had felt strongly that her main priority lay in caring for her future husband. If only she had been able to see into the future she would not have hesitated to apply. She would then have had more income at her disposal to fund a decent place of her own, not the seedy bed-sitter that was about all she could stretch to as matters stood – once she had found a way to make her departure from under Edna Peel's roof without causing offence to her or her daughter and being responsible for a family rift.

Conscious that Marjorie Evans could possibly be fishing to confirm that Isabel was not angling after her job now, she chose her response carefully. 'I was happy with the position I had then and I still am, Mrs Evans. I didn't want the responsibility and I'm still of that mind.'

She seemed satisfied by Izzie's answer. 'Well, yes, I can see your reasoning in that supervising any department, especially a busy one like this in such a large company, does tend to come with its share of sleepless nights. Other departments see ours as the least important in the company, but where would they all be without us, Isabel, just tell me that?'

The four women Izzie was sitting with in the canteen while she ate her cheese and onion sandwich were chatting animatedly about their weekend activities. All around Izzie's age, all having worked for the company since leaving school, three of them were now happily married with growing children. They'd already had a good gripe to the others about how time-consuming it was having a family to care for, all the chores it involved, and now it was Nita Adams' turn. An attractive thirty-five-year-old divorcee and mother of two, whose household chores were not high on her list of priorities, she was moaning about her current boyfriend.

'I'd parked the kids on me mother and thought I was in for a good Saturday night with Harry, a session down the pub followed by one in bed. What I got was a night in by the telly with a couple of bottles from the offy and a packet of salt and vinegar crisps. And as soon as we got into bed he fell asleep! When I tackled him next morning he said he was tired from working hard all week. He's an account clerk, for Christ's sake! How can he be tired from sitting on his fat arse all week? I work hard as a typist *and* have a house and kids to look after, but I ain't tired enough not to want a bit of fun at the weekend. He was never tired all the time he was getting his feet under me table. My ex-husband had more life about him than Harry's got, and I got rid of *him* because he was a boring old fart. My old granddad of eighty-eight has more life in him! Well, I'll give Harry the benefit of the doubt for a bit longer, but if things don't improve then he's going the same way me old man did.'

She fixed her attention on Izzie. 'I don't suppose it's any good asking if you did anything exciting at the weekend, gel? I expect the most exciting thing you got up to was teking yer nieces to the park on Sunday afternoon.'

'If that's how Izzie wants to spend her Sunday afternoons then that's her choice,' said Pauline Stone in her defence. 'I wish my sister would take my two gels off me hands on a Sunday afternoon and give me a bit of peace and quiet, but it'd never enter her head.'

'Well, I think Izzie's got her eye on the park keeper meself and that's why she's so obliging,' Nita quipped. 'I have to say, I always had an inkling there was something going on between you and that bloke that worked in the design department, Izzie. Well, you used to sit with him most lunchtimes. But then I realised I was wrong when he got married and left to emigrate to Canada.' She pulled a face. 'If I was to emigrate, I wouldn't plump for Canada. Too bloody cold for my liking. Australia would be my choice. I fancy the idea of having Christmas on the beach with all those hunky, tanned, half-naked men prancing round me.'

'I tried to talk my old man into emigrating to Australia a few years back,' said Angie Bradley, a wistful tone in her voice. 'He wouldn't even consider it, though. Said he had no intention of being buried anywhere but in the soil of the country he was born in.'

'Your old man sounds as boring as my ex,' said Nita dryly, then looked at Izzie enquiringly. 'Have you ever heard how that chap that went off to Canada is getting on?'

Izzie inwardly groaned. Was she never going to be allowed to forget Lawrence? She wondered what the other women would think if they knew that for fifteen years she had been so besotted with him she had blindly allowed him to dupe her into becoming an unpaid skivvy, leaving him free to pursue his own social life? She didn't need to guess, she knew. They would think her stupid, and quite rightly so.

She responded hurriedly, 'No, and I don't expect to.' Not wanting her workmates to see this conversation had struck a raw nerve with her, for fear they would probe further and discover her shameful secret somehow, she picked up her empty lunch box, saying, 'I'd best get back. I've urgent work to finish

23

for the personnel department. I'll see you all at lunchtime tomorrow if you're eating in the canteen.'

At just before six that evening Isabel stood before the back door of her new abode and took a deep breath to steel herself. Living under Edna's roof was already proving to be a trial. It had been late on Saturday evening by the time all her belongings had been boxed up and carried round there. As soon as the family had departed, Edna had made it very apparent to Izzie that, regardless of the fact that she would be paying her way here, this was *her* house and Edna made the decisions about what went on inside it.

The room that had been Pat's bedroom up until her marriage was small, facing the drab yard and the backs of dilapidated terraced houses. The decorative order of the rest of the house was poor but this room, having been left unused for so long, had a dreadful air of neglect about it. The once white paintwork was now a dingy grey and was flaking in parts, and the once bright blue forget-me-not wallpaper was faded and showed numerous damp patches. Izzie had only to look at the bed to know it would be far from comfortable. No matter how hard she tried, she knew immediately she stepped into the room that it would never feel homely to her, a place of sanctuary, unlike her old room. When she suggested to Edna that she should move the bed and wardrobe around to make more use of the space, the look she'd received back was more than enough to tell her that such suggestions were not appreciated. Where Edna had placed her furniture was where she liked it and where it would stay.

The meals Izzie had received from Edna were not the filling kind that Pat had produced, there hadn't been enough on the plate for that, but then Izzie had appreciated that no money for her keep had been settled upon or exchanged before the shops shut for the weekend and therefore Edna would not have had the finances to cater for two and was splitting her own supplies. They had now settled that Isabel would pay three pounds a week, the same as she had handed over to her brother and his wife, which she felt was fair enough even if the accommodation could not compare to what she had left behind. Sunday had been

24

spent settling properly into her room and getting organised for work the next morning though this had been regularly interrupted by Edna's requests for help with menial chores the older woman was more than capable of tackling herself, and had done before Izzie's arrival.

Only a day into her new lodgings, already Izzie was sorely missing being part of a family and all that it entailed. She knew without a doubt she had a lot of adjusting still to do.

As soon as she entered the kitchen Edna pounced on her.

In an accusing voice she said, 'You didn't take the list and the money when you left this morning.'

As she was stripping off her coat, Izzie stood looking at her, non-plussed. 'Sorry, Mrs Peel. List? What list?'

'The one I made you last night for tonight's dinner. Well, I can't be expected to carry groceries for the two of us, and it's no trouble to you to get what we need in yer lunch hour, is it? I'll come with you for the weekend shop on a Saturday afternoon, though, up the town. Anyway, the shops will be shut now but luckily I've a few spuds and a couple of eggs in the pantry so we'll have to make do with egg and chips tonight. I was so looking forward to liver and onions. Oh, well, we'll have it tomorrow instead.'

Izzie was looking at her in astonishment. Edna was expecting her to use her lunch hour to do their daily shopping! But by the time she'd reached the shops, a good walk from her workplace, queued for their requirements and then returned to work, there'd be no time left for her to eat her lunch. Edna was in fact quite capable of going to the shops herself, the same as she had done before Izzie's arrival, and more than physically capable of carrying the extra supplies for her lodger. Izzie didn't mind helping Edna with the weekend shop as she had often accompanied Pat but she had a strong suspicion that this meant she would be trailing after her landlady carrying the bags while she chose what she wanted, giving Izzie no opportunity to browse the shops she wanted to herself.

But Edna wasn't going to allow her to argue the toss, she was too busy issuing instructions. 'You peel the spuds while I get the pan on to heat and set the table.'

The few potatoes turned out to be two medium-sized ones, producing a handful of chips each, the eggs were small and there was no bread as Izzie hadn't done the shopping. Edna droned on throughout their meal about matters most people wouldn't consider important, and should Izzie even have wanted to make any contribution to the conversation or strike up a topic of her own, Edna did not draw breath to allow her to do so. The thought of spending an evening in her company did not appeal so as soon as the meal was cleared away Izzie planned to make her escape to the privacy of her bedroom to listen to her radio. But she had reckoned without the plans that Edna had already made for them. They were expected at her neighbour Florrie's so Edna could introduce the new lodger to her.

Wheelchair-bound Florence Liddle, a tiny, skeletal woman, sat looking at Izzie with deep interest. 'It's lovely to meet you, dear,' she twittered in a reedy voice. 'Edna's told me all about you, how good you are with us older people. She said you helped to look after a friend's crippled mother. Not many people would offer to help us older ones out these days ... too busy getting on with their own lives. The home help comes in every day to do me cleaning and get me shopping but she never gets the right things. I was so pleased when Edna said you'd get mine for me when you was shopping for yer own. I'll have my list and money ready for you tomorrow. You can collect it before you go to work tomorrow morning. Since my husband died I've hardly left this house. No one to push my wheelchair, you see, me never having been blessed with family, so you can't imagine how excited I was when Edna told me you was moving in with her. She said you'd be happy to offer your services to take me to visit my husband's grave whenever I wanted to go. I'd like to tomorrow as it's the fifth anniversary of his death and due to my predica- ment I haven't been able to visit since his burial. I do appreciate you work so early-evening would be better than nothing. You are sure yer don't mind, dear?'

'Of course she doesn't mind, Florrie,' piped up Edna. 'She was happy to help look after her friend's mother, and I'm family. As my friend you're family too, Florrie.'

Izzie did mind her spare time being commandeered like this without the courtesy of being asked first. She might be Edna's lodger but that didn't give her licence to take over Izzie's life. She would speak to her as soon as they returned home.

Back inside the kitchen at Edna's, Izzie said to her, 'Mrs Peel, I wish you'd asked me first before volunteering my services.'

Edna looked at her, surprised. 'Well, how could I as you wasn't there at the time? Why, had you got something planned for tomorrow night?'

'Well, no, but . . .'

'Well, no harm done then. Florrie's so looking forward to visiting her husband's grave, and I'm coming too. Oh, by the way, the community centre are taking us all out for the day to Belvoir Castle. It's three weeks on Sunday and I put your name down as a chaperone.'

She'd done what! 'Oh, but weather permitting I take Suzy and Sally to the park, as you know, Mrs Peel.'

'They won't mind giving up a Sunday so their gran can have a day out. Besides, if you let us down then the whole coach trip can't go as we were short of a volunteer to accompany us.' She looked at Izzie reproachfully. 'I'll tell the organisers then, shall I, it'll have to be called off 'cos you have to take your nieces to the park?' Edna knew her emotional blackmail had worked by the resigned expression that filled Izzie's face. 'Good, that's settled then. Now, I'm ready for me cocoa. Make sure the milk is properly boiled, I like it nice and hot. Oh, and by the way, when we went to bed last night I couldn't get off to sleep. I could hear your radio through the walls.'

Izzie stared after Edna as she shuffled off into the back room to settle herself in her armchair and await her cocoa. She knew that these parting words were a warning not to play her radio at night. Edna retired at nine o'clock and had made it obvious to Izzie that she expected her to do the same. But she hadn't been ready to settle down for the night at that early hour. Conscious that Edna was in the room next to hers, she had respectfully kept the radio on low as background music while she read. She could hardly hear it herself, let alone it being loud enough to keep Edna from getting off to sleep in the room next door. She must only have been guessing Izzie had had the radio on and this complaint was by way of conveying that Izzie was a guest in her home and her rules were to be abided by.

Isabel sighed. Her nature dictated she be considerate to others, adapt herself to whatever surroundings she found herself in, but living under Edna's stringent house rules, her whole life being commandeered in any way her landlady felt fit, was going to prove too much for her. Izzie was aware that Edna felt she was entitled to treat her this way because her new lodger was beholden to her for somewhere to live. But the alternative of a tiny bed-sitter was looking increasingly attractive to Izzie. She might find it cramped after living in a house all her life but at least there she'd have free rein to live her own life the way she wanted.

She had to get out from under Edna's roof, whether her departure caused offence or not, and the sooner the better.

The next night, as soon as they returned from their trip to the church yard – not the sort of place Izzie would normally choose to go in the dark, and hardly a pleasant outing as Florrie snivelled all the way there and back and Izzie also had to endure Edna's constant instructions on how to push a wheelchair – she escaped to her room to study the Property to Let column in the *Mercury*.

Edna's prophecy that finding accommodation was going to be difficult proved true. Very little was on offer that fell into Izzie's price range, but regardless she did find three properties that were.

Telling Edna she had been kept back late at work, over the next few nights she viewed two small flats and a bed-sitter. All proved to be dire to say the least, needing a lot of money spent on them before they were even partway liveable. She felt the landlords were showing bare-faced cheek to be asking the amounts they were for accommodation hardly fit for dogs, let alone human beings. But she would not be despondent, she decided. Her increasingly desperate need to get from under Edna's roof would keep her looking until she achieved success.

CHAPTER FOUR

The following Sunday afternoon, a bright fine day that was unusually warm for the middle of October, Suzy was casting a miffed look in the direction of her grandmother sitting several rows ahead, ramrod-straight on a wooden chair beside Florrie in her wheelchair. Both of them were dressed in their Sunday black coats and hats, clutching bulging black handbags on their knees.

'Did they have to come with us, Aunty Izzie?' she sulkily demanded of her aunt.

'Yeah, did they have to?' piped up her sister, sitting the other side of Izzie, cradling her doll in her arms.

When she had informed Edna she was taking the girls to the park, her landlady had automatically assumed she was invited along, as of course was her friend Florrie. 'Well, someone had to push Mrs Liddle's wheelchair.'

'Why couldn't Grandma do it?' asked Sally.

'Well, she's too old for pushing wheelchairs, sweetie.'

'She wasn't before you moved in with her, Aunty Izzie. I've seen her pushing Mrs Liddle down the road lots of times when Mam made us go with her to visit.'

It seemed both Edna and Florrie had kept her in the dark about that fact, letting her believe that if Izzie didn't do the honours then Florrie was permanently housebound.

'By the time the band's finished we'll have no time for playing on the swings before we have to go home for our tea. And we ain't had our ice cream. I don't like this music. Can't they play "Puff the Magic Dragon"?' Suzy asked.

Izzie wasn't overly fond of the type of music the band was

29

playing herself. She didn't think it very likely that the Ratby Brass Band had 'Puff the Magic Dragon' in their repertoire, though. To pacify her niece she said, 'Well, you never know, they might.'

'Do you like living with Gran, Aunty Izzie?' Sally unexpectedly asked her.

How could she tell her beloved nieces she hated every minute? 'Well, I've only been living with her a week but so far I do,' she fibbed.

Both girls' faces fell.

'Oh, but we were hoping you hated it,' said Sally.

'Yeah, we were,' said her sister. 'So you'd come home.'

'We don't half miss yer, Aunty Izzie, don't we, our Suzy?' said Sally, her bottom lip trembling.

'Yeah, we do.'

A lump formed in Izzie's throat 'Do you, darlings?' she mumbled. 'Well, that's nice to hear. I miss you both too.'

'Well, come home then,' they urged.

She wished it was that simple. 'But you and Mum and Dad are a family. It's not really right, your aunty living with you too.'

'Why not?' Suzy asked. 'Jill, my friend at school, well, her gran and her uncle live with them.'

How could she explain to them that their mother had decided her extended family had outstayed their welcome? 'Oh, well, your friend's parents obviously have a bigger house. Now you're both growing up, you need a bedroom each and you couldn't have that with me still living with you, could you?'

'But Suzy doesn't sleep in her bedroom, Aunty Izzie. She hates sleeping on her own. She sneaks in with me every night, don't yer, our Suzy?'

She nodded vigorously. 'I never wanted a bedroom of me own anyway, it was Mam that told me I did. She tells me off every morning for sneaking in with our Sal, but I still do it. Mam shouts at us more since you ain't been with us, Aunty Izzie, for not doing more round the house for her. I heard Dad saying to her that she was missing the help you gave her. She said she wasn't, but as we're girls we should be helping her more round the house ready for when we leave home ourselves. But I don't need to learn housework, I'm having servants to look after me. Mam laughed at me when I told her that.'

'Well, servants cost a lot of money, sweetie.'

'Why, do you buy them?'

'No, but you have to pay their wages.'

'Well, that's all right. I'm going to be rich with my own hair-dressing shop. I'm not going to have children. They get on yer nerves and make yer hair go grey, don't they? Mam says they do, anyway.'

Izzie smiled to herself. Suzy's dreams for the future changed daily. Last week she was going to be living in a castle in the country with her children. She had no idea where the money was coming from to fund her lavish future or of the fact that to have children at all a man had to be involved, and eight-year-old Suzy had vowed never to have anything to do with them. Oh, to be young and innocent again, she thought wistfully

'So being's Suzy don't sleep in her room and plays in mine all the time, you could move back in, couldn't you, Aunty Izzie?' Sally informed her aunt.

Izzie had no answer to give her that wouldn't blacken their mother in the girls' eyes. She thought it a good idea to steer them away from this conversation. Casting a quick look over at Edna and Florrie to satisfy herself they were too engrossed in the concert to notice them slipping away for a few minutes, she grabbed the girls' hands and said to them, 'Come on, we'll go to the van and get you an ice cream each. We'll be back before Grandma and Mrs Liddle know we've gone.'

With both girls happily licking their overflowing cones, strawberry sauce tricking down their hands, Izzie started to lead them back to the grassy knoll where the bandstand stood which was beyond an area of dense shrubbery.

As they rounded a bend in the path they automatically moved aside to allow a couple strolling in the opposite direction room to pass by. As the male member of the couple drew in line with Izzie, recognition made her gasp in shock and her heart start to race. She not believe what her eyes were seeing. It couldn't be him. He was four thousand miles away in Canada . . . But it was, there was no doubt. Before her, as large as life, stood Lawrence Clayton.

He looked most surprised to see her too but nevertheless smiled and greeted her. 'Hello, Izzie. I forgot you brought your nieces to this park on a Sunday afternoon. Anyway, how are you?' He patted both the girls' heads. 'Hello, girls.'

Their mouths were too full of ice cream to reciprocate.

Before Izzie could respond the woman accompanying him spoke up. 'Oh, Lawrence darling, is this the lady you told me was so good about helping you look after your mother? The only one your mother took to out of all the ones you took home and introduced her to?'

Without batting an eyelid, he replied, 'Yes, it most certainly is. Izzie was marvellous with Mother.'

She had to fight with all her might not to scream at him that she only undertook the onerous task of being a virtual slave to his mother's selfishness because he had brazenly led her to believe they had a future together, flirting outrageously with her and wording his future plans in such a way as to lead her on. She was still angry with herself for being such a willing pawn, so blinded by love for him she never for one moment realised the truth. She didn't, though, want to cause a scene in a public place. And after all Lawrence's wife was innocent in all of this and also Izzie had her beloved nieces with her.

Janet Clayton was smiling warmly at her. 'You really must be a saint. From what Lawrence has told me his mother wasn't an easy person at all. That's the reason he never took me round to meet her. He said she'd not like the fact we were courting and do her utmost to split us up.'

'Well, after my father died she focused all her attention on me. She had no one else,' he said complacently. 'She was terrified I would abandon her to fend for herself.'

Janet looked up at him lovingly. 'Darling, as if you'd know-ingly do anything to anyone that would cause them grief, let alone your own mother.' She then looked back at Izzie.

32

'Lawrence told me he paid you well for what you did, but if it wasn't for you we wouldn't have been able to see each other regularly and I was always so grateful. I wanted him to introduce us at our wedding so I could express my own appreciation to you, but with so many people turning up to wish us well I never got chance to get round everyone.'

Izzie couldn't believe that Lawrence had said he had paid her to care for his mother when all the time he had done no such thing. She did wonder if Janet would feel the same about him if she knew what a manipulative man he really was, seemingly with no compunction over his abuse of Izzie's good nature to achieve his own aim. She did, though, genuinely hope that his wife never had cause to find out this particular trait in his character.

Janet was looking at her questioningly. 'Not that I doubt my husband for a moment, but I sometimes wonder if he was exaggerating his mother's domineering ways. Was she really that difficult?'

'She was an old dragon, Mrs,' piped up Sally before Izzie could respond. 'My mam said it was a pity she wouldn't do us all a favour and attend her own funeral.'

Izzie was gawping at Sally, mortified by this innocent repetition of her mother's words. 'Oh, I'm sure Pat never said that,' she blustered.

'She did,' said Suzy, backing up her sister. 'I heard her say it, lots of times.'

A red-faced Izzie glared at them both by way of warning them not to say any more and dearly hoped they took the hint. She looked apologetically at Janet. 'Please excuse my nieces, they do tend to get things muddled up like most children do after they've been eavesdropping. I'm positive my sister-in-law would never have said any such thing,' she lied, knowing very well Pat would have. She then hurriedly changed the subject by responding to Janet's question. 'Mrs Clayton could be very trying at times but most old people can be, can't they?' Edna came popping into her mind then. She also felt the need to know what Lawrence and his wife were doing back in Leicester when they were supposed to be four thousand miles away in Canada, getting on with their new lives together, but she was more desperate to get away from this appalling situation and the man who could still cause her such misery. It wasn't doing her any good at all to witness how happy together he and his new wife were. 'Well, I must be getting the girls back.' Graciously she added, 'It was lovely to meet you in person, Mrs Clayton. Excuse us, won't you?'

Urging the girls forward, she made to depart but was stopped in her tracks by Lawrence saying, 'Good to see you again, Izzie. I suppose we're bound to cross paths again when I start back at Jones and Shipman a week on Monday.'

'Oh, and I most likely will too,' said Janet. 'I'm hoping to get a job there as a secretary. Lawrence told me that with my qualifications I should have no trouble, the company is always on the lookout for good secretaries, but I prefer to err on the side of caution, to avoid disappointment. But should I be successful, it'll be nice to think I already know someone who works there.'

Izzie's thoughts ran wild as she stared at both of them, stunned. Lawrence couldn't just have told her he was returning to work at Jones and Shipman and his wife was hoping to work there too? This couldn't be happening. It was bad enough having to contend with the ghost of his memory in her workplace, but to have to face him in person, day in, day out, and not only him but his wife too . . . She couldn't, she just couldn't.

'But . . . but . . . what about your new life in Canada?'

'We gave it a good try but we just couldn't settle,' said Lawrence, 'so we decided to cut our losses and come back.'

'Lawrence is being gallant,' Janet said, flashing him a tender look. 'He settled very well over there, loved his job and the way of life, but unfortunately I'd never realised how much I would miss my family. I was so homesick.'

'Oh, I see. Well, I . . . er . . . welcome back home.' She forced a bright smile to her face. 'We really must be going. Come along, girls.'

As they hurried down the path leading back to the bandstand

area, Suzy's young face was wreathed in concern. 'You all right, Aunty Izzie? Only yer look really upset.'

Upset was an understatement. After such an unexpected encounter with Lawrence and the news she had received, Izzie knew that not only was she urgently seeking a new place to live but a new job too. The thought of leaving a position she enjoyed, and working amongst new people, did not appeal but she had no choice if she was to stand the best chance of coming to terms with Lawrence's abuse of her good nature and get on with her life.

She smiled down at her niece warmly. 'What have I got to be upset about, sweetie, when my two favourite nieces are with me?'

The band were packing their instruments away, the audience dispersing, by the time they began to retrace their steps to the seating area. Izzie's plan to return before Edna discovered their absence was foiled. She was awaiting their return, her stony expression showing her displeasure.

'Where have yer bin?' she demanded when they arrived.

'We went for an okey, Gran,' Suzy told her.

In an accusing tone Edna snapped back at Izzie, 'Well, you could have said. We thought you'd forgotten about us and gone home.'

'Oh, Mrs Peel, you've known me long enough to realise I wouldn't do that,' Izzie said, hurt.

'Maybe I have, but there's a first time for everything. I'd appreciate you letting me know yer doing a disappearing act before yer do it next time.'

'Well, we didn't want to disturb your enjoyment of the concert and I thought we'd be back before you noticed we'd gone.'

'Huh! Well, I wouldn't have minded an okey meself, and you wouldn't have either, would yer, Florrie?'

'Well, yes, an okey would've been nice,' twittered the wheel-chair-bound woman.

'We'll go back to the van now and get you both one,' Izzie offered.

'Too late, I've gone off the idea,' Edna said sulkily, much to Florrie's obvious disappointment.

Her encounter with Lawrence and the resulting problem this had presented her with sat heavily on Izzie who was in no mood to deal with childish behaviour from Edna. Smiling politely at her she said, 'It's turning chilly, I suggest we make our way home.'

CHAPTER FIVE

'What yer looking down the Job Vacancies for?' Edna demanded the next night, walking unannounced into Izzie's room.

Sitting on her bed, that evening's copy of the *Leicester Mercury* spread out before her, Izzie jumped, startled. 'Oh, Mrs Peel, you gave me a fright,' she said, clutching her chest with one hand. She gave a sigh. Edna really was taking her landlady's privileges too far. Why she was looking down the jobs column was purely Izzie's business. 'I just like to keep abreast with what's on offer, Mrs Peel.'

'Well, you could have done that downstairs instead of hiding yerself away up here. Anyone would think yer didn't like my company.'

And anyone would have been right but Izzie was too polite to tell her so. 'I was just respecting the fact that you were listening to your programme on the radio, Mrs Peel, and the rustling of the paper would have irritated you, that's all. Did you want me for something?'

'Er . . . just checking you was okay, that's all, as I couldn't hear any sounds from you.'

Izzie smiled warmly at her. 'I'm fine, Mrs Peel. I appreciate your concern. Maybe next time, though, you could knock? Then that way you won't risk giving me a heart attack.'

Izzie could tell by the tight look on Edna's face that the older woman realised this was a polite way of asking her to respect her lodger's privacy.

She said gruffly, 'Well, I'll expect yer down at just before nine for yer cocoa.'

Izzie quite fancied a cup but she knew Edna was expecting her to offer to make it and felt the woman needed a strong hint that she wasn't going to jump whenever she clicked her fingers, just because she was living under her roof. 'I think I'll give it a miss tonight, Mrs Peel. Goodnight. I hope you sleep well.'

Edna wasn't pleased to realise Izzie was dismissing her or by the fact she would have to make her own cocoa that night. 'Oh! Oh, er . . . er . . . I hope you sleep well too,' she mumbled.

As soon as Edna had left Izzie resumed her job search. There were plenty of clerical positions on offer but all offering less money than she was receiving due to her long service with Jones and Shipman. She might urgently need to make her escape from her workplace but to take a lesser-paid job would be madness on her part as then she'd never be able to afford a place of her own. Despite this being her first search, she was despondent not to have come across anything suitable as Lawrence was returning to work on Monday week and if she wanted to have moved on before then, it only left her another four days to secure something and a week to serve her notice. She was just about to concede defeat and hope tomorrow evening might yield better results when an advertisement caught her eye. It was for a clerk to be solely responsible for running the post room of a small but busy plastics manufacturer based a short bus ride away. The wage offered was ten shillings more than she was getting now. Not a great deal, but ten shillings more towards the rent on a place of her own. She immediately gathered together her writing implements to apply for it.

The following Friday evening Frank Miller looked at Izzie, impressed.

Though outwardly cool, she was dearly hoping he could not tell how nervous she was to be attending her first interview in over twenty years. She feared that at any moment she might say or do something that would make him think she was unsuitable for the position. She had applied for two other jobs advertised in the *Mercury* since applying for this one but as yet had received no reply from either of them. Those two jobs had been of interest to her, both clerical positions in large companies offering about the same wage as she was getting now, but this particular post was so well suited to her in every way that she'd be disappointed if she didn't get it. She was also conscious that time was running out for her to achieve her aim of having left Jones and Shipman before Lawrence returned.

'Well, you certainly have the experience we've looking for, Miss Jenkins,' Frank Miller said to her, a warm smile on his fatherly face. 'After twenty years in the post room of a company the size of Jones and Shipman, handling our requirements should be no trouble for the likes of you. I'd just like to ask you why it is you want to leave your job after being with them such a long time?'

Thankfully she had anticipated this question and was prepared for it. 'I'm quite happy in my job, Mr Miller, but I feel like a change, working with new people.'

'I can appreciate that. Mrs Watson, whose post we're inter- viewing for, has been very happy with us for seven years but is leaving for the same reason. Well, the people here are a good bunch, and from what I've observed of you I don't see any reason why you won't fit in here very nicely, Miss Jenkins.' He spent several minutes going over terms and conditions, before asking her, 'Is there anything else you'd like to ask me about the job?'

She thought for a moment then shook her head. 'I think you've covered everything, thank you, Mr Miller. I'd just like to say, though, that I do appreciate your arranging my interview for after working hours.'

'My pleasure, Miss Jenkins. It served to show me you're conscientious and didn't wish to take advantage of your present company by making an excuse such as a fictitious dental appoint- ment.' He folded his arms and looked hard at her. 'Well, I don't see the point in wasting any more of my time in seeing further candidates when the ideal one is sitting in front of me. I'd like to offer you the job, Miss Jenkins, and hope you like the sound of working for us enough to accept it.'

She hadn't expected this, had fully expected to be told she'd be informed of her success or failure by letter in due course and have an agonising wait for its arrival. A broad smile lit her face. 'Oh, I do like the thought of working for this company. I do accept the job, yes, I do. Very glad to.'

'Good.' He rose, holding his hand out towards her. 'We'll look forward to seeing you at eight-thirty a week on Monday.'

She was walking on air as she left the building. The prospect of starting her new job, meeting her new work colleagues, proving to Mr Miller he'd done right in taking her on, was daunting to her, but regardless she had been spared having to face Lawrence on a daily basis and possibly having to be friendly with his wife which was a far worse prospect.

Edna pounced on her when she arrived home. 'Yer very late. Yer never said yer'd be late when yer left this morning.'

Izzie hadn't because she had known Edna would grill her for the reason why. 'Well, I didn't want to tempt fate, you see.'

Her landlady looked both puzzled and intrigued. 'Tempt fate! In what way?'

'Well, I went for a job interview.'

'A job interview? What for? You've a perfectly good job.'

'I fancy a change. I got the job and I start a week on Monday.'

'Oh, I see. Well, I suppose congratulations are in order.' A worried look crossed her face. 'Is it . . . er . . . more money you'll be getting?'

Izzie knew why she was worried about that. More pay meant Izzie would be able to fund a place of her own more easily, just when Edna was getting used to having her around and enjoying the benefits of using her to fetch and carry. 'A little, but not enough to make a major difference.'

Edna seemed pleased with her response. 'Oh, well, a little is better than nothing. At least you ain't like me and have to manage on the bit of pension I get and me small amount of savings. Well, I'm famished. Where's the shopping? Then we can get cracking on with the dinner.'

Izzie inwardly groaned. In her haste not to be late for her interview she had rushed straight off at finishing time, completely forgetting to pick up the carrier of shopping she'd stowed under her desk containing two mutton chops and bag of potatoes which she had fetched during her lunch hour. 'I left it behind at work. Never mind, I'll treat us both to fish and chips and we'll have the chops tomorrow.'

Edna seemed pleased with her offer. 'Well, if you're paying, make mine a piece of skate. And make sure they don't mix scratchings in with my chips. Oh, and put plenty of salt and vinegar on. I'll have the plates warmed for when you get back.'

With Edna's strict instructions still ringing in her ears, Izzie rushed off.

She was just about to cross the road opposite the chip shop when she stopped short. Two figures caught her attention. They were passing the shop, illuminated by the bright lights beaming through the large plate-glass windows, both weighed down by an overflowing carrier bag in each hand. They looked familiar . . . They should do, they were her nieces.

Frowning, she kicked up her heels and ran across to them, calling out loudly, 'Oi, you two! What on earth are you doing out at this time of night by yourselves?'

At the sound of their aunt's voice both girls abruptly stopped, gawping at her, horrified.

As she arrived to join them Isabel demanded, 'Well?'

They both gulped, guilty looks flooding their young faces.

'Well, what, Aunty Izzie?' Suzy asked her, looking innocent.

'Don't play games with me, madam,' Izzie replied tartly. 'I asked what you two were doing out at this time of night by yourselves?' She gave a suspicious glance towards the carriers they were holding. 'And what have you got in those bags?'

They both looked at her blankly.

'Just stuff,' Suzy finally said cagily.

'What stuff?' demanded Izzie.

'Our stuff,' said Sally.

'What sort of *our stuff*?' Izzie commanded.

Suzy eyed her aunt boldly. 'Clothes, that sorta stuff.'

'And my dolls,' added Sally. 'And some tins of peaches and a packet of biscuits.'

Izzie frowned at them, confused. 'What's going on?'

Sally nudged her sister. 'You tell her, Suzy, you're the eldest.'

Suzy's face set defiantly. 'We're running away.'

'I see,' said Izzie. 'Your mam and dad will be worried about you both.'

'It's all right, we left 'em a note telling them what we were doing and why,' Suzy told her.

'Oh, I see. They'll still be worried, though, when they find it, if they haven't already and . . . well . . . I dread to think how they'll be feeling. Anyway, where were you running away to? Your gran's? Because you're going the wrong way for her house.'

They both looked horrified at the very thought.

'Not likely,' Suzy blurted. 'She'd only clip us round the ear and make us go back home so we ain't gonna let her know what we're doing. We was going to go up the park and make a den in the bushes.'

'Oh, I see. Well, I wouldn't fancy being you two. It gets very cold at night there and it doesn't look to me like you brought any blankets with you.'

'Couldn't carry 'em,' said Sally. 'But I brought my dolly hers so she wouldn't get cold.'

'That was kind of you,' said Izzie, hiding a smile. 'Er . . . just why are you running away?'

''Cos Mam said if she finds out I've slept with our Sally and not in me own bed again, she's gonna chain me to it each night to make sure I do,' Suzy blurted out. 'Well, we ain't going back until Mam lets me move back in with Sally,' she said resolutely.

'No, we ain't,' piped up her sister determinedly.

Pat might threaten that in frustration though Izzie knew she'd never do such a thing in reality, but obviously Suzy wasn't taking any chances. 'Your mother often threatens to beat you senseless when you don't do what she asks you to first time, but she never has so far, has she?' Isabel squatted down on her haunches and looked Suzy in the eye. 'You know, lots of girls your age would give anything to have a bedroom to themselves.'

'I know,' she muttered. 'Katie at school was right jealous when I told her. She has to share with her three sisters.'

'What frightens you about sleeping in a room by yourself, sweetie?' Izzie gently probed. 'Truth now, then maybe I can help you.'

Suzy stared at her thoughtfully. 'Well . . . nothing really, Aunty Izzie.'

'So why do you keep sneaking in with Sally?'

A look of shame filled her face. 'Dunno.'

Izzie looked at Sally then. 'Do you know what frightens your sister?'

'Our Suzy ain't scared of n'ote,' she responded matter-of-factly. ''Cept Mam when she's in a temper, 'course.'

Izzie frowned at them, confused. 'Neither of you is making any sense to me. Now what's going on? Come on, tell the truth,' she ordered.

They both looked at each other then Sally spoke up. 'It was our plan, Aunty Izzie, so you'd get your bedroom back and could come home.'

'Oh, girls,' she uttered, choking on the lump in her throat. Taking a deep breath, she said, 'Now listen to me. I know you miss me and I miss you both, dreadfully I do, but I couldn't go on living with you forever. I'm only living with your grandma temporarily until I find a place of my own. I want somewhere you'll be able to come and visit me and stop over whenever you want to. It might not be a big place but I'll always be able to find somewhere for you two to sleep.'

'Oh,' they both mouthed, excited at the thought of stopping over at their beloved aunt's house.

'Whenever we want, can we?' asked Sally.

Isabel nodded. 'As long as it's all right with Mam and Dad.'

'Can you hurry up and get somewhere then?' Suzy urged.

'As soon as I can, sweetie, I promise. Now your mum is insisting you have a room each because she knows you're both growing up and need your privacy. Like when she tells you to sit up straight because she's worried you'll grow up round-shouldered if you don't. And while we're on the subject, she's right to want you to help her with some chores or how will you know how to do them when you get a place of your own?' She smiled at Suzy. 'I know you're having servants to do your house-work, sweetie, but you can't check they've done things properly for you if you don't know how to do it yourself, can you?'

She gave a shrug. ''S'pose not.'

'And another thing, girls. If you did what your mum asked

43

you to do first time, then she wouldn't have any reason to shout at you or threaten to murder you, would she? Looking after a family is hard work, all that washing, cleaning, cooking, shopping and ironing . . . well, she gets tired so the least you can do is give her a hand now and again.'

Looking shame-faced, they both gave a shrug. 'S'pose we could.'

Izzie stood upright, looking down at her nieces with a twinkle in her eye. 'Right, well, best let you get to the park before the keeper locks the gates. Oh, and mind you're careful not to wake any of the tramps on the benches as you pass, they don't take kindly to children who disturb them.' She was pleased to see this have its desired effect as a look of terror crossed both faces. 'Oh, and did you bring a tin opener for the tins of peaches?'

They both shook their heads.

'Oh, dear. Well, the amount you two eat, that packet of biscuits isn't going to last you long. I'll try and bring you a food parcel when I finish work tomorrow lunchtime but I can't promise. I have to accompany your gran up the town for her weekend shopping so it might not be until well after six. I'd try and eke the biscuits out, if I were you.'

Sally's bottom lip was trembling and Suzy was staring at her, frozen-faced.

'I don't wanna leave home no more, our Suzy,' Sally blurted out to her.

'I don't either,' wailed her sister.

Izzie once again squatted down on her haunches and gathered the girls to her, kissing them both on their cheeks. 'I'm sorry I frightened you but I needed to make you see that what you were planning on doing is dangerous, my darlings. It's not safe for little girls to be out on their own at night. I really appreciate what you were trying to do for me but you must promise me you'll not think of leaving home again? Well, not until you're old enough, that is.'

They both vigorously shook their head.

'Mam's gonna kill us,' muttered a worried Suzy.

'Murder us black and blue,' uttered Sally, gulping worriedly.

Izzie smiled. 'She might threaten to, and I can't say as I blame her. I don't think your dad's going to be very happy either.'

'Maybe if you come with us, Aunty Izzie, they won't be so mad at us,' Suzy begged her.

Izzie was going to anyway. Edna would have to wait a bit longer for her supper. 'Well, I can't promise anything but of course I'll come with you.' She relieved them of their carriers. 'Come on then, let's get this over with.'

The girls, not at all relishing what was facing them, nor Izzie for that matter, unlatched the back gate, and as they were trooping through it, the back door burst open and Pat, pulling on her coat, charged out, followed closely by Arnold. On spotting the little group illuminated by the jetty street lamp just inside their yard, both of them stopped short.

'Oh, thank God you're safe,' Pat cried. Relief at seeing his daughters home safe and sound was very apparent on Arnold's face too. Then Pat erupted. 'What the flipping hell do you both think you were playing at? Get inside and up to bed now, I'll deal with you both later.'

They didn't need another telling. Kicking up their heels, the girls shot up the path, skirting their parents as widely as possible for fear of a clip around the ear, which thankfully they didn't receive, before disappearing through the back door.

Izzie hurried up the path to join Pat and Arnold. She thrust the carriers containing the girls' belongings at Arnold and looked at Pat pleadingly. 'Don't be too hard on the girls, Pat. I know what they did was wrong and dangerous but they only did it because . . .'

'I know why they left home,' she interjected. 'I found the note they left me on Sally's bed when I went up to check on them both a couple of minutes ago. I obviously can't let it go unpunished, but don't worry, I won't be too hard on them.' Izzie was shocked to see Pat's features soften then and hear her give a deep sigh before adding, 'Izzie, I'd really like to have a chat with you, if you've got time?'

If Pat knew why the girls had done what they had, why did she want to talk to her? 'Yes, of course I have.'

The girls safely tucked up in bed, and Arnold settled in front of the television set in the front room, Pat joined Izzie at the kitchen table, picking up the cup of tea Izzie had made for them all while their mother had gone up to make sure the girls were in bed and to kiss them goodnight for the second time that night.

Cradling the cup in her hands, Pat looked at Izzie for several long moments before she began. 'I can't tell you how I felt when I discovered the girls had gone. I can't tell you either how I felt when I read their note, telling me why they'd left.' Tears glinted in her eyes. Her face puckered with shame and her voice faltered as she uttered, 'Suzy said I was a horrible mummy, making her Aunty Izzie live with their gran. I had no idea the girls even knew I was behind you leaving, Izzie. Either the little tykes were eavesdropping or they worked it out for themselves ... well, anyway, that's by the by. My daughters are right, though, it *was* wicked of me, dumping you on my mother. I love her but she was bad enough when I lived with her, always wanting to know everything I did and forever letting me know that it was *her* house and *her* rules I lived by. She's grown worse as she's got older, and I've always thanked God I've never had reason to move back in with her.' Pat took a deep breath. 'The girls have missed having you around terribly since you went, but they aren't the only ones. Arnold has, of course, but ...' She paused for a moment before adding softly. 'I have too, Izzie.'

This admission came as such a shock it struck Izzie speechless.

Eyeing her remorsefully, Pat continued, 'You see, I thought I'd be glad to see the back of you and have my family to myself, be the most important woman in their lives instead of having to share them with you. I resented you living with us, Izzie. But it's not like you ever interfered with the way I ran this house. From the day I married Arnold, you graciously stepped down and allowed me the freedom to do things my way, never once knowingly tried to interfere. I should have been grateful I had such a wonderful sister-in-law instead of seeing you as an intruder. I feel ashamed to admit the number of times I prayed to God for Lawrence's mother to die so you and him could get married and I'd get my wish. When it came out that he'd been leading you up the garden path all those years, believe me, Izzie, I was so hurt for you, I wanted to go round and knock him for six. You tried to make light of it, insisting it was your own fault for making out

46

the relationship between you two was more than just friendship. But I knew how devastated you were and I never offered you the support I should have as all I could think of was that now marriage to Lawrence was no longer on the cards, you could be living with us forever if I didn't take matters into my own hands. So I hatched that plan with my mother to get you out.'

With a look of shame on her face she added, 'You must hate me for the way I've treated you since I married your brother. I shudder sometimes when I think of the nasty comments I made about you when I knew you could hear. I hardly ever thanked you for the help you gave me or showed you how much I appreciate what you do for the girls, even though I do, very much. I'm sorry, Izzie, so very, very sorry. I had no right to make you feel uncomfortable in your own home. This was your family's house, and if anyone is the intruder here it's me. Oh, Izzie, I do like you, always have done, it's just that I haven't been able to show it. It's taken my kids' daft behaviour tonight to make me take stock and see what a stupid woman I've been, what a friendship we could have shared if I hadn't been so pig-headed. I can only hope you'll forgive me, and ask if we can start again?'

Pat's genuine remorse for her past behaviour and heartfelt apologies for it brought a choking lump to Izzie's throat. 'Oh, Pat, there's nothing to forgive.' She smiled kindly at her sister-in-law. 'I think you've been a saint, putting up with me living with you all these years. If I hadn't been such a fool about Lawrence I would have made my own way in the world years ago and then you wouldn't have had any cause to resent me.' She reached across the table and clasped one of Pat's hands, squeezing it affectionately. 'Let's do as you suggested, put all this behind us and start again.'

Pat's gratitude was apparent on her face. 'Only a woman like you could forgive so easily, Izzie. Thank God my girls did what they did tonight. We'll all come around tomorrow afternoon after you and Arnold have finished work for the weekend, help you pack your stuff and carry it back round here.' With a grin on her face, she added, 'That's if you can stand another night under my mother's roof?'

Izzie smiled warmly at her. 'Pat, I'd like nothing more than to move back in and it's nice to know you all want me back, but it's time I found a place of my own. Anyway, I've no choice now. I've promised the girls they can come and stop over with me, providing it's all right with you and Arnold, of course? I can't let them down.'

'Izzie, the girls can come to see you and stop over whenever you want them to. But the type of place you can afford . . . well, I wouldn't rest at night, knowing you were living in some hovel. At least come back while we find you something half-decent in your price range.'

What was so comforting for Izzie was that she knew Pat genuinely meant this. And she was right. Judging by the accommodation in her price range that Izzie had viewed this week, hovel was definitely the word. Part of her would dearly have loved to take Pat up on her offer as spending another minute under Edna's roof felt like a prison sentence, but Suzy and Sally were just coming to terms with not having her permanently around. When the time came for her to leave, it might unsettle them all over again and she didn't want that for them.

Smiling brightly, she said, 'I haven't told you my good news.'

Pat looked keenly at her. 'Good news? Oh, I could do with a bit of that. What good news?'

'I've got myself another job.'

She looked confused. 'But why? You liked your job at Jones and Shipman, and you've been there so long.'

Izzie realised that if she and Pat were ever going to forge a sister-like relationship she would have to take the other woman into her confidence, and after all these years of not having anyone to confide in and ask an opinion of, the thought was very welcome. Taking a deep breath, she told Pat of her encounter with Lawrence and his wife the previous Sunday.

When Izzie had finished Pat sat back in her chair, folding her arms, her face tight. 'That man is beneath contempt, Izzie. He's no conscience,' she hissed. 'It's a pity we can't let everyone at Jones and Shipman know how badly he treated you. I could tell Arnold and he'd tell his mates in the firm and so on. Lawrence would soon get his comeuppance, believe me. But that would mean everyone knowing your business and pitying you . . .'

'And them all seeing how stupid I've been, and I don't want that, Pat,' Izzie insisted. 'And don't forget, Lawrence's wife is hoping to get a job there. She'd get to hear, too, and that's not fair on her as she's innocent in all this.'

'You weren't stupid, Izzie. You were in love with the man, for Christ's sake, and had absolutely no reason not to believe he meant to marry you once his mother died. I appreciate your point about his poor wife, though. Look, don't worry, this is between you and me, you have my promise it won't go any further. That man's put you through enough. Well, look on the bright side. New job, new start. So tell me about this job then. Where is it? Doing what?'

Izzie obliged.

'Sounds all right,' Pat commented when she had finished. 'Nothing you can't handle. I really hope you're happy there, Izzie.'

She smiled warmly. 'Thanks, Pat. The extra money I'll be getting isn't going to make me rich but it will at least give me ten shillings more a week to put towards rent.'

'Well, I'll keep checking shop window cards for you, and when you do get somewhere I'll help you all I can to make it homely. I'm a dab hand at running up curtains as you know from the ones I've done for this place.'

'Thanks, I appreciate that.' She drained the dregs of her cup of tea and stood up. 'Well, I'd better be off.' Izzie saw the look of remorse cross Pat's face again and in order to ease her conscience lied, 'It's not that bad for me, Pat, honestly. I'm not Edna's daughter, just her lodger. She can't lord it over me so much, not like she did with you.' Actually she wasn't really lying to Pat, she reminded herself, as she had in her own diplomatic way asked Edna not to invade her privacy so much.

As Izzie began to make her way back to Edna's the negative feelings about her future that Lawrence had left her with were beginning to be shoved aside to make way for brighter ones. She had a new job to look forward to, and all the new people she would meet through it. There were extra means to fund a more comfortable place to rent, and the excitement of making her new home comfortable and inviting her nieces to come and stay. But most importantly she had her new understanding with her sister-in-law and a real friendship to look forward to there. Her future certainly did look far better than it had when she had risen that morning.

It wasn't until she had turned the corner of Edna's street that a man hurrying past her and the smell emanating from the newspaper-wrapped parcel he was clutching reminded her of the reason she had ventured out tonight in the first place. She had promised Edna fish and chips for her supper! Isabel inwardly groaned, flashing a quick look at her wrist watch. The longest it should have taken her to collect the fish and chips and return home was twenty minutes and by now she'd been keeping Edna waiting over an hour and a half. Her mood was going to be bad enough without her returning empty handed. Spinning on her heel, Isabel ran back towards the chip shop.

Thankfully the shop was empty and as though he'd had a premonition that a customer in a hurry was about to descend, the owner had just finishing frying a fresh load of chips and a couple of pieces of fish, albeit they were cod as he'd had no delivery of skate that day.

As she'd been expecting, Edna launched herself on Izzie the moment she entered the back door.

'Where yer bin, for Christ's sake? I'd have bin quicker to have gone meself.'

Handing over the parcel to Edna so she could take off her coat, which was snatched off her, Isabel said, 'I do apologise for taking so long but I remembered I had an urgent errand to do, Mrs Peel.'

Edna's nose twitched nosily. 'Errand? What errand?'

Izzie felt that if Pat wanted her mother to know what had happened tonight then she would tell her herself. 'Just an errand, Mrs Peel.' She smiled sweetly at the old woman. 'Shall we dish out the supper before it gets cold?'

CHAPTER SIX

I zzie hadn't relished the thought of her interview with Marjorie
Evans to hand in her notice the following Monday morning,
had been convinced she would be put out at being lumbered with
the time-consuming task of finding a replacement. She hadn't at
all expected the reaction she did receive. Marjorie looked posi-
tively stunned, but more surprisingly to Izzie, upset.

'Oh, Isabel, when you asked to see me privately, of course I
wondered what you had in mind but I never thought it'd be to
give your notice in. Why do you want to leave? Are you unhappy
with me in some way as a supervisor? If so, I'm sure we can
talk about it and sort it out.'

Many supervisors wouldn't care a jot if their underlings were
unhappy with their method of management. Isabel smiled warmly
at the woman. 'I've been very happy with you as my supervisor,
Mrs Evans, it's just that I'm ready for a change of scene.'

'Well, I can appreciate that, dear. I left the Post Office for the
same reason and that's what brought me here. Oh, dear, I shall
be so sorry to lose you. I've been very lucky and had myself a
happy little team here. Well, I know young Marilyn can test my
patience at times, but on the whole she pulls her weight. Still,
nothing lasts forever, does it? I just have to hope I can find a
replacement as conscientious as you've proved to be. I wish you
the best in your new position, I really do.'

As word began to spread of her impending departure at the
end of the week, via Marilyn's loose tongue, Izzie began to
wonder if she'd done the right thing. So many of her colleagues
seemed sincerely sorry that she was going and insisted they would
miss her. She'd had no idea she was so well thought of and felt

it was a shame that it had taken her resignation to discover the fact, but then she reminded herself of why exactly she was leaving, which was a far stronger incentive to go.

She had just finished helping Edna dish up the dinner that night when the back door burst open and Pat charged in.

It was very apparent to Izzie that she was excited about something but before she could say why she had called, Edna, automatically assuming her daughter had called to see her, snapped, 'You've called at an inconvenient time, we're just about to have our dinner. You're usually having yer own at this time, what's so important it couldn't wait 'til later?'

Izzie could see that Pat was holding back from giving Edna a piece of her mind out of respect for the fact she was her mother. 'I just need to see Izzie about something, Mother.' Before Edna could respond she ordered, 'Get your coat, Izzie, I've something to show you. Come on, quick!' She smiled sweetly at her mother. 'You won't mind putting Izzie's dinner in the oven to keep hot, will you? We shouldn't be that long.'

Edna looked most put out. 'Well, it seems I have no choice, doesn't it? But when you get back, I shall expect to be told exactly what's going on.'

Outside in the street, facing a bewildered Izzie, Pat erupted. 'My mam is a nosey old bat, and when yer don't want her to know summat 'til you're good and ready to tell her, she doesn't half take it personally. If only she hadn't been so embittered by me dad's death! Anyway, we'd best get a move on as she's expecting us at six-thirty,' she said, hurrying off, obviously expecting Izzie to follow her.

When she caught up, falling quickly into step, Izzie asked, 'Who's expecting us, Pat?'

'Nan Willett is.'

'Nan Willett? Oh, the woman who's got the alterations shop just before the railway bridge on Narborough Road, that Nan Willett?'

'That's right. She owns that shop, but more importantly the flat above it too which I found out this morning from Ada Shawditch who owns the corner shop. How *she* found out is anyone's guess, but the fact is the previous tenants have just done a moonlight owing two months' rent and taking all the furniture Mrs Willett provided, cheeky buggers, which means the flat is vacant. I went round and saw Nan about it and told her all about you, how reliable you are and everything, and got her to agree to give you first option on it.'

Izzie gasped. 'Oh, Pat, you have? Oh, thank you, thank you!'

'Don't thank me 'til you've seen it. I've no idea what it's like or what rent she wants, but I do know that it's a one-bedroomed and you don't have to share the outside lavvy.'

Trying not to build their hopes up too much, silence fell between the two women as they hurried along to their destination.

The flat was accessed around the back of the two-storey building by a flight of steep rusting metal stairs. Nan Willett, a slim, smartly dressed fifty year old, opened the door when she heard their footsteps clanging up the metal steps.

'Nice to see you promptly,' she said to them. 'Tells a lot about a person does promptness.' As Pat and Izzie joined her she glanced her prospective tenant over and, seeming to like what she saw, smiled. 'You must be Miss Jenkins. Well, after my experience with my last tenants, I hope you're as reliable as your sister-in-law promised me you were. Before I take you around to view, I must warn you that they've left the place in a bit of a state.'

As Nan led them both inside they saw she had grossly under-stated the condition the last tenants had left the place in. Instead of a 'bit of a state' she should have said 'rubbish dump'. Piles of old newspapers, empty tins, smeared milk bottles and food wrappers, along with all manner of other items, lay everywhere, the stench they emitted powerful enough to take breath away. It was a wonder to Izzie that there wasn't an infestation of rats although she did suspect from a trail of small brown droppings she observed that mice were in residence. The walls of each room were covered in brown marks, obviously the result of having cups of tea thrown at them. It was clear the last tenants' relationship had been a volatile one. Hanging from the windows were filthy-looking, sun-faded curtains, nets yellowing and falling into holes, the panes in the windows themselves grimy from lack of a wipe.

But looking past all the debris and filth, the flat itself excited Izzie. The front door led straight into a decent-sized living room off which was a reasonable kitchen, big enough to take a small table for four, and off the other side of the living room was a bedroom big enough to hold a double bed and wardrobe and still leave room to move around. It was perfect for her simple needs, in the right area for her, and all she hoped was that the rent was affordable.

'It's ideal for me. How much do you think Mrs Willett will want?' Isabel whispered to Pat.

'For us to help gut this place out or rent-wise after the fumigators have been in?' Pat answered sardonically. 'I know you meant rent-wise.' She gave a shrug. 'Best we ask.' She called across to Nan Willett who had tactfully waited by the entrance door while the two women had taken a look around. 'How much rent are you charging for the flat, Mrs Willett?'

Instantly she answered, 'Three pound ten a week, tenant responsible for the gas and electric. Rent's payable a week up front, and four weeks' rent as bond which is refundable on vacation, depending on the state the place is left in.'

'I take it the last tenants didn't get a penny of their bond back?' Pat said dryly. She turned to Izzie. 'What do you think then?'

Izzie rubbed a hand over her chin, her face thoughtful. 'Well, it could be made to look like a little palace once it's cleared out and the walls are given a coat of emulsion. But I'll be cutting it fine. Even with my extra ten shillings a week, it's not leaving me much over. But I've some savings put by for furnishings and household stuff when I thought I'd be marrying Lawrence.'

'Good job you didn't spend it willy-nilly on clothes then, like some women would have. Now it's affording you the means to set yourself up in a place of your own. Anyway, to save some money, I can help you out with a set of bedding, a few towels and a couple of pans, and I might have a few other things I can spare too. None of it's up to much after twelve years of marriage but it all helps and you're welcome to it, Izzie.'

She smiled gratefully. 'Thanks, Pat. Your offer is much appreciated.'

Pat looked across at Mrs Willett. 'Are you flexible on the rent? I mean, let's be honest, it's in a lot of a state not a bit as you said.'

'Soap and hot water and elbow grease will soon have this place looking spick and span,' she responded firmly. 'The rent is what I said it is. I won't have any trouble letting it.'

Pat glanced at Izzie. 'She ain't as daft as she's cabbage-looking, is she? She might only be a seamstress who managed to land herself a husband that set her up in business, but she's enough brains to know she's got you over a barrel if you want this place. Oh, well, getting her to reduce the rent was worth a try but she's obviously not going to. So, are you taking it or not?'

'Well, it looks like my next few evenings are going to be spent shifting the rubbish and dirt from this place and sprucing it up before I move in, Pat, because yes, I'm taking it.'

Pat grinned at her. 'Good, 'cos it's not too far for me to pop around for a cup of tea when I need to escape me family for a bit of peace and quiet and a natter with you. And you won't be tackling this lot by yourself, me and Arnold will give you a hand.' She looked excited. 'Oh, I can't wait to traipse around the second-hand shops with you and help you choose furniture. Right, come on, let's do the business with Mrs Willett so we can get out of here. I don't know about you but that smell is beginning to make me feel sick.'

The deal done, Izzie strode alongside Pat as they made their way to her house. Pat had asked her back to tell the others and share a celebration cup of tea. Already the two women's new understanding was proving its worth to Izzie. After her years in the wilderness after Freda's departure, it felt good to have another woman's friendship and support at her disposal.

A while later Izzie was sitting at Pat's dining table, nursing a mug of steaming tea. Suzy had her arms around her neck, cheek pressed against hers, and was excitedly demanding, 'Can we come and stop in your new flat tonight then, Aunty Izzie?'

'Yeah, can we?' Sally piped up, perched on a chair beside her father, cradling her favourite dolly in her arms.

'The flat needs a lot of work doing to it before it'll be fit enough for Aunty Izzie to move into, so have patience,' their mother chided them both. 'Now skedaddle up to bed, the pair of you, and leave us adults in peace to discuss what we have to do to get Aunty Izzie moved into her new place.'

Isabel smiled at them both in turn. 'I promise you can both come and stop over with me the first Saturday night after I move in. Provided it's okay with your mam and dad, of course.'

'While you was making the tea and Mam was telling us and Dad all about yer new flat, she told us that if we didn't stop interrupting her with questions so she could finish her news, she'd let you adopt us, Aunty Izzie,' Sally matter-of-factly told her.

'I meant it as well,' Pat confirmed. 'Trouble is it's no sort of threat to them. They think that living with their Aunty Izzie would be all play and no work.'

'Oh, do they?' With a twinkle in her eye, Izzie said in a serious tone, 'Well, if they think that, then they think very wrong. If you want me to take the girls off your hands then that's fine with me, Pat, I could do with a pair of skivvies. I've enough cleaning and cooking to keep them occupied when they're not at school. And children their size will come in very handy for shoving up the chimney to clean it. I could lend them out to my new neighbours so they can do theirs for them too. They can sleep in the coal shed with the spiders and mice.'

Both her nieces were gawking at her by now.

'Do you mean that, Aunty Izzie?' Suzy asked her worriedly.

'Well, keep not doing what your mother asks you first time and you'll find out, won't you? And that includes doing what she's just asked you to do – go to bed.'

They didn't need another telling.

Over in his armchair by the fire, Arnold drained the dregs of his tea then stood up and walked across to the table to address his wife. 'Look, you two don't really need me here. We men don't get a say in anything anyway, just do as you women tell us, so I'll leave you to it and go for a couple of pints, if that's okay, Pat?'

She smiled at him. 'As long as you don't complain when I hand you the list of jobs that need doing for Izzie by Friday night?'

He gave an ironic laugh. 'Being the sensible man I am, I know there's no point in me complaining. You'll still make me do what you've ear-marked me for anyway,' he said, tongue in cheek.

As he left Pat looked questioningly at Izzie. 'You look worried, gel?'

'Pardon? Oh, I was just wondering if we'll really manage to get the flat ready for me to move into by Friday night. There's such a lot to do, isn't there?'

'Yes, there is, I grant you, especially shifting the thick grease on that cooker . . . did you notice, Izzie? It was disgusting, didn't look like it had been cleaned for years. But either we do manage it or the alternative is you spend another week at my mother's.'

Pat could tell by the look on Izzie's face that that thought did not appeal to her one iota. She laughed. 'I'll get a pencil and paper and we can start making a list.'

A while later Izzie made her way home. In her pocket was her own list of things she needed to do before Friday. Pat had very kindly offered to rally round some of her neighbours and make a start on clearing out all the rubbish during the day while Izzie was at work. First, though, Izzie had to go to the Post Office to draw out of her savings the amount she needed to hand over to Nan Willett to secure the flat. Both she and Pat had gasped in shock when Nan insisted she wanted rent for the days preceding Izzie's move in while they cleared the place out and spruced it up. No rent, no keys, had been her words. Pat was ready to argue the toss but Izzie had not wanted to risk Nan's taking umbrage and revoking her offer. Much to Pat's chagrin she had agreed to Nan's terms.

Despite the hard graft and running around that faced her over the next few days, Izzie was excited about her impending move into a place of her own and was already in her mind's eye planning the best layout of furniture in order to maximise the space as well as make it all homely and inviting.

As she entered the kitchen Edna was making herself her nightly cup of cocoa. Seeing that tight expression, Izzie's excitement faded as she knew she was in for a rough time from her landlady.

'You said you wouldn't be long,' she snapped. 'Not long to me means a half hour, hour at the most. You've bin gone nearly three. So what was so urgent and secret Pat couldn't even let her own mother in on it?'

'My new flat, Mrs Peel.'

The shock this information gave the older woman was plain.

'Your what? New flat, did you say?'

'Yes, that's right, Mrs Peel,' she said, taking off her coat to hang it up on the back of the door. 'All being well, I'll be moving into it on Friday evening.' She added, trying to lighten the situation, 'I expect you'll be glad to get the house back to yourself.'

'Well, yes, there's that. Having someone living with yer is always a hindrance. But this is a turn up, I must say. You kept the fact you was flat hunting quiet. I mean, I open my house to you, make you welcome, and you repay me by moving out without even the courtesy of a warning.'

'Oh, but you knew I was looking for a place of my own, Mrs Peel. You knew my living here would only be temporary.'

'Yes, but . . . but . . . Well, I've got used to having you here now.'

Used to me fetching and carrying for you and feeling free to utilise my time as you feel fit, Izzie thought. 'Well, once I've moved I'll try and pop in to see you as much as I can, and if you need anything doing then I'll gladly do it,' she offered.

'Huh! Yer say that but I doubt you will,' Edna ungraciously responded. 'You young ones get too tied up in yer own lives to think of us older ones.' She gave Izzie a disgusted look. 'I had to chuck yer dinner away, it was all dried up. Waste of good food. You won't be so wasteful when yer scratting to pay all yer bills by yerself. If yer hungry, yer'll have to help yourself from what's in the pantry. Don't touch that egg, I want it for me breakfast, and make sure you leave me some bread.'

With that she snatched up her mug of cocoa and departed, leaving Izzie with a feeling of profound gratitude that come Friday evening she'd no longer have to deal with any further such encounters.

CHAPTER SEVEN

Over the next three days it amazed Izzie to see how much had been achieved towards her move. True to her word, Pat had commandeered the services of several of her female neighbours. As soon as Izzie had sealed the monetary side with Nan Willett during her lunch hour and been handed the keys, they all moved in. By Tuesday evening, when Izzie went around after work expecting to do her share, she was shocked to find that hardly any of the stinking rubbish the last tenants had left behind remained. Thankfully a fresher smell now filled the rooms and the flat was almost clean enough to receive a coat of emulsion throughout. The next evening, she herself, Arnold and Pat, the girls having been left with a neighbour much to their displeasure, set to to tackle the emulsioning. All that was left for Izzie to do by Thursday evening was scrub the shabby linoleum covering the floors, clean the windows, unblock and spruce up the pot sink and degrease the cooker, then the flat was ready for her to move into. On the previous evening Izzie had persuaded Pat she could manage the rest of the cleaning herself and her sister-in-law should take a much-deserved evening off to be with her family, ready for helping again with the actual move on Friday evening. A sofa, easy chair, bed frame and mattress, wardrobe, chest of drawers, gate-leg table and four chairs, sideboard and kitchenette for storing food – although its lime green colour wasn't to her taste but it was the only kitchenette they had – and a free-standing cupboard for her pots and pans, had been purchased by Izzie from a local second-hand shop and were awaiting collection by Arnold in a borrowed van as soon as he'd finished his shift on Friday afternoon. Pat had sorted through her linen cupboard and piled up for Izzie a set of sheets, three blankets, pillow case and pillow, a couple of pans, and some odds and ends of crockery and cutlery to tide her over until she bought her own.

As Izzie walked through Edna's back door that Thursday evening to have her dinner before going over to the flat, her landlady greeted her as coolly as she had been doing since she had learned of Izzie's impending move. 'I expect you'll be wanting to rush off to this new flat of yours so we'd best get cracking on the dinner. You did find time to get the sausages from the butcher's at lunchtime, I take it?'

It wouldn't have hurt Edna to offer to shop for their dinner herself as she knew Izzie had been using her lunch hours to find things for her new place from shops that would have been shut by the time she got to them after work, but then Edna had not offered to lift a finger in any way towards her move or offered a word of encouragement to her in her new venture. It was obvious to Izzie that she was taking her departure as a personal slight against herself and not taking on board the fact that Izzie was a grown woman who needed a place of her own to live in.

She handed over the carrier. 'Yes, of course I did, along with the fresh loaf you asked me to get. I'll do the potatoes, shall I, Mrs Peel?'

This meal, like all the others they'd shared since Izzie's announcement, was conducted in awkward silence. Izzie was mortally relieved when the clearing away had been done and she had tackled the household jobs Edna had left for her as then she could make her escape to the new flat for a few hours and be out of the strained atmosphere Edna was deliberately creating.

She was just ready for the off and had gone into the back room out of courtesy to inform Edna she was going and wish her a good night's sleep should she already have retired by the time Izzie returned, when she noticed a letter on the table addressed to herself. It hadn't been there before and she wondered what Edna had gained by holding it back until now.

'Oh, is this for me?' she asked, picking it up.

'It's got your name on it so it's not for me, is it?' Edna gruffly responded, manoeuvring herself around in her armchair and looking fixedly at Izzie by way of telling her she expected to be told who the letter was from and what it contained.

Despite being intrigued herself, Izzie felt she once again needed to remind Edna that her business was her own so thrust the letter in her pocket, saying, 'I'll read it later. If I'm not back before you go to bed, I wish you a good night, Mrs Peel.'

Ignoring her scowl of indignation, Izzie left the house.

Inside the flat, she flicked on the lights and made to take off her coat to ready herself for the tasks ahead. As she put the flat keys into her pocket for safe-keeping she felt the letter she had put there earlier. Still with no idea who it was from or what it contained, she pulled it out of her pocket, slit it open and took out the contents. She began to read it. As she did so, a groan of anguish escaped her lips and her shoulders sagged despairingly as the impact of the words she was reading registered.

The letter was from Mr Miller who had interviewed her for her new job. He was most apologetic but said he was having to retract his offer of employment due to the fact that the woman it was intended she should replace had withdrawn her notice, after a change of heart. He apologised for any inconvenience this may have caused Isabel and wished her well for her future.

Inconvenience this may have caused her! This was far more than a minor inconvenience. The news put paid to her planned move into this flat instead of a crummy bed-sitter. No, worse than that, she couldn't even pay rent on a bed-sitter as she was now jobless.

Retracting her own notice was not an option as her replacement had already been recruited from another department. Izzie had been showing her the rudiments of the job for the last two days and it would be most unfair of her at this late stage to disappoint Fiona Blackman who had always made it very plain she hankered after a position in the post room, a step up from her job in the basement filing department. She had been over the moon when Marjorie Evans had offered Izzie's place to her. Besides, Fiona's job had already been filled by someone else in the works and *her* post was being advertised in the *Leicester Mercury*. The powers that be at Jones and Shipman did not hang about when it came to running the firm efficiently. Besides, she wouldn't have retracted her own notice even if she'd had no such considerations as there was still the problem of Lawrence.

She was distraught at losing her new job, but even worse was the thought of losing this flat.

Her mind raced frantically to find a solution. She could manage on her savings for a while until she landed another job. Getting one shouldn't be too hard as there was plenty of clerical work on offer. But what if the wage she was offered was the same as she'd received at Jones and Shipman? She could top up her wages each week out of her savings to keep on the flat. But what would she do once her savings ran out if she hadn't received a pay rise by then to cover the shortfall?

As matters stood, it seemed to Izzie that somewhere along the line she was going to lose this flat. She felt she had no choice but to cut her losses now and give it up before she settled in and the place became home to her. Then it would be an even bigger wrench than it was now to part with it. Once it was clear what her future earnings would be she would just have to begin her search for her own place again.

That painful decision made, a thought struck her. This meant she would have to go cap in hand to Edna and ask if she minded letting her stop on for a while longer. Of course Edna wouldn't really mind at all. She'd have Izzie back on board to fetch and carry for her, treat in any way she liked, knowing Izzie was beholden to her for a roof over her head. The thought filled her with dread. She knew Pat would have her back willingly, and so would the rest of the family, but that still left the problem of Suzy having to go back to sharing a room with her sister just when she was getting used to having a room of her own. No, she had no choice but to stay put at Edna's while she secured herself another job and then saw what accommodation she could find on her new wage.

She wondered if the woman who'd changed her mind about leaving that job had any idea what a dramatic effect her decision had had on the future of the woman who had been going to replace her?

Isabel gave a heavy sigh as she looked at her wrist watch to see the time was just after seven-thirty. Good sense dictated that she inform Nan Willett she was no longer in a position to rent the accommodation as soon as possible. She ought to go now and get it over with, then straight round to tell Pat the planned move was off and explain why. Her nieces would be disappointed but she hoped they'd be able to understand why they wouldn't be spending time in their aunt's new accommodation, for the foreseeable future at least. She would deal with the furniture tomorrow lunchtime. Hopefully the shop would take it back off her, albeit at a lower price than she'd bought it for, but hopefully she wouldn't be too much out of pocket there as she already was on the bond for the flat and all the cleaning materials, and paint.

Taking a last longing look around the rooms that had been going to be her home, trying not to think of the happy time she knew she would have spent here, with a heavy heart Isabel locked the door securely behind her and set off for Nan Willett's house, the address of which was known to her via the tenancy agreement she had signed before Nan handed her the keys. It was a decent walk away on Wingate Drive.

Nan Willett looked very surprised to see who her caller was. 'Not a problem already, Miss Jenkins?'

Izzie took a deep breath. 'Not with the flat, Mrs Willett, but yes, I do have a problem. You see, my circumstances have changed. I'm no longer in a financial position to rent the flat.'

'Oh! Oh, I see. Well, I'm sorry to hear that as I know you'd have made a damned sight better tenant than my last proved to be. Well, I'll keep next week's rent as your notice. As for your bond, I'll need to do an inspection of the flat to make sure there's no damage before I hand you that back.'

'The flat is in a far better state now than it was when I took it on, Mrs Willett.'

'I don't doubt your word but I'd prefer to be the judge of that. Call in at the shop next Friday and we'll settle up.'

Izzie pulled the keys out of her pocket and handed them over. Then, after telling Mrs Willett she was very sorry for the way matters had turned out and wishing her goodnight, she made her way back down the path.

Shoulders hunched, feet dragging, it was only with great difficulty that she managed to keep at bay the flood of miserable self-pitying tears that threatened to engulf her. This morning she had risen with thoughts of a new job and a first home of her own to look forward to. Now, through one faceless woman's decision, that whole future had dissolved into ashes. Life certainly seemed to have a grudge against her at the moment, she thought, a cloud of doom settling upon her.

Suddenly she stopped short as a terrible thought struck her. She was in danger of turning herself into the likes of Edna if she continued to think like that. Edna had ignored the fact that all human beings have their fair share of cruel blows to deal with, not just herself. Isabel had overcome the far greater disappointment over Lawrence, hadn't she? She could overcome this too. There would be another job out there for her and another place to live. Dwelling on her losses wouldn't get those found.

With new determination, she resumed her journey.

The street lighting being poor on this street meant she didn't see the well-dressed old lady standing in the middle of the pavement looking around bewilderedly until she had almost collided with her.

Flashing the woman a quick courtesy smile as she made to skirt around her, that lost air struck Izzie. Forgetting her own plans, she stopped and asked, 'I'm sorry to bother you but are you all right? Only you look like you're lost.'

The woman stared at her for several long moments, weighing her up. Seeming satisfied at last that the young woman before her was no threat, she responded, 'Well, yes, I am, my dear.'

Izzie smiled kindly at her. 'If you tell me where you're looking for then maybe I can help you. I know these streets well.'

The old lady looked mortally relieved. 'Oh, do you? Oh, thank goodness. I've been wandering around for hours trying to find my way back. It was light when I came out and now it's dark and everywhere looks so different in the dark, doesn't it?

I was beginning to give up hope and worrying I'd be out all night until you came along.'

'So where is it you're trying to get back to?' Izzie gently probed.

She looked worried. 'Well, that's it, you see, dear. I can't seem to remember. I've only lived in this area of the city for a few days . . . just over a week, in fact.' Her face grew wistful. 'The house was far too big for me after my husband died, God rest him, and we'd no children so I've no son or daughter to move in with. In fact, I've no living relatives left, so I was quite delighted when I found out about the place I'm in now as the lady who owns it likes to think we're all one big family. And it is a very nice place . . . so much better than some I went to see, and actually very reasonably priced compared to some homes that wanted extortionate fees. So the money my husband left me plus what I got from the sale of the house should see me well through until my time comes. I've a lovely room and they look after you so well. Nothing's too much trouble for the staff.'

A look of shame filled her lined face then. 'Mrs Johnson isn't going to be very happy with me now, though. She was most insistent that for the first few weeks new residents coming from outside the area shouldn't go out without a member of staff accompanying them. Not until she's happy we're familiar with our new surroundings. But the staff member assigned to me, I can't quite recall her name now . . . oh, dear, my memory really *is* playing me tricks today . . . but anyway, she never turned up and I thought she'd forgotten. I so wanted a walk around my new neighbourhood, and I did need to visit the chemist for a few bits and pieces which another resident very kindly gave me directions to, so I decided I could manage by myself. But I must have taken a wrong turn out of the drive . . .'

'I take it you live in an old people's home?'

'Lodge, dear. Mrs Johnson is of the opinion that her residents have enough to remind them they're in their twilight years without the name of the place they live in adding to it. But another name comes before Lodge and I just can't seem to recollect what it is. The name of the road is the same as the Lodge, you see, and that's why I couldn't stop anyone and ask them for directions.'

Well, on the evidence so far her place of residence could be anywhere, Izzie thought. 'Er . . . is there any landmark that you can remember seeing nearby? A church maybe?'

'A church? Yes, there is as I intend to go on Sunday with some of the other residents who attend. Mrs Philpots has very kindly said I can sit next to her. She's very nice and has the room next to mine. We share similar tastes in things so I know she and I are going to get along very well together. Her husband was a doctor, you know, so she understands a lot of medical things through helping him run his surgery and it was her who advised me to get some . . .' She stopped in mid-flow, looking worried. 'Oh, dear, Mrs Philpots told me the name of it but I can't seem to recall it at the moment, though I do have it written down in my handbag. Anyway, some linament for my knee to help ease the pain I suffer from it. That's why I was planning to visit the chemist.'

'So this church,' Izzie prompted her, 'do you remember any features about it that could help me recognise it?'

The old lady thought for a moment. 'Oh, yes, I do,' she jubilantly proclaimed. 'It had a cross on top of the spire.'

Not very helpful, Izzie thought privately, as most churches did and there were numerous places of worship in Leicester. 'What about a park? Can you remember if there was a park nearby?'

She shook her head. 'Fraid I can't, dear.' Her worried expression returned. 'I'm never going to find my way back, am I?'

'Yes, of course you are,' Izzie insisted, the old lady's plight beginning to upset her too. 'We just have to work this through, that's all. I won't leave you until I've seen you safely back to the Lodge, I promise you.'

'Oh, you're so kind,' she gratefully uttered.

It struck Izzie then that if this woman had been out for hours then she had missed her evening meal and her stamina would be ebbing by now. It was also turning very cold. Izzie needed to get her into the warmth or her health would be at risk. It was more than likely that her absence had now been discovered by the staff where she lived and the alarm raised. An idea came to her. 'Look, it's quite possible that the police have been informed that you're missing. I'm on my way to my sister-in-law's. Why don't you come with me? You can have a warm and a cup of tea there while I pop to the nearest police station and make enquiries.'

'Your sister-in-law wouldn't mind my turning up unannounced?'

'She'll make you most welcome,' Izzie assured her.

'Well, in that case, a cup of tea would be most appreciated, and I am rather cold as it happens. The nights are fairly drawing in now, aren't they? I should have put my heavier coat on but I didn't intend being out so long.'

Izzie took her arm. 'It's not too far, I'll soon have you there.'

They had only gone a short distance and had just turned the corner of the street into the main Narborough Road when the lady pulled Isabel to a stop and started looking searchingly at a large four-storey Victorian house on the corner of the road. A short well-lit drive led up to a double oak door.

'Is there something wrong?' Izzie asked.

'Wrong? No, no. It's just that this place looks familiar to me . . . The place I live in has pretty shrubs in the beds underneath the windows and a sundial in the middle of a circular patch of lawn, just like this place has . . . Oh, but this is it!' she proclaimed. '*This* is where I live. I can't believe I was so close.'

Relief flooded Izzie. 'Well, thank goodness for that. You're home safe and sound. I'll just watch from here to see you make your way inside then I'll be on my way.'

'Oh, but you must come inside and allow me to reward you for your kindness. I could have been wandering around all night if you hadn't offered me your services. I wouldn't insult you by offering you money but I've a nice little scarf in my room that I'd like you to have as a token of my appreciation.'

'There's no need really,' Izzie insisted. 'It was my pleasure.'

'But I must reward you,' she insisted back. 'My mother raised me to acknowledge good deeds. She might have passed long ago but it wouldn't be right of me to go against her teachings.'

Izzie couldn't bring herself to upset this sweet old lady. She sighed resignedly. 'All right.'

As soon as they entered the imposing, immaculately decorated and furnished tiled entrance hall, a middle-aged woman dressed in a nurse's uniform burst out of a room off the hallway and rushed up to them.

'Oh, Mrs Austin, thank goodness you're safe,' she blurted in genuine relief. 'When I heard the outer door open I was so hoping it was you and not one of the night staff coming on duty. When Nurse Beattie went to meet you to accompany you out and there was no sign of you, she thought that as she was late due to an emergency you'd got tired of waiting for her and gone up for an afternoon sleep in your room. Then, when you never turned up for your tea, we went to your room and found it empty with no sign of you anywhere else in the building. None of the other residents could remember seeing you all afternoon so we realised you'd obviously gone out on your own. We've all been frantic since. Mrs Johnson is out now, searching the streets for you, and the police are too. Where have you been, Mrs Austin?'

Just then the outer door opened again and a smartly dressed mature woman hurried through.

'Oh, Mrs Johnson . . .' the nurse called across to the new arrival.

'Oh, Joyce!' Mrs Johnson cut her off. 'I've looked everywhere and there's no sign of her. Oh, I'm so worried about the poor dear. She must be so cold, tired and hungry by now. I can't imagine what state of mind she must be in. I've just popped back in case the police have turned up anything. But I don't know where to try next. Where could she have got to?'

The nurse put a hand on her arm. 'But, Mrs Johnson, Mrs Austin is safe. She's here. Look,' she said, pointing across at her.

Jennifer Johnson's frantic eyes darted to where Joyce was pointing and her relief at seeing the return of her missing resident was readily apparent. 'Oh, Mrs Austin, thank goodness you're safe! I was beginning to imagine all sorts had happened to you.' She turned to address Joyce. 'We'll deal with the whys and wherefores later. It's imperative we get Mrs Austin to her room. Help her out of those cold clothes, please, and dress her

68

cosily in her night attire. She'll need a hot water bottle put in her bed. Will you see to that for me? Then check she gets a hot drink and some food, and stay with her until you're sure she's suffering no ill effects. I need to inform that nice constable at the station that our lost lamb has returned to the fold, safe and sound.' For the first time it registered with her that a perfect stranger was amongst them. Looking quizzically at Izzie she asked, 'I'm sorry, I don't know you, do I?'

'She's the nice young lady who took the trouble to help me find my way back here, Mrs Johnson,' Amelia Austin spoke up. 'I got lost, you see, and in my confusion I couldn't remember the name of this place. The young lady was so patient with me. Did her best to coax me into remembering, and when I still couldn't she offered to take me to her sister-in-law's house for a cup of tea while she went to the police station to ask if I'd been reported missing. Wasn't that kind of her? You were so right, Mrs Johnson, in telling me I shouldn't go out unaccompanied until I was more sure of my surroundings. But I thought . . . well, excuses can't disguise my stupidity but after today I will take heed of your advice to me, you can rest assured. Meanwhile I want to reward this young lady for her kindness, it's the very least she deserves. I've a little scarf that will do nicely. My dear late husband bought it for me on one of our anniversaries. It's very precious to me. It's in a drawer in my chest.'

'That's very nice of you, Mrs Austin,' Jenny Johnson responded. 'Kindness certainly does deserve reward. If you give it to Nurse Joyce she will make sure this lady gets it while you're making yourself comfortable. Oh, and should you require any medical aid to get you off to sleep after the excitement of today, let Joyce know and she'll see to it for you.' Turning to face Izzie she asked, 'Would you like to come into my office and take a seat while you wait? I must make a call to the station before the police waste any more of their valuable time.'

With that she turned and walked purposefully across the hall, obviously expecting Izzie to follow her.

'Thank you again, young lady,' she heard Mrs Austin call.

She smiled back. 'Again, my pleasure, Mrs Austin.'

'I'll be back down with the scarf as quick as I can,' Joyce told Izzie before she patiently began escorting Amelia Austin across the hall towards a gated lift at the back.

Jenny Johnson was already on the telephone talking to the desk sergeant at the local police station when Izzie arrived inside her office and seated herself on the comfortable chair before the desk as she had been invited to by a wave of Mrs Johnson's hand. Conversation ended, she replaced the receiver in its cradle and gave Izzie her full attention. 'The police were very understanding. Well, I know Mrs Austin is rewarding you for what you did for her but I hope you'll accept my sincere thanks too?'

Izzie was getting a little tired of being thanked for what she perceived as something anyone would do in the same circumstances. 'I really appreciate Mrs Austin's gesture but I'm not comfortable about accepting something so precious to her. Or anything, in fact.'

'Oh, but you must accept it . . . er . . . I'm sorry, I don't know your name, dear?'

'Isabel Jenkins. I'm known as Izzie.'

'Well, Izzie, as I was saying, you really ought to accept the scarf. A refusal will, I'm sure, upset Mrs Austin. If it's any consolation, after all my years in this business, I know for a fact that elderly people do not give their treasured possessions away unless they have really good reason to, and more importantly want to.'

Izzie knew then she had no choice but to accept the scarf. 'I'll make sure I take great care of it.'

Jenny looked at her appraisingly. 'Are you a nurse?'

'A nurse? No, I'm in clerical work. Why do you ask that?'

'You have the qualities about you that, in my experience, good nurses possess. A calming air and patience. I was a nurse in my youth and a Matron told me then I had those qualities too. Said they made the difference between a good nurse and a great one. You must have had some experience with the older generation, though, from the way Amelia said you dealt with her situation?'

'Well, no, I . . .' Izzie stopped short then, remembering the years spent keeping Lawrence's mother occupied and coping with her picky ways. Then there was Edna and Mrs Liddle . . . 'Well, actually, I suppose I have. I used to help a . . . friend keep his crippled mother amused, and I lodge with an elderly lady at the moment.' Before she could stop herself she added, 'You need the patience of a saint to cope with Edna as she can be very trying.'

Jenny gave a laugh. 'Oh, my dear, I know all about cantankerous elderly people. Not all my residents are as sweet-natured as Amelia Austin is, I can assure you.' She glanced at her wrist watch. 'Joyce shouldn't keep you much longer. I expect you're wanting to get off home to your husband and children. They'll be wondering where you are.'

'I'm not married, Mrs Johnson.'

'Aren't you? Oh, I would have thought a lovely woman like you would have been snapped up long ago. Just not found the right one, I take it?'

She had thought she had. 'Yes . . . yes, that's right.'

The other woman smiled warmly at her. 'There's plenty of time for you. I didn't marry until I was in my late-twenties. Unfortunately my dear husband died five years later.' She flashed a wan smile. 'I still miss him dreadfully. He was a great man.' She looked across the room as there was a tap on the door and Joyce stepped inside. 'Ah, here's Joyce now. Our wanderer all right, is she?'

'She's no worse for her excursion, I'm glad to say, Mrs Johnson,' said the nurse, walking across to them. 'As soon as I've done this errand for her I'm off to the kitchen to get her a cuppa and some food.' She handed Izzie the neatly tissue-wrapped scarf she was holding. 'Mrs Austin asked me to thank you once again for your kindness towards her. She also told me to tell you that if you're ever passing and have time, maybe you'd like to call in and have a cup of tea with her. Be nice for her if you could. Makes the old dears' day when they're expecting a visitor, especially those in Mrs Austin's situation with no living relatives, and friends increasingly fewer due to their advancing years.'

Izzie smiled up at her. 'I'd like that. Please tell Mrs Austin

I'll call in to see her as soon as I can manage.' Joyce departed and Izzie carefully put the tissue-wrapped scarf in her handbag then stood up. 'Best be off.'

Mrs Johnson rose too. 'I'll see you out.' As she walked around her desk to join Izzie she said, 'If you ever fancy a change of job, maybe you should consider one with old people. I think I'm right in saying you'd be an asset to the profession.'

Izzie looked stunned by this suggestion. 'A job looking after old people! Oh?'

'Don't look so horrified at the thought, my dear. It has its rewards, you know.'

'Oh, I wasn't horrified by your suggestion, Mrs Johnson, I was merely surprised by it as doing a job like that has never crossed my mind before. I'm looking for a new job at the moment, in fact, and I'll give your suggestion some serious thought.'

Mrs Johnson's eyes lit up keenly. 'Looking for a job? Well, if Lady Luck isn't shining on me today . . .'

At the prospect of work in any guise, Izzie eyed her keenly. 'Do I take that to mean you have a vacancy here for someone like me?'

'As a matter of fact, I do. My last day shift assistant, who was an absolute little treasure, left three weeks ago to take up her nurse's training. I encouraged her, much to my own detriment as I've been struggling ever since to find the right replacement for her as well as trying to ease the strain on the other day staff. I've had quite a few applicants, but although they could do the job adequately they didn't display the temperament I'm looking for in any member of my staff. The sort of qualities you displayed with Amelia Austin this evening. If you're seriously interested in a job here then I'd like to discuss it with you further.'

'You would!' Isabel exclaimed. 'Well, I'd like to find out more about it, yes, certainly I would. Would you like me to make an appointment, Mrs Johnson?'

'Well, there's no time like the present. That's, provided you can spare the time?'

'Yes, most certainly I can,' she eagerly responded.

'Then please sit down,' Jenny said, going back around her desk to resume her seat. Sitting comfortably in her chair, she clasped her hands in her lap and began. 'Becoming a nurse was all I ever wanted for myself. My mother was against it as she'd set her heart on me joining her in her fashion shop. She was a brilliant designer. Her clothes were worn by all the high society women in Leicester and beyond.

'Anyway, during my subsequent nursing career it always grieved me to see the way older people were treated by many others in my profession, and their own relatives too, some of them. Some people seem to be of the opinion that when you reach a certain age, you no longer deserve any show of respect or posses any dignity. Just because Nature is being unkind to you by slowing down your faculties and you start to suffer from age-related problems, it doesn't mean you're any less of a human being, does it?'

'No, it doesn't,' Izzie readily agreed.

'Well, I so wished I could do something about it but I knew I couldn't singled-handedly educate all the people who thought this way, or those to come in the future. What I could do, though, when I had the finances at my disposal, was provide a facility for at least a few elderly people who I could make sure did not suffer the same fate in their remaining years.

'I found myself in a position to buy this place nine years ago, and realised my dream. It had been a family home originally but in the twenties was bought up by a property developer who also purchased the house adjoining and combined the two into a hotel. The entrances adjoined, fortunately, and the two hallways were combined to make the spacious one we have now. The original staircases were taken out and a wider one leading to the first-floor landing installed. I understand the hotel was very popular for quite a few years, but during their last few years of ownership, for whatever reason the owners lost interest in the place and repairs of any kind were not tackled. It needed quite a bit of work doing to it when I bought it, and of course fitting the lift proved very expensive but highly necessary as not all our elderly residents find walking upstairs at all easy. Anyway, it took just about every penny I had but the result is this and I'm very proud of it.

'I have twenty residents' rooms altogether in what were the old guest rooms. Sixteen of those are on the first floor served by two bathrooms. The second floor has four rooms and one bathroom. The rest of the second-floor area is taken up by my own accommodation, which I share with my daughter, and of course I have my own private bathroom. All the residents' rooms are fitted out with the needs of the elderly in mind. Downstairs, this room and the one next-door are offices for myself and my daughter Leonie who deals with all the paperwork for the place. Opposite is the residents' lounge, and through the archway cut into what used to be the dividing wall is the television room. The large room next to that is the dining room, and behind that is the kitchen, laundry room and staff room. At the back of this side of the property is a conservatory leading out on to a large garden.

'Altogether I employ five trained nurses and five assistants. The day shift starts at seven-thirty and finishes at six and is staffed by two trained nurses and two nursing assistants. One assistant's job is vacant at the moment and hopefully you will be filling it. Then there is the cook and her helper, plus a full-time cleaner and two ladies who take care of all the laundry. I haven't included the gardener but he comes in once a week to tend the grounds and also any repairs or maintenance. I also have the services of a very reliable carpenter-cum-odd job man named Brian Knowles, and a good electrician and plumber.

'I'm jack of all trades, lending a hand where and when neces-sary, but most of my time is spent checking food supplies with Cook, dealing with any staffing problems, and of course any non-medical problems the residents may have, like repairs to their rooms. They come and report these to me and they don't like to rush. Usually a visit involves a cup of tea and a chat. I also arrange entertainments in the lounge as often as I can. Film shows on interesting subjects, topical talks, demonstrations, that sort of thing, for any residents who wish to attend. For the less able ones, I have an arrangement with the local library and a very nice librarian comes in every Wednesday morning to collect books and take requests.

'The nurses' assistants' duties are simple really. They fulfil any request a trained nurse or resident asks of them. That can be anything from helping a nurse soothe a resident while she tends them, helping to bathe them if they require help, making them a cup of tea should they want one in between our normal times, reading to those with very poor eyesight or accompanying them on shopping trips should they request. At all times I expect my staff to display the attitude that nothing is too much trouble.

'We have twelve ladies and eight gentlemen with us at present. All of the residents suffer a certain number of age-related ailments, some make more of an issue of these than others, but none is suffering from any terminal illnesses according to the doctor who attends them. Should that transpire, we do our best to care for a resident until it gets to a stage where the only answer is hospital care.'

Jenny paused long enough to unclasp her hands and lean forward to rest them on her desk. She looked questioningly at Izzie. 'I'd like to hear about you now.'

Izzie obliged.

When she had finished divulging her work background and some facts about herself, Jenny looked impressed. 'You are most certainly just the sort I've been seeking to fill Alice's shoes. Does joining us here appeal to you, Izzie?'

Izzie stared back at her thoughtfully. The job she was being offered was totally different from how she'd earned her living previously or had ever expected to, but it involved nothing she hadn't done before for Lawrence's mother or Edna. Mrs Johnson did seem nice and so had the nurse she had met, and from what Mrs Johnson had told her the rest of the staff were good people too. If she didn't find the job suited her then she could always return to what she had done before, couldn't she? And she did need a job that started as soon as possible if she didn't want to dig further into her precious savings. She had nothing to lose by giving this one a trial.

She smiled brightly at Jenny. 'It does appeal to me.'

'Oh, I'm delighted. So you could start a week on Monday?'

'I could start this coming Monday, if you would like me to. You see, I did have a job lined up but I received a letter today informing me that the lady I was to replace had withdrawn her notice. I couldn't do likewise as my position has already been filled and I've been training my replacement up for the last two days.'

'Might be remiss of me to say so but that lady's change of heart about leaving her job has proved to be my good fortune.' Jenny gave a laugh. 'Maybe I need to thank Mrs Austin too for getting herself lost like she did or our paths might never have crossed. Oh, goodness, I've mentioned nothing about pay, have I?'

Izzie had been wondering.

'Five pounds a week for a six-day week, and two weeks' holiday a year.'

Izzie's face fell. Working a six-day week against the five and a half she already did didn't concern her. But what did was the wage. Five pounds a week was not a bad wage for the duties involved but she had been getting six from her job at Jones and Shipman and could expect the same from another firm for her skills. She wasn't worried about cutting down on her outgoings to accept a job she would enjoy and be happy doing, but on five pounds a week she would never be able to afford to rent even the most dilapidated bed-sitter and risked having to live with Edna not just for the foreseeable future but years ahead. That thought did not appeal one little bit.

The disappointed expression on Izzie's face did not escape Jenny's notice. 'I take it you're used to earning more than I'm offering?'

'Well, yes, Mrs Johnson. A pound a week more. If it wasn't for the fact that I need that pound to be able to pay rent on a place for myself, it wouldn't be such an issue.'

The manageress's disappointment at this news was readily apparent. 'Oh, I see. Yes, you did mention your rather difficult landlady. Even though I imagine you are very tolerant with her, everyone reaches an age when they want and deserve a place of their own, not having to consider how others feel because they are living under their roof.'

Jenny Johnson really did know old people and their ways, thought Izzie. Without her having to go into great detail, on the scant information Izzie had divulged, Jenny had deduced for herself exactly what life with Edna was like.

Jenny gave a heavy sigh. 'Well, I would dearly like to entice you to accept my offer by offering you more money, but you see, I already pay ten shillings a week above the normal going rate for a nurses' assistant to secure the best staff, and there's the fact that if I did pay you more then in fairness I'd have to up the other assistants' wages too. My finances wouldn't stand it unless I raised the residents' rates, which I try my best to keep reasonable so some can afford to live here who otherwise wouldn't. My accountant is always on at me to cut corners or risk bankruptcy, but the residents' welfare is far more important to me than lining my own pockets.'

Izzie picked up her handbag from the side of her chair and stood up, holding out her hand. 'I appreciate the time you've spent telling me about the job, Mrs Johnson. I really am disappointed that it isn't possible for me to accept the position.'

Jenny rose too, leaning over the desk to accept Izzie's hand and shaking it firmly. 'Me too. I just wish the outcome could be different. I'm sure you would have fitted in very nicely here and proved an asset. Such a pity I couldn't have offered you a live-in post and that would have solved the financial problem, wouldn't it? Still, it's just one of . . . Oh!' she suddenly exclaimed as a thought struck her. 'Oh, but maybe I can do something about your accommodation situation. Please sit down again, Izzie, and hear me out.'

When Izzie had done as requested she said, 'Look, I told you that this place used to be a hotel, didn't I?'

Not having a clue where Mrs Johnson was heading with this conversation, she said, 'Yes, you did.'

'Well, when the two houses were originally combined, the attics were still kept separate to provide accommodation for the male and female hotel staff. When I bought it I couldn't see any point in spending money turning them into residents' accommodation . . . too high up and the lift can't reach that far. Anyway, both attics are accessed from a back staircase in the corridor by the kitchen. When I had my own accommodation designed, I had the access to the attic above my flat bricked up to make my flat completely private. The attic rooms the other side, though, are fully accessible and, more important, lying empty. There are three rooms which would make you a nice little flat. One room for a bedroom, one a sitting room, and a kitchen. I'd have to get the plumber in to put a sink in the room that's to become the kitchen, and the electrician to wire in a cooker point, but that's not a major undertaking. Actually there's a bathroom too that the hotel staff used to use, although it's rather antiquated, I'm afraid.'

Izzie was gawping at her. 'Are you saying I could rent the rooms from you?'

'Well, there's no point in them remaining empty when someone needs them, someone who'd accept a job here. The only problem is that the rooms are unfurnished. I can't promise to put new stuff in there but I could see what I could . . .'

'But I have furniture, Mrs Johnson, so all I'll need to get is a cooker,' Izzie excitedly cut in. 'You see, I was about to move into a flat of my own, tomorrow night in fact. I took the flat on the strength of the new job I was going to start on Monday. But then I received the letter today informing me the job was no longer mine so I had no choice but to cancel the tenancy. Oh, Mrs Johnson, I can't believe what you're offering me. Well, it's the answer to a prayer.' But there was still one important factor that hadn't been mentioned, the outcome of which would be the deciding factor as to whether she would be able to accept Mrs Johnson's offer. 'How much rent would you require from me?'

'Oh, I haven't thought. I don't know.' She stared at Izzie thoughtfully for several long moments. 'Does two pounds a week sound all right to you?'

Two pounds! Was that all she wanted? Izzie had feared it would be more in the realms of what Nan Willett had charged. This meant she'd be left with the same amount each week to manage on as she would have at the plastics factory and renting Nan Willett's flat. She couldn't believe her luck. 'Two pounds is fine by me, Mrs Johnson. And of course we'll come to some arrangement about the electric.'

'Oh, I can't imagine for a minute you're the sort that would run up a huge bill so shall we say ten shillings a week? The only problem is that the central heating wasn't extended up to the attics when I had it installed, so would a couple of two-bar electric fires be all right for you?'

This arrangement was getting better and better. 'Oh, Mrs Johnson, I don't know what to say.'

Jenny beamed broadly at her. 'I do. Confirm to me that you'll be starting on Monday with us?'

'Oh, yes, most definitely I will.'

'Well, that's settled then. I'll get the plumber and electrician to come tomorrow and do the necessary. If the worst happens and they can't manage to fit the jobs in at such short notice, I'm sure you won't mind managing without your own kitchen sink and cooker for a couple of days. You can use the main kitchen meantime. Sunday morning would be the best time for you to move in as many of the residents attend church so the comings and goings won't disturb them. The back entrance to the premises is accessed by a gate in the boundary wall around the corner in Westleigh Road which I'll make sure is unlocked as I will the door leading into the attic rooms at the top of the stairs. I'll have a set of keys cut for you so you can secure your accommodation when you're not in residence and for the back gate so during your free time you can come and go as you like.'

At the mention of Sunday a thought struck Izzie, a problem that had completely escaped her until now, and a worried look crossed her face.

Noticing the look, Jenny asked her, 'Is there something wrong, dear?'

Izzie took a deep breath. 'I'm so grateful for the way you've bent over backwards to make it possible for me to accept your job offer, and I want to so very much, but you see I have two nieces, lovely girls they are, Suzy and Sally, aged seven and eight.

I promised them faithfully that as soon as I was settled into a place of my own they could come and visit and stop overnight with me on occasion. Having made a promise to them, I would never break it.'

'And so you shouldn't. A promise is a promise whoever it's to, especially to children or how can we expect them ever to honour their own promises? No, it certainly wouldn't be right for you to break your promise to your nieces.' Her face was wreathed in thought. 'I have no objection to your nieces coming to visit you or stopping overnight as long as they're respectful towards the residents should they come into contact with them while they're here. The residents themselves are a different matter. Some elderly people have a great affinity with children, but some have a positive aversion to them. If those living here with an aversion outnumber the ones that don't, I could have a mutiny on my hands.'

A feeling of foreboding filled Izzie again. This was one problem she couldn't see Mrs Johnson being able to resolve for her. She was going to lose this job and all that it brought with it because of the promise she had made to her nieces, but regardless that promise would stand firm.

Then to her surprise she heard Mrs Johnson say, 'Well, if I have your promise that whenever your nieces are visiting you, you will use the side entrance to access your accommodation and not the main building we shouldn't have a problem, should we? The residents don't use the side entrance as it's where the bins are kept and household deliveries by tradesmen are made.'

'Yes, of course you have my promise I will, Mrs Johnson,' she exclaimed.

'Your word is good enough for me. So, Izzie, are you now completely happy with our arrangement?'

'Oh, yes, Mrs Johnson, I couldn't be more so.'

'And I couldn't be more happy that you're joining us.'

Just then Jenny Johnson diverted her eyes to look past Izzie and said, 'Hello, Leonie. Oh, you're dressed for going out. But I thought we were having supper together?'

Izzie automatically turned her head to see a young woman

of about twenty framed in the doorway. She would never have guessed this was Jenny's daughter as she looked nothing like her mother. It was obvious she took after her father who must have been handsome as she was very attractive in a delicate English rose kind of way, having fair skin and light blonde hair which was dressed fashionably in a bouffant on top, the sides fixed up in a French pleat. She was about five foot six and dressed very fashionably in a full white skirt and bright green short-sleeved scoop-necked blouse, a wide black belt pulled tight around her middle to accentuate her trim waist. She wore high black patent stilettoes and carried a coat over her arm.

'I thought so too, Mother, but it's after nine and I'm already late for meeting my friends at the skiffle club.'

Jenny flashed a look at her wrist watch. 'Oh, dear, is that the time? I didn't realise it was so late. Been one of those days today. Still, you'll be pleased to hear that Mrs Austin is back safe and sound with us, Leonie, all due to this young lady,' she said, smiling at Izzie. 'Oh, I haven't introduced you both, have I? Leonie, this is Isabel Jenkins, Izzie to us. Izzie, this is my daughter Leonie.' Both girls nodded a greeting as Jenny continued, 'Izzie is going to be starting with us on Monday as Alice's replacement. She's also going to be living in the attic rooms. Be nice to know those rooms are being put to good use after lying empty so long, won't it?'

Leonie smiled at Izzie. 'I hope you'll be happy here.' Then she said to her mother, 'Look, I must dash. I might be late, don't wait up.'

With that she turned and left.

'I was just like her when I was young,' Jenny said. 'Always dashing here and there, friends to meet, things to do. Right, well, I'd better let you get off too.'

They shook hands again and Izzie left the premises, hurrying off in the direction of her sister-in-law's house. She couldn't wait to tell her newfound friend what had happened to her tonight and see her face when she did so.

Pat was most surprised to see who her caller was.

'Good God, our Izzie, I wondered who on earth could be

knocking me back door down at this time of night,' she said, standing aside to let her in and shutting the door behind her. She gave a yawn before adding, 'There was nothing worth watching on the telly and me and Arnold were both tired so we decided to have an early night. We're going to be busy tomorrow night, moving you. He went up ten minutes ago and I was just finishing locking up, about to join him. Anyway, I'd have thought you'd have been bushed and in bed yerself by now after tackling what was left to do in the flat before your move tomorrow.'

'Ah, well, the move is off, Pat, because you see . . .'

'Oh, my God, Nan Willett has changed her mind about renting it to you, hasn't she?' Pat interjected. 'That's what you've come around at this time of night to tell me, isn't it? But who would she ever get who'd be as good a tenant as you, and after all that hard work we've put in too. I know what's she's done. After all our hard work she's letting it out to another tenant at a higher rent. She can't do this. I'll go . . .'

'Listen to me, Pat,' Izzie cut in. 'It's not Nan that's changed her mind about renting the flat to me, it's the other way around. You see . . .'

But Pat wouldn't let her finish. 'What do you mean, you've changed your mind about moving in there?' she asked incredulously. 'But why, Izzie?'

She knew she'd burst if Pat didn't allow her to tell her story. 'Look, Pat, sit down and shut up while I tell you everything.'

Pat stared at her gob-smacked. Izzie had never told her to shut up before, and there'd been many times in the past she would have had every right to. Now, obediently, Pat pulled a chair out from under the kitchen table and sat down. As soon as Izzie was seated opposite her she demanded, 'Well? I'm all ears, and I promise not to utter a word until you've finished.'

Izzie began her tale, starting from the letter she had received earlier that evening and finishing with shaking hands with Jenny Johnson a few minutes ago.

Pat was stunned by it all. 'Bloody hell, what a turn up!' she exclaimed. 'You're in the depth of despair one minute 'cos you've lost yer job and through that had to give up your new flat, and the next minute yer jumping for joy because you've landed another job and another place to live. I can't believe this new job and place to live really came about through you stopping to help an old dear who'd got lost. This Mrs Johnson sounds a saint from how you've described her. One thing's for sure, she obviously wanted you to work for her considering how she's bent over backwards to sort things out for you. You'll have to tell Arnold all this, I'm sure he'll think I'm exaggerating. Eh, but Izzie, are you really serious about wanting a job looking after old people? I'd have thought you'd have had a bellyful of pandering to old folk after Lawrence's mother and then mine.'

Izzie smiled at her. 'I thought I had too. But not all old people are as cantankerous as those two. Mrs Austin was a lovely old lady and very grateful for the help I gave her. More importantly, Pat, I got a great deal of satisfaction from what I did for her. Anyway, if I do come across any who show the same traits as Lawrence's mother and Edna, then because of the experience I've gained handling their tantrums and demanding ways, I'll know how to handle them, won't I? In a way, all those years spent with Mrs Clayton and then your mother have been like an apprenticeship for me.'

Pat looked at her as though she was mad. 'Huh! Well, I suppose that's one way of looking at it though only the likes of you could see it all that way. Still, if you find the old dears too much to cope with, day in, day out, you can always fall back on what you did before and you'll have a roof over your head here with us meantime.'

Izzie smiled gratefully at her. She had a feeling, though, that she wouldn't be taking up Pat's offer. From the way this had all come about, she felt destiny had guided her towards going to work for Jenny Johnson at Westleigh Lodge and she was going to be very happy there.

CHAPTER EIGHT

Monday morning at seven-fifteen Izzie locked the door at the top of the back stairs that led to her accommodation and proceeded to make her way down to join the other day staff in the nurses' room to begin her first working day at Westleigh Lodge.

Her last Saturday-morning shift at Jones and Shipman, after her twenty years of service to them, had proved very emotional for her. Departmental staff she'd hardly been on nodding terms with previously stopped by the post room to wish her well and she'd been choked to receive not only a leaving gift from Marjorie Evans – an ornamental brass pillar box along with a card expressing her thanks for Izzie's efforts – but also a collective gift of a red cyclamen pot plant from the four women she had regularly shared her lunchtime with since Lawrence's desertion of her. Carrying her gifts, a feeling of loss and sadness had enveloped Izzie when she had walked through the firm's gates for the last time. Not all her memories of work over the last twenty years were soured by one employee's abuse of her feelings. But that sadness and loss were soon mixed with anticipation of what the future held for her in her new place of work.

Her move the previous morning had gone far more smoothly than she'd dared to hope it would. Arnold, despite being somewhat miffed that he'd to forgo his Sunday morning lie in and lunchtime pint at the pub, had nevertheless thrown himself into Izzie's relocation by rearranging the use of his friend's van and roping him into helping too. He'd also arranged for the second-hand shop to open up especially on the Sunday morning so they could collect the furniture Izzie had purchased from them, along with the cream enamel three-plate electric cooker she had added the previous afternoon after finishing her last shift at Jones and Shipman. Unbeknown to Izzie, he'd slipped the reluctant owner a backhander of ten shillings by way of a bribe.

Suzy and Sally were told they would be spending the duration of their aunt's move with a neighbour, much to their fury as both were desperate to view and explore their aunt's new abode and help with the move. Both expressed their displeasure very vocally, only quieted by a severe threat from their mother that if they didn't do as she told them then she would not allow them ever to visit their aunt, let alone stay overnight with her. That had been enough to send them on their way.

While Arnold was collecting the furniture and packed boxes of Izzie's possessions along with a box of necessities she had shopped for after buying her cooker, she and Pat, armed with carrier bags full of cleaning materials, arrived in the attic of Westleigh Lodge all geared up for a session of hard labour in ridding the rooms of the dust and cobwebs of years ready for the furniture to arrive. They were both rendered speechless to find that not only was it all spotless, since Jenny Johnson had obviously commandeered the services of her own cleaner to do the honours, she had also used her persuasive charms on the plumber and electrician already as in the room Izzie would have chosen herself for a kitchen, a sink with running hot and cold water had been fixed to the wall under an eaves window and a cooker point been fitted on the wall opposite, ready for wiring in the cooker, a job Arnold was capable of doing for her. Propped against a vase of fresh late-flowering roses from the garden on the kitchen windowsill, her new employer and landlady had left a note welcoming Izzie to her new home and wishing her every happiness. There was also a set of newly cut keys. Izzie was very touched by such thoughtfulness.

On inspecting her new accommodation for the very first time Izzie had been delighted by what she had discovered. As her rooms were situated in the roof space of the premises she had been concerned they'd prove dark and pokey, but to her surprise all of them were much larger than she'd expected and an eaves window in each meant they were light and airy.

Pat too had been very impressed by it all, although in her opinion it would definitely benefit from a coat of paint throughout which she and Arnold would help Izzie with when she felt ready. She was, though, very impressed that Izzie had a bathroom to herself, albeit its fittings were very old-fashioned, and was somewhat envious that Izzie's was situated right next to the room she had chosen as her bedroom whereas Pat's bathroom, courtesy of a government moderisation grant a couple of years ago, had been placed in the old adjoining outhouse. It was accessed by a door at the end of the kitchen and was bitter cold in winter. Baths taken during those months were hurried and no pleasure. Here Izzie's ablutions would not be disturbed by anyone desperate for the use of the toilet and nor would she have to clean up after other people.

By twelve o'clock Pat and Arnold, plus Arnold's mate, had done all they could towards Izzie's move apart from unpacking her possessions. Once Izzie had insisted she could now manage by herself, they went off to enjoy what was left of their Sunday, but not before Izzie had firmly promised Pat she would visit her after work the next evening to tell her how her first day had gone.

At nine o'clock that night, before she had retired to bed in order to be up fresh and alert to start her new job next day, Izzie had wandered around the rooms to admire her efforts. She had only been in residence for a matter of hours but already the place was beginning to feel like home to her and she knew it would be even more so when she had picked up a few items to make it more homely. Izzie had worried she would feel a certain amount of loneliness living on her own after a life spent residing with others. She need not have worried, though. To her surprise it felt very liberating to have a place to call her own, to do whatever she liked in, whenever she liked, without having to consider the feelings of others. In essence a place where she could be herself.

Her accommodation felt right for her in every way and all she had left to hope for was that the job that came with it was right for her too, and more importantly she was right for it, so she could keep living in her new home for a very long time.

On tentatively tapping at the nurses' room door and entering, Izzie found the woman she knew as Joyce hanging her coat up on a row of pegs. She was a slim woman, in her early-forties, light brown hair pinned up into a neat French pleat and a nurse's hat pinned in place on it. She looked every inch the efficient nurse in her freshly laundered uniform.

Joyce smiled welcomingly at her. 'Ah, nice to see you're prompt.' She gave a laugh. 'Mind you, you can't use the excuse of the bus being late, can you, not living on the premises? If you do ever oversleep it's a short distance for one of us to come and knock you up.'

'Oh, I promise I'll make sure I don't oversleep,' Izzie assured her.

Joyce laughed. 'I was only joking, this is a good place you've come to work in. We all do things like that now and again – as long as they are only now and again, mind. I'd finished my shift by the time you left on Friday night but I was delighted when Mrs Johnson told me you were joining us here. It's been hard work coping with just the three of us on days after Alice left to take up her nursing training so it's great that we're up to full complement again.'

Izzie smiled back at her. 'I just hope I can prove my worth to you all.'

'Oh, you've already done that with the way you handled Mrs Austin. We couldn't have arranged a better test of your suitability if we'd done it on purpose. The old duck was still singing your praises when I left her an hour after taking up her tea to her. She's suffering no after effects from her wanderings.'

'I'm glad to hear she's all right.'

'You can see for yourself when you come across her later. It'll make her day when she finds out you're working here now. Oh, I'd better introduce myself properly to you. I'm Joyce Hill. Call me Nurse Joyce when we're on duty, but out of earshot of the residents plain Joyce will be fine. I understand from Mrs Johnson that you're known as Izzie?'

'That's right.'

Joyce held out her hand to her. 'Then welcome on board,

Izzie.' After they had firmly shaken hands she said, 'Well, we'd better get you kitted out.' She stood back and appraised Izzie before going across to a cupboard at the back of the room. Opening it up, she sifted through garments hanging inside until she found what she was looking for. Walking back to Izzie, she held out two blue-striped dresses, two belts and two white frilly caps. 'Two of each. One for wearing, one for the wash, and if necessary there are spares in the cupboard. I've a good eye so they should fit you. You can change in here or if you hurry you've time to change in your flat before our shift starts.'

Izzie felt it would be very prudish of her to go back upstairs, after all they were both women, albeit she secretly wished she had such a shapely figure as Joyce possessed to show off in her underwear instead of her own well-padded one.

As she was changing, Izzie asked, 'Have you worked here long?'

Joyce, the skirt of her uniform pulled up to her thighs, was refastening a suspender which had popped on her black stocking. 'Just coming up for six years. After my children reached an age when I could safely return to work, I'd been thinking of returning to the Royal Infirmary but trying to organise my family around the shifts, especially the night ones, well, I thought better of it. Especially when a day shift was advertised for an old folks' home not far from where I lived. Nursing the old is not everyone's cup of tea but I'd always found it very satisfying, so I applied. Bad mistake on my part.'

'Oh, why do you say that?' Izzie asked her quizzically as she pulled her uniform over her head and down over her body. Joyce certainly did have a good eye as it fitted her perfectly.

Having straightened her own uniform, Joyce was now checking her appearance in the mirror on the wall. 'It was a bloody awful place to work. The couple who owned it, Pain their name was, seemed very nice at my interview but as soon as I started it was obvious to me they were in it only to make as much money as they could for themselves. They treated their residents appallingly. The poor dears were got up early each morning and left sitting on commodes in the lounge all day. They were only moved at mealtimes when they were taken into the dining room. They were given no stimulation at all to keep their brains active. They used to force drugs down the ones who complained about the treatment. If relatives questioned the zombie-like state of those they were visiting, those that had visitors that is, then they were fobbed off with the excuse that they'd been forced to administer drugs on doctor's orders to quieten them as they'd become abusive to the staff through senility setting in. Of course, the relatives believed them. And the food they dished up . . . well, it was hardly better than pig swill. The other staff I worked alongside were a lazy lot and saw it as a place to make an easy living.

'I felt so sorry for the residents but it was a case of put up and shut up or else get out. It was obvious any pleading to the management to change their ways was going to fall on deaf ears, so I left. It still grieves me even now when I think of those poor folks in that home and others run just like that. Anyway, I was about to apply to the Infirmary for a position when I heard about this job going.'

'After your experience in that awful home, what made you apply for a job in another old people's home?' Izzie asked her as she cinched together the silver metal clasps on the elasticated belt round her waist.

'Well, to cut a long story short, the nurse who worked here before me was leaving because she and her husband were moving to a house in a village outside Leicester and it was too far for her to travel. When it came to her leaving time, Mrs Johnson asked her if she knew of a suitable replacement amongst her nursing friends. Well, the grapevine amongst the nursing profession travels as fast as any other and I got to hear about it. I have to say, Mrs Johnson sounded too good to be true but curiosity made me apply. And here I am.

'The rest of the staff have worked here since Mrs Johnson opened her doors to the first residents eight years ago, except for the young assistants who've replaced those who've left to further their careers, that is. I can safely say you will enjoy working for Mrs Johnson, Izzie. She's one in a million and that's no exaggeration. There's a waiting list of people wanting to spend their remaining years here, though most never get their wish granted as you can imagine, it being such a lovely place. Once lucky enough to get a room, the residents don't leave voluntarily, only in a box.'

Just then the door opened and a young girl of about sixteen entered. Underneath her open coat she was wearing an identical uniform to Izzie's. Joyce took one look at her and immediately launched in with: 'Just what the heck do you think you're playing at, miss, turning up for work like this?'

The new arrival looked innocently back at her superior. 'What do you mean?'

Joyce scowled at her. 'You know fine well what I mean, Alma.'

Alma obviously did too as she wailed, 'Ahh, just this once, Joyce. I promised to have it brushed out by the time I turn up for work tomorrow. Me friend's an apprentice hairdresser and she did it for me after work on Saturday 'cos I'd got a date with a new chap I'd met down the youth club on Wednesday night. I'm seeing him again tonight and I like him everso much. I don't want him to think I'm old-fashioned. Please, Joyce?' she begged.

'I'm no killjoy, Alma, but a beehive is not a suitable hair-do for the kind of job you do. What it is, is a health hazard. All that sticky hair lacquer keeping it in place.' She looked suspiciously at the mass of backcombed hair that rose inches above the young girl's forehead. 'There's no telling what's lurking inside it. A nest of mice for all we know. Nor are those stilettoes suitable footwear either,' she added, casting a look down at the girl's feet.

'Well, I'm going to change those for me flatties, Joyce.'

'Like you're going to brush out your hair and fasten it back, neat and tidy, like it should be. You want to be thankful, young lady, that you're dealing with me and not Matron at the Royal. She would have had you marched off the premises and not allowed to return until your hair was dressed according to hospital rules, *and* she'd have put you on a week of sluice duty by way of punishment. Now you're a good gel, Alma, and have never given any of your seniors here cause to speak to you about your appearance for work before, so let this be the first and last time.'

Just then the door opened again and another woman bustled

through. She was middle-aged, very round of figure, and had a jolly look about her.

'Morning, all,' she called out as she hung her handbag on a coat hook while she took off her coat. 'Hope you all had a good weekend, unlike mine with the surprise party for me dad's eight-ieth birthday coming up. I'm helping me sister organise it and with the worry of it all I hardly had a wink of sleep. I need to nick a couple of Mogadons out of the stock bottle 'cos if I don't get a good sleep tonight, I'm gonna be fit for nothing.' Having replaced her handbag with her coat, she turned to face them all and spotting Izzie, dressed as she was, exclaimed: 'Oh, Joyce lovey, make my day and tell me we have at long last found a replacement for Alice?'

'We certainly have, Beattie. Meet Isabel Jenkins. Izzie to us.'

Holding out her hand in greeting, broad welcoming smile on her rotund face, Beattie came over to Izzie. As they shook hands she enthused, 'I'm pleased to meet yer, ducky. Welcome on board. I'm Beatrice Coleman. Nurse Beattie in front of the resi-dents, plain Beattie otherwise.'

She then noticed Alma's hair-style but before she could voice her disapproval, Joyce said, 'I've dealt with it already, dear. Alma's just going to brush it all out. Weren't you, Alma?' she added meaningfully.

The girl immediately began to take out the black velvet ribbon fixed in the back of her beehive as a prelude to brushing it out.

'Whose turn is it to do the handover with the night shift, Joyce?' Beattie asked her. 'Mine or yours? So much has happened to me since last Friday I can't remember.'

'Mine,' Joyce told her. 'And I'd better get off now so the night staff can get home. You're happy to give Izzie an introduction to the place, Beattie?'

'Yes, 'course I am.' A thought seemed to strike Beattie then and she said to Joyce, 'Can I have a quick word in private?'

Over by the cupboard, she whispered something in Joyce's ear and Izzie saw her face light up and heard her exclaim, 'Oh, fancy me forgetting about that. You can deal with it, can you, while I'm doing the handover?'

Beattie nodded. 'Leave it to me.' As Joyce hurried off to attend to the handover with the night staff, Beattie addressed the younger woman. 'Right, Alma, hurry up and get that mess on the top of your head sorted, then get yourself off to the dining room for breakfast duties. Izzie, I'm sorry to abandon you, dear, this being your first morning, but I've a quick errand to do first so wait for me here and I'll be back to collect you shortly. I'll give you a tour around the place then assign you your first duty. That all right with you?'

Izzie nodded. 'Yes, of course it is.'

With that Beattie turned and followed Joyce out.

'They both seem very nice,' Izzie said to Alma, who was engrossed in fishing a hairbrush out of her handbag. Having found the brush, Alma began dragging it through her hair, grimacing as it immediately became entagled in the mass of back-combing her hairdresser friend had had to do to create the hair-style. 'Oh, bloody hell! Help me get this brush free from me hair, will yer, Izzie? It won't budge for me.'

Izzie went across to her and took hold of the brush, gently trying to ease it free.

Realising her new colleague was having difficulty fulfilling her request, Alma worriedly asked her, 'Oh, you won't have to cut it out, will yer?'

Izzie was beginning to fear that drastic action might be the only answer when thankfully the brush came free and she handed it back.

A mortally relieved Alma accepted her brush. 'Oh, ta, yer a lifesaver.' As she began brushing it again, far more carefully this time so as not to repeat what had just happened, she said, 'I ain't going to all this trouble again for any man. Beehives might be all the rage but this is one fashion I'm gonna give a miss in future. Anyway, what was it you said to me, Izzie?'

'That the nurses both seem nice,' she repeated.

'Yeah, they are. Like mums to me, the pair of them. My own mam died when I was three and I've been brought up by me dad since, so it's great to have them to turn to when I need mumsy sort of advice. Although they can take it a little too far sometimes, for my liking. Now I've opened me trap about me new fella they'll both be wanting to know all about him, to check they think he's suitable for me. Anyway, I knew I'd get it in the neck for coming in with me hair like this but I thought they might let me off for once. I was wrong, weren't I?'

Izzie laughed before saying to her, 'I've met Mrs Johnson's daughter, only briefly when I was being interviewed, but she seems nice too.'

Alma gave a shrug. 'From what I see of her she's pleasant enough. Don't see much of her, though, hardly anything in fact as she's in her room all day doing all the office work Monday to Friday. It's Mrs Johnson herself who deals with all us staff. The rest of them are lovely. Cook's a treasure. She always makes more cakes than she needs each day for the residents so us staff get one with our afternoon tea, and the night staff get their share too. You'll love working here, Izzie. Worked in a place like this before, have yer?'

She shook her head. 'No, I haven't. I was in clerical work before.'

Alma pulled a face. 'Didn't like the thought of office work myself when I came to leave school and get a job. I didn't fancy factory work either so I thought I'd end up working in a shop or something. I found out about this job through a mate of mine whose sister worked here as an assistant straight from school and was only leaving 'cos she was six months into expecting her first baby. I couldn't believe it when Mrs Johnson offered me the job out of quite a few other gels my age who'd applied. She told me I'd got all the qualities she was looking for,' Alma said proudly. 'Mrs Johnson, Joyce and Beattie are always trying to encourage me to train as a nurse.' She gave a laugh before adding, 'Anyone would think they wanted rid of me! But I'm happy doing just what I am. I had enough sitting exams at school and never passed them so there's not much chance of me passing me nursing exams, despite them telling me I could easily if I applied meself. Do you live far away?'

'No, I don't. Upstairs in the attic actually. When Mrs Johnson found out I was looking for a place, she very kindly offered to rent the empty attic rooms to me.'

'Really? Oh, that was good of her. I shouldn't be surprised though as Mrs Johnson is like that, bend over backwards to help her staff if they need it and she can. When she found out it was me dad's fiftieth birthday and I wanted to do something special for him but couldn't really afford to, Mrs Johnson got Cook to make a cake and some sausage rolls and other bits and pieces so I could have a little party for him, and she wouldn't take any money off me.' Her once tangled hair now brushed smooth, Alma swapped her brush for an elastic band she'd got on her wrist. Having swept back and fixed her mid-length blonde hair up into a pony tail, she said to Izzie, 'I'd better get off to the dining room to make sure everything's ship-shape before all the old dears start arriving to tuck into their breakfast. Thank God you're on board now and this is the last mealtime I'll have to manage by meself. Anyway, we'll probably bump into each other during the morning but otherwise I'll see you at coffee break at eleven. Hope you get on all right.'

And with that she too left the room.

So far Izzie liked what she was seeing. Her colleagues on the day shift did come across as a friendly bunch and she couldn't have wished for a better reception from them. All she had to hope now was that there was nothing involved in the duties attached to her job that proved beyond her.

Izzie was left twiddling her thumbs for over ten minutes before Beattie popped her head around the door.

'Izzie, can you do me a favour, ducky, as none of the rest of us are free? I know it's putting on you as we haven't even shown you around the place yet, but Joyce is still doing the handover with the night staff; I'm just about to go and check our medical supplies to see if we're running short of anything so Mrs Johnson can get the order in earlier enough for delivery on Thursday, and Alma is showing her face to the residents in the dining room and lounge. Only I've just remembered we haven't got Mr Danvers up yet. It's usually the night staff's duties to see to all the residents who need a hand getting up but Mr Danvers won't rise before eight in the morning, so seeing to him falls to us day staff.'

'Yes, of course I'll go and help him,' Izzie willingly responded. 'He just needs support getting out of bed?' she asked Beattie to confirm she'd understood her instructions properly.

The other woman smiled appreciatively at her. 'Yes, that's right. His room is on the second floor, number twelve. Turn left at the top of the main stairs and you'll find it all right. Meet me back down here. As soon as I've finished with Mrs Johnson, I'll pop back and collect you.'

Izzie found room number twelve easily enough and gave a purposeful tap on the door, waiting respectfully for a response from the occupant. Several seconds passed before she heard a deep, very cultured baritone voice command, 'Enter.'

Opening the door, she walked in. This being her first glimpse inside a resident's room, she couldn't stop herself from having a quick glance around. Mrs Johnson had indeed not exaggerated when she had told Izzie she had gone to much trouble to ensure the comfort of her residents. This room had obviously been designed with a man in mind. It was tastefully decorated in a rich blue and cream Regency stripe; a dark blue and cream woollen carpet covered the floor; plain Draylon drapes hung from the window, the colour a near-perfect match to that in the stripes of the wallpaper. The furniture consisted of a comfortable-looking double bed, side cabinets with matching bedside lamps on each, double wardrobe and chest of drawers all of which were in dark oak, plus there was an easy chair by the window along with a bookcase and writing desk. There was a sink in an alcove by what had once been a fireplace but was now boarded up, a large radiator before it. Several shelves had been fixed to the wall above the sink for holding toiletries. Sitting under the window was a large trunk, garments piled on top of it as though Mr Danvers had been in a rush to get to bed the previous evening and not taken the trouble to hang up his clothes. What surprised Izzie was that the item on top, she assumed a shirt as it was a man's room she was in, was very feminine in colour, not at all the sort she would have thought a gentleman would wear.

She was so engrossed in her thoughts she almost jumped out

of her skin when a deep voice boomed out, 'I don't recognise you.' It was more an accusation than a question.

Her eyes went to the bed to see a pair staring warily back at her. The face they belonged to was long and narrow, dark hair greying at the temples. He looked to be a very distinguished man, though what the rest of him was like was not evident as the bed covers were pulled up under his prominent chin. It did strike Izzie that he appeared very clean-shaven for a man who'd been in bed all night.

Shutting the door, she made her way over to the side of the bed and smiled down at him. 'Mr Danvers?'

'I am indeed he. Peregrine Danvers at your service, madam. And who might you be?'

'My name is Isabel Jenkins. I like to be called Izzie, though. It's my first day here. Nurse Beattie sent me to help you up. Are you ready to get up, Mr Danvers?' she asked politely.

'Ready as I will ever be, my dear.'

'Would you like to tell me what you'd like me to assist you with then?'

She listened intently while he issued instructions to her. He wanted her to pull the bed clothes clear of his body, then slip her arm under his armpit and around his back to ease him up into a sitting position. Then, taking hold of his knees, she should swing him round until the backs of his knees were in line with the edge of the mattress, lowering his legs gently until his feet touched the floor.

She nodded by way of informing him she was quite clear in her mind just what he wanted her to do. She then took hold of the edge of the covers under his chin, pulling them down, and with her back to him walked her way down the bed taking the covers with her, which as he was a tall man, she had to do right down to the bottom to clear them completely off him. As she turned around to face him and make her way back up to the top of the bed in order to carry out the next stage of the operation, she stopped short, face wreathed in shock, her brain unable to accept what her eyes were seeing. She blinked rapidly several times to confirm that her mind was not playing tricks on her.

But it wasn't. Mr Peregrine Danvers really was wearing a woman's winceyette nightdress and not men's pyjamas as she had automatically expected him to be. With him being so tall, the ankle-length nightdress only came down to the top of his calves, exposing the rest of his very hairy legs.

'Is there anything the matter?' he demanded. 'Only you're standing staring at me as if I've three legs or something.'

'Pardon? Oh, er . . .' Her mind raced frantically, not knowing what to say to him that wouldn't offend him. At Jones and Shipman she had heard rumours about one of the female staff who was divorcing her husband because she had arrived home from work earlier than normal one day and found him in their bedroom, dressed in her clothes, and not just her outerwear but underwear too. She had been in her teens at the time and in her naivety had chosen not to believe it, it never crossing her mind for a minute that it was indeed no rumour but the truth. But faced with what she was now, obviously there were men who liked to dress as the opposite gender. How did she react? Did she openly show her shock at this discovery? Did she pass a complimentary comment that she thought his choice of night-wear very becoming? Did she pretend to ignore it and act like nothing was amiss, all in a day's work in fact.

In truth what residents chose to wear in privacy was their choice and nothing to do with her. Aiding people in personal situations was part of her job now, and this situation was a warning that she must learn to expect the unexpected on occasion in future.

She planted a smile on her face and said brightly, 'I'm sorry, Mr Danvers. I just had a momentary lapse of concentration. I was reminding myself of your instructions before I proceeded any further.' Resuming her position at the top end of the bed, she said, 'Right, if you can raise yourself up a little, Mr Danvers, so I can slip my arm around your back, I'll have you sitting up in a jiffy.' It took several moments to complete the manoeuvre, all the time making sure the nightdress didn't ride up to protect his dignity and spare her own embarrassment. Once satisfied Mr Danvers was sitting comfortably on the edge of the bed, she asked him, 'Anything else I can do for you before I leave you in peace to get yourself dressed?

'Well, as a matter of fact there is, my dear. I'd appreciate it if you stayed and help me dress.'

'Yes, of course I will, Mr Danvers. Clothes in your wardrobe, are they?'

'Er . . . no. I sorted out my attire for today last night before I retired to bed. They're on top of the trunk under the window. Would you fetch them over for me?'

Going over to the trunk, she bent to scoop up the pile of clothes, shaking each item out to lay over her arm. As she did so it was a great shock to discover that the item she had thought to be a shirt was indeed a woman's day dress, the item underneath it a full petticoat. She turned to face him. 'Er . . . Mr Danvers, I think you've made a mistake. These clothes are . . .'

'No mistake,' he cut in. 'I picked that dress 'specially, it's my favourite.' He flung out his arms in a dramatic gesture and added, 'You see, my dear, I cannot go on hiding my true self any longer. I'm fed up with having to hide behind closed doors. It's time the people I live amongst saw me as I truly am. We're no longer living in the Dark Ages. People are far more accepting of others' idiosyncrasies these days. It is rumoured that Hitler used to dress in women's clothes and his followers did not condemn him for it.'

Wouldn't have dared, Izzie thought.

'Bring the clothes to me, child,' he demanded.

She stared at him, frozen. Was Mr Danvers serious? Was he really going to present himself in the dining room dressed as a woman? How on earth would the rest of the residents take this revelation about someone who was living amongst them? It could shock some of them so much heart attacks might result. People were definitely beginning to become far more liberal in their thinking these days, but it was the younger generation leading the way in the revolt against Victorian attitudes, not the older. She feared dreadfully that Mr Danvers was about to make the biggest mistake of his life, one which could result in the termination of his residency at Westleigh Lodge when the rest of the guests presented a united front to Mrs Johnson and demanded his expulsion from their midst. She had to try and make him reconsider what he was about to do, make him realise the possibly serious implications for him.

'Oh, but Mr Danvers, are you sure about this? I mean . . .'

'Absolutely positive, my dear girl. You will support me, won't you? You will escort me down and stand firm by me when I present myself to the world as the real Peregrine Danvers, not just the sham I've been presenting for all my life?'

She gulped, her mind racing frantically. He was seriously requesting she accompany him down and stand by him, showing all the other residents that she fully approved his preferred mode of dress? But what would they think of *her*? Quite possibly it would not only be Mr Danvers faced with eviction in a very short time. Oh, God, what a dilemma she had unwittingly found herself in. Then she remembered why she was employed here. To support the residents. Mr Danvers had requested her support and that was what she was here to give.

Smiling weakly at Peregrine Danvers, she said, 'Yes, of course I'll accompany you down.'

Just then the sound of giggling reached her ears. Confused, she looked around to realise it was coming from the corridor outside. She turned her head to glance across to the door, surprised to see it was now open a good few inches when she distinctly remembered pushing it to as she had entered. The giggling increased to loud laughter and the truth suddenly dawned on Izzie. Now she knew what Beattie's errand had been about and why she'd been left on her own in the staff room meanwhile. It was to arrange all this with Peregrine Danvers and hope he'd be willing to put on a performance, which he obviously had been. She spun her head back to look at Mr Danvers who was now sporting an amused expression on his face. 'Oh, my God, this is a set up, isn't it?' Then she immediately launched herself across to the door and pulled it fully open to reveal Joyce, Beattie and Alma, clinging to each other, convulsed in mirth. 'Why, you rotten lot!' she shot at them, before seeing the funny side herself and joining in with their laughter.

Joyce was the first to regain her composure. 'You passed your initiation ceremony with flying colours, Izzie dear. Oh, what a hoot! I've not had such a laugh since we put Alma through hers.'

'Me neither,' said Beattie.

'I never laughed at my initiation ceremony,' said Alma, drying her eyes on a Kleenex.

'No, you screamed blue murder,' Joyce said to her as she stepped inside the room to address Peregrine Danvers. 'You were your usual brilliant self, Mr Danvers, your retirement is indeed a loss to the theatrical world.'

'Indeed I agree with you, dear lady, but there comes a time in everyone's life when tough decisions have to be made. When it came to the point when parts for handsome males were only being offered to younger men, and all I was offered were small supporting roles, I knew it was time I closed the lid of my tin of grease paints and returned to live out my remaining days in the town of my birth, my acting days over, except of course for leading roles such as today's and my monthly one-act plays to a captive audience here.'

Izzie looked at Peregrine Danvers with awe despite his comical appearance in the woman's nightdress. 'You're a real actor then, Mr Danvers?'

'Unfortunately, my dear girl, not in the league of our truly greats such as Olivier and Gielgud, but I was good enough to be cast in roles on Drury Lane alongside Peggy Ashcroft, Flora Robson, Edith Evans and Anna Neagle. In my heyday I was once cast in a play directed and written by Nolly himself – *Blithe Spirit*. I played the husband,' he said proudly.

Having noticed the puzzled expression on Izzie's face, Joyce nudged her in her ribs and whispered, 'Humour him, he's referring to Noël Coward.'

'Oh, Noël Coward,' Izzie exclaimed, impressed. Her admiration was no act as she was aware of Noël Coward herself and knew he was revered by all his colleagues in the acting profession, having read about him in the *Tit Bits* she used to buy weekly when younger. 'Really?'

'I certainly was. He's a homosexual, you know.'

Beattie clapped her hands together, thinking it was time this conversation was halted before it became embarrassing for them all. 'Well, we've work to do, ladies, and we need to leave Mr Danvers to dress himself . . . in normal men's attire . . . before he risks missing his breakfast, which he was about to go in for when I waylaid him to help us over this. Thanks again for another wonderful performance, Mr Danvers.'

'My pleasure,' he boomed back at her.

As they gathered together outside in the corridor, having shut Peregrine's door to afford him his privacy while dressing, Joyce asked Izzie, 'Would you really have accompanied our Mr Danvers downstairs dressed as a woman if we'd allowed your initiation ceremony to continue? Not that we would have, of course. There's a line to be drawn as far as things like this are concerned.'

'Yes, of course, I would have,' she answered with conviction. 'My job is to support the residents, isn't it? I can't say I was looking forward to it, though. I was worried about Mr Danvers ending up tossed out on the streets.' And she added, tongue in cheek, 'I didn't think the dress he'd chosen to parade himself in would really have done him justice.'

Joyce turned to Beattie. 'She'll do, won't she?'

Beattie grinned. 'I'll say.'

Joyce then said to Izzie, 'Right, I'll take you down to the dining room and introduce you to the residents in there plus the ones who've already breakfasted and are in the lounge, then give you a quick tour around the place, then you can assist me with some dressings I have to do. You can accompany me for the rest of the day. By the end of it you should know your way around and have a good feel for what your duties will be. That all right with you, dear?'

'I'm looking forward to it,' she eagerly responded.

CHAPTER NINE

Later that morning Izzie was in the medical supplies cupboard to collect an eye patch for an old gentleman with a nasty sty when Alma popped her head round the door.

'Hiya, Izzie. How's it going?'

Izzie turned and smiled at her. 'Fine up to now, Alma, thanks. Well, I've received no complaints from Joyce yet. I'm just trying to find an eye patch then I'm going to help her rebandage an ulcerated leg.'

'The eye patches are behind the finger bandages.'

'Thanks. I couldn't see what I was looking at.' Coming out of the cupboard, she locked the door behind her and turned to face Alma. 'So what are you up to?'

'Well, I've got to set out the seating in the lounge ready for the visit from the WI ladies who are giving a flower arranging demonstration this afternoon for those who want to watch, but first I'm off to help Mrs Miller find her purse. She wants to buy herself a new nightdress, and when old ladies make up their mind they want to do something, another time won't do. I'm just off up to her room to help her look for it. She's probably put it somewhere safe and can't remember where. Under the mattress is the favourite place.'

'Oh, don't mention nightdresses to me,' said Izzie, giggling as memories of earlier came back to her.

Alma laughed too. 'That was so funny, Izzie. I can't wait to tell me dad tonight, he loves to hear tales of the life and times in an old folks' home.'

'As a matter of interest, Alma, just what did you have done to you for your initiation?'

'Oh, bloody hell, don't remind me. It still haunts me when I think back on it even now,' she exclaimed, pulling a horrified face. 'That pair of buggers, Joyce and Beattie, I mean, told me that during the night an old chap had died and out of respect for the dead I was to sit with the body until the funeral directors came to collect it as they were all too busy. They told me not to worry as it was covered up. Well, I wasn't happy but I had to do as I was told, didn't I, 'cos I thought if I refused I'd lose me job.

'So there I was, sitting in this near pitch-dark room as the curtains were closed tight, with what I thought was a dead body with a sheet pulled over it, suffering a terrible dose of the willies and praying that the funeral man turned up quick so I could get out of there. It was dead spooky, believe me. Then all of a sudden the bloody corpse let out a loud groan, shot upright and boomed out "Boo" at me. Well, I was out of there before you could say Jack Robinson, screaming blue murder, and like with you this morning, them pair, along with Alice who you replaced, were outside the room laughing their bloody heads off. It was one of the old blokes they'd got to put on a performance for me as Mr Danvers wasn't with us then. The old chap, Harry Franks his name was, well, he's dead now, bless him, but what a character he was. He used to call me his sweetheart and tell me that if he'd been sixty years younger he'd have whisked me off to foreign parts and had me treated like a princess.

'Anyway, thank God you only get put through one initiation ceremony, that's all I can say, as me nerves wouldn't stand another trick like that playing on me. Oh, I'd best be off or I'll have Mrs Miller bending me ear for keeping her waiting. I'll see you at coffee break.'

Three hours later Izzie was back at the medical supplies cupboard, this time with Joyce. 'Well, that was a marathon this morning,' she said as she stacked unused medical sundries back in their relevant piles. 'It's not normally quite so busy. It's my opinion half of them were made up symptoms so they could get a butcher's at the new nursing assistant. I hope they all appreciated the fact we missed our own coffee break to make sure we saw to them all. I'm sorry about that, Izzie.'

'You've no need to apologise to me for a missed cup of coffee. The residents' needs come first.'

Joyce smiled at her. 'You've the right attitude for working here, lovey. You really have a knack of putting people at their ease. Mrs Hopgood was really quite het up about me tending her ulcerated leg as she knew it wasn't going to be a pain-free experience for her, but without me having to tell you, you took her hand and used just the right words to calm her and talk to her throughout so she hardly noticed what I was doing.'

'I'm pleased you're happy with what I've done so far.'

'More than happy, ducky. I know Beattie will be too when it's your turn to accompany her on her rounds. Oh, I've just realised that in this morning's rush, what with fitting in your initiation ceremony, I haven't got around to explaining to you how we work that. Me and Beattie take it in turns to do the medical round each morning. The one who's not on rounds holds court in the nurses' office between the hours of nine-thirty and twelve, to have a chat to any of the residents who feel they want the advice of a nurse.' She gave a laugh. 'And that can be on anything that's bothering them, mostly nothing medical at all. But that's what we're here for. We also take it in turns to accompany the doctor on his visits to those who need to see him when he comes in twice a week ... that's on a Tuesday and Friday afternoon and he's on call the rest of the time. It's Beattie's turn to accompany him tomorrow so I'll remind her to seek you out when he arrives and introduce you to him so he knows who you are. He's a nice chap is Doctor Landers, I'm sure you'll find him very approachable, same as we do.

'Only us qualified nurses dish out the actual medicines and those are kept in a cupboard in the nurses' room. We have stock bottles for common or garden medicines like aspirin and sleeping pills which Doctor Landers replenishes for us when we're running low, but other medicines for residents' individual ailments, like blood pressure and heart complaints and many more too numerous to mention, are kept in the bottles provided by the chemist with residents' names on so there's no mix up. It's part of us qualified nurses' duties to make sure the residents get their prescribed doses each day. We can't leave it to them because there is a danger they might forget. Oh, if you ever find yourself in need of something to help you sleep or have a headache or whatever, as we all find happening to us at some time in our lives, then we staff are trusted enough to help ourselves from the stock bottles.

'Anyway, when me and Beattie aren't attending to medical duties we basically keep ourselves occupied by doing what you assistants do unless we're called upon for an emergency, and you can guarantee that in a place like this there's usually an emergency at least three times a week on average. Apart from the age-related ailments they suffer, the old dears are always maiming themselves in some way or other, falling over, that sort of thing. Of course, if it's serious then we need to take them to the hospital and either me or Beattie go with them. And we have our share of hypochondriacs. Mrs Naylor is the worst one we have with us at the moment. It took me over an hour to convince her on Friday afternoon that she hadn't been poisoned by the fish at dinnertime but her nausea was caused by the whole one-pound box of chocolates she'd gorged all in one go in her room after her daughter brought them in for her the previous afternoon.' She paused long enough to look at the watch pinned on her chest. 'Oh, let's hurry and get the rest of this lot put away, it's nearly the residents' dinnertime and we have ours straight after.'

'Shall I meet you back in the nurses' room after our lunch, Joyce?' Izzie asked as she passed her the remaining supplies she was holding to put back in the cupboard.

Joyce looked at her quizzically. 'Oh, are you not having dinner with us then?'

'Well, I'm having my dinner tonight as it's a bit of a rush cooking it then eating it inside an hour at lunchtime. I was going to bring a sandwich along with me this morning but then I thought I didn't need to as I could go back up to my flat and make it fresh.' The very last thing Izzie wanted was for her colleagues to think she was aloof, not joining them while they all ate their sandwiches. 'Once I've made it, though, I could bring it back down and then join you to eat it, if you don't mind me joining you, that is?'

'Of course we expect you to join us,' she said, looking at Izzie as if to say how could she think otherwise. 'Mrs Johnson always joins us too. Her daughter doesn't. I understand from Mrs Johnson that she only takes fifteen minutes over her dinner so she can leave earlier at night. It's good when you work for your own mother and can arrange your work time to suit yourself, unlike us mere employees who are governed by set working hours. Leonie, I should imagine, has a hectic social life as most young things do these days and likes plenty of time to get herself ready if she's going out, especially with a boy. Anyway there's no need for you to make yourself a sandwich or dinner tonight as it's provided for us. We eat the same as the residents.'

Her dinner provided every day! This job was just proving better and better to Izzie.

'What day is it today?' Joyce mused. 'Oh, of course, it's Monday, so it's shepherd's pie today made with the remains of yesterday's roast. Believe me, Hilda Williams makes the best shepherd's pie you'll ever taste. She's the cook, by the way, and before we go in for our lunch I'll take you into the kitchen and introduce you to her. So you know, Cook comes in at eight and finishes as soon as the staff sit down to eat their dinners. Her assistant, Rita Smith, leaves as soon as all the washing up is done about two-thirty. The plates of sandwiches and cake for tea are prepared by them in the morning and left under cloths in the cold storeroom. It's the night shift assistant's job to clear the tables of the crockery and wash up once all the residents have retired to their rooms for the night. Cook and her assistant both have Saturday off and a retired cook and her widowed daughter come in to see to the meals then and the clearing up afterwards to earn some extra money. Not working weekends myself, I've never met them but I understand they're nice enough.'

'Does Mrs Johnson ever take a day off?' Izzie queried.

Joyce shook her head. 'Not while I've worked for her, she hasn't, just takes a few hours off here or there when she needs to do some personal shopping or get her hair done. She's never had a holiday to my knowledge neither. Her business is her life and it's not like she's a husband to look after, her being a widow and her daughter old enough to take care of herself. Anyway, while you assistants are occupied overseeing the residents at their dinner, me and Beattie go and see Mrs Johnson in her office for a confab to catch up with each other's morning so we all know what's going on. I'd better get off or they'll have started without me and have to go back over anything they'd discussed beforehand.'

'And what would you like me to do meantime?' Izzie asked Joyce.

'Well, it's part of your duties to join Alma in the dining room at twelve-thirty. She will put you straight on what's expected of you.' Before she departed Joyce smiled warmly at Izzie. 'Mrs Johnson is bound to ask you how you're getting on over dinner, but she'll ask me when we have our confab too. I shall take great delight in telling her that once again her choice of staff has come up trumps.'

Izzie arrived at the bottom of the thickly carpeted stairs just as Alma appeared from the door leading to the back of the house.

On spotting Izzie, she called over, 'Ah, there you are. I was just reminding the residents sitting in the conservatory that it was five minutes to dinnertime then coming to find you so you can help me get them all settled at their tables. Be nice to have another assistant again helping me do that so we're not so rushed.'

'So what happens at dinnertime?' Izzie asked her as she walked along with Alma towards the dining room.

'Same as teatime which is at five. We help the residents find a seat and settle down comfortably. Some like a pillow in their back. Refill water jugs, make sure anyone who wants mustard with their meal has it, that kind of thing. Then we serve them their dinners, soup first, then the main meal, then pudding which we collect from Cook and her assistant through the hatch. Takes about an hour all told. Once they've finished and gone up to their rooms for a nap or a rest in the lounge, we have some peace to have ours.'

'Sounds easy enough,' said Izzie.

'It is until you get some awkward cuss who finds fault with something and nothing you do is right and you know they're just being awkward for the sake of it. It doesn't happen often, thank God. All the residents here at the moment are nice enough, but some are a bit nicer than others, if yer get me drift.'

'When you say we help the residents find a seat, do they not all have their own designated places?' Izzie asked her.

'Oh, no. Mrs Johnson is dead set against that. She likes people to get to know each other and one good way of them all mixing together is at mealtimes. Otherwise they get cliquey, don't they, and some people can get left out, especially new residents coming in. Mrs Johnson wants everyone here to feel like they're part of a big family.'

Mrs Johnson had really thought things through when she had been planning how to run her old people's home, Izzie thought to herself.

By this time they'd arrived at the entrance to the dining room. From what she could see of the inside it was a bright room decorated in calming pastel shades of creamy yellow and light blue, matching drapes at the double French windows that overlooked the garden, which she imagined were open wide in warmer weather. Five round tables, each with plenty of room for the residents to move safely around, were big enough to seat four comfortably. A larger round table over in the far corner was set for five which Izzie assumed was for the staff.

Residents were beginning to arrive and Alma said to Izzie, 'Right, here we go. If yer get stuck on anything, just ask me.'

When Amelia Austin made her entrance a moment later she made a beeline for Izzie and said excitedly to her, 'Oh, my dear, I've been hoping to bump into you all morning but I believe you've been helping Nurse Joyce on her rounds. I was so delighted when I learned you'd be joining us here. I've told all the other residents I've been in contact with today all about you and how lovely you are and they're dying to meet you too.' She waved across to two women already seated at a table close by and called out, 'Cooee, Nora, Katherine, this is the lovely young woman I told you about who made sure I got home safely on Friday night. Silly me to get myself in such a tizzy. Now she's come to work here.'

Izzie smiled over in greeting before turning her attention back to Amelia. 'Would you like me to see you comfortably to your seat, Mrs Austin?'

'Oh, would you, dear?' She produced a cushion from under her arm which she handed to Izzie. 'If you could help me position my cushion in the small of my back, I would be most appreciative. I don't mind where I sit. It's the only way to make friends, isn't it, to mingle? Especially as I'm the newest arrival here. I told you I'd already made a friend in Mrs Philpots, didn't I, dear? That's her over there,' she said, pointing at the woman she had just addressed as Katherine.

'Yes, you did,' Izzie patiently responded.

'Well, I'm also getting quite friendly with Mr James too. He says there's a local bowls club nearby and he'll take me along one afternoon if I fancy going. He said I don't have to play if I don't want to, can just sit and watch, and you can have tea afterwards in the small pavilion.'

'Are you going to go?' Izzie asked her.

She looked coyly at Izzie. 'I might. Mr James really is a very nice gentleman.'

Romance wasn't just for the young then, thought Izzie as she took Amelia's arm and guided her over to a vacant seat.

A few minutes later most people had arrived and either seated themselves or been aided by Alma or Izzie when she happened to notice a woman standing just inside the door, looking around for a vacant seat. She was very smartly dressed in a tweed skirt and twinset, a pair of sensible shoes on her feet. She stood ramrod-straight, showing no signs of an elderly stoop to her shoulders. Her silver-grey hair was pulled back into a bun at the base of a long slender neck. To Izzie, this new arrival had a headmistressly aura about her.

Izzie made her way across to her. 'Hello. I'm Izzie, the new nurses' assistant. I see you're looking for a seat. If you'd like to come with me there's a seat next to Mr Granger or there's one . . .'

Before she could finish the woman exclaimed brusquely, 'Has no one told you that I am not averse to sitting anywhere, so long as it's not in that despicable man's company?'

Izzie was stunned by her harsh tone and surprised to hear her describing Frederick Granger as a despicable man. He'd come across as very pleasant when Izzie had introduced herself to him on his arrival a few moments ago. 'Oh, I see. I do apologise for suggesting it then, Miss . . . er . . . Mrs . . .'

Just then Alma arrived and blurted, 'It's okay, Miss Stringer, there's a seat over there, well away from Mr Granger's table. It's my fault Izzie didn't know not to suggest you sitting with Mr Granger, I forgot to tell her.'

Miss Stringer looked at her meaningfully. 'Well, I trust now you know it won't happen again.' With that she moved off to take her seat at the table Alma had pointed out to her.

'I'm sorry about that, Izzie,' Alma said to her apologetically. 'I don't know what it is with those two, and none of the other staff do either. They both came to live here around the same time a year or so ago and seemed to hit it off at first.' She confirmed Izzie's suspicions when she continued, 'Miss Stringer used to be headmistress at a posh girls' school before she retired. Some of her old pupils still come and visit her so she must have been well liked, and the other residents don't seem to have a problem with her or she with them either. Mr Granger was in local government, so I understand. They never used to have a problem sitting at the same table at mealtimes, and I've seen 'em strolling round the garden together many times, chatting away to each other. Then, a few months ago, suddenly it seemed they couldn't stand the sight of each other. What went off between 'em, well, they ain't telling. Anyway I'd love to know what happened between them 'cos it must have bin summat bad to cause them to hate each other, mustn't it?'

'Yes, I suppose it must have been,' mused Izzie, curiosity making her wonder herself. 'But unless one of them spills the beans then we'll all have to continue wondering. Anyway, now I know the state of play between those two, I won't make the same mistake again in trying to seat them together.'

The rest of Izzie's first stint of dinnertime duties passed without incident and, as soon as the staff were all seated around the table to eat theirs, Jenny Johnson asked Izzie how her morning had progressed and if she was enjoying her duties so far, but not before informing her that some very favourable opinions had reached her from those she worked alongside plus the residents she'd had contact with that morning. Izzie was delighted to receive this praise and pleased also to be able to respond sincerely that so far she was loving every minute and couldn't see that changing.

Later that afternoon Izzie opened the door leading into Mrs Austin's room and stepped inside. Amelia Austin had requested Izzie to fetch her gloves for her as she and another two residents were going for a walk around the garden, and having fetched her coat she had forgotten to pick up her gloves which were on the top of her chest of drawers. She didn't want to risk catching a chill and neither did she like the thought of the journey back up to her room again, which a younger person could manage a lot quicker than she could.

When Izzie had queried the fact that she had noticed the residents never locked their doors behind them, Joyce had explained to her that due to the age of the occupants and the accidents that frequently befell them none of the rooms was kept locked so that easy access could be gained by the staff to deal with mishaps quickly. Izzie saw the wisdom of this but then questioned the fact that the rooms were not really private as anyone could walk in. That was how she learned that a strict rule was enforced that no resident entered another's room without an express invitation, and never when that occupant was not in residence. To break this rule meant immediate eviction for the guilty party. Any staff member caught in a room without the resident present who could offer no valid or substantiated reason for being there, was immediately sacked. In all the eight years Jenny Johnson had been operating her business, no resident or staff member had been asked to leave for this reason.

Izzie was therefore stunned on entering Amelia's room to find it was not empty as she'd expected but that a man was present. He was over by the window and so engrossed in what he was doing, which seemed to Izzie to be fiddling with the window fastening, that he didn't hear her come in. She was on the verge on demanding who he was and what he was doing when she noticed he was wearing workmen's overalls and, judging by the type of tools hanging from a belt around his waist, was obviously the carpenter-cum-handyman Mrs Johnson had told her about at her interview. Unfortunately at this moment Izzie couldn't recall his name.

'Don't mind me,' she said by way of acknowledging him. 'I've just come to fetch Mrs Austin's gloves.'

At the unexpected sound of her voice, he spun round to face her, his own face wreathed in shock, almost toppling off the work stool he was standing on. 'Oh! Oh, my God, but you frightened the shi . . . er . . . life out of me, I didn't hear you come in.' A flash of guilt crossed his face and he eyed her in concern. 'Look, er . . . well, you see, I'm not exactly supposed to be in here but I was called in a couple of days ago to fix the window as Mrs Austin complained of a draught coming through. While I was doing it I noticed that the catch had warped over the years and wasn't fastening properly. It needed replacing. I was on the premises doing another job in the room down the corridor and, as I passed this room, remembered about the faulty catch. I did knock to check if Mrs Austin was in but obviously she's not and it seemed such a shame to charge Mrs Johnson for a second visit just to remind myself what type of catch I needed so I popped inside to have a quick look.'

Now Izzie knew the reason for his guilty look. 'And you're worried I might mention you've been in a resident's room without permission?'

'Well, yes. I could lose the money from the work I do here. I need all I can get to support my wife and three children.'

She looked at him searchingly. He was a big-made man, at least five foot eleven, not handsome but with facial features pleasantly arranged. He must be trustworthy for Mrs Johnson to allow him to carry out repairs and maintenance on her premises unsupervised. Izzie knew how particular her employer was about her staff and had no reason to believe this did not extend to the tradesmen she called in.

She smiled warmly at him. 'It's nice of you to try and save Mrs Johnson some money.'

He looked mortally relieved. 'I'm Brian Knowles, by the way. Carpenter-cum-handyman.'

'Isabel Jenkins. Izzie. Nurses' assistant. Started today.'

'Well, as I'm here on average at least once a week, I expect I'll be seeing you again.' He eyed her enquiringly. 'Er . . . will Mrs Austin be returning to her room in the next few minutes, do you know? It's just that I thought I might as well find out from her if there're any other jobs she wants doing in here that she's not had time to report to Mrs Johnson yet. She seems a nice old dear, Mrs Austin. While I was fixing her window last week we had a nice chat. She told me all about where she used to live. She hasn't any children, in fact not a relative left living. I feel sorry for those that are left alone like that.' He gave a laugh. 'When I'm doing repairs to their rooms some of the residents make a pretence of having something to do at the same time. I know it's because they want to have a chat so I let them rattle on. They love to talk about the good old days, don't they? I suppose it's because they haven't much of a future to look forward to. 'Course, not all of them are friendly. Some see me as an intruder in their room and want the repairs done quick so they can get rid of me, but I'm on friendly terms with several here and always give their doors a knock as I'm passing, just to say hello when I'm on the premises.'

He was coming across to Izzie as a very nice man.

'Anyway, is Mrs Austin on her way up?' he asked her again.

'No, I'm sorry, she's not. I did announce when I came in that I had come to fetch her gloves but you obviously never heard what I said as you were engrossed in what you were doing.' She went over to the chest and collected them. Making her way back to the door she said, 'Well, I'll leave you to it, Mr Knowles, as Mrs Austin will be wondering where I've got to.'

'Brian, please. I've nearly finished here so I won't be seconds behind you. In future I'll make sure I get proper permission from Mrs Johnson to enter an unoccupied room. Rest assured, I won't be putting you in a compromising position again.'

She flashed him a smile of appreciation before she turned and left.

'Oh, there you are, dear,' Amelia Austin greeted her as Izzie arrived back with her gloves. 'I was beginning to think you'd got lost. The others have gone on ahead as it starts turning chilly about four now autumn has well and truly set in, I'd better hurry to catch them up. Did you bring my hat?'

'You never asked me for your hat, Mrs Austin.'

'Didn't I? Oh, I thought I had.'

'Would you like me to go and fetch it for you?'

'No, dear. I've imposed on enough of your time. Er . . . now which way again is it to the garden? I can't quite seem to remember. In a large place like this it does take a while to get your bearings, doesn't it?'

It wasn't just Amelia still getting used to her new surroundings, Izzie was too. In fact she had got lost herself several times that morning so sympathised with the old woman. She smiled kindly at her. 'Down that corridor and on through the conservatory.'

'Ah, yes, I remember now.' She made to depart but stopped, looking thoughtful. 'Oh, I've just remembered I need to see Mrs Johnson about something. Now what was it?'

'If it's about your faulty window catch, then that's being dealt with, Mrs Austin.'

She looked blankly at Izzie. 'What faulty window catch?'

'The one in your room.'

She looked confused. 'I didn't realise it was faulty. It works perfectly well for me when I've opened and shut my window.'

Just then an elderly gentleman came up to Izzie. She had not been introduced to him before so didn't know his name. In a very loud voice he said, 'Excuse me, miss, but have I missed the start of the film show in the lounge?'

She looked quizzically at him. 'Do you mean the flower arranging demonstration by the ladies from the WI?'

He cupped his ear. 'What? Speak louder, girl.'

She repeated her words several decibels louder.

'Flower arranging!' he boomed out disgustedly. 'You've got your wires crossed, girl. Why would I want to go to a demonstration of that? That's for women, that is. The film show is on the Historic Houses of Leicestershire. I saw it advertised on a notice on the board in the residents' lounge. Monday the twelfth, it said, at . . . I think it was three but I'm worried now it was earlier than that and I've missed the start.'

'The twelfth was last Monday, Isaac,' an old lady supported by a Zimmer frame informed him. 'It's the nineteenth today.'

'Is it?' he exclaimed. 'The nineteenth, really? You sure?'

'Yes, it is,' Izzie confirmed to him.

He scratched his head. 'Oh! I was really looking forward to that film show. Got a packet of mints to suck during it 'specially,' he grumbled as he moved off.

Izzie turned her attention back to Amelia just as her face lit up and she exclaimed triumphantly, 'Ah, I remember now what I wanted to see Mrs Johnson about. It was your mention of the conservatory, dear. Someone is moving chairs around in there and not replacing them in their right places afterwards. It's a lack of consideration towards other residents. I need to inform Mrs Johnson about it so she can find out who it is and get the matter resolved.'

She then walked off in the direction of the office, totally forgetting that she already had a meeting fixed in the garden.

That evening Pat was convulsed in hysterics when Izzie related the trick her new colleagues had played on her that morning.

'Oh, Izzie, I'd love to have seen your face when you pulled back those bed covers and saw that chap wearing a woman's nightdress. I'd have fallen about laughing, I know I would.'

'Can we see that man dressed in a nightdress when we come to visit you, Aunty Izzie?' Suzy's voice piped up.

Pat's head swivelled round to see both her daughters looking back at her through a crack in the door leading to the stairs. 'Oi, you two! I've told you so many times about earwigging. Anyway, I thought I'd tucked you both into bed an hour ago, what are you doing down here?' she demanded.

They looked shamefaced.

'Well, we heard you telling our dad that Aunty Izzie was

coming round after work, to tell you all about her new job, and we wanted to see her,' said Suzy.

'Yeah, we did,' agreed Sally. Her small face puckered. 'We don't half miss yer, Aunty Izzie, so we've bin listening out for you coming.'

'I've missed you both too, sweetheart,' Izzie told her. 'Now if you both go back to bed like good girls and behave yourselves for the rest of the week, if it's all right with your mam, you can come and stop with me on Saturday night and we'll spend all day Sunday together.'

'Can we really?' they said excitedly.

'You can keep them until they're both old enough to earn their keep, if you want to, Izzie,' Pat said to her dryly.

Izzie laughed. 'I think your mam means by that that it's all right with her for you to come on Saturday,' she said to the girls. 'Now come and give me a hug and a kiss goodnight and I'll pick you both up on Saturday after I've done my weekend shopping.'

The girls both swooped on her, whooping in delight.

As soon as they'd been ushered off back to bed Pat leaned her elbows on the table, rested her chin in her hands and looked at Izzie keenly. 'Now, where were we before those little tinkers interrupted us? Oh, yes, you were telling me about the man in the nightdress. So what happened after?'

Izzie obliged, then proceeded to describe all the other things that had happened to her that day.

When she had finished Pat leaned back in her chair, folding her arms under her shapely chest. 'Well, you've certainly had an eventful day. You do seem to have taken to your new job.'

'Oh, Pat, I've really enjoyed what I've done today and it gives me such pleasure to know that what I've done, even little things, has contributed to making a resident's day better for them. Mrs Johnson said that caring for older people was very rewarding, and I have to say she was right as far as I can see.'

Pat looked at her quizzically. 'But don't their pernickety little ways get on your nerves, 'cos I know they would grate on mine? I'd end up losing me rag with the cantankerous ones. Having said that, you've got the patience of a saint, Izzie. Look how you were with me for all those years, never rising to my bait when I used to drop hints about you leaving this house, and how you put up with my mother during those weeks you lived with her. I'm just sorry I never appreciated you before, Izzie, and I'm so glad I was made to by my daughters. Anyway, this home you work in sounds more like a hotel to me from your description of the place than an old folks' home.'

'Well, from what Joyce told me of her experience in the other home she worked in, Westleigh Lodge *is* like a first-class hotel. I'd be happy paying hard-earned money to stay in it myself and be looked after and catered for like the residents are there. There's a waiting list to get in,' Izzie told her.

'I'm not surprised. Anyway, you can add my name to that list for when I get old enough, and as you're working there, I'll expect discount.'

Izzie laughed. 'You're thirty-three, Pat, far too young to be planning for your old age for a long while yet. Anyway, I'd best be off.'

Pat looked disappointed. 'Oh, so soon? But Arnold's not due home from his Union meeting for another hour and I'm so enjoying our natter.'

'I am too, Pat, but I want to pop in and see your mother on my way home.'

Pat eyed her as though she was mad. 'You want to visit my mother voluntarily? I popped in to see her this morning on my way home from the shops. She was her usual miserable self. Never thanked me for the jobs I did for her, jobs I had a reprieve from doing while you lived with her, by the way.'

'She's lonely, Pat.'

'And whose fault is that but her own? She's only got her neighbour next door as a friend because she's a cripple and can't get out to meet anyone else. It's my mother or no one for her.'

'Well, I think your mother is the way she is because she was so devastated by your dad's death that she was frightened to get close to anyone again.'

'We all get hurt at some time or another. Me mam's n'ote special.

Look what happened to you over Lawrence, Izzie, but you didn't let it sour you for life, did you?'

'I could easily have done, Pat, but thankfully I remembered how your mother allowed the bitterness she felt to affect her life. I might be wary of falling in love with another man until I'm absolutely sure his feelings for me are genuine, but the last thing I want is to alienate my family or friends from me as your mam has done. Anyway, thanks for the tea. Give Arnold my love. I'll see you on Saturday afternoon when I come to collect the girls.'

Getting up to see her sister-in-law out, Pat replied, 'I'm looking forward to it.'

Izzie wasn't sure whether Pat meant she was looking forward to seeing Izzie herself again or to being child-free for almost twenty-four hours at the weekend.

When Edna didn't answer her summons at the back door a short while later, Izzie realised that she wouldn't be expecting anyone so wouldn't be listening out for a knock. Having lived with her, she knew Edna's habits. At this time in the evening she would be watching her programmes on the television. Letting herself in, the sound of the television set immediately greeted Izzie. Despite calling out to Edna to announce her presence as she went through into the back room, it wasn't until she touched Edna's arm that she realised someone else was in the room with her.

'What the hell?' she cried out, her head spinning around so she could stare wildly at Izzie. Realising who her intruder was, her face tightened and she hissed, 'Oh, it's you. What do you want?' Before Izzie could answer a smug expression had formed on her face. Folding her arms under her matronly bosom, she said, 'I know why yer here. You've come tail between yer legs to ask me for yer room back as yer new place ain't working out for you, is it? Well, I need to think on it. Come back tomorrow and I'll let you know me decision. Now, if you'll excuse me, I'm missing *The Likely Lads*.' She then turned her attention back to her television set.

'Well, actually, I haven't come to ask if I can move back in, Mrs Peel.'

Edna looked taken aback. 'Eh? Well . . . er . . . what have yer come for?' she brusquely snapped.

'Just to see how you are.'

'Well, you can see how I am. I'm fine.'

'You're keeping all right then?'

'I managed fine before you came here, why wouldn't I now? The few odd jobs you did for me, when you could be bothered, didn't make that much difference to me. It was no skin off my nose when yer left.'

Edna really did make it difficult for people to like her and want to do things for her. Did it enter her head, Izzie wondered, that should anything happen in any way to take her daughter and neighbour from her, she would find herself completely alone in the world? Izzie was no blood relation so was not morally obliged to Edna in any way. By putting herself out to visit tonight, she was offering the hand of friendship. But Edna had not even tried to make her welcome by asking her to sit down or offering any refreshment. She gave a sigh. If only Edna would see just what she was doing to herself and change her ways, life would be so much more pleasurable for her. It was obvious to Izzie that her own impromptu visit tonight was viewed as inconvenient.

'I'm sorry I disturbed your evening. I'll let myself out, shall I?'

Without taking her eyes off the television, she gruffly responded. 'Well, you let yourself in without any help from me so I'm sure you can manage to let yourself out. Oh, and don't be late on Sunday. Eight-thirty sharp. Me and Florrie will be ready for yer.'

Izzie stared at her, taken aback. 'I'm sorry?'

Edna turned her head and glared over at Izzie. 'For the trip to Belvoir Castle.'

Izzie froze. She had forgotten all about Edna's volunteering her services for that trip. Now she had promised her nieces they were coming to spend the weekend with her. She couldn't disappoint them. 'Oh, Mrs Peel, I'm so very sorry, I can't manage it.'

'You can't? Why?'

'Well, I . . .' Her mind raced frantically. Edna would not be happy Izzie was putting her grandchildren before her and by her manipulative ways would make Izzie feel guilty, forcing her

to cancel her own arrangement with her nieces so she was free
to oblige Edna instead. 'Well . . . er . . . you see, I have to work,'
she lied. 'We're short-staffed at work. I'm sure in the circumstances another voluneer to replace me could be found.'

Edna scowled at her. 'Not one who'd stay with me and Florrie
all day and help push her around.' Izzie should have realised
that was why Edna had put her name forward, so she would
have a personal attendant. 'But if you've got to work, you've
got to work, there's nothing I can do about it,' she added sarcastically. 'I hope you can live with yer conscience that our day
out could end up not happening 'cos you've backed out. Florrie's
going to be so upset when I tell her.'

As Izzie closed Edna Peel's back door, she knew she wouldn't
be calling on her again. It was very clear to her that Edna hadn't
appreciated her visit and never would in the future. It was silly
of Izzie to keep putting herself in a position where all that was
achieved was her own discomfort. So she wouldn't call anymore,
not when there were those who did appreciate the time she spent
with them and showed it too.

CHAPTER TEN

The following Saturday evening, on the pavement outside the side gate of Westleigh Lodge, Izzie put down the bag of her nieces' belongings and squatted before them. 'Here we are, girls. Now, you will remember what Aunty Izzie told you, won't you?'

They both nodded.

'That we're not to cause havoc while we're here?' said Suzy.

Izzie inwardly smiled. What she had asked them not to do was make loud noises; what Suzy had done was to interpret these words in the way her mother would have expressed them. 'Well, yes, that's right, darling. And what else?'

'We're not to go anywhere else in the house but your flat.'

'That's right. No exploring.'

'Why can't we, Aunty Izzie?' Sally asked her.

'Weren't you listening?' her elder sister scolded her. 'Because we might annoy the old folk Aunty Izzie helps look after and she could lose her job.'

Sally's freckled face puckered up. 'But I ain't annoying.'

'Yes, you are,' her sister chided her. 'You annoyed Mrs Gillows when yer went into her back yard without asking her first to fetch yer satchel after Jimmy Dale threw it over the jetty wall yesterday. And you annoyed Mam last night when you wouldn't put yer comic down to come to the table for yer dinner.'

'Well, you're annoying too,' Sally shot back at her. 'You . . .'

'That's enough, girls,' Izzie cut in before a war of words broke out between them. 'Look, lots of old people don't mind children at all, but some . . . well, they find children irritating. Some older people you like and get on well with but some irritate you, don't they?'

'Like Gran irritates us, you mean?' asked Suzy.

'What's irritate mean?' Sally put in.

'Gets on yer nerves,' Suzy told her.

'Oh, yeah, Gran gets on mine all right,' Sally blurted. 'She's always telling me off and she never cuddles us or plays with us like other kids' grans do and she's always telling us to be quiet. She tells us that children should be seen and not heard. She annoys Dad too when she sits in his chair. I hate it when she visits and we have to visit her.'

'Yes, well, that's just the way your gran is unfortunately.' Feeling it best that this particular topic was halted, Izzie asked them, 'Look, are we straight on the rules then?'

Both girls nodded.

There were many things about their aunt's new abode that delighted the girls as they wandered from room to room on their first exploration of it. Sally loved most the fact that it was so high up she could see over the rooftops opposite, and far beyond when she looked out of the sitting-room window. Suzy liked best the fact they would all be sleeping in Aunty Izzie's bed together until such time as she bought them fold-up camp beds from the Army and Navy Store, to put up and take down when they came to stop with her. But most exciting for both of them was the fact their aunt said she would allow them to stay up later than their normal bedtime. They would all play games of Snakes and Ladders which they had brought along with them, and she would read stories to them that they chose themselves from a children's short story book Izzie had purchased on her shopping trip that afternoon.

She never needed to chide them once for even the most minor of misdemeanours and early Sunday afternoon, after helping their aunt clear away the delicious roast beef dinner which they had helped her prepare, both girls were very subdued after packing up their belongings for their return home.

'Why the long faces, girls?' Izzie asked them. 'It's not like you're never coming again, is it? Anyway, I'm not taking you home just yet as thankfully it's a dry day. We can still go to the park.'

That information put smiles back on their faces and both of them scampered off happily to fetch their coats. Izzie had enjoyed their visit so much herself she was already looking forward to the next time she had them to stop over.

As they were making their way through the side door to cross the paved area towards the back gate, Izzie was most surprised to see Amelia Austin, her back towards them, trying to unlatch the gate. Ordering Suzy and Sally to stay put in the doorway, she went across to old lady. Very conscious of making her approach quietly so as not to startle Amelia, Izzie asked her softly, 'Mrs Austin, what are you doing in here?'

She looked mortally relieved to see Izzie. 'Oh, my dear, thank goodness you're here. I was beginning to worry I'd never get out of this yard and end up spending the night here.' She looked puzzled to see Izzie, though. 'I haven't seen you around today, dear. I was looking for you before we set off for church this morning as I'd arrived downstairs to join the others and found I'd forgotten to pick up my prayer book. It was all right, though, as the other nice young nurse's assistant helped me, the one who comes in on a Sunday with the other nurse. Her name is Thelma, I think. Yes, that's right, it's Thelma. Or is it Thora?'

'It's Thea, short for Dorothea,' Izzie told her. 'Sunday is my permanent day off, that's why you couldn't locate me today, Mrs Austin.'

'Oh, yes, of course it is. My husband always used to say I was dizzy at times but my mind really is playing tricks on me just recently, isn't it?'

'We all get mixed up sometimes, Mrs Austin, whether we're young or old. I'm sure that it's all to do with getting used to your move here,' Izzie reassured her. 'So how come you are here? I'm sure Mrs Johnson would have told you this part of the grounds is not for residents' use. It's where the dustbins are kept and the tradesmen come in and out with their deliveries.'

'Well, yes, she did tell me there was a section at the side of the building that was out of bounds to residents, and the reason why, but I didn't realise that the gate I've often passed by outside in the street actually led into it directly. I wasn't sure where it led to, possibly a short cut into the garden that I hadn't been told existed, so I thought I'd satisfy my curiosity after dinner today before I went up to have my nap.'

It appeared exploring wasn't just for the young.

'When I entered the gate and realised where I was, I immediately made to go back out the way I'd come in but the gate had slammed shut behind me and I couldn't open it,' Amelia Austin continued. 'My hands are arthritic, you see, dear, and the latch is very stiff. So I tried to find my way back inside the building through the entrance you've come out of but the only door inside leads into the kitchen and the stairs opposite look very steep. I wasn't sure if I climbed them where I would end up.'

'In the attic where I live,' Izzie told her. 'Although you can also get into the main building through a door on the third floor. You could have gained access to the rest of the building through the door at the other end of the kitchen. Anyway, never mind, I'll unlatch the gate and escort you through to the front so I know you've got back safe and sound.'

She looked gratefully at Izzie. 'Oh, will you, dear? That is so good of you.'

After silently motioning to Suzy and Sally to stay put until she returned, Izzie unlatched the gate, then hooking her arm supportively through Amelia's, guided her through. As they made their way down the remainder of Westleigh Road and around the corner where the front entrance of the Lodge was situated on the main Narborough Road, Amelia said to her companion, 'Izzie dear, did you notice two little girls standing in the back door entrance? Do you think they're got themselves lost like me and need your help too? Maybe they wondered where the gate led to and wanted to find out for themselves. Then once they were inside couldn't unlatch the gate like I couldn't because it was too stiff for them?'

'The two children are my nieces, Mrs Austin. They were staying with me.'

'Were they, dear? Oh, and they are such pretty little things. Look like angels. Why haven't you brought them down to meet us?'

'I would really like to have done that, Mrs Austin, but you see, some of the residents might not take kindly to children amongst them.'

'But I like them. I was very sad when none came along for me. I know Mrs Philpots does too because she has three grand-children and so looks forward to being collected by her daughter to go and visit them every fortnight. I'm sure many of the other residents do too. After all, we were young once. When you're living so closely with people you have to be tolerant of others, don't you, give and take? I'm not so keen on a Sunday evening after tea on having to listen to Mrs Peters singing her old-time songs accompanied by Mr Waters on his accordion, because despite her thinking she can, she really can't sing, dear, and Mr Waters' accordion is very out of tune. But I don't object as I know many of the other residents do like the performances they give. Anyway, I could always go and sit and read or listen to my wireless in my room during that hour, couldn't I, just like the residents who really cannot abide children don't have to stay around if they don't want to. So next time you have your nieces to stay, you will bring them down to meet us, won't you?'

Izzie would have liked nothing more. 'As much as I'd like to, Mrs Austin, I'm afraid rules are rules and no children are allowed in the residents' areas. I have to abide by that. Careful of the steps,' she warned as they arrived at the front entrance. Inside the hallway, Izzie politely offered, 'Would you like me to see you to your room or can you manage from here by your-self?' She hoped her offer was declined as she needed to get back to her patiently waiting nieces.

'Well, I think I've gone past having a nap now, dear, so I'm going to sit in the lounge and have a natter with whoever is in there, or I just might go into the television room and see what Sunday afternoon film is on today. I would be obliged, though, if you'd help me off with my hat and coat and take them up to my room for me?'

The girls were just going to have to be patient a little longer. 'Yes, of course I will, Mrs Austin,' Izzie politely responded.

Typical of her generation, Amelia would not be hurried, and

despite Izzie's assistance it took a good five minutes for her to retrieve the old lady's hat and coat during which time Izzie was very conscious she really should be somewhere else. Finally in possession of Amelia's outerwear, and after seeing her on her way to the television room, Izzie made to hurry to complete her task, but just as she was about to put her foot on the first stair, she was stopped short by Amelia calling over to her.

'Oh, Izzie dear, while you're up in my room could you please bring me back down my library book? It's on my bedside table. Or is it on my tallboy? Well, it could be on my writing desk. It's in my room somewhere. Oh, and my reading glasses. Just in case, you see, the film on the television is something that doesn't appeal to me. I hope it's not a Western. Nor a gangster type. Too much violence for me.' Her aged eyes lit. 'Unless Ray Milland's in it.' A girlish look crossed her face. 'I've rather a liking for him, dear, he's a very handsome man.' She then looked expectantly at Izzie. 'You will get my book and glasses for me, won't you, dear?'

Izzie told her that of course she would then made to hurry off urgently to complete her tasks, but before her foot had contacted the first step another voice demanded, 'Are you going upstairs, Izzie?'

She turned her head to see Muriel Peters over by the entrance to the lounge, looking expectantly back at her. 'Yes, I am, Mrs Peters.' Oh, please, don't ask me to fetch you something too, Izzie inwardly prayed.

Her prayer went unanswered. 'Oh, good, could you save me the trouble of going up myself? The stairs wear me out and the lift frightens me to death when it judders so. I only go up in it when I absolutely have to. Anyway, Mr Simmons would really appreciate me singing a favourite song of his dear late wife's tonight as it would have been her birthday today, only he can't remember the title and I can't make out what it is from his humming of it. He denies it, of course, but he's tone deaf. I should know, I used to be a music teacher. Anyway, could you go into my room and fetch my song book down for me? It's on my chest.'

Izzie smiled politely at her. 'Yes, of course I will, Mrs Peters'.

In order not to be waylaid by anyone else she immediately ran up the stairs, careful to ensure no resident was on their way down so she didn't collide with them.

Amelia's book was neither on her bedside table, chest of drawers nor her writing desk. Izzie eventually found it behind the cushion on her easy chair by the window where she must have been reading it last. Her glasses were another matter. She couldn't find those at all. Having spent a good ten minutes in Amelia's room, thankfully Muriel Peters' song book was where she'd said it was.

She was just closing Muriel's door behind her, when to her surprise she saw Doctor Landers approaching down the corridor. He was carrying his doctor's bag.

On spotting Izzie, he smiled warmly at her. 'Hello,' he said as he came up to her. 'I didn't expect to bump into you today, it's your day off, isn't it?'

She had only met Doctor Steven Landers on one previous occasion and for no more than a couple of minutes. That was on her second day of working at Westleigh Lodge when Beattie had made a point of introducing their newest member of staff to him. He had seemed very pleased to meet Izzie and she had instantly warmed to his very pleasant, easygoing nature. About her own age of thirty-five, maybe a little older, he was a stocky man of medium height with a thatch of thick black curly hair framing a round, chubby-cheeked face. His complexion was ruddy. He appeared more like a struggling country farmer to Izzie than a prosperous town doctor. He was dressed in a green tweed woollen suit – years old by the looks of it – off-white shirt, showing signs of wear around the collar, and a snagged brown sleeveless V-necked pullover. Izzie was pleased that she had made enough of an impression on him during their short introduction for him to have remembered her name.

'Yes, it is my day off, Doctor Landers, but I was just on my way out when two residents asked me to do an errand for them. Is today not a day of rest for you too, Doctor Landers?'

He gave a laugh. 'Oh, my dear, a GP is very lucky not to be called out sometime on a Sunday.'

A worrying thought struck her. 'Has one of our residents taken ill, Doctor Landers? Oh, I hope it's nothing serious.'

'All the residents are hale and hearty as far as I'm aware. Well, apart from the normal age-related ailments and some they've convinced themselves they have, that is. I was called out by a patient of mine who lives in the next street. It was thought she had broken her leg in a fall but thankfully it turned out to be a sprain. So while I was passing on my way back home, I thought I'd pop in and check Mr Danvers' blood pressure. It was rather high when I checked it on Thursday and I want to satisfy myself that the change of tablets I prescribed is bringing it down. I understand from Mrs Johnson he's in his room rehearsing his next performance for the residents in a couple of weeks. I suppose I shall be on the receiving end of a display of the dramatics from him for daring to disturb a thespian at work but his health comes before a performance, whether he agrees with that or not.'

With a twinkle in his eye he added, 'While he's under my care I will do my best to ensure he doesn't die on stage.' With an even brighter twinkle then he said, 'Anyway, I understand you've had experience of Mr Danvers' acting abilities yourself.'

He obviously noticed the look of embarrassment flood Izzie's face at this reminder of her initiation ceremony at the hands of her colleagues because he added, 'Don't look like that. I understand you gave back a command performance yourself. Anyway, Nurses Joyce and Beattie have expressed nothing but praise for your work since you've been here and the residents seem to have taken to you, especially Amelia Austin. According to her you're her guardian angel. I don't need to ask if you think you did right, leaving your office career behind and entering the caring profession. I can tell you think that.'

She smiled warmly at him. 'You're right, Doctor Landers.' A thought then struck her. The doctor didn't appear to have anyone along in a nursing capacity to assist him with his check on Peregrine Danvers. Automatically she asked, 'Would you like any assistance with Mr Danvers, Doctor Landers?'

'Thank you for your offer, it is very kind of you, but your day off has already been disturbed enough. Mrs Johnson is aware

I'm here but I declined her offer of assistance as well as Nurse Marion's as both of them were busy and I don't really need any help to check blood pressure.'

The people under Doctor Landers' care were as important to him as Jenny Johnson's were to her, Izzie thought. He was obviously also considerate of others as a man in his position could have insisted that either Mrs Johnson or Nurse Marion drop what they were doing, regardless of how important it was, to assist him. She suddenly found herself very much liking this doctor and wondered if he'd a wife awaiting his return? Then she realised that at his age of course he would have and possibly several children too. Even if he hadn't, and her type of woman happened to appeal to him, a professional man would never consider a relationship with a mere nursing assistant from the back streets of Leicester. Regardless, though, he didn't seem in any hurry to excuse himself from her company.

But a sudden vision of her nieces waiting patiently in the back entrance doorway for her return flashed before her eyes. 'Oh, please excuse me, Doctor Landers, but I have to dash. My nieces are waiting for me to take them to the park.'

In her haste to depart she did not notice the look of disappointment that flashed across his face before he replied, 'I hope you have an enjoyable time with them.'

As she went Izzie was totally oblivious to the fact that a very thoughtful Steven Landers was watching her hurry off down the corridor, his eyes not leaving her until she turned the corner to take the stairs.

As she reached the bottom, prepared to make her way first into the television room to give Amelia Austin her library book and inform her that her glasses were nowhere to be found so were possibly in one of her drawers, which Izzie would never go into unless specifically given permission, then quickly hand over the song book to Muriel Peters in the lounge, she noticed Jenny Johnson standing just before the entrance to the lounge, her hands clasped before her, deeply engrossed in whatever was going on inside. To capture her employer's attention so completely, something very interesting was obviously going on.

Curiosity getting the better of Izzie, she went across to stand beside Jenny and look inside the room.

The sight that greeted her had her gawping in horror.

At one of the two card tables where residents played their games of bridge and whist sat four people: Katherine Philpots, Jean Merridew – their oldest resident at eighty-seven, Cuthbert Swann, and last but not least her own niece Suzy. They were all playing a game of Ludo. Nearby, in comfortable high-backed chairs, sat four elderly ladies, among them Amelia Austin. Seated in the middle of them was Sally, proudly showing off her favourite doll, Elizabeth. Amelia Austin, the reading glasses Izzie had searched her room high and low for perched on the end of her nose, was leafing through one of the copies of *Woman's Weekly* Jenny provided for them.

It was obvious to Izzie that her nieces had grown worried over being left alone so long and gone in search of her, somehow ending up in the lounge. She couldn't be cross with the girls for disobeying her orders in the circumstances. A feeling of foreboding swamped her. When she returned from taking them back home, she would be packing her own belongings, no doubt, having been dismissed from her job.

'Oh, Mrs Johnson, I am so very sorry,' she blurted out to her employer. 'I'll take the girls home immediately and return to pack up my things. I'll need to make arrangements to have my furniture . . .'

Jenny was looking at her, confused. 'You're leaving us?' she interjected. 'But why, Izzie? I was under the impression you were very happy here with us.'

'Oh, but I am, Mrs Johnson. Couldn't be more so. But you specifically asked me not to bring my nieces into contact with the residents . . .'

'Yes, I did, dear,' she cut in. 'But only because of a worry that the number of residents objecting to having children in their midst might outnumber those in favour. Well, so far no one has said a cross word and, besides, look at the joy they've brought to eight of the residents in the short time they've been here. I bought the Companion Box of Games when I opened eight years ago and this is the first time it's been used. The other three residents in the lounge are carrying on with reading the Sunday papers and don't look as though anything else going on in the room is particularly disturbing them. Besides, Izzie, had I discovered your nieces causing any sort of disruption, I would not have sacked you. I would merely have asked you not to bring them on the premises again as our arrangement was not working out, that's all.'

Just then Sally spotted her aunt in the doorway. 'Oh, Aunty Izzie, these ladies are gonna knit 'Lizabeth some clothes. They're looking through the magazines to see if there's some doll's clothes patterns so I can choose what I like best. Ain't that nice of 'em? And they're gonna knit me other dollies some clothes too. They want me to bring them all in after school tomorrow so they can measure up. I said I'd read from me book to 'em then. Mrs Austin said she'd loved *Brer Rabbit* when she was little and she'd help me with the words I don't know. Mrs Austin ain't got no grandchildren of her own, Aunty Izzie, and said me and Suzy could be like her 'dopted ones. I can be, can't I, Aunty Izzie?'

Suzy too had now become aware of her aunty's presence. 'I can come too, can't I?' she called over. 'Mr Swann's gonna teach me how to play chess.'

'Oh, well, I don't . . .' she began.

Jenny cut her short. 'If the ladies have asked you to do that then you must oblige them, young lady,' she said to Sally. To Suzy she said, 'And of course you must come too. I play chess myself, and when Mr Swann has taught you maybe you'd like a game with me?' She turned to Izzie, smiling brightly. 'Seems my judgement was wrong on this one. Do the children live far from here?'

'Er . . . well, no, just a couple of streets away.'

'Well, then, as far as I'm concerned your lovely nieces can come any time they like out of school hours, as long as they continue to conduct themselves as they are now, and of course as long as their parents know where they are and approve. It's not only the residents themselves who will benefit from having such well-behaved youngsters around them, the girls also will gain a broader experience of life. So it's a good thing all round, isn't it? Maybe I should relax the rule of no grandchildren visting those residents who have them in future, as long as all the children are as well behaved as your nieces are, of course. Yes, I shall think on it seriously.'

Izzie was reeling from this turn of events. It would be wonderful for her to see her beloved nieces on a regular basis again and not just when she managed to visit them and their parents after work or had them over for the weekend. She would make sure the girls were in no doubt that whenever they were on these premises they must be polite and well mannered at all times.

'I'm taking the girls to the park before I take them home so . . .'

Amelia Austin might be a little forgetful but it appeared there was nothing wrong with her hearing when she cut in, 'Oh, Izzie dear, you're off to the park with the children? Can I come along too?'

'Oh, yes, me too, please,' asked Katherine Philpots, looking expectantly across at Izzie.

'I wouldn't mind a stroll in the park myself,' piped up Cuthbert Swann. Addressing the other two elderly people at the table with him, he said, 'We can finish this game of Ludo when this young lady comes after school tomorrow.' He got up. 'I'll just fetch my hat and coat.'

Twenty minutes later, Jenny Johnson waving them off on the outside steps, Izzie, Suzy and Sally set off for the park accompanied by seven residents all determined to enjoy themselves.

CHAPTER ELEVEN

When Joyce announced to the gathering around the table at coffee break a few weeks later that Jenny Johnson would like to convene a meeting with them all to discuss arrangements for Christmas, Izzie realised with a sense of shock that she had been at Westleigh Lodge for over a month. How time seemed to have flown by as she accustomed herself to what was required of her, immensely enjoying what she was doing while getting to know the different residents and members of staff. No day was exactly the same as the next, both residents and her superiors saw to that, and not that Izzie minded but both taking full advantage of her obliging nature. Up to now she had no regrets whatsoever about coming to work and live at Westleigh Lodge, and from what Mrs Johnson had told her she herself had no regrets either about employing Izzie. In fact, blessed the day she did. So content was she with her life now that her trauma over Lawrence had been pushed right to the back of her mind and she rarely thought of him.

On evenings she had no particular plans of her own, after clearing away her evening meal and seeing to any of her own household chores, she would return back downstairs to spend time with the residents: watching the television with them, reading to them, joining in with games of cards, or just generally chatting to those who sought her company. She had grown to know the night staff well, and they were always very appreciative of her offers of help to them.

Suzy and Sally regularly visited out of school hours and so far had not had to be spoken to about their behaviour. All but a couple of the residents, who found other places to be at those times, very much looked forward to the appearance of their little faces. Sally's dolls each had an ever-expanding wardrobe, and her reading abilities were dramatically improving due to the help she was receiving from her elders as she read her books to them. Suzy was becoming very competent at chess due to Cuthbert Swann's patient teaching of her, and could also play a short, just about recognisable, tune on Walter Waters' accordion. Of course, Pat was delighted to have the girls less under her feet as she could now indulge in her own passion for reading or stay longer when visiting friends.

Izzie was well aware that her employer always did everything her finances would allow to provide the best care and social stimulation for her residents every day of the week and therefore assumed that Christmas would be extra-special, especially for those residents with no living relatives.

'What happens at Christmas?' she asked her colleagues.

'Well, we trim up in the lounge and dining room and we have two trees,' Alma told her excitedly.

'Two trees?' queried Izzie.

'One in the lounge and the other outside by the entrance complete with lights,' Joyce told her. She took a sip of her scalding milky coffee and grimaced. 'Ugh! I haven't put sugar in. Pass the bowl over please, Beattie?'

As she went to oblige she noticed it was empty. Making to rise she said, 'Needs filling, I'll just go and do it.'

'I'll do that for you,' Izzie offered, getting up and taking the bowl from her.

As she went off to the kitchen Beattie and Joyce looked at each other as if to say they both knew Izzie would do that.

Hilda Williams smiled on seeing her enter the kitchen a moment later. Noticing the empty sugar basin Izzie was holding she immediately knew what she was after.

'You'll have ter open a new bag, lovey, I've just used the last of one making the apple crumbles for pudding. Help yerself out the cupboard.' She then called over to her assistant at the sink, busy peeling a mound of potatoes, 'Rita lovey, just check those apples stewing on the stove haven't boiled dry. I've me hands caked in pastry crumbs.'

'Right yer are, Mrs Williams,' the younger woman willingly responded.

Meanwhile Izzie was staring into an empty cupboard. Turning to face Mrs Williams, she said, 'This cupboard is empty.'

Looking across at her, the older woman laughed. 'That's not the cupboard I meant, lovey, but the one next to it. Actually what you're looking in ain't a cupboard at all, it's the dumb waiter. Didn't you notice the pulley ropes?'

Shutting the door of the dumb waiter, feeling dumb herself for her mistake, she asked Hilda Williams, 'Is it still in use?'

'Not as much as it used to be when the building was originally a house as in those days the dining room would have been upstairs on the first floor. Dishes would have been placed on it by the cook and taken off by the servants upstairs to serve to the owners and their dinner guests. And I suspect it was used a lot by the hotel staff too for guests having meals in their rooms. Mrs Johnson still uses it now and again for transporting stuff up to her flat that's too heavy to carry up the stairs as she likes to keep the lift free for the residents.'

Izzie had now found the bag of sugar, refilled the basin and returned the bag to its place in the dry food cupboard. 'I'll tell Alma it's apple crumble for pudding today, she'll be pleased as it's her favourite,' she said to Hilda. 'Thanks for the sugar, Mrs Williams.'

The amiable cook waved a pastry-caked hand at her. 'My pleasure, ducky.'

Having retaken her seat at the dining table, she passed the refilled basin over to Joyce and said, 'You were telling me what happens at Christmas?'

Having tipped two heaped spoons of sugar into her coffee and given it a stir, Joyce took a sip and said, 'Ah, that's better. Well, as we've already told you, we trim up the lounge and dining room and have two trees. On Christmas Eve the church choir comes in to sing carols and afterwards have a glass of sherry and mince pies. Mrs Williams prepares as much food as she can leading up to Christmas as she always has the actual day off to spend with her family. Mrs Johnson herself prepares the rest of it on Christmas Day and it's usually a cold buffet for tea, plus the usual iced cake and pork and mince pies.' She gave a laugh. 'And me and Beattie are kept busy on Boxing Day dealing with the usual belly aches from residents who've stuffed themselves with too much rich food!' She looked across at Beattie. 'It's my turn to work Christmas Day this year as you did it last.' She glanced at both Alma and Izzie then. 'Alice worked last year so you two can toss for it.'

'I don't mind doing it this year, Alma,' Izzie offered. 'You have your father and brother at home, whereas I'm just myself and can visit my family in the evening.'

'Oh, d'yer mean that, Izzie? Oh, ta,' said Alma, delighted. 'That means we can have our dinner at the usual time instead of me dad and brother having to wait until I get home in the evening.'

'Don't forget the visit from Santa on Christmas afternoon,' said Beattie. 'All we staff come in for that, Izzie. It's the only time we actually all get together. Mrs Johnson always buys each resident and all of us staff a present. I had a box of my favourite chocolates from her last year. What did you get again, Joyce?'

'Barbara Cartland's latest book, Mrs Johnson knows she's me favourite author,' she told Izzie.

'I got a record token,' Alma told her. 'I bought the latest Ricky Valens with it.'

'Does Mrs Johnson play Santa?' Izzie asked them.

'No, Doctor Landers does,' Alma told her. 'Him being plump, he don't half make a good one. He's lovely is Doctor Landers, not at all gruff like the doctor that took over from him while he was on holiday in the summer. He used to look at me like I wasn't good enough even to be in the same place as him whenever I bumped into him during me work. I avoided him as much as I could. He gave me a peck on me cheek under the mistletoe,' she said, beaming at the rest of them.

They all looked at her, taken aback.

'You don't get mistletoe in summer, Alma,' Joyce said to her. 'So how could Doctor Bickerstaff have pecked your cheek under it? I can't imagine him pecking anyone's cheek. He treated me and Beattie like we were his servants. Why did you let him anyway?'

'Eh! Oh, no, Doctor Bickerstaff never! It was Doctor Landers what did. The mistletoe was hanging up under the doorway into the lounge and I just happened to be standing beneath it when he came back from changing out of his Santa suit into his own clothes. He said it was a shame to waste an opportunity to kiss a pretty girl and pecked me cheek,' Alma said coyly.

'Well, I've a feeling he'll be hoping to catch someone else under the mistletoe this year,' said Joyce matter-of-factly.

'Me too,' Beattie agreed.

'Who?' asked Izzie, intrigued.

'You,' they both said simultaneously.

Izzie noticeably blushed. 'Oh, don't be silly,' she scoffed. 'What on earth makes you say that?'

''Cos he don't look quite so pleased to see me, Beattie or Alma when he's here as he does you,' said Joyce.

'No, his eyes definitely don't light up in quite the same way when he looks at us,' Beattie agreed.

'And I think I ain't mistaken when I say your eyes light up just like his when you catch sight of him,' said Joyce.

'Yer right, Joyce, I've noticed that too,' Beattie confirmed.

'Oh, stop it, the pair of you,' Izzie scolded them. 'I'm sure his wife wouldn't like to hear you talking about her husband like this.'

'He's not married,' Joyce told her. 'As far as I know he's never even been engaged.'

'You're right, Joyce, he's not,' said Beattie.

'How do you know?' Joyce asked her.

''Cos I asked him, that's how. I was on rounds with him one morning a couple of years ago and he was asking how my husband was after his bout of influenza. Pretty nasty dose, he had, do you remember, Joyce? I was really worried about him pulling through at one stage.'

'I do,' she said. 'I was worried myself. Nice man, your Pete. As good a husband to you as my Ronald is to me.'

'Well, I told the good doctor that I was sure it was his tending to him and not some other doctor that ain't so conscientious towards their patients that got my Pete through,' continued Beattie. 'He said nonsense, it was the love of a good wife that did the trick. It was then I asked him how long he'd been married for. Never found a good woman who thought my ugly mug fanciable, was his reply to me. Oh, but Doctor Landers, I told him, there's someone for everyone, it's just that you ain't met her yet.' She looked fixedly at Izzie. 'Maybe he has now.'

Izzie gave a disdainful tut. 'A man like Doctor Landers wouldn't look at the likes of me.'

The other women stared at her blankly.

'Why ever not?' Joyce demanded.

'Well, because he's a doctor for a start.'

'Unlike Doctor Bickerstaff and many others I've had the pleasure, or misfortune, to work under during my hospital career, Doctor Landers is not the sort to let his own status in life dictate the kind of woman who takes his eye,' said Joyce. 'He's a lovely man whose fancy's been taken by a lovely woman, namely you, Izzie. I bet you half a crown he's asked you on a date before Christmas Eve.'

'You can count me in on that too, Izzie,' said Beattie. 'Like Joyce, I'm long enough in the tooth to know when a man and woman have taken a fancy to each other.'

'Oh,' mouthed Alma excitedly. 'When you get married, can I be a bridesmaid, Izzie?'

'Stop jumping the gun. At least let the man ask her out before you start planning the wedding,' Joyce chided her then glanced at her wrist watch. 'Oh, time we was off. Come on, you lot. Chop-chop.'

As Izzie followed them all out her of the dining room her mind was far from the next task she was about to tackle. It was firmly fixed on Steven Landers. She had convinced herself that a man like him would never consider an association of any sort with the likes of herself and therefore her interest in him was just one-sided. She loved her job here but had to admit that on the days Steven Landers was due to visit it was even more enjoyable. Knowing she might see him, on those days she made an extra-special effort with her appearance, despite telling herself that his friendly attitude towards her was no more than he showed towards the rest of the staff. But maybe she had been wrong. Joyce and Beattie might be prone to practical jokes but she knew them well enough to realise they would never go as far as toying with someone's emotions, just for a bit of fun.

Her heart began to race. Were they right? Did Doctor Steven Landers have a fancy for her? Oh, she hoped so. If Joyce's saying was true and there was someone for everyone, then Izzie would be absolutely delighted to discover that her someone was Steven.

CHAPTER TWELVE

On rising the next morning Izzie sincerely wished the discussion of yesterday regarding Doctor Landers had never taken place as all it had achieved for her was a sleepless night, tossing and turning, trying to clear her mind of visions of when and where he might broach the subject of a date with her. She knew she'd be terribly disappointed if Joyce and Beattie happened to be wrong and he never did. Also there was the danger that when she knew he was definitely due on the premises she would want to make a point of bumping into him, and as a result her work could be affected which wasn't fair to the people she helped care for.

Somehow she had to put that conversation out of her mind, pretend it never took place, and carry on as she had before. If Steven and she were to get together then it would happen without her instigating it.

As she checked her appearance in her mirror before she set off downstairs to start her shift, she thought it a good job Steven wasn't due for a visit that day. She looked terrible due to her lost night's sleep.

A while later, with great interest, Izzie was watching Cyril Cox eating his breakfast, or rather not eating it, when she felt a hand touch her arm and turned her head to see that Alma had joined her.

'I checked on Mrs Naylor and she ain't coming down this morning, Izzie.'

Izzie looked at her, bothered. 'That's not like Mrs Naylor, missing a meal. She's a proper hypochondriac and swears blind she's a delicate stomach but no one here enjoys her food as much as she does. She's not ill, is she? Did she look all right to you?'

'I never actually saw her, Izzie. I knocked on her door and called out to her that it was me but before I could pop me head around she called back to me that she was sleeping and wanted to be left alone. But you know what she's like. The slightest twinge and she's demanding Doctor Landers' attention, so she's not ill. Although . . .'

'Although what?'

'Well, she did sound a bit funny,' Alma mused.

'Oh! In what way?'

She shrugged. 'Not sure, just funny. Her voice sounded different, kind of lispy and mumbly.'

Izzie smiled at Peregrine Danvers as he walked past her on his way to take a seat. 'Morning, Mr Danvers,' she greeted him.

'And good morning to you, my good lady,' he boomed theatrically, grandly bowing his head at her.

Izzie then returned her attention to Alma. 'Mrs Naylor's voice sounded mumbly, did it? Mmm, not sure what that means but as soon as breakfast is over I'll pop up and see her. Now, does Mr Cox looks as though he's eating strangely to you, Alma, or is it my imagination?'

Alma's attention was already elsewhere. 'Oh, God, Izzie, Miss Stringer's just arrived and the only seat available is on the table with Mr Granger! You deal with it, Miss Stringer frightens me to death she's so royal-acting.'

Izzie quickly scanned her eyes around the room. Alma was right. There were only two empty seats and both were at a table occupied by Frederick Granger. It wouldn't be right of Izzie to request another resident to move seats just to accommodate Elinor Stringer, whatever her problem with Mr Granger was. An idea came to her.

Making her way across to Elinor Stringer and smiling welcomingly, she said, 'Good morning, Miss Stringer. How are you today?'

The tall aristocratic-looking woman gave a slight nod of her head to Izzie before replying, 'I'm very well, thank you, Isabel. I trust you are too?'

'Very, thank you, Miss Stringer. Er . . . as you can see, everyone

144

else is down before you this morning, except Mrs Naylor, but the only seats left are at Mr Granger's table. Knowing how you feel about him, I was wondering if you'd care to sit at the staff table this morning? It would mean sitting by yourself, though.'

'That will suit me fine, in the circumstances. Thank you for being so thoughtful, Isabel.'

After making sure Elinor Stringer was settled comfortably and had everything she needed to enjoy her meal, Izzie returned to Alma's side. 'Well, that's one potential disaster averted. Now, as I was asking you before Miss Stringer came in, do you think Mr Cox is acting strangely?'

Alma looked over at the man in question but before she could make an assessment, Cyril Cox, a frustrated look on his face, slammed down his knife and fork on the table. Abandoning an almost full plate of bacon and eggs, he got up and hurried out of the dining room.

Izzie looked at Alma. 'Well, there's nothing wrong with the food, no one else has made any complaints, but obviously something has put Mr Cox off it. I'll go and check on Mrs Naylor first, just to make sure she's having a lie in and not ill, then I'll find Mr Cox and find out why he left his breakfast and hurried off like he did.'

A few minutes later Izzie tapped lightly on Jessie Naylor's door. 'Mrs Naylor,' she called out. 'It's me, Izzie. I'm just checking why you've not come down for breakfast?'

'I don't want any. Now go away and leave me alone,' came the muffled reply.

Izzie wasn't happy with her response. 'Are you feeling poorly, Mrs Naylor, is that it? Do you want me to get Nurse Beattie to come and see you?'

There was silence for a moment. 'Yes . . . no . . . oh, I don't know.'

There was something the matter with Jessie Naylor, Izzie was in no doubt. 'Look, Mrs Naylor, I'm worried about you so I'm coming in.'

Without waiting for a response she opened the door and walked inside.

Fully dressed, Jessie Naylor was perched on the edge of her bed, one gnarled hand clamped over her mouth. She looked very distressed. Izzie walked across and sat down on the bed beside her.

'What's wrong, Mrs Naylor?' she gently probed.

A tear trickled down her cheek and through her hand as she blurted, 'Oh, Ithie, I think there'th really thomething theriouthly wrong with me.'

'Wrong in what way, Mrs Naylor? Something to do with your mouth, I take it, since your hand is covering it?'

She nodded. 'It's suddenly got bigger.'

Izzie looked at her, confused. 'Got bigger? I don't understand. What do you mean?'

'Bigger inside. My teeth don't fit me anymore. They did before I took them out to clean them thith morning but when I went to put them back in, they don't fit becauth they're too thmall.'

Izzie frowned at her, deeply puzzled. 'It's not that I don't believe you, Mrs Naylor, but are you sure they don't fit you? Is there any chance you weren't putting them in right?'

'I've had dentureth for over twenty yearth,' she snapped. 'Of courth I wath putting them in right. Look, I'll show you, they don't fit me.' Taking her hand from her mouth, she picked up a bulging handkerchief that was lying in her lap, unfolding it to reveal a top and bottom set of dentures. Izzie looking on, she selected the top set and tried to position them in her mouth. It was very apparent to Izzie that the denture was too small to fit over her gums.

She scratched her head, puzzled. 'This doesn't make sense to me, Mrs Naylor.'

'Me neither,' she wailed. 'What am I going to do? There'th thomething theriouthly wrong with my mouth, I just know there ith. It's thome dreadful ditheathe I've got, ithn't it? I'm going to die, aren't I?'

Izzie reassuringly patted her hand. 'Stop worrying yourself unnecessarily, Mrs Naylor. Now, apart from your gums expanding, do they hurt in any way at all?'

She shook her head. 'No. They feel jutht like they normally

do. I know they're bigger, they have to be or my teeth would thtill fit, but they don't feel thwollen or anything. I feel fine apart from worrying that my teeth thuddenly don't fit me anymore.'

'Nurse Beattie is on duty this morning. I'll go and find her and ask her to come and see you, maybe she'll have an answer.' Izzie hoped so because she certainly didn't.

As she closed Mrs Naylor's door behind her, she remembered she needed to call in on Mr Cox to check on him. It might transpire that the reason for his abrupt departure from the table at breakfast was something medical and he might need the attention of Beattie too, so she may as well kill two birds with one stone.

His room was two down from Mrs Naylor's. Arriving outside it, she tapped lightly on the door, calling out, 'Mr Cox, it's Izzie. Are you there?'

The door shot open to reveal a stooped old man, peering up at her through thick-lensed glasses. He said something to Izzie that was inaudible to her. 'I'm sorry, Mr Cox, what did you say?'

A look of frustration filled his face and to Izzie's amazement he whipped out his dentures and said to her in a toothless lisp, 'I thaid, what can I do for you?'

'Well, I called to see what I can do for you, Mr Cox. I wondered why you left the table so abruptly this morning, without eating your breakfast?'

'Becauth I couldn't eat my breakfast, that's why. For thome reathon thith morning my dentureth don't fit right. They keep dropping down as thoon as I open my mouth and I can't theem to keep them in. They were fine when I took them out lath night and put them in my glath.'

Izzie stared at him. Surely two people on the same day having trouble with their dentures was more than just a coincidence? Suddenly a thought struck her. 'Er . . . Mr Cox, did you happen to visit the bathroom this morning?'

He frowned at her, insulted 'I vithit the bathroom every morning for my full bodily wathdown.'

'Do you happen to know who was in there before you?'

'Yeth, I do, that Jethie Naylor. Taking an age too. I kept having to bang on the door to get her to hurry up so I wathn't late down for breakfath. In a right tizzy when thee finally came out, thaid thee didn't apprethiate me hurrying her and would have a word with Mrth Johnthon about it. But I reminded her that the bathroom ith not herth alone to hog. That thoon thut her up.'

'Just one more question, Mr Cox. I presume you don't take your spectacles in the bathroom with you?'

He eyed her strangely. 'Well, I can hardly wath my face properly with them on, can I?'

Izzie was then sure she knew what had happened that morning. Jessie had taken the glass holding her teeth into the bathroom with her. After being hassled by Cyril to hurry up, she had forgotten to pick up the glass with her dentures in when she had left, having to return for them after Cyril had finished his ablutions. Short-sighted Cyril had not noticed there was already a glass containing dentures on the wash stand when he had put his own down close by. He'd put in the dentures from Jessie's glass instead of his own, leaving his own glass and dentures for Jessie to find later on.

Izzie smiled at him. 'Mr Cox, would you mind if I borrowed your dentures for a moment?'

'What on earth would you want with them? You've got a perfectly good thet of teeth of your own.'

'Well, I think I know why they suddenly don't fit you. I just have to take your dentures somewhere for a minute to check if my assumption is right. Hopefully, when I return they will fit you again perfectly.'

Looking uncertain, he handed the dentures over.

Izzie returned to Mrs Naylor's room. Jessie was still perched on the edge of her bed, looking very worried.

'You've come back to tell me Nurth ith on her way to thee me?' she asked Izzie hopefully.

Izzie smiled kindly at her. 'If I'm right, Mrs Naylor, you might not need to see her. Bear with me a minute,' she said before she went over to the sink. After giving the dentures Cyril had handed to her a thorough clean, she returned to Jessie Naylor, holding them out to her. 'Try these again, Mrs Naylor.'

She looked dubiously at the dentures in Izzie's outstretched hand. 'I'm not putting thtrange teeth in my mouth. Whoth are they?' she demanded.

'If I'm right, Mrs Naylor, they're yours.'

'Eh?'

'Please, just try them,' Izzie urged her.

Jessie grabbed the set of dentures from out of Izzie's hand and put them in her mouth. 'Why, they *are* mine. They fit perfectly,' she exclaimed, and looked bewilderedly at the set wrapped in the handkerchief in her lap. 'But then, whose are they?'

Izzie looked worriedly at her for a moment. How were both Jessie Naylor and Cyril Cox going to take the fact that they'd had each other's dentures in their mouth? Neither was going to be happy, that was for sure, and it could cause bad feeling between them. A story came to mind. She just hoped Mrs Naylor was so relieved to have her own teeth back, and Cyril his, they both believed it.

She took a deep breath. 'Well, you see, Mr Danvers had the dentist make him a new set of dentures for a character he has in mind to play at the next residents' performance. Yesterday afternoon the dentist had them delivered and I was the one who signed for them. I thought I'd give them a clean before I gave them to him, and did it in the bathroom. Afterwards I put them in a glass of water I'd taken with me. I put the glass with the dentures on the side of the sink while I washed my hands and then, like you this morning, I was disturbed by another resident wanting to use the bathroom, and . . . well . . . I left without picking the glass up. Until now I had forgotten all about it. The same thing happened to you this morning, didn't it, Mrs Naylor? You forgot to pick up your denture glass because another resident was hurrying you, and when you went back to collect it after Mr Cox had vacated the bathroom, you didn't notice there were two glasses containing dentures and picked up the one containing Mr Danvers' new ones by mistake.'

'Oh, well, I was in a hurry to get down to breakfast,' Izzie said defensively.

'Well, all's well now. So if you'll let me have Mr Danvers' new set, I can make sure he gets them.'

She looked at Izzie worriedly 'You won't tell him I've been wearing them, will you? It's an easy mistake to make, anyone could have, but . . . well, Mr Danvers might not take kindly and demand I buy him a new set.'

'No, of course I won't. It's our secret.'

Several minutes later Izzie left both Jessie Naylor and Cyril Cox in a much better frame of mind than they had been earlier that morning now each of them had their own dentures back.

As she was making her way down the corridor towards the stairs she noticed Brian Knowles at Mrs Foster's door. He seemed to be having a conversation with her, although from where she was Izzie couldn't actually see Mrs Foster herself. She then saw Brian take a white envelope from out of his pocket and hold it out. She saw a hand come from inside to take it from him, and assumed it was Mrs Foster's. She was close enough now to hear him say, 'It's all done and dusted and just as you wanted, Mrs Foster. You can rest easy now. Just glad I could be of help.'

Brian then sensed the presence of someone else in the corridor and spun his head to look at Izzie, staring frozen-faced at her for several long seconds before a bright smile spread over it. Walking over to meet her, he said jocularly, 'Hello, Izzie. I was just letting Mrs Foster know that I'd done the repair to her door as it was sticking. So how are you then?'

Her own state of health was the last thing Izzie was thinking about. It was what could possibly be inside the envelope Brian had handed to Mrs Foster? What would a carpenter-cum-handyman need to have put in writing to a resident in an old people's home?

All those thoughts, though, flew from her head at the appearance of Alma rounding the top of the stairs and exclaiming, 'Oh, there you are, Izzie. Hello, Brian,' she acknowledged him as she arrived to join them. 'Izzie, I wondered where the hell you'd got to as the last thing you told me was that you'd gone to check on Mrs Naylor and Mr Cox and that was ages ago. Are they both all right?'

'I'll leave you to it,' Brian said to Izzie. 'I've a shelf to refix over the wash basin in room five. 'Bye, both.'

Both women reciprocated accordingly.

'So are the two old dears okay now?' Alma asked Izzie again.

Smiling brightly at the younger woman, she said, 'Oh, yes, they are now. Nothing serious ailing either of them, I'm glad to say. I'm sorry I left you to clear the dining room after break-fast on your own.'

'Oh, that's all right, Izzie. It wasn't like you was skiving off for a crafty fag. I'm glad you sorted the old dears out. So what was wrong with both of them?'

'Oh, nothing worth wasting your time with, Alma.'

'Oh, I see, something and nothing then, just time-consuming for us. Right, I'm off to help Mrs Merridew take the hem up on a new frock she's bought.' She pulled a face. 'I never was any good at sewing at school so I'll probably end up sticking more pins in her than in the hem of the frock. Anyway, what you up to now?'

'Accompanying Mrs Austin on a trip to the shops for some new underwear.'

'Sooner you than me, it's bloody freezing out there today. Cook reckons we're in for some snow. See you later then.'

Izzie smiled at her as she hurried off to Mrs Merridew's room.

A hour and a half later in a ladies' lingerie shop on Cart's Lane, just off the main shopping area of the town centre, much to the assistant's frustration Amelia Austin had been engrossed for half an hour in deliberation over whether her usual style of cotton Aertex would be the best choice or if she should try out a new brand of woollen garments the shop was now stocking? Izzie, having several times declined to make Amelia's decision for her, was gazing out of the window, amusing herself watching the passers by. A man and a woman sitting in the window of the café opposite caught her attention. They were deep in conver-sation. There was nothing unusual about two people of the oppo-site sex having a cup of tea and sharing a plate of fancy cakes together. What *was* unusual was that the couple in question was none other than Frederick Granger and Elinor Stringer!

Izzie had been under the impression that they couldn't stand the sight of each other. Miss Stringer had referred to Mr Granger as 'that despicable man'. It seemed they had made their differences up. That was good, she thought to herself, as it meant she and Alma would no longer have the problem of keeping them apart at mealtimes.

Amelia, now having made her choice to stick with the Aertex and paid the bill, was ready to leave.

That evening at teatime Izzie was confused to note that Miss Stringer sat as far away from Mr Granger as she could, in fact with her back to him. The making up of their differences had obviously been short-lived.

CHAPTER THIRTEEN

Three weeks later Izzie was in the hallway just about to go and check all was well in the dining room as teatime was almost upon them, then she was going to remind her nieces it was time for them to go home for their own, when she felt a tug on her arm and saw Suzy looking worriedly up at her.

'Can I talk to you, Aunty Izzie?'

Izzie squatted down to address her face to face. 'Can it wait, sweetie, or is what you want to speak to me about urgent? Oh, you're not fed up with coming here, are you? Is that what you want to tell me?'

She vigorously shook her head. 'Oh, no, Aunty Izzie. I love coming here, and so does Sally. My friends at school are ever so jealous 'cos they can't come here too and do the things we get to do with the old ladies and gentlemen.'

'I'm glad to hear it, sweetie, because I know you'd be missed if you and Sally didn't come any longer. Your friends here enjoy seeing your happy smiley faces, and all the things you do with them. So what is it you wanted to talk to me about?'

Suzy gave a heavy sigh. 'Well . . . it's Mr Waters, Aunty Izzie.'

'Oh, what about him, dear?'

'He told me he wasn't feeling himself today and asked me if I minded if he didn't give me a lesson on the accordion. I didn't mind anyway 'cos Mr Danvers told me before that he was going to bring his box of wigs down that he used to wear on stage and let me try them all on.' Her face lit up and she giggled. 'Oh, I had so much fun! Mr Danvers said we can do

153

it again sometime. Did you know he used to be an actor, Aunty Izzie?'

She gave a wry smile. 'Yes, I did. So what is concerning you about Mr Waters, sweetie?'

Suzy's face screwed up. 'Well...I think he's upset about something and that's why he's not feeling himself.'

'And what makes you think that?'

She gave a shrug. 'He looks just like Mam does when summat's upset her. Yer know, Aunty Izzie, her face all screws up. Mr Waters' face is all screwed up like Mam's does. I don't like to see him upset, Aunty Izzie, as he's been everso nice to me. Do you think if I gave him a sweet out of me poke at the weekend, that would cheer him up?'

'Oh, darling, that's a lovely idea, I'm sure it would.' But more to the point, if Suzy was right and Walter Waters was upset about something it had to be bad for a child to notice.

Just then Sally dashed up to them and grabbed Suzy's arm, tugging urgently on it. 'Come with me, our Suzy, I've got summat to show yer!'

'Where did you come from?' Izzie asked her. 'It wasn't from the lounge or the television room or I would have seen you coming out when I was talking to Suzy.'

She looked innocently at her aunt. 'I was just in the kitchen, getting meself a glass of water.'

Izzie frowned at her. 'You sure that's all you were doing, young lady? You have a look of guilt about you to me.'

She gave a shrug. 'Yeah, honest, Aunty Izzie. I put Cook's chair back after I'd used it to stand on, and I made sure I turned the tap off proper.'

'Mmm. Okay, I believe you, missy. Thousands wouldn't. So what is so exciting that you have to show your sister?'

'Eh!' Sally looked blank, then gave a shrug. 'Oh, I've forgotten now.'

Izzie shook her head at her. 'It couldn't have been that important then, could it? Anyway, it's time for you two to get your coats and make your way home.'

'Oh, do we have to?' they both wailed.

'No fuss now or you won't get back. Go and say cheerio to everyone and tell them you'll look forward to seeing them on Thursday after school.'

'I wish we could come every night,' moaned Sally.

'Me too,' mumbled her sister.

'Well, if you did come every night you'd not have anything to look forward to on the nights you didn't come, would you?'

'No, s'pose not,' they both muttered.

'Are we still coming to stop overnight on Saturday?' Sally asked her aunt.

'Unless you know a reason why not?'

'Oh, we don't, we've been good,' they both insisted. 'You can ask Mam when you see her.'

Izzie feigned a stern expression. 'Oh, I will, and that'll be tonight as she's expecting me in for a cuppa and a natter.' A smile then broke over her face. 'I've no reason whatsoever to think for a minute your mam's report on your behaviour isn't going to be a good one so I was thinking of treating you both to Chipperfield's Circus on Saturday afternoon at the Granby Halls.'

The excitement this news provoked was immediate. 'The Circus! Oh, wow!' they both exploded, gleefully clapping their hands.

'Did I hear someone mention the circus?' an elderly voice said.

Izzie turned her head to see Amelia Austin coming towards them. Izzie knew what was coming next. 'You'd like to come too, Mrs Austin?'

Excitement kindled her old eyes. 'Oh, my dear, I'd love to. Thank you so much for offering. Oh, how thrilling!' Looking down at Suzy and Sally she said, 'The last time I was at the circus was with my father. I was a little girl of seven, about your own age in fact. Oh, I so enjoyed it! There were elephants and tigers and bareback riders on white horses and trapeze artists and . . . oh . . . and . . . we had candyfloss. Like eating sugared clouds, I remember. Girls, we will have candyfloss at the circus on Saturday and it'll be my treat.' She looked enquiringly at

Izzie. 'They still have candyfloss, don't they? I mean, it's such a long time ago since I went . . . well over seventy years in fact, and fashions change, don't they, dear?'

'I'm sure candyfloss is one of the things that the passing of time hasn't changed, Mrs Austin,' Izzie assured her.

She looked pleased to hear that, then much to Izzie's astonishment announced, 'I'll pass word around the others and see how many of them want to come too.' She smiled down at Sally, holding out a doll to her. 'You forgot 'Lizabeth, dear.'

Sally took it from her. 'Oh, ta, Mrs Austin. I can't sleep without 'Lizabeth.'

The old lady smiled fondly at her. 'My memory has a habit of playing tricks on me sometimes but I do remember your telling me that and that's why I came after you with her. I'll have 'Lizabeth's new jumper finished for you when you come again on Thursday.' She suddenly looked bothered. 'Now I was going to do something, wasn't I?' Then she beamed. 'Dear me, how could I have forgotten? I'm going to tell all the others about our trip to the circus. 'Bye-bye then, girls.'

''Bye, Mrs Austin,' they both responded

Izzie laughed. 'Well, girls, looks like a party of us will be going to the circus on Saturday afternoon. Right, go and fetch your coats and don't forget to pop your head around Mrs Johnson's office door and thank her for letting you come today.'

'Mrs Johnson said we don't have to keep thanking her, Aunty Izzie,' Suzy told her. 'She told us we was doing her a favour, helping her keep some of her ladies and gentlemen occupied so she could get on with other things.'

'Well, it's nice she told you that, but I'd still like you to thank her out of politeness. Now I'll just go and have a quick check on the dining room to make sure all is in order there then I'll meet you back here in five minutes.'

Ten minutes later Izzie was shivering in the cold November evening as she watched her nieces turn the corner of their own street a short distance away to disappear from her view. As she made to hurry back inside she noticed Walter Waters standing an arm's length away. He appeared to be staring hard in the opposite direction from the way her nieces had gone. Suzy's concern for the old man came to mind and Izzie looked at him closely. From his anxious expression and nervy manner, it seemed to Izzie her niece was right. Walter Waters did appear very bothered about something.

She stepped across to him, laying a hand on his arm gently. 'It's rather cold for you to be out without a coat, Mr Waters. Would you like me to go and fetch yours for you?'

He looked startled for a moment before saying, 'Oh, er . . . thanks for the offer, Izzie.' He gave a resigned sigh before adding, 'He's obviously not coming today.'

Walter had only one regular visitor as far as Izzie was aware and that was his son. 'Well, maybe something cropped up and put a stop to your son's visit today. Have you checked with Mrs Johnson that he hasn't telephoned and left a message for you?'

He nodded forlornly. 'Several times, and he hasn't.'

'Well, maybe he just hasn't been able to get a telephone. I'm sure he will as soon as he can, Mr Waters.'

He gave a wan smile and patted her arm. 'Yes, yes, I'm sure you're right, my dear.'

She took his arm. 'Come on in before you catch your death,' she coaxed. 'It's just about teatime. I know Cook has made sausage rolls to go with the sandwiches today and you're partial to sausage rolls, aren't you, Mr Waters?'

He nodded distractedly. 'Yes, I am.'

A while later, from her stance by the serving hatch, Izzie was monitoring Walter Waters as he ate his meal. Or rather picked at it. This wasn't like Walter. To any casual observer it might have seemed as if the small, wiry eighty-one year old hadn't eaten a decent meal for years due to the taut stretch of the skin over his bones, but in fact the opposite was true. His appetite was as healthy as a man's half his age and usually he tackled every meal put before him with relish, hardly leaving a crumb. His worry over the non-appearance of his son today seemed to be far more acute than Izzie would have expected.

As Walter made his way out of the dining room, Izzie waylaid him. 'Mr Waters, I just wondered if you'd received word from your son yet, to tell you why he couldn't manage today and put your mind at rest?'

Eyes grave, he shook his head. 'It's very kind of you to ask, Izzie, but no, I haven't.'

'Well, there's still time tonight but if not, I'm sure you will hear from him tomorrow.'

He flashed a brief smile at her. 'Yes, I'm sure you're right.'

The thought that this old man was going to spend the remainder of the night worrying over the absence of his son, and possibly not sleep, concerned her. Regardless of the fact Walter was far from stupid she asked him, 'Have you tried to telephone your son, Mr Waters? Provided he's on the telephone at home, that is?'

'I have, several times, but there's no answer.' He wrung his hands. 'What I can't understand is why his wife . . . my daughter-in-law . . . or one of my grandchildren haven't answered the tele-phone, but they haven't. They're not on holiday or anything so even if my son were out, one of them would have been at home all the times I tried.' He aged face screwed up in anxiety. 'I'm beginning to think they've all had a terrible accident and no one's told me.'

His thoughts mirrored her own. Her mind raced frantically for what she could do to help ease his mind. 'Look, Mr Waters, I'm going out later to visit my sister-in-law but if you give me your son's address, I'll pop and see him first. Hopefully I'll find out what's going on and can put your mind at rest. I'm sure the reason he's not showed today is something to do with work, and when you telephoned the house his wife and children just happened to be out.'

He was looking at her expectantly. 'Oh, would you do that for me? I'd be so obliged, I really would.' His face clouded with worry. 'But it's two bus rides away from here. Too far to expect you to go.'

She smiled warmly at him. 'I don't mind, Mr Waters, really.'

His eyes filled with gratitude. 'If you're sure then I'll write the address down for you. You will come and see me as soon as you return? I'll wait up for you.'

'Yes, of course I will.'

Two hours later, Izzie was knocking on the front door of a well-maintained pre-1940s semi-detached house in the residential area of Evington. She cast her eyes down to the slip of paper she was holding to check the details on it before looking back at the house. This was definitely the address Walter Waters had written down for her. But it was empty. Whoever had lived here had packed up and gone, leaving the premises vacant for new owners to move into. An estate agent's board with Sold plastered on it stood in the front garden; the echo that had resounded when she knocked on the front door and a glimpse through the bay window into the empty room beyond confirmed this.

In his worry for his son's missed visit Walter must have made a mistake when writing down the address. There was no other explanation that Izzie could think of to explain what she had found.

'Must be awful to start losing yer memory when you get old,' Pat mused to Izzie a while later, as both women faced each other across the kitchen table armed with cups of steaming tea. She put her cup in its saucer and looked earnestly at Izzie. 'If I ever get to a stage when I ain't in control of me faculties or it's obvious I'm losing me marbles, you're to take me outside and shoot me. I don't want to be a burden on me family, Izzie, that's the last thing I want.'

'Me neither, Pat, but we've a few years yet before either of us has to start worrying about old age getting the better of us.' She gave a distracted sigh. 'But Walter Waters hasn't before now shown any signs of that.'

'Well, this is obviously the start for him then,' Pat said.

Izzie felt sorry for Walter if her sister-in-law was right. But then in her opinion it was probably better to suffer steadily increasing memory loss rather than endure a debilitating, painful illness that rended you reliant on others for your every need,

159

and which you were all too aware of. She downed the contents of her cup and stood up. 'Well, I'd better get back and let Mr Waters know that in his worry he gave me the wrong address. I know he's desperately waiting for news of his son.'

Pat looked at her reproachfully. 'I suppose I should feel miffed that once again our natter's being cut short by the needs of one of your old dears, but I'm just glad you stopped by to tell me what was happening instead of not showing up. I'd have been worried about what had happened to you.'

Izzie beamed at her, aware that she meant every word. The close friendship she had now with Pat was very precious to her, and it warmed her to know her sister-in-law felt likewise.

The door to Walter's room swung open almost the second Izzie tapped lightly on it. It was obvious he'd been waiting on the other side, desperate for her return.

Ushering her inside and closing the door behind her, Walter took one look at Izzie's face and said, 'They've gone, haven't they?'

She looked at him, taken aback. 'You already knew the house would be empty, Mr Waters?'

She watched in bewilderment as Walter's face drained to a deathly grey and he slowly backed away from her, to collapse heavily on the edge of his bed. It seemed to Izzie that his whole body was shrinking inside his suit, as though his very life was draining from him, before he uttered, 'Not knew for certain but I had a terrible suspicion it would be the case after Victor not showing up for the past three weeks.' His voice lowered to a choking whisper, he said, 'I prayed I was wrong, though. Didn't want to believe my own son would do this to me.' He began to shake visibly. 'I signed the papers for the sale of the house over three weeks ago. Victor was to come and see me with a bank draft for half the proceeds of the sale the day after. I haven't heard a word from him since. There's no other conclusion I can draw than that he's absconded with my share, wasn't happy with just the half I was giving him.'

While Izzie looked helplessly on he began pacing the room,

wringing his hands, distraught. 'When I told my son six months ago that my funds were running low and I'd need to look at selling the house, although he tried to hide it from me I could tell he wasn't very happy. I knew he saw the house as his inheritance, he's never hidden that, was always joking about the time when he'd have the money to do what he wanted after he got his legacy. But it's not my fault I'm living longer than the expected three score and ten, is it? Of course I was sorry that my having to sell the house meant he and his family would need to get a place of their own, but he'd have had a substantial deposit from his half of the proceeds to put down on a new place. I assured him I'd give him that.'

'Oh, I see, so your son and his family lived in your house?' Izzie said.

Walter stopped his pacing, looked at her and nodded. 'When my dear wife passed on ten years ago, Victor insisted on moving in with me so I wasn't on my own. I wasn't stupid, though. I knew the main reason was because he was struggling to support his family on his wage as a clerk with the Gas Board and it would be cheaper to live with me than carry on renting his own place. I was bereft at the time and had no heart to stand against this decision. Very soon life in my own house was intolerable to me. My son's wife is the bossy sort and it was as if I'd become a guest in my own home, never having a say in anything that went on. That's how I came to live here.

'After becoming thoroughly despondent about all the homes I went to view, I couldn't believe my luck when I saw what Mrs Johnson was offering here, and luck was on my side again because she was just opening for business so had vacancies. I'm her longest surviving resident, you know,' he said proudly. 'Eight years I've been here, and due to Mrs Johnson's dedication to her residents I feel as much at home here at Westleigh Lodge as I did in my own house before Winnie passed on, God rest her. Anyway, when I told my son it was best all round I move into a retirement home, it was obvious he wasn't happy and he tried his best to talk me out of it. He said he didn't like the thought of me being looked after by strangers, but I knew he wasn't being truthful. It was the fact that the fees to live here would be eating away at his precious inheritance.' He gave a deep sigh. 'Victor never made any secret of the fact that his dream was to have a little Post Office and general store in a pretty village on the Lincolnshire coast. Half the money from the house sale wouldn't have bought him that without his having to take out a substantial mortgage, but all of it would.'

Izzie was staring at him, stunned. Surely his own son wouldn't leave him unable to pay his keep here?

'I was upset at the time about having to sell my home and let Victor persuade me into having the bank draft from the sale put in his name, for convenience's sake . . . he kept going on about trips back and forth to the solicitor and bank telling on me at my age, and he did have a point as it doesn't take much these days. Anyway, once the money was in his account he was going to arrange payment of my half to me. But he hasn't been to see me for three weeks and with you telling me the house is empty . . . well, there's no other conclusion I can draw. He's gone off with the lot.'

Walter sadly shook his head. 'I should be angry with Victor for what he's done. But he's my son, Izzie, my and Winnie's only child. If I choose to believe he's done this to give his family a better future, it makes it easier for me to accept. I suppose he views me as an old man who's had my life now whereas he still has a good part of his left.' He gave a wan smile. 'Well, thank you, my dear, for doing that errand for me. You must let me refund your bus fare.'

'It was no trouble, Mr Waters, and I won't hear of you refunding my bus fare. Er . . . what will you do now?' Izzie asked worriedly.

'I have enough money in the bank to pay my fees here for the next couple of weeks. After that . . . well, I'll have to do what other people in my position do. I'll warn Mrs Johnson of my intention to leave tomorrow so she can start seeking a replacement for my room.'

Izzie knew Walter was referring to seeking a place in a homeless refuge. Despite those places being a better option than actually living on the streets, the conditions offered were very austere and in fact hardly improved on what they had been when their name had changed from 'workhouse' to 'homeless refuge' a few years before. The thought of anyone elderly being reduced to seeking shelter in one of those places grieved Izzie, let alone a lovely old gent like Walter Waters who was in the latter stages of his life and the financial predicament he found himself in not of his own making. Fighting back her own tears at his plight, she said, 'I'll see you at breakfast tomorrow, Mr Waters.' She had been careful not to wish him a good night's sleep because she doubted that with what was facing him in a couple of weeks' time he'd get a wink.

Closing his door behind her, a deeply distracted Izzie made her way down the corridor towards the main staircase en route to her own accommodation. In an alcove just before the top of the stairs, a small sofa had been placed for residents to rest on should they feel the need after their climb up. Arriving by the sofa, Izzie absently sank down on it to explore her thoughts. How she wished she had the money to pay Walter Waters' fees at Westleigh Lodge, something she would gladly do sooner than see the dear old man spend the rest of his days in a refuge. Then a thought struck her. She *did* have funds. About three hundred pounds of savings left after her move. It would be better used helping to ease Walter's plight than lying doing nothing in a Post Office account. She was trying to work out how many weeks' fees three hundred pounds would take care of and how she could get this proud old man to accept her offer, when she jumped on feeling a hand touching her arm. She looked up to see Jenny Johnson staring at her in concern.

'Izzie, what on earth are you doing sitting here at this time of night, looking so pensive?' her employer asked. 'I've spoken to you twice, and twice you've ignored me.'

'Oh! Mrs Johnson, I'm so sorry, really I am. I . . . well, I never expected to bump into you at this time of night.'

She smiled. 'Well, I usually have retired by this time but I'd gone down earlier to check with the night staff that all was well with them and got chatting to several of the residents still in the lounge. They're all very excited about this trip you're taking them on to the circus with your nieces on Saturday afternoon.

It's a lovely thing you're doing, Izzie, and you have my thanks for offering them this. We must look into transport arrangements and also the possibility of getting the tickets cheaper with a block booking, but all that can wait until tomorrow. You haven't answered my question, Izzie. Apart from the fact I hadn't expected to bump into you at this time of night, just what has upset you? Oh, it isn't anything to do with a member of your family, is it? The girls aren't ill, are they?'

Izzie shook her head. 'My family are all well, thank you, Mrs Johnson.' She shifted uncomfortably in her seat. She herself might have come up with a way to resolve Walter Waters' financial problem in the short term but as proprietor Jenny Johnson needed to be made aware of what was going on in her establishment. The corridor was hardly the place to discuss the personal details of a resident, though. 'There is something I need to tell you but . . .'

Just then the sound of elderly voices filtered up from below.

Jenny leaned over and took her arm. 'Quickly, dear, let's get to the privacy of my flat. You can tell me all about what's troubling you over a cup of tea.'

As Izzie trotted alongside Jenny to her private quarters, her respect for her employer rose even higher. Despite having worked a long day and needing her own rest, Jenny Johnson was prepared to use what was left of her evening to try and help Izzie with what she thought was a personal problem.

Izzie was not at all surprised by her employer's accommodation. It looked welcoming and comfortable, just like Jenny herself.

'I always find problems are best aired over a cup of sweet tea at the kitchen table. What about you, Izzie?' Jenny asked as she closed the door of her flat behind them.

Izzie smiled at her. 'My sentiments exactly, Mrs Johnson.'

Minutes later Jenny placed a tray on the kitchen table and took a seat opposite Izzie. As she poured out the tea she said to her guest, 'Izzie, just because I'm your employer doesn't mean you can't . . . well, tell me to mind my own business, so to speak.'

Izzie smiled. 'Mrs Johnson, if I had a problem I would not

hesitate to share it with you and would certainly appreciate your advice.'

Jenny looked confused. '*If* you had a problem? Oh! I've obviously got it wrong. I could have sworn by your face you were extremely worried about something.'

'I am worried, very much so, Mrs Johnson, but it's not over a problem I have personally. It's one of our residents who has the problem.'

Jenny looked aghast. 'One of our residents! Oh, but how terrible of me. I hadn't noticed and it's taken one of my staff to point it out.'

'It wasn't me that noticed Mr Waters was deeply bothered about something,' said Izzie. 'It was my niece Suzy who put me wise, that's how I got involved.'

'Suzy was the one who noticed? Well, that dear child puts us all to shame, she really does. I shall make sure she's aware of my gratitude for bringing this to our notice. What a good decision I made that day I allowed your two lovely nieces access here whenever they wish. But Mr Waters is worried over something. Just what is it, Izzie?'

She took a deep breath and told her employee of Walter Waters' plight.

As she told her tale, Jenny's expression changed from one of shock to extreme concern. At the end she exclaimed, 'Oh, how could Victor Waters do that to his own father? I've met him on several occasions and he always came across as being a very upright sort of man, devoted to his father. Oh, Izzie, it just goes to show you never know what is lurking beneath the surface of some people.' She rubbed a hand across her chin. 'Oh, the poor old man,' she uttered. 'Well, one thing is for certain, there is no way I'm going to allow him to spend his remaining days in a homeless refuge.'

'No, me neither,' said Izzie. 'I've some money put by and whether Mr Walters agrees or not, I'm going to give it to you to pay his fees for the number of weeks it'll cover. At least that will give us some more time to try and sort out a better alternative than a refuge for him.'

Jenny looked at her, impressed. 'Oh, Izzie, what a kind offer. But you will not need to do that. Walter Waters can stay here free from fees for the remainder of his days.'

'Mother, are you mad?'

Jenny's head jerked around. Her daughter Leonie stood in the kitchen doorway.

'You can't mean what you said about Mr Waters living here for nothing?' she demanded.

'Yes, I did, dear.'

'You're not running a charity, Mother.'

'I know that, but we do need to show charity in this case, Leonie.'

'Mother, the business is running on a knife edge as it is. I do the books, remember, and I keep telling you that the low prices you charge, and all the extras you pay for yourself, hardly leave us any profit. If you start giving away free board and lodging, you'll end up bankrupting us.'

Jenny sighed. 'Leonie dear, you know I did not come into this business to make a fortune. As long as we break even every month, that's fine with me. The satisfaction I get from seeing how happy my residents are here means far more. You've no need to worry about your own future, Leonie.'

She gave a deep sigh. 'Yes, Mother, so you keep reminding me whenever I bring up the financial state of the business. But as I said, I do the books and from the figures on the balance sheet it seems to me I do need to be worried.' She looked fixedly at her mother for several long moments before she shook her head in resignation and said, 'I'll leave you to it.'

As Leonie walked out of the room, Jenny said distractedly, 'I suppose I should tell Leonie . . . No, she's too young to handle that yet.' She gave herself a mental shake. 'Sorry, Izzie, for having to witness that exchange between Leonie and myself.' She gave a heavy sigh. 'Having the care and protection of a child isn't easy. Sometimes I feel as if I'm floundering in the dark. You're never quite sure whether your decisions in respect of them are the right ones and can only hope they are. When you have your own children, you will see exactly what I mean.'

Time was marching on for Izzie at nearly thirty-six. As matters stood she doubted she ever would have the problems associated with the care of a child to contend with. Her hope that something might transpire between herself and Steven Landers was starting to fade. Maybe the observation of a spark in his eye by her colleagues had been a mistake. Since the night she had talked to him in the corridor circumstances hadn't brought her in his company again, apart from a glimpse of his back as accompanied by either Joyce or Beattie he had done his rounds of the residents. Regardless, though, Izzie counted herself extremely lucky. She had a job she derived a great deal of satisfaction from, a lovely place of her own to live in, and her nieces did provide an outlet for her motherly feelings.

'Now,' Jenny was saying, 'we have to make a plan of campaign because Mr Waters is not the sort to accept a handout in any guise.' She stared thoughtfully into space for a moment. 'Izzie, I don't like the thought of lying to him at all but I can't see we have any choice in this case. The only other option I can see is that I tell Mr Waters that before he left for pastures new, his son arranged with the bank that the fees for his keep are transferred to my bank each month, so he's nothing to worry about in that respect. Then we just have to hope Mr Waters never discovers my deceit. How we handle the lack of contact by his son . . .' Her face clouded over. 'Oh, Izzie dear, there is no way I can shield that dear old man from the fact his own family has abandoned him, but at least he won't live the rest of his days thinking his son robbed him as well, will he?' She gave a shudder. 'Oh, the thought that Mr Waters could have ended up in a refuge for the homeless . . . it doesn't bear thinking about. I just wish I had the means to take all of those poor people residing in those dreadful places out of them and give them a decent place to live. Still, at least the ones under my roof are as well cared for as I can manage.' She smiled warmly at Izzie. 'I'm just so grateful you took the trouble to discover all this and allow me to do something about it before it was too late.'

'I was just doing my job, Mrs Johnson.'

'Oh, my dear, if you were just doing your job you wouldn't

be sitting here with me at this time of night. Again I bless the day Amelia Austin brought you to my door.'

'I bless her too, Mrs Johnson,' Izzie said with conviction. 'Absolutely I do.'

CHAPTER FOURTEEN

The next morning as Izzie was making her way towards the dining room to commence breakfast duties she saw Walter Waters coming out of Jenny Johnson's office. She was very glad to see that the look of doom she had left him sporting the previous evening had vanished and he looked near enough his normal chirpy self.

Catching sight of Izzie, he signalled to her that he'd like to speak to her.

Pulling her out of earshot of any other residents, he said, 'It seems I was mistaken about my son, Izzie. It was very wrong of me to think so badly of him, it really was. He hasn't done at all what I thought he had. I don't know how I could even think it. To save me the trouble of having to deal constantly with the bank over my fees here, he's arranged with his own to transfer the money direct to Mrs Johnson's account each month. Isn't that thoughtful of him? She told me not to worry about not hearing from him yet as he's obviously tied up with getting himself and his family settled, wherever it is they are. He just hasn't got round to me yet. But then, he knows I'm safe and well cared for so he doesn't have to worry about me, does he? I shall get a visit from him soon or a letter, I've no doubt. Anyway, my dear, thank you for putting yourself out for me last night.'

'It was my pleasure, Mr Waters.'

He patted her hand. 'Well, I'm very peckish this morning so I'm off to get my breakfast. Oh, when your niece comes tomorrow, I will give her a longer lesson on the accordion to make up for the time she missed yesterday, should she so wish.'

Izzie watched the wiry little man hurry off in the direction of the dining room with mixed feelings. She was very relieved Walter Waters had been saved from the fate that could have befallen him by Mrs Johnson's own generous intervention, but how she would like the opportunity to give Victor Waters a piece of her mind for what he had so callously done to his elderly father.

A short while later Izzie glanced at her wrist watch then across at the two empty chairs on separate tables that should have been occupied by Elinor Stringer and Frederick Granger. Both of them were extremely late down this morning. If they didn't arrive soon they would miss their meal altogether. She looked at her watch again. She had given them both long enough to show. It was time she went and checked on their welfare, just in case their lateness was due to more than a simple case of over-sleeping.

Having told Alma, who was busy helping an arthritic old lady cut up her food, she made her way up to the first floor where both Elinor Stringer and Frederick Granger's rooms were situated. Elinor Stringer's was the first door she tapped on.

'Morning, Miss Stringer,' she called out. 'It's me, Izzie. Are you all right, only time's wearing on and I'm worried you'll miss your breakfast?'

She received no reply so tapped again.

When again she received no reply, she frowned, bothered. The upright ex-headmistress in her early-seventies had appeared to be in perfect health when Izzie had wished her good evening in the lounge the previous evening. Her silence must surely mean she had been taken ill during the night.

Fearing the worst and prepared to make a rush to fetch medical help, she opened the door and poked her head around. Fully expecting to be greeted by the sight of an unconscious Elinor Stringer, she was shocked to see that her bed was empty and there was no sign of the old lady at all. Entering the room, Izzie flashed a hurried glance around. Elinor's wash bag and towel were on the shelf by the sink so she wasn't in the bathroom, although strangely there was no sign of her dressing gown. Elinor wasn't downstairs, so where was she? Maybe the answer was simple. On her way up to check, Izzie had somehow missed Elinor on her way down.

She then made her way to Frederick Granger's room.

Tapping on his door she called out, 'Mr Granger, it's Izzie. Are you all right? Only time's wearing on and I'm worried you'll miss your breakfast.'

She received no reply and was just about to repeat herself when she heard a very faint, 'Help me. Oh, please help me.'

Without further ado she burst into the room to stop dead in her tracks, mouth opening in utter astonishment at the sight that greeted her. Frederick Granger was still in bed, asleep by the look of it, but he was not alone. Lying beside him was Elinor Stringer. The bedclothes were partially dragged off, revealing her body. She was naked.

The elderly woman was extremely distressed but also obviously mortified at the predicament she had been discovered in.

'Oh, Izzie, thank goodness it's you.' Her tone was desperate. 'Please shut the door. Izzie, quickly, please, before anyone else comes in. Izzie!'

'Pardon! Oh, er . . . yes, of course, Miss Stringer.'

Having done the deed she turned to face the bed and it was then it struck her that something was not right with Frederick Granger. His skin had a deathly pallor and his lips were blue. The man was dead.

Through her frozen stupor she heard Elinor beg her, 'You have to help me, Izzie. Frederick . . . oh, poor Frederick, he's . . .' Her voice trailed off and it was obvious she was fighting with all her might to keep control of her emotions. 'My arm is pinned under him, I can't move.'

Pulling herself together, Izzie rushed over to the bed and pulled up the covers, very mindful of keeping Elinor's dignity as much as she could, then quickly assessed the situation. A naked Frederick lay nestled against Elinor, one arm across her, his head beside hers. Her arm was trapped underneath him.

'Right, Miss Stringer, I'll try and lift Mr Granger up as far as I can and hopefully you'll be able to slip out from beneath.'

Elinor nodded her understanding.

Going around the other side of the bed, Izzie leaned across and placed both hands firmly on Frederick Granger's left shoulder. She tried not to recoil at the cold stiffness of his skin. Heaving with all her might, she pulled him up enough for Elinor to slide free her arm and escape the bed.

Immediately the older woman collapsed on the floor, clutching her stomach, rocking backwards and forwards, desperate tears pouring down her face. 'Oh, Frederick,' she sobbed. 'Oh, my dear, dear Frederick.'

As respectfully as his heavy weight would allow, Izzie let Frederick's body fall back against the mattress and pulled the covers over his nakedness. Then she raced around the bed to find Elinor's dressing gown which was on the floor by the side of her. Draping it around the distraught woman, Izzie then fell to her knees, threw her arms around Elinor and gently pulled her close, smoothing her hand over the loose flowing grey hair. A wet patch spread across Izzie shoulder where her tears fell.

'There, there, Miss Stringer,' she soothed. 'There, there.'

After what felt like an age to Izzie, Elinor's heart-wrenching sobs eased up and she tremulously uttered, 'I know what this must look like. Two elderly people caught naked in bed together. It's disgusting, isn't it? Having sex at our age. But it wasn't just sex, and it certainly wasn't disgusting. We loved each other,' she whispered. Pulling away from Izzie, she wiped her wet face on the sleeve of her dressing gown. 'We wanted desperately to get married and spend every minute of the time we had left with each other, but when Frederick told his children about me, thinking they'd be delighted for him, they wouldn't hear of it. They were revolted. Threatened never to speak to him ever again if he dared embarrass them by marrying again at his age. Worse than that was the fact he could even be thinking of betraying their dead mother's memory by taking another wife. They warned him that if he didn't agree to stop this nonsense with me, then in their eyes he wouldn't exist anymore.

'Frederick was devastated by their reaction but prepared to be alienated from his family to be with me. I wouldn't hear of it. I knew how much he loved his children and grandchildren and the hurt it would have caused him never to see them again. We daren't appear to be even friends in public in case any of his children should ask the residents here about us and realise we were still secretly seeing each other. The only way we could be together was by sneaking into each other's room at night. It is criminal that upstanding people such as we two were reduced to acting like thieves in the night due to the small minds of others.'

As Izzie listened to Elinor's heart-breaking story she couldn't believe that for the second time in less than twenty-four hours she had become involved in a tragic situation caused purely by the selfishness of a resident's offspring.

Elinor gave a deep shudder and looked across at the bed where her dead lover lay. A fresh wave of tears flowed. 'Oh, Frederick,' she moaned. 'How am I to carry on without you, my dear love?' Her shoulders sagged despairingly. 'We fell asleep last night and I didn't even know he'd gone until I woke about six this morning. At least, though, he died in my arms knowing how much I loved him and not on his own.' She took a shuddering breath. 'Before I met Frederick when I moved in here I'd never been in love, or even felt what it was like to be loved by a man. I'd dedicated my life to my job. In my day teachers at private schools, especially ones like me with ambitions to be a headmistress, didn't marry and have families. It was one or the other. I had led a fulfilling life, so I had thought, until Frederick made me see how empty it had really been.' She lifted her head and looked at Izzie beseechingly. 'I will have to leave here as soon as I can. It will be bad enough mourning my loss for the rest of my life without having to endure the fact that the residents and all you staff will be thinking of this as a sordid liaison, when in truth there was nothing sordid about it. I don't care for my own reputation but I can't bear the thought that people will think badly of Frederick.'

Izzie didn't care whether what she was about to say to Elinor Stringer was right or not. As far as she was concerned, no crime had been committed here. This woman was suffering enough over the loss of the only man she had ever loved and been loved by without causing her any more distress. If Izzie could spare her, then she would.

'No one will think badly of either of you, Miss Stringer,' she said softly. 'There's no need for anyone to know about this relationship. As far as anyone else is concerned, Mr Granger died in the night alone in his bed. You being with him at the time will be our secret, Miss Stringer. You'll be able to mourn your loss in private but remain here in your home amongst your friends. Mr Granger will be remembered by everyone for the lovely man he was.'

Elinor looked at Izzie in disbelief then her eyes filled with a deep gratitude she was too moved to voice.

Izzie got up, and helped Elinor up also, wrapping her dressing gown around her. 'Now I'll go and check the corridor is clear and you can slip along to your own room. After I've dealt with the necessaries here, I'll come to check on you. I'll tell the other staff you've had a bad night and are feeling under the weather so have decided to stay in bed. That way you don't have to face anyone until you're ready to. In the meantime, would you like me to send Alma up with a tray of tea? I'll tell her to leave it outside your door and tap and tell you it's there.'

Elinor nodded and whispered, 'You're so kind. I can't tell you how much I appreciate your response to all this.'

Unexpectedly she grasped Izzie's hands and gave them a tight squeeze, then gave her a kiss on her cheek.

As Izzie went across to the door so she could check the corridor, she had to fight back tears of her own.

A while later Izzie was alone in the laundry room at the sink, arranging winter greenery from the garden in vases to be displayed around the premises. Prior to tackling this task she had been up to check on Elinor Stringer, gratified to find the old lady had drunk the tea taken up for her and was now in an exhausted sleep. Sleep, Izzie felt, was the best thing for her. Jenny Johnson had been deeply grieved to learn of the death of Frederick Granger and had immediately taken responsibility for dealing with the situation. She had also shown deep concern for Izzie's own welfare as the one to have discovered the body. Izzie had repeatedly assured her that she was suffering no ill effects but promised her boss she would take a break from her duties long enough to have a cup of sweet tea.

Despite the staff's endeavours to keep Frederick Granger's death from the other residents so a proper announcement could be made to them all, somehow one of them had cottoned on to the fact that something was amiss, investigated, and within a very short space of time everyone was talking about the loss of a respected resident. Thankfully, however, as far as Izzie was aware no one had discovered Elinor Stringer's involvement in the situation and she prayed it stayed that way, for the old lady's sake and to protect Frederick Granger's memory.

As Izzie heard the door to the laundry room creak open she automatically looked across to see who had entered. To her surprise it was Steven Landers, the last person she'd expected to see. Immediately her heart began to race and she dearly hoped he didn't witness the effect his presence was having on her. Despite thinking she stood no chance with him on a romantic, level, she still found herself very drawn to him.

As he walked across to join her he was smiling at her warmly. 'Ah, just the lady I was looking for. I was told I should find you in here.'

She couldn't think what he would want to speak to her about. She couldn't tell him anything more than she had told Jenny Johnson about finding Frederick Granger dead in his bed. Then it struck her. Jenny Johnson had asked him to check on her, just to confirm she wasn't suffering after her ordeal. How lucky she was to have such a wonderful caring boss, she thought. Laying down the pair of scissors she was trimming stems with, she said to him, 'Mrs Johnson worries too much. It's good of her to ask you to check I'm okay but, as you can see, Doctor Landers, I'm fine. I am sad, though, for Mr Granger and feel sorry for his family and what they're going through now.'

Having joined her by now he said, 'I'm glad to hear you're okay but shock can be delayed. Don't hesitate to ask me for something to help you should that happen. What I'm here for is to ask you a couple of questions regarding Mr Granger's death that are puzzling me. Just to put my own mind at rest.'

She was staring at him warily. 'You think something isn't right?'

'No, no, not at all,' he reassured her. 'I've no doubt whatsoever he died from natural causes. It's just that there's a bit of a mystery about the way he was lying which I'd like clearing up if possible.'

'Oh, what mystery?'

'Well, Mr Granger was obviously asleep when he died and that was in the early hours of the morning as rigor mortis had set in when I examined him. But he was lying in a funny position. His arm was crooked, as though it lay over something . . . well, cuddling it. I just wondered if you'd removed something he was holding when you found him?'

Izzie stared at him. 'Oh, I see.' Her mind raced frantically. In her endeavours to stop Elinor Stringer and Frederick Granger's secret affair from becoming common knowledge she had not mentioned that Frederick had not been alone when he died. She hadn't had to lie about that fact because Jenny Johnson hadn't asked her if anyone else had been present in the room when she had found him. A doctor wanting to unravel this mystery could investigate further and then her cover up would come to light and along with it the scandal of the affair between Frederick and Elinor. She had to come clean to Doctor Landers about what she had done. Knowing he had a duty to report anything he felt was amiss to the authorities, she'd face the consequences herself but did hope that the relationship between Elinor and Frederick could remain private, for their sakes.

Taking a deep breath, she clasped her hands together. 'I did remove something, Doctor Landers . . . well, helped to . . . and if what I did was wrong then I'm fully prepared to face whatever punishment I deserve. You see . . .' She proceeded to take him fully into her confidence over the whole story of that morning. When she had finished she said, 'That's all of it, Doctor Landers. I'm not sorry for what I did. Miss Stringer is suffering enough, through no fault of her own. Is it possible to find a way to keep the affair from his family and the residents here?' She blushed then. 'Oh, I'm sorry, I shouldn't have asked you that, it's putting you in a compromising position. Please forgive me, Doctor Landers.'

He smiled warmly at her. 'We doctors are human beings, you know, Izzie. I think it's very compassionate of you to have acted as you did. It seems love isn't just for the young, doesn't it? You have my word that what you've told me stays between you and me. I will, however, pop up and see Miss Stringer while I'm here, ask if she needs any medical assistance. It's bad enough grieving in the open, but having to keep your bereavement to yourself is a hard thing to do. I will tell her I heard she wasn't feeling well and took it upon myself to check on her. That way she won't know I'm aware of what she's really suffering, unless she chooses to tell me herself.'

Deeply relieved with this outcome, Izzie couldn't find the words to express her thanks.

Steven was looking at the vases she had already filled with winter greenery. Bringing his eyes back to rest on her, he said, 'They look very nice. Woman of many talents, aren't you, Izzie?'

She felt herself blushing again. 'Thank you,' she muttered. He was looking at her as though he really liked her, but she reminded herself that the doctor was a friendly sort of man and he was just being so with her.

'Well, better leave you to it,' he said and made to depart then hesitated, seeming to be deliberating over something before he blurted, 'Look, Izzie, this really isn't the time or place but I never seem to catch you on your own. In fact, we haven't really crossed paths since that night we had a chat in the corridor. Anyway, I . . . er . . . well I was wondering if . . . er . . . if you'd like to have dinner with me one night?'

She was totally shaken by his offer and just stared at him.

He mistook her response for dismay. 'Oh, I've embarrassed you. I'm so sorry. Just forget what I said.'

'No, you certainly haven't embarrassed me, Doctor Landers. Not at all you haven't. It's just that I wasn't expecting . . . , well . . . you being a doctor and me just a nursing assistant, I . . .'

'You think you're not good enough for me!' he cut in incredulously. 'Izzie, I'd be proud to share a table with you.'

'You would! Well, I'd love to then.'

He beamed in delight. 'Tomorrow night?' Then he burbled, 'Well, that's if you're free, of course?'

She'd have cancelled tea with the Queen to go out with Steven. The only thing she wouldn't was an outing with her nieces. 'Tomorrow night would be just fine with me.'

'Really? Oh, that's just great. I'll make reservations for a nice table at the Coach and Horses. It's a lovely little pub in Anstey. Old world charm and they do really good food. What time would you like me to pick you up? Oh, and I'd better give my old jalopy a clear out, it's full of medical paraphernalia.' His latter remark was more of a reminder to himself than to inform Izzie his car was a mess.

She had long wished to have a male friend with his own transport so she could find out what it was like to be taken out for trips. It seemed she was to get her wish. Nervous excitement was creating havoc with her insides. She felt in dire need of a stiff brandy to calm her down. 'Will eight o'clock be all right?' she asked him, fighting to keep her voice from betraying her nervousness.

'Eight o'clock it is then.'

CHAPTER FIFTEEN

Dorothy Landers, a five-foot-one-inch, homely sixty-two year old, looked with a certain amount of suspicion at her son at just after one o'clock that afternoon. She was sitting opposite him at her dining table in a small two-up, two-down, shabby but comfortable terrace house opposite a busy clothing factory in a small street at the bottom end of the Narborough Road.

'Pie all right, son?' she asked.

He nodded, smiling. 'As delicious as all your meals, Mum. You know chicken and mushroom is my favourite.'

She looked gratified then addressed her husband, a man only a few inches taller than his wife but with the same roundness and homely pleasant face, who was sitting at the head of the table. 'More gravy, Linus?'

He nodded appreciatively at her. 'If there's some going, I won't say no.'

She rose up, bustling off into the kitchen, and returned with a jug which she put before him. 'Help yourself, lovey.'

Sitting back down again, she picked up her cutlery, preparing to resume eating her own meal, then laid it down again. 'I can't bear the suspense any longer. Come on, who is she, son?'

Steven stared blankly at her. 'I've lost you, Mum.'

She gave a snort of disdain. 'You know exactly what I'm talking about. You've got that look in your eye, a way about you, like you're bursting at the seams. You've met someone, haven't you? For a few weeks now I've suspected you'd a woman on your mind but today . . . well . . . something's happened and I think you've a date with her arranged. Oh, I'm so pleased for you, son,' she enthused. 'What's her name? What's she like? What

179

does she do for a job? When are you going to bring her around to meet me and your dad?'

'Whoah there, Mum,' he ordered. Then he shook his head at her. 'Might have known I was on a sticky wicket, trying to keep this from you. All right, I have met someone. She's lovely, Mum. I'm taking her out for a meal tomorrow night. Now can I finish my dinner before it gets cold?'

Dorothy beamed at him in delight. She adored her son. Couldn't be more proud of him. Steven had been a caring and thoughtful child, and hadn't lost those qualities in adulthood. Factory workers like themselves didn't usually have sons who became doctors, but she and Linus did.

Steven's desire to join the medical profession had been fuelled by the loss of his beloved younger sister whose death at the age of seven might never have happened had their doctor not decided that the needs of an affluent paying patient, suffering heartburn at the time, were more important than attending a child from a working-class background. It was only a temperature, after all. But it turned out to be a killer strain of meningitis. As the bereaved family gathered around the graveside to say their good-byes, Steven vowed to his dead sister that he would study medi-cine when he grew up and commemorate her death by making sure that all patients under his care received equal attention from him, whatever their status in life.

He worked hard at school, achieving top grades, and his entry into university was partly funded by a well-deserved scholar-ship and by the labours of his parents who worked all hours at their factory jobs without complaint to ensure their son should gain his medical degree. Steven was eternally grateful for their unwavering support so that he could achieve his ambition. He kept from them the fact that the reason he could not now stand the sight of beans on toast or macaroni cheese was because he'd virtually survived on such cheap food during his five years of study. They were also unaware that he had taken a variety of menial part-time jobs in order to take as little money from them as he could. Nor did they know that he'd continually had to endure nasty taunts and pranks from upper-class students whose view was that the medical profession was not for the likes of Steven Landers.

Knowing of their son's vow to his sister, neither Dorothy nor Linus was surprised when after graduating – and there were no prouder parents attending that ceremony than those two – their son turned down the offer of a surgical post under a very prominent heart surgeon to open up a general practice in his own neighbourhood and serve the community. Ten years he'd been running it now and Dorothy was well aware that all her son's patients felt themselves very fortunate to have the services of a doctor who actually cared about their health, about them as people in fact, and no matter what time of day or night was always there for them with a smile on his face and some kindly words.

Dorothy was very content that her son had a good livelihood his own little house nearby that she kept clean for him, and that he was well liked and respected by all who knew him. All she wanted for him now was the love of a good woman who would share his life.

Trouble was, he was now thirty-five and she was beginning to worry that her own ambition for herself and Linus to become doting grandparents was not going to materialise. Steven had had several girlfriends to his credit, nice enough women who seemed very attached to him, but none of them had been wife material. Dorothy was therefore excited to think that maybe this one could be the one with that extra-special something her son was looking for in the woman he chose to spend the rest of his life with.

'Are you taking her somewhere nice, Steven? Wear your blue suit, that one you bought for your cousin Janet's wedding last year, as you look so handsome in it.'

'Leave the lad alone, Dorothy,' Linus spoke up. 'Remember how your mother drove you daft when you first met me, and how pressured you felt that she was practically arranging our wedding after our first date? Mind you, I can't blame her for recognising the good catch that I was,' he added, a mischievous spark glinting his eyes.

Dorothy looked at him reproachfully. 'My mother had all the family round and lined up to inspect you on the night of our first date. I'm just showing a motherly interest – you can hardly compare that to what my mother put us through. I want our son to look his best on his date and he will, in his blue suit.' He fixed her attention back on Steven. 'It'll need an airing so I'll take it out of your wardrobe when I pop around to your house tomorrow morning to do your cleaning.'

Other men might see their mother's interference in their personal life as pure meddling but Steven knew she had his best interests at heart and was happy to keep her informed as to what was going on with him. Besides they were a family that didn't keep secrets from each other 'I hope you approve, I'm taking her for a meal at the Coach and Horses in Anstey – where I took you and Dad for your wedding anniversary last month. At least I know already it's a lovely place, the food is good and the staff are obliging.' To change the subject he asked her, 'Still going to visit Aunty Ada on Saturday afternoon?'

'Well, that's providing you haven't other plans on Saturday afternoon,' she said, looking at him meaningfully. 'I'm quite capable of catching the bus.'

'I wouldn't dream of allowing you to catch the bus when I've a car to take you in,' he told her. 'Besides, I'm fond of Aunty Ada and like to see her myself. I also want to check that the cream I gave her to help ease her eczema is doing the trick. Oh, and that reminds me, I need to renew the prescription for your insulin as you've only another couple of days' supply left. I've a busy afternoon ahead of me so I'll make a mental note to get it done tomorrow.'

His mother pulled a face. 'This dratted diabetes of mine is a hindrance.'

'It's not like it stops you from doing anything you used to,' he said to her.

'I meant a hindrance to you, having to come here every day to give me my injection.'

'Well, I'm your doctor, it's my job. Besides, you repay me by giving me my dinner every day to save me cooking for myself

when all most doctors get is a lukewarm cup of tea offered them.'
He grinned mischievously at her. 'I reckon that's why you and
Dad were so keen to help put me through my medical training –
so you'd have your own private doctor on hand to deal with your
ailments in old age.'

She snorted at him. 'Cheeky monkey!'

As he continued to eat his meal Steven had difficulty disguising
his elation at Izzie's acceptance of his invitation. He'd had several
girlfriends in the past but had a strong suspicion that Izzie was
going to become a special person in his life, she had that extra
something about her his other girlfriends hadn't possessed, something invisible that drew one person to another. He was anxious
to get to know her better.

He was aware that his comfortable green tweed work suit,
though respectable enough for visiting his patients in, wasn't
suitable for an evening out so was thankful for his mother's
recommendation and agreed with her that the wearing of his
smart blue suit was called for on this occasion. He'd wait until
he'd finished his meal, though, before he asked Dorothy what
colour shirt she suggested he team with it to ensure his appearance was as immaculate as he could manage. It was so important to him that Izzie formed the best possible impression of
him. He was hoping that tomorrow night was the first date of
many, and prayed Izzie felt the same.

Later that evening Izzie couldn't tell who was more excited
about her date the next night with Doctor Landers, Pat or herself.

'Oh, Izzie, your day has certainly been eventful! It must have
been awful, finding that dead man like yer did, but you can tell
me about that another time. Now I want to know more about
Doctor Landers. You're a right dark horse, not having mentioned
him to me before. A doctor, eh? Fancy you having a date with
a proper doctor. Oh, not that I don't think yer good enough to
be taken out by a professional man, Izzie, though you've every
right to be thinking I meant that after the way I used to treat
you, but I never really meant those wicked things I said about
you. I was just saying them . . .'

'I know you didn't mean them,' Izzie cut in reassuringly, patting her hand. 'That's all in the past, Pat, so please leave it there.'

Her sister-in-law looked gratefully at her before launching off again. 'So what's he look like? Short? Tall? Fat? Thin? Good-looking, is he?'

She smiled coyly. 'Well, I think so. He's not much taller than me and he's . . . well, I think you'd say cuddly. He's such a lovely person, Pat.'

'Like you then,' she said warmly. 'You'll make a wonderful pair.'

'Oh, they will, Mam,' an excited voice suddenly piped up. 'We know Doctor Landers, don't we, our Sally? He's everso lovely. He gave me a lolly out of his bag the other day when I banged me leg on the corner of a table in the lounge, and he put some cream on it. He said I was everso brave as I didn't cry when I done it.'

Both women spun their heads to see Suzy and Sally peering at them from around the stair door.

'Oi, you two, how long have you been earwigging?' Face stern, Pat shook her head at them. 'You heard me telling your dad, didn't you, that Aunty Izzie was coming tonight for a natter, so he could go for a pint down the pub to give us peace? You two have obviously been listening out for her. Look here, I won't tell you again, adults have conversations when kids are in bed because it's about stuff kids shouldn't be listening to. Come and kiss your aunty then get back up to bed.'

Galloping into the room to throw herself on her beloved aunt, Suzy proclaimed, 'But we wanna hear all about Aunty Izzie's date with Doctor Landers, Mam. Don't we, our Sally?'

'Yeah, we do. What you going to wear, Aunty Izzie?'

'Her birthday suit,' answered their mother.

They both looked quizzical for a moment before Suzy asked, 'What colour is the suit yer got for yer birthday, Aunty Izzie?'

She laughed. 'Sky blue pink with duck yellow spots on. Oh, don't hold me so tight, both of you, I'm having trouble breathing.'

'They'll have trouble breathing if they don't get themselves back up the stairs and into bed where I put them an hour ago.'

They both looked at their mother and knew by her tone and facial expression they had pushed their luck far enough.

'Okay, Mam,' they said in unison.

The girls safely back upstairs and out of earshot, Pat said to Izzie, 'I always seem to be saying this when you come for a visit, but where were we before we were interrupted . . .' Before Izzie could respond she mouthed, 'Oh . . . but I've just had a thought. Most doctors have cars, don't they? Has Doctor Landers got one?'

She nodded. 'He's taking me for a meal at a pub in the country. I can't remember the name of it now, I was so knocked side-ways at the time. Well, to be truthful, I couldn't care less where he's taking me, I'm just looking forward to being with him.' A worried look then clouded her face.

'What's wrong, Izzie?' Pat demanded.

She took a deep breath then slowly exhaled. 'If you want the truth, I'm terrified, Pat.'

'What of?'

'Everything. That I'll not be dressed right. That I might not find enough interesting things to talk about. That . . .'

'Eh, you can bleddy pack in thinking like that for a start,' she interjected, looking at Izzie sternly. 'In fairness to you this is your first proper date with a man as you can't really count having yer lunch in the works canteen or sitting with his mother as Lawrence taking you out on dates, can you? You're just nervous, that's all, Izzie, like all women are on their first proper date. Don't forget, though, he'll be as nervous as you, mark my words. Now, let's decide what you're going to wear so you can stop mithering about that.'

After mentally going through Izzie's entire wardrobe they both agreed she should wear her power blue shift with navy court shoes and matching handbag. Blue was Izzie's favourite colour and it suited her. Plus the fact that the dress was simple and comfortable, the sort of style that could be worn on most occasions except when an expensive evening dress was called for.

'You'll find plenty to talk about but should you be stuck for words just pretend to be interested in what he has to say. That way he'll think you're a good listener, which in fact you are, Izzie,' Pat advised her, then added tongue-in-cheek, 'All you really have to do is make sure you don't spill the gravy down you and make a right idiot of yourself. Eh, and before you start worrying about that, I was only trying to make you laugh, forget your nerves over tomorrow night.'

Izzie appreciated her effort but it didn't work. She was in such an inner turmoil she doubted she'd sleep a wink that night.

CHAPTER SIXTEEN

S he was right, she didn't sleep at all. Well, it certainly felt like she hadn't when she rose the next morning. Rising above the fatigue though was a flood of adrenalin and nervous anticipation of what the evening would bring.

Over elevenses Jenny Johnson took advantage of all the day staff being together to discuss the details of Frederick Granger's funeral, which was taking place two days later.

'I don't know whether we're invited to the wake afterwards as nothing was mentioned when his daughter was going over the details with me this morning. She'd called in to collect her father's belongings. I assume it's just family and long-standing friends but I'll ask Cook to lay something on here for us for when we get back. Just a few sandwiches and cakes and a glass of sherry each, to make sure we send Mr Granger off properly in our own way.' A look of sadness filled her face. 'This is the part of my business that I hate. Losing a resident for me is like losing a member of my family. I don't think the residents' families appreciate that we all suffer the bereavement too.'

'Well, I'll miss Mr Granger,' mused Joyce. 'He was a pleasant man. Always a thank you from him for what yer did for him.'

The others all agreed.

'Elinor Stringer won't miss him,' said Beattie. 'She hated the sight of him, didn't she? She's probably toasting his passing.'

They all murmured their agreement apart from Izzie who appeared to be studying the cup of coffee she was holding so hoping no one could witness the look of guilt that crossed her face.

'Well, I have my suspicions that someone could be devastated by Mr Granger's passing,' said Jenny.

They all looked at her quizzically apart from Izzie as panic filled her. Did Jenny suspect there'd been an affair between Elinor and Frederick and was about to divulge her suspicions? She tentatively asked, 'Er . . . what do you mean, Mrs Johnson?'

'Well, it's just that something very odd happened when I was handing over Mr Granger's personal effects to his daughter. I mentioned to her that as I was parcelling up his books a card fell out of one of them. His bible, I'm positive it was. I gave it to her as . . . well, it wasn't in an envelope and not that I was being nosey but it would have been obvious to anyone it was a Valentine card. It must have been very important to Mr Granger or he wouldn't have kept it. I thought maybe it was a love token from his dear late wife but she died quite a few years ago and the card wasn't yellowed with age so it was obvious to me it was from someone he'd met after her death. When his daughter looked at it she immediately threw it in my waste bin, saying that it wasn't her father's and she had no idea what it was doing in his personal effects. Quite aggressive about it she was. Anyway, after she had left, out of curiosity, I suppose, but more for the fact that the card ought to be returned to its rightful owner if it wasn't Mr Granger's, I rescued it from the bin and it obviously *was* meant for Mr Granger. It had a very intimate verse and in handwriting it said, "To my darling Frederick, I bless the day we met each other and will always treasure the love we share. Yours forever, E."

'I know from his details that his wife's name was Sarah so it wasn't from her, was it? Then I wondered if the card was from someone he'd grown . . . well, considering the type of card and the words on it . . . more than a little friendly with here at Westleigh Lodge. During the time Mr Granger was residing with us we've had a couple of ladies with names beginning with E, but the only one fitting the bill recently would have been Elinor Stringer. Now I know they used to be on good terms when they first moved in, but it was a well-known fact that something happened between them to sour their relationship and they openly despised each other. It can't have been from her. Mr Granger was always going out and about. Now I'm worried he was having a relationship with someone locally who might not know he's passed on if she hasn't seen the announcement in the *Mercury*. Poor woman, I do feel sorry for her, finding out he's died in this way.'

Izzie was feeling most uncomfortable as she was well aware of the identity of Mr Granger's mystery woman and could put Jenny's mind at rest that she knew of his death, but she couldn't unless she broke her promise to Elinor Stringer and she wasn't prepared to do that.

All the rest of the staff had been riveted by Jenny's tale.

'Well, it might be a relationship that's over and Mr Granger just kept the card for sentimental reasons,' mused Joyce.

'Oh, yes, it could well be, and in view of what's happened to him I do hope so, for the sake of the woman concerned,' agreed Jenny.

'Well, Mr Granger was a very nice man and I'm glad he found a bit of happiness to ease his loneliness after losing his wife,' said Beattie with conviction.

'Most of my friends think it's disgusting but I think it's lovely meself when old people get together,' said Alma.

Jenny smiled at her. 'My sentiments exactly, dear. Love isn't just for the young. I'd like nothing more than to help arrange a wedding between two residents who met through being here. I'd have no objection to their sharing a room as a married couple. Anyway, as for the arrangements for all those who want to attend Mr Granger's funeral . . .'

As Jenny departed a short while later Joyce said to Beattie, 'On a lighter subject, did you notice that Doc was looking rather pleased with himself yesterday when yer did his rounds with him?' She then focused her attention on Izzie. 'It was me who pointed him in your direction yesterday morning when he told me he'd a query he wanted clearing up over Mr Granger's death. What was that query, by the way?'

How Izzie hated being evasive with her colleagues!

'Oh, er . . . just . . . er . . . what time I found him, that's all.'

'Oh, I thought I told the doctor that,' said Joyce, puzzled. 'Still, as long as you put him straight so the information is correct on the death certificate. Anyway, after he'd spoken to you I happened to catch sight of him and he did look very happy with himself, in my opinion.'

'Yes, he was certainly very chirpy on our round,' said Beattie, looking at Izzie quizzically. 'Well, he's always good-humoured but was even more so yesterday.'

'So it must be something to do with you,' said Joyce. 'I told you the doc had a twinkle in his eye for you.'

'Has he asked you out then and that's why he was all cock-a-hoop after he'd left you?' Alma blurted.

Izzie gulped. She'd like nothing more than to share the information with her colleagues but had no idea whether Steven wanted their date together becoming common knowledge. If he asked to take her out again after tonight, which she dearly hoped he would, then she must clarify this with him. Until then, out of respect for him, she had no choice but to play on the safe side. Picking up her empty cup and getting to her feet, she said, 'I don't know about you but I've work to do.'

They all looked disappointed by her evasive response. Izzie knew without a doubt they liked her and the doctor and would take great delight in discovering there was a romance blossoming between them both. Well, hopefully she would be able to give them the news they were desperate to hear after her date tonight.

Just before lunchtime after helping an excited Julia Gregson, a seventy-seven-year-old resident of three years' standing to dress for her Christmas shopping expedition with her daughter that afternoon, Izzie was making her way down the corridor towards the stairs when she noticed Brian Knowles at Amelia Austin's door. He had a white envelope in his hand which she saw a hand from inside the room take from him. She assumed it was Amelia's. Izzie then heard him say, 'Just as you wanted, Mrs Austin. Now you can rest easy in your bed, knowing that your house is properly in order.' He then obviously sensed a presence in the corridor as he spun to face Izzie, looking startled for a moment before addressing her with, 'Hello, Izzie. I was just checking with Mrs

Austin that she's had no more trouble with her window catch now I've fixed it.'

Izzie had joined them now and smiled warmly at both Amelia and Brian, but it didn't escape her notice that Amelia was hiding the envelope she had seen him give her behind her back and was looking flustered.

'Everything all right, Mrs Austin?' she enquired.

'Oh, yes, everything is fine, thank you.' Amelia then said to Brian, 'I appreciate what you've done for me.' Then looking back at Izzie said, 'I'd better hurry and freshen myself up ready for dinner.' With that she disappeared inside her room, shutting the door.

'Well, I'd better report to Mrs Johnson that I've done the jobs she asked me to today. See you, Izzie.'

'Yes, see you, Brian,' she called after him as he dashed off down the stairs.

She stared thoughtfully after him as a question she had already asked herself once before posed itself again. Just what was in those envelopes she had witnessed him hand over to two of their female residents? Nothing she could think of explained it. Suspicion reared within her. It all seemed very cloak and dagger to her. Then she reasoned with herself that Jenny Johnson was very particular as to who she employed, and wouldn't have Brian Knowles on the premises if she wasn't satisfied he wasn't trustworthy. There must be a simple explanation of what those envelopes contained. Then she reminded herself she was employed here to care for the residents, not to pry into their private lives uninvited.

She heard her name being called and looked over towards the staircase to see Alma grinning over at her. 'Come on, Izzie. Dinner duties call.'

She was just about to call back over to Alma that she'd be right with her when she heard another voice calling out to her from behind. She turned to see Katherine Philpots heading her way.

'You wanted me, Mrs Philpots?'

'Not you in particular, dear, any staff member would have

done, but being's you're here you can do something for me to save me the trouble. The bathroom that I use at the far end of this floor, well, the hook we hang our bathrobes on on the back of the door has fallen off and needs reporting to Mrs Johnson.'

'I'll make sure she's aware of it, Mrs Philpots.' Izzie then had a thought. If she hurried she might catch Brian Knowles still on the premises and he'd be able to do something about it while he was here, save Mrs Johnson calling him in again.

She made her excuses to Katherine Philpots and hurried off to try and catch him before he left. Downstairs in the foyer she was just about to knock on Jenny's office door before she entered, hoping Brian was inside with her, when the sound of voices reached her ears. They belonged to Jenny and Leonie.

'I don't agree, dear, that laying on transport for the residents who wish to attend the two forthcoming outings is an unnecessary expense,' Jenny was saying. 'Standing around the graveside in this bitter weather is arduous enough, let alone having to wait around at bus stops to ferry them all backwards and forwards. The journey from the church to Gilrose Cemetery involves two bus rides and you know the local bus service isn't always reliable. As for the trip to the circus, Well, I feel it is kind enough of Izzie to offer to take along those residents who wish to go without her having the task of supervising them all on the bus as well. The Circus is on at the Granby Halls site which again is two bus rides away from here.'

'But these occasions aren't isolated ones, Mother. You're always funding expensive extras for the residents which constantly eat away what little profit this business produces,' Leonie sharply responded. 'And while we're on the subject, I think your decision to wait until after the funeral before you fill Mr Granger's room is unsound. That's a week's fees we've lost.'

'Oh, Leonie, it would have been very disrespectful of me to have filled Mr Granger's room as soon as his body was taken away to the funeral home. It would be as though he meant nothing to any of us here. But he was part of our family, we all need to grieve his departure before someone else moves in to take his place. And, Leonie dear, isn't knowing the residents have the best quality of life we can give them more important than a few extra shillings' profit on the balance sheet?'

'All you care about is the residents, Mother! As long as they're all right, that's all that counts, isn't it? Will it take the bailiffs knocking on the door to make you see sense? Oh, I know I'm wasting my breath, you won't listen to me. I'll leave you in peace to squander what little profits we've left over this month on transport for the blessed residents!'

Izzie hadn't at first thought the conversation she was over-hearing to be unduly private but it had suddenly become very personal between mother and daughter and out of respect she was just about to depart, meaning to return later to speak to Mrs Johnson about the broken hook in the bathroom. But before she could take her leave Leonie, appearing not to see her, was rushing past her and on into her own office, shutting the door behind her none too gently. Next thing Izzie knew, Jenny had almost collided with her.

'Oh, Izzie, er . . . did you want me?' Jenny asked her, flustered.

'You're on your way somewhere, Mrs Johnson, it's not urgent. I can see you about it later.'

Jenny looked worriedly in the direction of Leonie's office for several long moments before she sighed distractedly. 'Oh, when she learns what I have to tell her when she comes of age, she'll understand I was only trying to equip her in the best way I know, how to handle her future. The young are so impetuous.' She then gave herself a mental shake and looked remorsefully at Izzie. 'Oh, I'm sorry, dear, I was speaking out loud. Now come into my office and tell me what you came to see me about.'

Thankfully for Izzie the rest of the day she was kept busy dealing with the residents so had little time to dwell on that evening's outing.

At seven-forty-five she was having a final check on her appear-ance in the mirror hanging on the living-room wall. Even if she wasn't happy with what she saw it was too late for her to do anything about it now unless she wanted to keep Steven waiting. Thankfully, though, she was pleased with her reflection. Despite its plainness she felt smart in her blue sleeveless belted shift dress, and her unruly curls for once had allowed her to tame them and sat becomingly around her face in a curly bob. She had never been one for overdoing her makeup and the light application of blue shadow and black mascara she had applied enhanced her eyes but did not overstate them. The younger generation seemed to go in for thick layers of panstick coating their skin and liberal amounts of black eyeliner emphasising their eyes, along with false eyelashes like Alma sported when she went out. Not that she was against modern trends but Izzie had never been the type knowingly to invite attention to herself.

As her eyes caught the tin clock she kept on her window sill and the time registered, her nervousness heightened and she dearly wished she had asked either Joyce or Beattie for a pill to calm her down out of their stock in the medical cupboard. But then they would have wanted to know why she was in need of such medical aid and that would have meant having to fabricate an excuse to them.

If she didn't want to keep Steven waiting for her, she ought to be making a move. Taking a very deep breath, she picked up her coat and handbag and made to depart then stopped suddenly as a thought struck her. She hadn't actually arranged the exact spot where she was meeting him as he'd just said he'd pick her up at eight. She presumed he'd meant at the front of the building as she didn't know whether he was actually aware that out of working hours she usually used the side entrance to come and go. It was very dark in the yard at this time of night and not without its hazards, the dustbins and the catch on the back gate proving troublesome at times. Izzie kept meaning to report it for repair but had never quite got round to it. She decided that sooner than risk the chance of spoiling her appearance by colliding with the bins she would make her exit via the main part of the building.

She had just reached the bottom of the stairs when Amelia

Austin, accompanied by Nora Hopgood, came out of the lounge.

'Oh, you do look nice tonight,' Amelia said to Izzie, glancing her over appraisingly. 'Going anywhere interesting, dear?'

'Well, I wouldn't advise anyone with a figure like yours to wear a belted dress,' said Nora, looking at her meaningfully.

Izzie's jaw dropped, her face clouding with worry. 'Oh, do you think . . .'

Before she could finish, Amelia glared at Nora and cut in, 'What do you mean by that remark?'

A haughty expression crossed Nora's aged face. 'Well, it's just that Izzie isn't exactly what you'd call slim, is she? Having been in the fashion industry, I would strongly advise her to wear a dress without a belt as they're supposed to draw attention to a trim waist and Izzie's isn't what we in the industry would call trim.'

'Nora Hopgood, you had a second-hand dress shop, that's hardly being in the fashion industry! And if that's the way you dished out your advice then I'm surprised you had any customers at all or ever made a living.' Amelia snapped.

In Izzie's experience some members of the older generation felt they had a God-given right to voice their opinions out loud, regardless of what hurt they would cause the recipient. When aimed at herself, despite any inward hurt, usually she managed to ignore such remarks. Tonight, due to her desire to look her very best for her date with Steven, she frantically asked, 'Oh, does this dress make me look fatter than I am?'

'You're not fat,' Amelia assured her with conviction. 'You're nicely rounded, dear. Womanly.' Izzie wasn't sure what to make of her next words. 'You are inwardly pretty, Izzie. Beauty is only skin deep, remember that, dear.' She then glared at Nora again. 'How dare you upset Izzie? Not everyone is a bag of bones like you, Nora.'

Shame clouded the other woman's face. 'I never was known for my diplomacy, Izzie. My husband was always telling me I spoke before I thought. I'm sorry, I didn't mean to upset you. You do look lovely in that dress. I was just being spiteful because

I've had an upset today and was taking it out on you. Wanted to hurt someone like I'm hurting, I suppose, to make myself feel better.'

Immediately Izzie's natural concern for others rose up. 'Oh, Mrs Hopgood, what's upset you? If I can be of any help at all . . .'

The old lady smiled appreciatively at her. 'It's just that I was expecting to spend Christmas with my daughter and her family as usual, only to be told today they are going away to spend Christmas in a hotel in the Cotswolds. My daughter said I'd have a perfectly good time here with my friends but I know she was just saying that to appease me.'

Izzie felt sad for the old lady that her family had seemingly abandoned her at the one time of year families did generally get together. 'Oh, but your daughter is right, you will have a great time here. I know Mrs Johnson pulls out all the stops to make Christmas really special. Even Santa pays us a visit.'

The old woman's face brightened. 'Really! Oh, thanks, Izzie, you have made me feel better.'

Amelia addressed her then. 'So where are you off, all spruced up?'

'Oh, er . . . just off to dinner with a friend,' Izzie said lightly.

Amelia looked disappointed. 'Oh, shame I've eaten or I could have come with you. Let me know next time you're dining out, it's ages since I've been out to dinner.'

'Me too,' said Nora, looking equally disappointed. 'I would like to have come too.'

Worried that they would ask to come along regardless, Izzie quickly said, 'Yes, I will. Well, best be off. I don't want to keep my friend waiting.'

She had just arrived on the pavement outside the front entrance when an old black Ford Popular pulled up, the driver's door crashing open and Steven bursting out, looking delighted to see her.

'Oh, I was so worried I was keeping you waiting, Izzie. I was just about to get myself ready when I had a call out for a patient. By the time I got back I only had ten minutes to get washed and changed. I thought you'd be waiting in the entrance hall for me. You shouldn't have been standing out in this bitter cold. I haven't kept you waiting for me long, have I?'

Considering the fact he'd dressed in a hurry, he looked very smart in his suit. She did notice a small trickle of dried blood on his cheek where he had obviously not noticed he'd cut himself in his haste to shave. She appreciated the fact he was concerned he had kept her waiting. And he obviously wasn't concerned about anyone at Westleigh Lodge knowing he was taking her out if he'd been expecting to collect her in the entrance hall which was rarely without anyone in it, except in the dead of night. She found her own jangling nerves were calming down now as it was obvious to her he wanted the evening to go as well as she did.

Smiling at him, she said, 'You haven't kept me waiting at all. I've just arrived, Doctor Landers.'

He looked relieved. 'Steven, please, Izzie. Let's get you in my car out of this cold,' he said, taking her arm to guide her across to it and help her inside.

Settled in the driver's seat next to her, he asked, 'Comfortable, Izzie?'

She nodded. 'Yes, thank you.'

Never having had the privilege of being in a car before, she immensely enjoyed the journey. She felt like royalty being driven along until they reached country roads and drove the couple of miles to the village of Anstey, viewing areas of the town of her birth she had never seen before. They casually chatted along the way, mostly about the weather, both agreeing they felt there was a likelihood of snow for Christmas.

They were greeted warmly by the staff of the Coach and Horses, their coats taken, and settled comfortably at a table near a roaring fire. After furnishing them both with menus, their order for drinks was taken by a polite waiter.

Despite Steven's attentiveness towards her, Izzie still felt in need of a stiff drink to calm the remainder of her nerves but feared that, being unused to alcohol, she could make a fool of herself, so she decided to play safe and opted for an orange juice.

Izzie's usual calming effect on others didn't seem to apply to Steven who was interested in her on a more personal level. He felt a stiff drink might calm his nerves and afford him the ability to converse easily with her, not babble which he feared he was going to do. Then he risked her perceiving him as a bumbling idiot and would scupper his chances with her for good. Sensibly he opted for a pint of best bitter.

Izzie was very taken by the old worldly décor of the place. 'It's lovely here,' she said to him. 'I've never been to a country pub before, I feel like I've stepped back in time.'

'I'm glad you approve of my choice.' His eyes were fixed on her, seeming to drink her in. 'You look lovely, Izzie. The blue of your dress really suits you.'

Lawrence had never looked at her the way Steven was, and although he'd paid her compliments – as she knew now just to keep her strung along until she was no longer useful to him – never had he said them so sincerely as Steven had just now. A surge of joy filled her being. This man sitting before her liked her as much as she liked him, she knew he did. Something magical was taking place between them. She beamed delightedly at him. 'Thank you,' she said graciously. 'You look very handsome yourself.'

It hadn't escaped Izzie's notice that two extremely attractive women were seated at the table next to them but as far as she had observed Steven hadn't noticed; his whole attention was focused on her.

'What takes your fancy?' he asked her, studying the menu. 'It all looks delicious, doesn't it?' He normally had a healthy appetite but in his anxiety tonight the last thing he felt he could stomach was a heavy meal. 'I think I might settle for chicken and chips.' Then he did just what he'd feared he'd do and babbled on. 'I've had a heavy meal already today as my mother makes sure I have a proper dinner every day, bless her. Doesn't matter how old you get, to your mother you are still their child, aren't you? We lost my sister when she was very young so my mother's only got me to fuss over now. I have a lot to thank her for. If it wasn't for the sacrifices she made, I'd never have been able to fulfil my ambition to become a doctor. I always joke with her that she only did so she had her own private physician on hand to minister to her in her old age. Oh, goodness, that reminds me. I never got around to replenishing her supply of insulin, I must do that tomorrow.'

He gave a nervous laugh. 'Some doctor I am, aren't I, forgetting my own mother's medication?' The very last thing he wanted was for Izzie to think he was forgetful towards his patients, especially his mother, but then neither did he feel at this stage in their relationship he could be honest about the cause of his forgetfulness, which was that all he'd been able to think about since he had made the arrangement was being with her tonight. 'I've had a very busy day today and not had time to catch my breath.' Which actually was the truth, he had been busy, all his days were in fact, Steven being the sort of doctor who did not hurry his patients. 'Anyway, I'm positive you'll like my mother, Izzie, everyone does. I've told her all about you and she can't wait to meet you.' He suddenly realised he was showing undue confidence that their relationship was going to progress as far as family introductions and murmured, 'Oh, er . . . I'm being presumptuous, forgive me. Er . . . er . . . so has anything on the menu taken your fancy?'

Concentrating on studying the menu again, Steven was unaware that Izzie was staring at him, frozen.

As he rambled on about his mother a dreadful vision of her first meeting with Lawrence reared up before her. It was like *déjà vu* for her. Over a meal Lawrence had fooled her into thinking he was interested in a romantic relationship with her when all he was really doing was cajoling her into becoming a companion for his mother, leaving him the freedom to pursue his own interests. Steven must be doing the same or why else had he sung his mother's praises so highly to her? He wouldn't realise, though, that due to her past experience she was able to see exactly what he was doing. Just like Lawrence's invitation to tea, this evening was no date, a prelude to a relationship between herself and Steven, merely a chance for him to assess her suitability as a companion for his mother. All she wasn't sure of was whether Steven hoped to lead her on into believing they had a future together like Lawrence had done and gain her services for free or would offer to pay her for her duties.

Oh, how stupid she had been to think for a moment a man like Steven would be in any way interested in her in a romantic way. She felt sick with humiliation that once again she had proved to be so gullible. The one saving grace was that no one at Westleigh Lodge knew of her liaison tonight so they would not be pumping her for news of how it had gone. She'd be spared their sympathy when she explained to them that he had never been looking in her direction in an amorous way but merely assessing her suitability as a carer to his precious mother.

She realised he was talking to her. Giving herself a mental shake she murmured, 'Sorry?'

'I was asking if you're all right, Izzie?' he worriedly asked. 'Only you have . . . well, all I can describe it as is a look of doom on your face.'

She couldn't sit here any longer, not now she was aware of what this whole evening was really about. In a stilted tone she said, 'Look, I'm sorry, Doctor Landers, but I've suddenly developed the most awful headache. Would you be kind enough to take me home?'

He looked stunned, bitterly disappointed that their evening was being cut short and also by the fact she had addressed him by his title and not his Christian name.

'Oh! Oh, yes, of course I will. I always take my medical bag everywhere with me but I haven't tonight. I could stop off at home on our way back and get you something from it?' he offered, summoning over the waiter so he could settle their bill.

'No, I wouldn't wish to put you to that trouble. I'm sure the medical cupboard at Westleigh Lodge will have something that will do the trick. Nurse Joyce told me the day I started to help myself from the stock bottles should I need to. I'm . . . er . . . just sorry I've wasted your evening.'

He looked quizzically at her. 'You haven't at all, Izzie,' he said, bemused, wondering why she would think she had. 'I'm just disappointed you've taken ill and our evening been put an end to.'

They were both silent all the way home.

As a doctor Steven was very sympathetic towards Izzie for what he thought she was suffering and didn't expect any conversation from her or that she would appreciate any from him, knowing that was the last thing she would feel like if she was enduring a debilitating headache.

Izzie was too upset over such a disappointing discovery to be able to offer any snippet of polite conversation. She just wanted this journey to end so she could be on her own to nurse her hurt pride.

As soon as Steven halted his car outside Westleigh Lodge, Izzie opened the door and leapt out almost as if her seat was on fire. Bending, she addressed him through the open door. 'Thank you for seeing me home safely, Doctor Landers. Look, I ought to save you wasting your time further by telling you that I love my job and am not looking to leave it. I'm not wanting anything part-time either. Goodnight.'

Before he could respond she had shut the door and was hurrying off, leaving him staring after her bemused. Why had she felt the need to affirm she loved her job to him? And what was all that about not wanting part-time work? He had no answer other than to suppose that her headache was so bad it was fuddling her brain. He wasn't her doctor but hoped that she'd seek his medical help if the pills she took proved not up to the job. As he drove off towards his own home he was only sorry she hadn't given him a chance to rearrange their evening for another time. But then, he would see her on his next visit to the Lodge and hopefully would be able to take her aside and ask her then. He would make sure he managed it.

As Izzie heard the car drive off she stopped and turned to look after it, a look of desperate longing filling her face. She knew she could have found happiness with the likes of Steven Landers but it had been silly of her to think he could feel the same way about her.

Suddenly the thought of spending the rest of the evening alone wallowing in self-pity did not appeal to her. What she needed now was the sympathetic ear of a good friend such as Pat was proving to be. As she about-turned Izzie hoped her sister-in-law wouldn't mind her turning up unannounced.

Pat was in the kitchen mashing a cup of tea when she heard the knock on the door and beamed in delight when she saw Izzie walk in.

'Oh, hello, Izzie. What a lovely surprise. You're just in time for a . . .' Then a thought struck her and her face clouded over. 'Oh, but aren't you supposed to be out with your doctor tonight?' The look on Izzie's face registered then and she knew something was dreadfully wrong. 'Take your coat off and sit down,' she ordered her sister-in-law, inclining her head towards the kitchen table. She then dashed over to the kitchen door and called through, 'Izzie's here, Arnold, and we don't want disturbing.' With that she shut the door and demanded, 'Right, what's happened? Did he have to cancel 'cos something had cropped up? Didn't he turn up? What?'

Izzie sniffed back the threat of tears. 'Oh, he turned up, Pat, but it soon became obvious to me that it wasn't a real date I was on with him but an interview.'

She looked confused. 'What?'

'He was sussing me out as a companion for his mother, Pat.'

She looked stunned. 'Eh? No, surely you've got it wrong, Izzie.'

'I haven't. As soon as we started studying the menus he started talking about his mother. How wonderful she was, and how much she was looking forward to meeting me.'

'Well, maybe he was just making conversation because he was nervous. On our first date Arnold rabbited on non-stop about his job making machine parts at Jones and Shipman. By the end of the evening I knew so much about it, I could have applied for a job on the shop floor myself.'

'Of all the subjects he could have rabbited on about, Pat, why his mother?'

She shrugged. 'Just coincidence.'

'Some coincidence. Some coincidence, too, that she's not a well person. Just as Lawrence's mother wasn't.'

'Look, Izzie, the way Lawrence treated you was despicable, but you can't allow yourself to believe that every man is going to do the same.'

'Pat, Steven wasn't just talking about his mother generally, he was singing her praises. She sounds a lovely woman, I have to say, from what he said about her and they're obviously close. But then Lawrence made *his* mother sound wonderful when he was first telling me about her. I can see why Steven thought I'd make a good companion for his mother. I work with old people, don't I, and he knows I enjoy my job? I can't blame him for looking in my direction, Pat. I was the fool, thinking he liked me for myself and was asking me on a date.'

'But why take you for a meal? That doesn't make sense to me.'

'I don't know either. All I know is that, for me, it was just like I was back in that canteen all those years ago, but instead of Lawrence it was Steven I was with.'

Pat looked at her sorrowfully. 'Oh, Izzie, I don't know what to say. You really like this man, don't you?'

She nodded. 'I was young and stupid where Lawrence was concerned. I should have known I wasn't the type of woman he would want to settle down with. Steven isn't like him in any way so it never entered my head he would be after the same thing with me that Lawrence was, but I should have known a man in his position wouldn't be interested in a nursing assistant who's not exactly the best-looking woman in the world. I've no illusions about myself, Pat. Anyway, at least I realised what was going on before I really made a fool of myself again.'

The tears came then, gushing unashamedly down her face.

Pat leapt up from her seat to rush round the table. She bent over to gather Izzie to her. 'Let it all out, it's the best thing for yer.'

'I'm just feeling sorry for myself, that's all, Pat,' she blubbered into her shoulder. 'Thank you so much for listening to me.'

'No need to thank me, Izzie. We're friends now, and I know damned well you'd do the same for me. Look, listen to me, you might not be the most beautiful woman in the world but you're beautiful inside and there's a man somewhere out there waiting for you, I just know there is.'

Izzie remembered how it had been when she'd discovered Lawrence's abuse of her good nature. At the time, because of the way her life had been, she'd had no close friend to share her grief with, hadn't had Pat's shoulder to cry on then or comforting arms encircling her. Now she had, and she was so grateful.

Pulling away from Pat, she grabbed at her handbag which she unclipped, delving inside to take out a handkerchief. After wiping her face and blowing her nose, she smiled gratefully over at her sister-in-law who had now retaken her seat opposite her. 'You're right, I feel better. A good cry is a good release. I wouldn't mind that cuppa now,' she said, eyeing the tea pot.

'Coming right up. I'd better take your brother one through before he dies of thirst.'

A few minutes later, both nursing cups of tea, Pat said to her, 'Look, Izzie, I appreciate you might not feel up to having the girls for the weekend or taking them to the circus so I'll take them instead, if you like, so as not to disappoint them?'

Despite her huge disappointment and wretchedness Izzie managed to laugh. 'And cope with half a dozen of the residents as well? Actually, maybe more as I'm not sure of the exact numbers yet. Old people have a tendency to change their minds at the last minute.'

Pat gawped at her. 'Eh! Are you mad, offering to take all those oldies along with you?'

'They invited themselves, Pat, and I hadn't the heart to deny them. Like the girls, they're so excited about a trip to the circus.'

Pat pulled a worried face and scratched her neck. 'Well, on second thoughts, I have to say that I've always found when I've had an upset it's best to keep meself occupied. That way I get over it quicker. A trip to the circus will certainly do that. And the girls will be good company for you for the rest of the weekend.'

Despite knowing this was Pat's way of revoking her offer, Izzie knew she was right and that keeping herself occupied was the best way to come to terms with her disappointment and put it behind her, the same as she had done with Lawrence. If Pat was right and there was a man waiting in the wings for her, when he appeared the first thing she would do was confirm without doubt it was herself he was interested in and not her skills as a care-giver.

CHAPTER SEVENTEEN

The next day as soon as he could find a few minutes in his busy schedule Steven paid a visit to Westleigh Lodge. Thankfully he saw the person he was seeking directly he entered the premises, which saved him having to scour the place in search of her.

Izzie had been dreading coming face to face with him. A personal relationship between them was just a dream, she knew, but that didn't mean she didn't still harbour strong feelings for him which would take time to fade. As she had lain in her bed the previous night, instead of dreaming of a future with Steven as she had thought she would have been after their first date together, she had been deliberating on the best way for her to handle the inevitable next meeting. She had decided to act professionally and be business-like. Steven's next scheduled visit was the following Tuesday which thankfully meant she should have several days in which to prepare herself for the encounter.

Instead, crossing the entrance hall on her way to the dining room to commence dinnertime duties, she was shocked to catch sight of him entering the premises. Her heart thudded, legs threatening to collapse beneath her. She feared if he saw her in this state he would surely not fail to guess her true feelings for him and then she would make a complete and utter fool of herself in his eyes.

Pretending she hadn't see him, she quickened her pace towards the dining room, hoping to escape inside before he saw her. But before she'd taken two steps she inwardly groaned to hear him call out her name. It wasn't in Izzie's nature to be blatantly rude and she couldn't bring herself to be so now. Clasping her hands together in an effort to stop them shaking and praying he could not hear the thumping of her heart, she planted a fixed smile on her face and turned to face him just as he hurried up to her.

'How nice to see you, Doctor Landers.' Izzie spoke briskly. 'Nurse Joyce is on duty today so I'll go and find her for you.'

She made to dash off but he stopped her by grabbing her arm and saying, 'It's you I came to see, Izzie.' He couldn't understand her stiltedness with him. What had he done to make her be this way with him? Withdrawing his hand from her arm, he placed it in his pocket. Shuffling his feet uncomfortably, he said, 'I . . . er . . . well, I wondered if you were feeling any better today or if I could be any use to you in my medical capacity, if you haven't had the chance to see your own doctor yet?'

With the same fixed smile on her face she said in the same brisk manner, 'I appreciate your concern but as you can see I'm fine, thank you, Doctor Landers. A good night's sleep did the trick.'

She was just about to excuse herself when she felt another hand on her arm and looked around to see Muriel Peters.

'Excuse me, Doctor Landers, I just need a quick word with Izzie,' the old lady said politely to him before focusing her attention back on Izzie. 'I wanted to check with you that the visit to the circus tomorrow is still on. I need time to decide what to wear, you see.'

She nodded. 'Yes, it is, Mrs Peters. Wrap up warm because the Big Top won't be heated.'

'I shall heed your advice, dear.' Then she addressed Steven. 'Isn't it good of Izzie, allowing us residents to accompany her and her nieces to the circus? We're all so excited about it.'

She shuffled off.

Steven was looking impressed. 'Mrs Peters is right, it is very kind of you to offer to take residents along with you to the circus, but in my opinion it's also very brave. I hope they all behave themselves for you. Pity I've already arranged to take my mother to visit her sister or I'd have loved to have come along myself, then I could have helped you supervise the residents.' He smiled. 'The last time I went to the circus was when my parents took me as a youngster. I was totally enthralled by it all. I remember for weeks afterwards I daydreamed of joining the circus when I was older. I'm not sure now what I had it in mind to do – a lion tamer, I think, or something equally as hare-brained. Anyway that daydream was replaced by wanting to become an ace pilot instead after discovering Biggles.' He looked thoughtful then. 'My mother would be happy to rearrange her visit to her sister's if she knew there was a visit to the circus in the offing. My father would most probably like to come along too. I shall see them both shortly at dinnertime, I'll ask them both and see about getting tickets.'

Izzie stiffened. If the circumstances had been different she would have liked nothing more than Steven's company but, as it was, the less time she spent in it the better as far as she was concerned or she'd never quash her feelings for him. He did seem hell-bent on her meeting his mother, though, one way or another. She had told him she wasn't looking to change her job or take on a part-time one but was he hoping she'd change her mind after she'd actually met his mother? It seemed, though, it wasn't only his mother he needed help in caring for but his father too. The sooner he stopped looking in her direction, the sooner he'd find someone else more willing to help him out.

'It might be too late now to get tickets for tomorrow's matinee, Doctor Landers. You should still be able to get ones for next Saturday's performance, though. Now, if you'll excuse me, I must get on.'

Desperate to make her escape, she spun on her heel and hurried off, completely missing the look of rejection that filled Steven's face and the disappointed droop of his shoulders.

Dorothy Landers pounced on her son as soon as he entered the back door a short while later.

'Yer a bit early today, son, but dinner won't be long. It's chicken casserole. Now, I'm desperate to hear how your dinner date went last night. When are you taking the young lady out again? I really can't wait to meet her.'

As he stripped off his coat and hung it on the back of the

door, he heaved a deep despondent sigh. 'You won't be meeting her, Mum. The evening didn't go well at all. It was cut short when she developed a headache only . . . well, the way she was with me today I'm not so sure she actually had one, to be honest. Anyway, I'm not seeing her again. Well, only for work. That's going to be hard as I really like her. But she's made it very clear to me she's not interested in that way.'

Dorothy was aghast. 'Oh, I don't believe that. You're a good catch, Steven.'

He smiled wanly at her. 'You're my mother, of course you think I am, but unfortunately for me the person I would like to, doesn't.'

She looked at him regretfully. 'Oh, Steven, I'm so sorry it didn't go as you hoped it would with her.'

'So am I, Mum,' he said sadly.

CHAPTER EIGHTEEN

E ven Izzie was taken aback by the number of residents gathered in the entrance hall waiting for her, Suzy and Sally to
arrive for the trip to the circus. As she counted all twelve of
them dressed ready for the off, talking excitedly in small groups,
she almost turned around and retraced her steps despite the
disappointment her doing so would cause her nieces and the
residents alike. She wondered how she was going to cope with
them all and just hoped they were going to be on their best
behaviour, not have her running around in circles after them.

A very astute Suzy sensed her aunt's concern and whispered
up to her, 'Don't worry, Aunty Izzie, 'cos me and our Sally will
help you look after them all.'

'Yeah, we will,' piped up her sister. 'And they'd better do as
they're told an' all or I'll send 'em to bed with no supper.'

Izzie fought not to laugh out loud. Sally had been mimicking
her mother. At least, though, with her nieces fully occupied
helping to keep the residents under control, they'd have no time
for getting up to mischief.

Izzie looked over towards Jenny Johnson's office. The door
was shut so it was impossible to tell whether Jenny was inside
or not. Val Mason, the weekend shift nurse, and her assistant
Thea had turned up to wave them off but Izzie was most surprised
her boss hadn't shown herself to do likewise. In fact, now she
thought about it, Izzie hadn't seen her at all that morning; she
hadn't even joined her staff for elevenses which was the first
time since Izzie had started her employment at Westleigh Lodge
that she hadn't. Something very important must be occupying
Mrs Johnson's time today and Izzie wondered what it could

possibly be as there was usually nothing more important to Jenny than her residents.

'Are we setting off then, Izzie, before we risk missing the start of the performance?' Mr Danvers' theatrical tones boomed out, ricocheting against the walls. 'Nothing worse, you know, for a performer than when their concentration is disturbed by late arrivals.'

All the gathering looked at her expectantly.

'Yes, you're right, we should be making a move,' she responded. 'Now has everyone got everything they need for this afternoon? Gloves, scarves, hankies . . .'

'Have you got the tickets, Izzie?' Walter Waters interjected.

She patted her handbag. 'All safe in here. Right, if none of you has forgotten anything, we'll be off then.' She was surprised the driver of the transportation Mrs Johnson had arranged to ferry them there and back had not come in to announce his arrival, but he was probably waiting outside for them.

'Oh, hold on a minute, Izzie, I need the toilet,' a voice suddenly piped up.

'Yes, me too,' piped up another.

'Well, if you're going to the toilet, I'm going back up to my room to change my silk scarf for my woollen one,' said another.

Izzie inwardly groaned as several of the gathering dispersed in various directions. This visit to the circus was turning into a pantomime. When organising the timing for their trip she was thankful she had taken Mrs Johnson's advice and allowed for just such a situation.

It was a good fifteen minutes before all of them were gathered together again and Izzie ushered them outside. Spotting no sign of a waiting mini-coach she frowned, checking her watch. She understood Mrs Johnson had organised it to pick them all up at two o'clock, allowing them an hour and a half before the matinee performance started for travelling there, buying of refreshments, visits to the toilet, finding those who'd wandered off and getting everyone settled in their seats. It was now two-fifteen.

'Where's the charabanc then, Izzie?' Peregrine Danvers bellowed across to her.

'Charabanc? Oh, the coach.' She shook her head. 'I don't know, Mr Danvers. It should have arrived by now.'

'We won't miss the start, will we?' Suzy asked her worriedly.

'Ahh, we won't, will we, Aunty Izzie?' Sally wailed, looking frantic at the thought. She had made all her school friends jealous with her bragging about this visit to the circus, an outing not many of her friends' parents could afford, and the thought of going in on Monday and being ridiculed by them for missing the performance because the bus never turned up did not appeal to her.

'Don't worry, sweetie, I'm sure the transport will be here in a moment,' Izzie reassured her. She knew Jenny used a reliable firm called Straw's and hadn't any reason to believe they would be let down by them.

'Well, I think it's appalling the transport company keeping us waiting,' snapped a disgruntled Katherine Philpots. 'I wasn't keen on going to the circus anyway, to me circuses are for children, but I was persuaded by Amelia.'

Amelia Austin flashed Katherine a hurt look. 'It didn't seem to me you needed that much persuading, Katherine dear, not when I told you Peregrine was coming along.'

Peregrine's eyebrows rose on hearing this. He'd always thought the Widow Philpots a fine-looking woman and had been waiting in the wings for just such an opportunity to ingratiate himself. The news she had come along on this trip because he was attending was very welcome indeed.

Katherine looked flustered. 'Oh, you do exaggerate, Amelia.'

She looked insulted. 'I admit to being forgetful sometimes but not to exaggeration. You were humming and hah-ing over coming until I mentioned Peregrine's name.'

He had by now moved to stand next to Katherine. 'Take my arm, dear lady. The pavements are a little icy today and we don't want you falling, do we?'

She gave a girlish giggle, looking up at him coyly as she slipped her arm through his. 'Oh, how gallant you are, Mr Danvers.'

Izzie, witnessing all this, wondered if Mrs Johnson was going to be granted her wish of arranging a wedding between two of the residents.

'Well, it doesn't look like the hire coach is coming to me. I can't see any sign of it and I'm getting perished out here,' grumbled Walter Waters, rubbing his gloved hands and stamping his feet in an effort to warm them. 'Oh,' he proclaimed, 'I can see a Corporation bus heading this way. Why don't we all catch it? It'd be better than us all catching our deaths, don't you think?'

Before Izzie could suggest she should seek out Mrs Johnson to telephone the transport company and enquire after the vehicle's whereabouts, the residents all started hurrying across to the bus stop where Walter Waters was now flagging down the Corporation bus.

As the bus pulled to a halt the conductor was stunned to find his platform suddenly invaded by a swarm of elderly people, all pushing and jostling each other to get on board and secure a seat. In the process he nearly lost his balance and fell off, and was only saved from abrupt disembarkation when he managed to catch hold of the pole.

'Can I collect all the fares from everyone to give to the conductor?' Sally begged Izzie as they boarded the bus themselves, looking excited at the prospect of performing a grown-up task.

A vision of the mayhem that would ensue as all the old dears sorted out their change from handbags and pockets, which in truth they hadn't expected to have to fork out so would be grumbling about during the proceedings, didn't bear thinking about to Izzie. Quickly she delved inside her handbag for her purse and pulled out a ten-shilling note which she handed to Sally, praying it was enough to cover all of their fares as she had only two pounds and loose change on her, that was supposed to last her until next pay day. There were still fares on three other buses to pay before they arrived safely back at Westleigh Lodge, plus the cost of refreshments for Suzy and Sally. Thankfully, she got some change back, albeit not much.

Finally, all clutching their individual bags of confectionery, except Izzie who was too fraught to consider eating anything, they were seated in the auditorium, chatting amongst themselves as they waited for the ringmaster to announce the start of the show. Settled into her own seat, flanked either side by Suzy and Sally, Izzie heaved a sigh of relief. Immediately they'd alighted at the stop nearest the Granby Halls, all twelve of the residents suddenly seemed to Izzie to transform themselves into unruly children. Keeping all of them together and heading in the same direction had been just about the most difficult thing she had ever had to do, and she would not have managed at all if she had not had Suzy and Sally helping her, continually herding them back together. At least, though, with them all in their seats she could relax for the duration of the performance. Then, of course, she was faced with the journey home but decided not to think about that until the time came.

The trapeze artists and acrobatic acts were exciting; the lions fearsome and the clowns hilarious. Now it was the turn of the knife-throwing act. A volunteer from the audience was being sought. To Izzie's horror Sally jumped up, waving her arms in the air, shouting, 'Me! Me! I'll do it. Pick me!' Izzie had leapt to her own feet, pushing Sally back down in her seat and beginning to tell her that she would not be allowed to put herself in such a dangerous situation, when she was suddenly grabbed by her arm and the next thing she knew she was being run down the aisle steps between the seats by the knife-thrower's leggy, sequinned assistant and into the middle of the arena. She was placed, arms akimbo, against the knife-thrower's target board and sternly advised by the assistant to keep perfectly still.

Flattened rigid against the board, she swallowed and her eyes bulged as across the other side of the ring she saw the knife-thrower readying himself to take aim in her direction, holding the most lethal-looking collection of long-bladed knives she had ever witnessed in her life. Her face paled to a deathly white. Closing her eyes, she silently and with great fervour recited the Lord's Prayer. As a continuous thudding of blades began hitting the board immediately surrounding her, the backdraft from one in particular near her left ear feeling dreadfully close, she squeezed her eyes together even tighter, her inward recital of the Lord's Prayer quickening so much the words tumbled into one another.

Then suddenly rapturous applause filled the air and she was

being walked into the centre of the ring and made to take a bow. The next she knew she was back in her seat and a very peeved Sally was grumbling to her. 'It ain't fair! Yer wouldn't let me do it, Aunty Izzie, but *you* did.' Then she beamed. 'Oh, but you were great, Aunty Izzie. Wait 'til I tell the gels at school my aunty was in the knife-throwing act, they won't half be jealous!'

'You were wonderful, Izzie,' the residents were telling her proudly, those sitting close by giving her pats on her back.

Other residents were clapping her, calling over how brave they considered her to be.

Izzie was still too much in shock after her terrifying ordeal to respond, she was just grateful to be back in her seat with no blood spilled.

The jugglers came next, straight after the sea lions had enraptured the crowd with their skills. Then the ringmaster was announcing the final parade. It was a spectacular affair, all the acts dressed in spangled costumes, taking their bows to the audience's appreciative clapping.

Outside the Big Top Izzie did a head count to make sure everyone was present and correct so they could begin to make their way home. To her dismay, she discovered one resident was missing.

'Does anyone know where Mr Nugent went?'

They all looked blank for a moment, then stared at each other and all shook their heads.

'Well, someone must have seen him. He was with us when we went in. Who was he sitting next to?' she asked.

'Oh, it was me, Izzie,' said Walter Waters. 'But after the lion-taming act he left.'

'Left? To go where?'

Walter shrugged. 'I don't know. I never asked him.'

Izzie inwardly groaned. This was the last thing she needed. It was nearing five o'clock, had grown dark, and the evening air had a strikingly wintry chill to it. Not the sort of evening for old people or those as young as her nieces to be waiting around while she went off in search of a missing resident who could be anywhere.

216

'We'll all start looking for him, shall we?' offered Walter.

'No,' said Izzie as visions of them scattering in every direction assailed her. 'Stay here while I go and search.'

'Don't worry, Aunty Izzie, me and Sally'll make sure none of them wander off,' said Suzy with conviction.

Sally pulled herself up to her full height of four foot one inch and, puffing out her chest, said importantly, 'We'll tek charge of 'em, Aunty Izzie. You go off now and find Mr Nugent.'

In other circumstances Izzie would have had a job to hide her mirth but as it was she was too worried about Reginald Nugent.

Looking around, she scratched her head. Where in this huddle of tents, lorries, vans and caravans would an old man be lurking? There was nothing for it but to search everywhere.

Rushing around, calling his name, she poked her head inside tents, under flaps, around vehicles and under them, as well as asking circus performers and stage hands she came across if any of them had seen a wandering old gent of Reginald Nugent's description. But no one had. She was beginning to despair when, thankfully, poking her head inside the tent that was the elephants' enclosure, she saw him squatting on a bale of straw, smoking a cigarette, seemingly staring into space.

Rushing over to him, she hunched down beside him and laid a hand on his arm. 'There you are, Mr Nugent. We were getting worried about you.'

He looked startled for a moment before saying, 'Oh, has it finished?'

She nodded. 'About ten or fifteen minutes ago. Didn't you enjoy it?'

'Oh, I did enjoy it, Izzie dear, very much so. It was all so exciting, wasn't it?'

'If you were enjoying it so much, why didn't you stay for all the performance, Mr Nugent?' she asked.

He heaved a sigh. 'Well, you see, dear, as I was watching I was taken back to when I was a child of about seven and my parents took me, my two brothers and sister to a circus performance.

Where I lived in the back streets of Leicester surrounded by factories . . . well, it was all grey and dreary. The circus was so colourful and exciting, I thought I'd gone to heaven. I decided to run away and join it. In the middle of that night when I knew everyone else was asleep I got up, packed my things together in an old rucksack and stole out of the house. I'd only got to the end of our yard when a hand grabbed my shoulder and I received a clip around the ear. My mother had heard the back door shutting and had woken my father up to investigate. He wasn't happy about having his sleep disturbed as he'd to get up at five to start his job so I didn't get off lightly. My parents are long gone now, bless them, as is my dear wife, God rest her, and all my children are happily settled. I've no one to stop me running away now, have I?'

'No, you've not, Mr Nugent. You can do exactly what you want,' she said softly then looked at him searchingly. The trip to the circus had obviously taken Reginald back to being seven years old again, young and impulsive, seeing the world as full of adventure through inexperienced eyes. It was said that the older generation, nearing the end of their lives, tended to relive past memories and that was just what Reginald was doing now.

She pursed her lips. 'Mmm, well, the show was certainly exciting and glamorous for us members of the audience. But for those performing I suspect it's just damned hard work, day in, day out, for whatever money they can make depending on the size of their audience. I don't think I'd like to live in a draughty caravan, having to get up at the crack of dawn in all weathers to tend to the animals and pitch tents. The constant moving from town to town, never settling anywhere long enough to make a friend outside the circus, wouldn't appeal to me either.'

He was staring at her blankly, then started chuckling. 'It doesn't appeal to *me* and I suspect that at seven, should I ever have caught up with the circus, I'd soon have been back home, desperate for a bowl of my mother's delicious rib-sticking stew and my warm bed.' He gave a wistful sigh. 'Just for a while, though, watching the performance and drinking in the whole atmosphere of this place, it took me back to when I was a little lad again, with my whole life in front of me.' He gave her knee an affectionate pat. 'Help me up, my dear, if you would. I seem to have set sitting here.' As Izzie obliged him he chuckled again. 'Some use I'd be to the circus, eh, with my old bones. Just like I would have been as a child. I'd no head for heights, and dogs scared the living daylights out of me. You can imagine what I'd have been like if they'd asked me to clean out the lions' cage, can't you?'

As they rounded the corner of the Big Top where she had left the rest of the group to go in search of Reginald, Izzie froze in her tracks to see no sign of any of them. Bewildered, she exclaimed, 'But where are they all? I left them with strict instructions not to move.' Just then the sound of laughter was heard coming from a caravan nearby, among it the theatrical tones of Peregrine Danvers.

Well, it appeared she had discovered the whereabouts of at least one of the residents. But where were the rest of them, and just as worrying if not more, where were her nieces? She prayed Peregrine knew.

Approaching the caravan, from the hum of voices that grew louder and louder the nearer she got, it was obvious to Izzie that many people were inside, probably a party going on. Although surely it was too early in the evening for a party, even for circus folk. She had to knock several times before the door was opened to her by a middle-aged woman dressed in a very gaudy silk dressing gown, her face heavily made up. Immediately familiar voices blared out at Izzie, and she was relieved to see all her charges were present, and by the sound of it all enjoying themselves hugely.

'Hello, dearie,' the woman was saying to her. 'I take it you've come to collect your belongings?'

By 'belongings' Izzie assumed she meant her charges. 'Yes, I have. Look, I don't know how they all came to be in here, but I do apologise for the intrusion.'

The woman gave a bellowing laugh. 'Intrusion! Not on your nelly, my lovely. They've been a pleasure. It's not often I get to mix with outsiders and I'm so glad those two little mites knocked on my door. They asked me if I could brew their friends a cuppa while they waited for their aunty to come back and collect them all after she'd found the missing one. They said they were worried because their elderly friends were getting cold. Not backwards in coming forwards them little gels, are they? They'll go far, I've no doubt. The tall man ... very loud, waves his arms a lot ... well, he's a character, ain't he? Been having us in tucks with his mimicking of film stars he has. Does a great Cary Grant. Oh, my name's Rosa by the way. I used to be a tightrope-walker but for obvious reasons ...' she said, patting her well-rounded stomach '... I man the ticket office and candy-floss machine now. As you can imagine, we're a bit squashed inside but we can make room for two more. Come on in and have a cuppa yourself.' She was doing her best to squash herself against the side of the door to make room for them to enter the caravan.

A hot cup of tea sounded very welcome to Izzie but she was mindful she needed to get her charges back to Westleigh Lodge. Mrs Johnson must be getting worried, wondering why they hadn't returned by now. 'Thank you so much for your offer, Mrs ... Rosa ... but ...'

'Oh, Izzie, you're not about to refuse this good lady's offer, are you?' Reginald Nugent spoke up, looking worried. 'I would dearly love a cuppa even if you won't have one.' Turning to Izzie he whispered, 'Besides, I'm never going to get the chance again to see inside a proper circus person's caravan, am I, so I'm not going to let this one pass me by.' Then he addressed Rosa. 'You're very kind, dear lady, thank you.' He held his hand out to her so she could help him up the caravan steps.

It seemed to Izzie that she was being given no choice but to accept the invitation. She smiled appreciatively at Rosa. 'A cuppa would be most welcome.'

An hour later a brightly painted circus lorry pulled to a stop outside Westleigh Lodge. The driver leapt from the cab to run around and let down the back board to allow his cargo to disembark.

As the old people were finally trooping their way inside, chatting animatedly between themselves, Izzie shook the hand of the kindly circus worker and said, 'I can't thank you enough for driving us all back.'

'Ahh, it wa' my pleasure, missus.' His accent was broad. Izzie had never heard it before and couldn't place it. 'Didn't take no persuading when Rosa came and asked me if I'd do the honours. I couldn't let old folks stand at a freezing bus stop at this time o' night, or a lovely lady like yerself and those two little angels either. The old lorry ain't as comfy as a sedan, not that I've ever had the pleasure of driving in one meself, but I did try and drive carefully so as not to jostle you all in the back too much.'

'And you didn't,' she assured him. 'The thick tarpaulin you laid down was quite comfortable to sit on, and the blankets Rosa borrowed from her friends to cover us up certainly helped to keep out the cold. They'll all be talking about this trip for weeks.'

After seeing the circus hand on his way, Izzie made her own way inside to be greeted by her waiting nieces and Val Mason.

'Well, you certainly gave them all a good afternoon out, Izzie,' Val said to her. She addressed Suzy and Sally then. 'You young 'uns enjoyed yourselves, did you?'

'It were great,' Sally enthused before her sister could utter a word. 'I'm gonna join the circus when I'm older. I want to be the lady that works the candy-floss machine. I love candy floss.'

Val laughed. 'And that's why you want to work on the machine that makes it, don't you, so you've got your own regular supply? You'd soon get sick of eating it, believe me, lovey.' Then she addressed Izzie. 'Well, the residents obviously had a great time 'cos they were absolutely full of it when they came in. They've all gone to their rooms to get out of their outdoor things before they come back down for their tea.' She gave a laugh. 'Typical of Mrs Naylor to be so worried we wouldn't have saved her any. You're back much later than we expected you to be.'

Izzie looked at her apologetically. 'Well, I am sorry about that, Val . . .'

'Oh, no worries, gel,' she cut in. 'These sort of things can't be timed down to the last minute. I just think it was brave of you, offering to take the residents along in the first place. Gave me and

Thea an easy afternoon, only having a handful of residents left to look after.'

'Mrs Johnson isn't annoyed that I've kept them all out longer than anticipated, I hope?' Izzie asked.

'I wouldn't know, Izzie. I haven't see her at all. This is the first afternoon since I started working here I haven't seen hide nor hair of her. It's very strange she's not checked how I am and even more so the residents. Must be something very important keeping her occupied elsewhere, that's all I can think. Right, I expect they'll all be down any minute, desperate for their supper, so I'd better go and give Thea a hand mashing their pots of tea.'

Izzie stared thoughtfully after her. She agreed that the absence of Jenny Johnson was very puzzling indeed and something important must lie behind it. She gathered her nieces to her and headed off with them, up to her own accommodation. She was looking forward to their company for the rest of the weekend as not only was she deriving the usual pleasure she did from having them, it was also helping her get over her cruel disappointment regarding Steven Landers.

CHAPTER NINETEEN

The following Monday morning, just before the start of their shift, Izzie, Joyce and Alma jumped as the door to the nurses' room burst open and Beattie charged in. Stamping her booted feet and rubbing her gloved hands together, she exclaimed, 'God, but it's bloody cold out there today.' Too cold even for snow, in my opinion. I've got thick icicles on the inside of me windows this morning. I just thank God my Keith had the foresight to replace the old lagging on the pipes this year with some thicker stuff. Talking of my bloody old man, he's always been a snorer but for some reason recently the sound level has risen to shattering proportions. I ain't had any sleep this weekend at all. Before I forget I'm gonna help meself to a couple of Mogadons 'cos if I don't get any sleep tonight it's the spare bed for him, whether he likes it or not.'

As she moved across to the medicine cupboard, she said, 'I started me Christmas shopping Sat'day afternoon, and so it seemed did everyone else in Leicester. The town was stuffed to bursting, you could hardly move. Oh, how I hate all that pushing and shoving. Still, it's got to be done, ain't it? I got my Greg a Magic Robot for his main present and my Sylvia one of them transistor radio things she never stops going on about.' She had the bottle of Mogadon in her hand now and was unscrewing the top. 'So all you had good weekends, did yer?'

'I was beginning to think all you cared about was what happened on yours,' said Joyce sarcastically. 'Mine was as busy as it normally is, catching up with chores. Then like you, Beattie, I went Christmas shopping on Sat'day afternoon. It's a pity you never mentioned you was going or we could have met up for a cuppa in the British Home Stores cafeteria. Anyway, yer right, the town was heaving but I did manage to plough my way through to a couple of counters and get me mam a bed jacket for her present. It's everso pretty, sort of a lacy knit, and her favourite colour of baby pink so she should be chuffed with it. I got my old man a new shaving brush and the usual couple of pairs of socks. And I topped me cake up again with another good dollop of whiskey. Smells good if I say it meself.'

'Oh, I prefer rum for my cake,' said Beattie. 'I put Guinness in me pudding, though.' She gave a fed-up snort and thrust the bottle of sleeping pills in Joyce's direction. 'Open this for me, will yer, ducky? Me hands are too cold to get a proper grip on the top.' Then a thought struck her. Looking at Izzie she said, 'Oh, how did the trip to the circus go, ducky? Any medical mishaps me and Joyce need to know about?'

Izzie laughed. 'No, I got them all home in one piece, unless of course something has happened to any of them between then and now. It was a lovely afternoon, the show was excellent, and all the residents who came really enjoyed themselves.'

Alma was looking at her regretfully. 'I really wanted to go to the circus with yer, Izzie, but yer know what it's like at home. I had chores to do and I'd an invite to me boyfriend's for tea.'

'Tea with his family, eh?' said Beattie, now she had the feeling back in her hands, stripping off her coat. 'It'll be an engagement you'll be telling us of next. Don't be in no haste, lovey. You're hardly just turned sixteen. If your mam was here she'd be telling you just the same.'

Alma sighed. 'I never said I had tea with his family, just that I was invited. His mam and dad weren't there as they'd gone to his married sister's for theirs.'

'Well, I hope you behaved yourselves, being's you was in the house by yourselves,' she said, alarmed.

Alma sighed again. 'I never said we was by ourselves. Jimmy's two eldest sisters were there and it was them that made us our tea.'

'Oh, that's all right then,' said Beattie, relieved. 'You know me and Joyce look out for you like your mother would have wanted us to.' She looked across at Joyce and asked, 'You got the lid off that bottle yet?'

'No, it's being a stubborn cuss. Ah, that's got it. Just a couple of pills, did you say?' She was tipping it up for the pills to fall out into her hand. Then she exclaimed, 'Oh, that's odd.'

'What is?' Beattie asked her.

Joyce addressed Izzie. 'Didn't you fill this bottle up to the brim on Friday with the replenishment prescription the Doc gave me when I asked him on Thursday?'

She nodded. 'Yes, I did, straight after the prescriptions were collected from the chemist.'

Joyce pulled a puzzled face. 'Well, the bottle is only half-full now. Val must have had a run on them over the weekend. Seems we have a plague of insomnia on our hands. Thank goodness we work days. We have enough to deal with while the old dears are awake, let alone plaguing the life out of us when they can't get off to sleep.'

Izzie gulped. She hoped the ones demanding pills to help them sleep weren't the residents she had taken to the circus. But then she reasoned the trip must have tired them out, some of them were nodding off during the journey back in the circus lorry. On alighting they had told Izzie they'd be going to bed soon after they'd had their tea because they were tired out, so she couldn't imagine any of them would have been in need of sleeping pills. Suzy, Sally and herself had certainly slept like logs that night. She felt it seemed strange as well that all the residents would suffer sleeplessness at the same time. She wondered what could lie behind it?

Just then the door opened and Leonie Johnson popped her head around.

'Mrs Davis, Mrs Owens,' she addressed Joyce and Beattie formally. 'Could I have a word with you in my mother's office now, please?'

'But I'm just about to go off and do the handover so the weekend night nurse can get off home,' Joyce told her.

'I've not changed into me uniform yet,' Beattie informed her.

'This won't take a few moments,' Leonie responded before withdrawing her head and closing the door.

'What on earth would she want to see us for?' Joyce quizzically asked Beattie. 'It's Mrs Johnson we take our instructions from. Miss Johnson just does the office work to do with the actual day-to-day running of the business, which is n'ote to do with us.'

'I can't imagine what she'd want with us,' said Beattie, giving a shrug. 'More to the point, what's she doing down at this time in a morning? Not that I've ever had much to do with her, but I've never known her show her face before eight-thirty. Did she look a bit worried to you, Joyce?'

Joyce pulled a face. 'Don't know her well enough to be sure what she looks like when she's happy, let alone worried.'

'Mmm, well, I suppose there's nothing for it but to go and find out what she wants. Come on, Joyce, best foot forward. Don't keep Miss Johnson waiting.' There was a hint of sarcasm in her voice.

Just before Joyce followed Beattie out of the door, she turned back and addressed Alma. 'You've a ladder in your stockings. I hope you've a spare pair on you but then, knowing you, I guess you haven't. Borrow the spares I keep in the uniform cupboard. And, eh, make sure you replace them and not with a cheap pair from the market. I only wear Pretty Polly from Lewis.'

Alma studied her legs and immediately saw the offending run. 'Oh, drat! These were new on this morning and she's right, I never brought a spare pair with me.' Her face clouded. 'But I can't afford to replace Joyce's, they cost half a crown against my one shilling and elevenpence off the market and I need every penny I can get for Christmas presents.'

Izzie went over to the cupboard and took out a packet which she handed to Alma. 'I happen to keep a spare pair in the cupboard too for emergencies.' Mindful Alma didn't have much money for herself after she had handed over half of her wages to help out her widowed father, she added, 'You're welcome to them and I don't need them replacing.'

Alma beamed her gratitude. 'Oh, ta, Izzie. You're a gem,' she enthused, taking them. As she made to start peeling off her damaged stockings, she said, 'Oh, I'm everso excited 'cos the

226

Christmas trees should be arriving any day now. It's only just over two weeks to Christmas and Mrs Johnson will want help trimming them up. I hope she asks me.'

Izzie was only half listening to Alma's chatter, conscious that time was wearing on. 'While you're changing your stockings, I'll go and make a start checking the dining room is all in order. It won't be long before the residents start coming down.'

She stopped short as the door opened and Joyce and Beattie came back in. It was apparent by the expression on their faces that they'd both been given devastating news.

Izzie immediately assumed that someone had died. Then a terrible thought struck her. Could it possibly be Jenny Johnson? Had she suddenly been taken ill over the weekend and that was why they hadn't seen her? Why else had it been her daughter who had requested an interview with Joyce and Beattie when normally she had nothing to do with the nursing staff?

Alma hadn't yet learned that it was polite to wait for her superiors to volunteer information when they were ready to, not demand it from them immediately.

'What's happened?' she asked bluntly.

Beattie looked as if she was about to burst into tears. 'You tell them, ducky, I'm far too upset,' she told Joyce.

A terrible feeling of foreboding flooded through Izzie. She dreaded that she was about to have her worst suspicions confirmed.

Joyce took a deep breath before saying, 'Me and Beattie have just been sacked.'

Alma was for once struck speechless.

There was some relief for Izzie in that she hadn't been told what she most feared but nevertheless she was shocked. Surely she hadn't heard Joyce right? 'Did you say you'd just been sacked?'

'Yes, you heard right, lovey. We're to leave immediately. Bad enough being dismissed at the best of times, but two weeks before Christmas . . . Look, I'm sure you can both appreciate that this has come like a thunderbolt to me and Beattie and we're both far too upset to talk about it now. Miss Johnson will put you straight. She wants to see you, Izzie. Asked us to send you straight through.'

Izzie froze. They were all being sacked. But why? And with no staff, how was the place going to be run? More worrying still for Izzie was how that would leave her accommodation-wise? She had never confirmed it with Mrs Johnson but had assumed the rooms went with the job.

Her mind was in a whirl all the way to Jenny Johnson's office. Tapping on the door, she waited patiently until she heard the summons from inside.

Leonie was sitting behind her mother's desk. She requested Izzie to take a seat in the chair opposite. As soon as Izzie was settled she began.

'I don't know how much Mrs Davis and Mrs Owens told you?'

'Just that they'd been sacked, Miss Johnson.'

She sighed. 'I never sacked them, I dismissed them, which is not the same. I didn't like it but I had no choice if Westleigh Lodge is to survive.' She paused and took a deep breath. 'You're maybe wondering why you haven't seen anything of my mother since Friday evening. Well, just after eight she got a telephone call out of the blue informing her that my aunt, my father's spinster sister, had been taken ill. As next-of-kin, the hospital were informing her. Of course, Mother said she'd go straight away and travelled over on the first train on Saturday morning. Anyway, it seems my aunt went to the hospital with what she thought was a minor complaint and it turns out she's terminally ill. Nothing can be done for her. As you can appreciate, my aunt is very distressed and my mother has taken it upon herself to look after her in her home for the duration. It isn't clear at this stage how long that will be for. It could be weeks, maybe months. You can't put a time on these things, can you? Mother meantime has put the running of the business into my hands and asked me to explain her sudden departure to the staff.

'Anyway, I know you were privy to a couple of conversations between me and my mother so I don't suppose that what I'm about to tell you next will come as that much of a shock. Since I took over the book-keeping side of the business, the lackadaisical way my mother runs things here has been worrying me more and more. Most of the profit is frittered away on extras for the residents. It's ludicrous when they already get a far better standard of living for their money here than they ever would in another home, without all that Mother provides on top. I've tried many times to get her to see that her generosity will leave us bankrupt if she doesn't learn to curb it. You yourself were present last week in our flat when I broached the subject again after overhearing her telling you she was going to allow Mr Walters to stay on here free of charge.

'Of course I'm very upset about my aunt, but with Mother out of the way I see this as an opportunity for me to get this business on the right track at last. I did nothing else all weekend but try and plan the best way to turn this place around. I have come up with quite a few ways to cut costs which really don't concern you, but cutting the staffing levels does.

'This is a residential home not a nursing home so we don't really need qualified nurses on the payroll. You nursing assistants are quite capable of dealing with cuts and abrasions, and anything more serious . . . well, the doctor is only a telephone call away or an ambulance ride to the Infirmary. The doctor really doesn't need a qualified nurse to aid him on his rounds, and I've never understood why the residents can't be responsible for taking their own medication instead of relying on an expensive trained nurse to remind them. I do appreciate that some of them can be forgetful, but you nursing assistants are quite capable of reading the timings of dosages on bottles, aren't you? The residents rely on staff members far too much to fetch and carry for them. They'll have to realise that just because they pay to live here, you staff are not their individual servants. In future they will have to do more things for themselves, as they would in any other residential home.

'As the elder of the nursing assistants, it's you I'm looking to to keep Alma on her toes. I do appreciate that with the departure of Mrs Davis and Mrs Owens you're going to be busier, but in truth you are only going to be as busy as any other nursing assistant would have been here had my mother not been so generous with staffing levels. And, of course, I don't need to remind you of Mother's generosity because you must appreciate that the rent you pay for your accommodation is cheap by any standards. I'm sure you won't blame me in the circumstances for putting it up another ten shillings a week – still far cheaper than you'd pay for the same rooms anywhere else.'

She paused for a moment and took a deep breath before continuing. 'Look, I appreciate you must be thinking me very hard about all this . . . I would be too if I was sitting where you are now . . . but I can assure you it really has grieved me to dismiss well-qualified staff, especially at this time of year. Nor do I like at all going behind my mother's back like this, but because of her attitude I really have no choice. I want to ensure she has a business to return to in the future. My mother thinks very highly of you, Izzie. I trust you will show me the same level of loyalty you show to her?'

Izzie, still reeling from what she had just been told, muttered, 'Oh, yes, of course I'll do my best for you.'

'I've written to the residents individually informing them of what's going on and slipped the notes under their doors last night. I requested them to deal directly with you as I will be busy enough keeping up with the paperwork and continuing to keep looking at ways of cutting our costs, without their interrupting me every few minutes like they did my mother.' Leonie stood up. 'Well, I appreciate I'm keeping you from your duties.'

As she made to walk out, Izzie hesitated and turned back to address Leonie. 'Miss Johnson, when you next speak to your mother, would you pass on all our good wishes to her, from both residents and staff, please?'

As she made her way back to inform Alma of all this a thought struck her. So that was why the transport for the trip to the circus failed to turn up. In her quest to cut costs Leonie had cancelled it. Izzie felt hurt that she hadn't afforded her the courtesy of telling her what she'd done, then reasoned with herself that after what Leonie had divulged to her today, the young woman had clearly had a lot on her mind so could perhaps be forgiven for this one lapse.

'Is it me to be told I'm sacked next, Izzie?' a deeply worried Alma babbled as soon as she opened the door to the nurses' office. 'Oh, I don't know what I'm gonna do,' she cried frenziedly. 'I doubt I'd get another job this close ter Christmas and . . .'

'You haven't been sacked,' Izzie cut in. 'Neither of us has.'

'We ain't?' she cried in relief. 'Oh, Izzie, thank God, thank God! Oh, but I'm so selfish, just thinking about meself. Poor Mrs Davis and Mrs Owens. They was both crying when they left. I ain't never seen 'em cry before. Why has Mrs Johnson done this to 'em? Well, she got her daughter to do the dirty deed, didn't she? I can't understand it of her, she's . . .'

'Mrs Johnson has been called away and knows nothing about this, Alma. Look, sit down and I'll explain to you what Miss Johnson said.'

Alma sat wide-eyed and wide-mouthed during Izzie's relaying of the situation to her. She finished off by saying, 'It's awful what's happened to all the nurses, particularly for us with Joyce and Beattie as we worked closely with them and they were like mums to you, Alma. We shall miss them, but we must now do our best to support Miss Johnson in her quest to make this place really pay its way, for Mrs Johnson's sake.'

Alma nodded. 'Oh, we must, yes, Izzie. I think the world of Mrs Johnson, she's bin good to me, and I'll work all hours God sends if necessary to help keep this place going for her.'

Izzie gave a wan smile. It was going to be hard for Alma and her to pull in the workload of Joyce and Beattie on top of their own duties, but she shared Alma's sentiment. Izzie didn't care how hard she had to work if it saved Jenny Johnson from facing bankruptcy through her own generosity. Her thoughts were also with Leonie. The usual worry for a young girl of that age was what she would be wearing when she went out that night, not thinking of ways to save her mother and herself from financial ruin. If Izzie could help ease her burden, then she would.

CHAPTER TWENTY

In the dimness of the corridor in between the entrances to the kitchen and the laundry room, Izzie paused for a moment to catch her breath and take stock of what needed her attention next. She had just delivered several bags of residents' washing which she had collected from outside their doors to the laundry for the two assistants to take care of. While Izzie caught up with the chores that neither she nor Alma had had an opportunity to complete this morning due to the demands being made on them by the residents, which previously either Joyce or Beattie would have taken care of, Alma was single-handedly handling the dinner duties and Izzie only hoped she was managing to cope by herself.

She decided that the next chore to tackle was checking the timings of residents' dosages of medicine, so none were missed. En route to the nurses' room she suddenly caught sight of a bundle lying against the corridor wall. At first she thought it was a large sack of potatoes or something similar that had been abandoned there for some reason, but as she made to walk past it it struck her with shock that this was no bag of potatoes but the hunched figure of a man. Then recognition struck. It was Walter Waters, staring vacantly into space.

Squatting down on her haunches in front of him, Izzie spoke softly. 'Hello, Mr Waters. What are you doing here? You should be in the dining room having your dinner.' When she received no response, she gave his arm a light squeeze and repeated herself.

He looked dazed for a few moments before uttering, 'Oh . . . oh, it's you, Izzie dear.'

'Are you feeling unwell, Mr Waters?' she asked him. 'Would you like me to have the doctor fetched to have a look at you?'

'Eh? Oh, no, dear. It's not pills or potions I need to help me.'

'If you're not ill then has something happened to upset you?'

To Izzie's horror she saw the glint of tears in his aged eyes and he began to shake. 'Oh, yes, Izzie, something has. Yes, indeed, and it's very upsetting. Mrs Johnson lied to me, you see. My son isn't sending my fees direct to her at all. I'm living here free of charge through her generosity. I was right in the first place, Izzie, my own son absconded with my money. I went into town this morning, you see, to do a spot of Christmas shopping, get a present each for my grandchildren, and I bumped into an old neighbour of mine. She was shocked to see me. Thought I was dead, apparently. I asked her why on earth she thought that. Because my son had told her, she said. She told him she was upset she wasn't asked along to my funeral to pay her last respects as we'd been neighbours for twenty years before I moved here, and he told her that I'd stated in my will I just wanted a quiet family do and he'd been respecting my wishes. Then he told her that now he'd come into his inheritance he was selling the house and buying a business on the Lincolnshire coast. He held a big party for all his friends and neighbours before they went apparently.'

Walter's face crumpled with grief. 'Oh, Izzie, how could my own son tell people I was dead? How could he do that to me? Well, now I know I can't go on living here. I've never accepted charity in my life. I'll leave here tomorrow. I will tell Miss Johnson I will somehow find the money to refund her for the weeks I've been living here for free. I don't know how at the moment but I will, if it's the last thing I do. I've never owed a penny in my life and I'm not about to now.'

Izzie was staring at him helplessly. With no money, the only place open to him was a homeless refuge. The harsh existence inside these places was bad enough for those used to such environments but Walter Waters wasn't and she deeply feared he wouldn't survive long there. She had just over three hundred pounds in her Post Office savings account and if she thought for a minute he would accept it to help tide him over until a better solution to his dire situation was presented she would gladly give it to him, but she knew he would flatly refuse her offer. Her mind whirled. Any alternative was surely better than Mr Waters living in a homeless refuge for the rest of his days. At the moment, though, if there was one, it was eluding her. Trouble was, she only had until tomorrow morning to find it – hardly any time at all. Then a vision of Pat rose before her. She was expected at her brother's for dinner tonight. Afterwards she would seek Pat's help with this problem and hopefully she might have the answer that was eluding Izzie. She dearly hoped so.

'Don't give up hope, Mr Waters, something will turn up, I'm sure it will.'

He patted her hand and smiled at her but Izzie could see that his eyes held the look of defeat.

'Thank you for trying to make me feel better,' he said to her. 'I know where I'm going, Izzie.'

Not if I can help it, she thought.

'I was beginning to think you wasn't coming,' Pat said when Izzie entered her kitchen later that evening. 'I thought you finished at six so I was expecting you as normal about six-thirty. It's nearly eight now. I've been keeping your dinner hot in the oven. I just hope it's not too dried up.' She grabbed a tea towel and took a covered plate out of the oven as she carried on talking. 'Arnold's already gone off to his darts night but he said to say hello. The girls were looking out for you and were so disappointed when I couldn't hold off their bedtime any longer, they've both school tomorrow. I told 'em it must be something important that's kept you from reading them a bedtime story and reminded 'em they'll see you tomorrow afternoon when they go to the Lodge after school.' Izzie, now disrobed of her thick layer of outerwear to fend off the bitter cold of the December evening, followed Pat who made her way into the back room and placed the hot plate on the dining table. 'Sit down, and while you're eating you can update me on life in an old folks' home.'

A while later Pat blew out her cheeks and exhaled loudly. 'Oh, Izzie, I feel sorry for the staff that've lost their jobs, I do really. It's worse so near Christmas. I just thank God you weren't one of them. But it's going to be tough on the rest of you covering all the work, isn't it? Well, let's hope Miss Johnson's efforts ain't in vain and Mrs Johnson will continue in her usual sweet way when she returns from looking after her ailing aunt. It's not going to be easy for her curbing her generous nature, just like me mam can't curb her miserable mean one, but maybe the drastic action being taken in her absence will make her sit up and take notice that if she does carry on spending money willy-nilly, she'll end up in Queer Street and her daughter with her. Then all her poor residents will be looking for somewhere else to live, and the rest of her staff looking for other jobs.'

Izzie gave a heavy sigh. 'It's ironic that Mrs Johnson's daughter is trying to save her mother from just the position that a resident's son has selfishly put his father in.'

Pat was looking at her blankly. 'Eh?'

Izzie eyed her keenly. 'Look, Pat, I need your help.' She told her then of the dire circumstances Walter Waters had found himself in and her own hope that between them they could come up with an alternative home for him than a refuge for the down and outs.

When she had finished Pat was looking at her non-plussed. 'Well, Izzie, that poor old chap has my sympathies, it's despicable what his son's done to him and I hope that rotter gets his comeuppance in some way, but if the old boy ain't got any other relatives he can park himself on nor any money to his name apart from a couple of quid and his few shillings a week pension, I can't see 'ote else for him but the old workhouse meself.'

'But Mr Waters can come and live with us, Mam,' Suzy's voice urgently erupted. 'He can have my room 'cos I'll move back in with our Sally.'

Both women spun their heads to see the girls standing in the doorway, dressed in their nightwear.

'How long have you two been earwigging?' Pat demanded of them.

Both of them shuffled uncomfortably on their feet.

'We were listening out for Aunty Izzie. We just wanted to say hello to her,' said Suzy. 'But Mr Waters can come and stop with us, Mam, can't he?' Her tone was pleading. 'He's been so nice to me, teaching me the accordion, and he don't shout when I get it wrong. I'd like to do something for him to say thank you. Anyway, he's my friend, Mam, and friends help each other, don't they?'

Sally piped up, 'He's my friend too. Mr Waters is always telling me stories about when he was in the war and had to fight in the . . . er . . .'

'Trenches,' Suzy finished for her.

'Yeah, that's it. He got medals, Mam, for being brave. He showed me 'em. He told me he's got two grandchildren, girls like me and Suzy, but he never sees much of them 'cos their mam and dad are too busy to bring them to see him. I asked him why he didn't go and see them and he looked everso sad. Said because they had moved and he didn't know their new address yet because they'd been too busy to write and tell him. Well, 'til he does get their new address, me and Suzy could pretend we're his grandchildren so he doesn't miss his own so much. We could, couldn't we, Mam, and that would make him happy.' Her face puckered then and her bottom lip trembled. 'Please don't make poor Mr Waters go to the workhouse, Mam. Teacher was telling us about those places at school and they're awful. They have rats and bugs and people are all ragged and die from 'sumption.'

'You mean consumption,' Pat corrected her, then tutted. 'Your teacher was talking about those places at the turn of the century, not now.' She looked at Izzie and whispered, 'Mind you, I don't think they've improved much since then.' She heaved a deep sigh and whispered again, 'My pair of little tykes have certainly put me on the spot, haven't they?' She heaved another sigh, this time resigned, and addressed her daughters. 'I suppose we could take Mr Waters in the meantime until we've sorted out some-thing else for him.' She turned to Izzie then. 'Though what exactly when he can't pay his way, I've no idea.'

The girls whooped in delight, swooping on her, throwing their arms around her neck and hugging her tightly.

'Oh, it'll be great,' Suzy enthused. 'Dad's always saying it's murder living in a house full of women. Well, now he won't be, will he?'

'We'll go up and start shifting our Suzy's stuff into my room,' offered Sally.

'No, you won't,' snapped her mother. 'You two will give your aunt a kiss then get your backsides straight back up the stairs and into bed. Look sharp now before I change my mind about having Mr Waters to stop with us.'

Only seconds later Izzie gave a chuckle. 'Well, that's the quickest I've ever been hugged and kissed by them both.' She cocked her head as the squeaking of bedsprings was heard through the ceiling. 'And they're both back in bed already. Must be a record.' She smiled tenderly at Pat. 'When I came here tonight, the last thing I was expecting was that you'd offer to take Mr Waters in. Are you sure about this? I mean, you're taking a stranger into your home.'

'I hardly feel he's a stranger after all you've told me about him, Izzie. He sounds a nice old chap. And the girls have spoken of him often enough before tonight. Mr Waters obviously likes them. Anyway, can you see my daughters letting me get away with changing my mind now?'

Izzie chuckled. Knowing her nieces, not without a fight. 'What about Arnold?

Pat looked at her knowingly. 'Do you need to ask? You know as well as I do that you and your brother are out of the same mould. He'd do anything for anyone if he could, just like you would.'

'Well, I'll make sure you're not out of pocket by seeing you right for Mr Waters' keep each week, it's the least I can do.' Izzie gave a thoughtful frown. 'Thanks to you the problem of somewhere to live for him had been resolved, but not how we're going to get him to accept this arrangement. He'll see it as charity.'

'Just you bring him round and leave that to me,' Pat told her. 'When Arnold gets back we'll put our heads together and come up with a list of light jobs an old body like Mr Waters can easily manage. And if I accept say a couple of bob a week from his pension, then he can't say what we're offering him is charity, can he? Anyway, by the time I've finished with Mr Waters he'll think he's doing us the big favour moving in with us, not the other way around. And you can forget handing over any of your money for his keep. I'm sure we can stretch to another plate at mealtimes.'

'I don't know how to thank you, Pat.'

'There's no need for thanks.' She looked meaningfully at Izzie before adding, 'It's like my daughter said, friends help each other.'

Izzie swallowed back the lump in her throat and rose. 'If you don't mind, Pat, I want to get back and check on him now. He went straight to his room after our talk in the corridor this morning, said he needed to see to his packing, and wouldn't allow anyone in. To stop his business from becoming common knowledge, I've had to fob the other residents off by telling those that've enquired about him that he's not well today and isn't up to visitors. No matter how hard I tried to persuade him, he wouldn't have any of his meals today because they hadn't been paid for. In desperation, before I left to come here tonight I made a plate of sandwiches and a large pot of tea and left them on a tray outside his room. I knocked and told him they were there and I just hope he's been sensible. Anyway, I'm so pleased he won't need to spend a sleepless night tonight when I tell him he's not going to a refuge. I've found a much better alternative for him and can reassure him it's definitely not charity.'

'I'll have the room ready for him, Izzie. Bring him any time you like after breakfast.'

After kissing Pat affectionately on the cheek and again expressing gratitude for the way she helped to resolve Mr Waters' dire circumstances, Izzie rushed back to Westleigh Lodge as quickly as the icy pavements would allow to give Walter his good news.

As she hurried through the entrance hall towards the central staircase, the evening shift nursing assistant came out of the lounge. She looked disappointed to see that the new arrival was Izzie.

'Oh, I thought it might be the doctor come back with news.'

Izzie stopped and looked quizzically across at her. 'News of what, Brenda?' Then the look on her face registered and Izzie began to feel afraid. 'What's happened? Has one of the residents been taken ill?'

Just then Peregrine Danvers, Amelia Austin and several other residents appeared behind Brenda, their old faces freshly creased with concern.

'Is it the doctor with news?' Peregrine boomed out to Brenda.

She turned and shook her head at him. 'It's Izzie coming back and I'm just telling her about it. I'm sure we'll hear some news soon, either from Doctor Landers in person or else by telephone. I'll tell you all as soon as I get it.'

They looked reassured and went back into the lounge.

Izzie hurried across to Brenda and demanded, 'Tell me what's going on.'

'Well, not long after you'd finished tonight Mr Danvers was on his way out to attend a performance at the Little Theatre. He was waiting at the bus stop when he saw the bus coming. Just as it approached he couldn't believe his eyes when he saw Mr Waters walk straight in front of it. Mr Danvers shouted out to warn him out of the way, but he didn't seem to hear. The bus driver couldn't stop and . . . Oh, Izzie, I don't know how bad Mr Waters is. Mr Danvers immediately ran to the telephone box and called an ambulance and they took Mr Waters to the Infirmary. I called Doctor Landers who was thankfully at home and he's gone to see what's going on. I went up to the flat to inform Miss Johnson but no one answered the door, then I remembered overhearing her on the telephone earlier. I'd tapped on the door to let her know I'd started my shift. She was on the telephone and looked annoyed . . . well, not annoyed, more guilty really. But I'd already heard her arranging to meet a Mrs Pain at seven tonight so she must have gone out. That's all I know, Izzie.' She looked bemused as Izzie ran for the door. 'Where yer going?' Brenda called after her.

But Izzie was too desperate to reach her destination to reply.

In the corridor outside the side room where Walter Waters was being treated, Steven Landers was engrossed in conversation with the doctor in charge when he spotted Izzie burst through the double doors at the end of the corridor and hurry headlong towards them. Excusing himself from the doctor, he walked over to greet her.

'How is he, Doctor Landers? He is going to be all right, isn't he?' she implored.

Face grave, he said, 'Izzie, would you like to come and sit down over there?' pointing to a row of chairs further down the corridor. 'I'll explain everything to you then.'

His whole manner revealed that what he had to tell her was not good news. Her face ashen, she asked him, 'Is Walter going to die, Doctor Landers?'

He took a deep breath and nodded. 'I'm afraid so, Izzie.'

'Oh, but there must be something you can do . . .'

He laid a hand on her arm. 'He's suffered complicated internal injuries that are beyond the surgeon's capacity to repair. And at his age I doubt he'd survive the surgery even if it were possible.'

Izzie froze. She knew that Walter's collision with the bus was no accident. He couldn't bear to face what he thought the future held for him. An urgent look suddenly filled her face. 'I need to see him, Doctor Landers. I've got some good news for him. It sounds stupid, I know, but what I have to tell him might do something to help . . . well, miracles do happen, don't they?'

He hadn't the heart to tell her that it was too late for miracles in Walter's case. His life was hanging by a thread that was about to break any minute. 'He's barely conscious, Izzie, and might be too weak to respond to you,' he warned her.

'But he'll know I'm there and hear me?'

Steven wasn't sure but nodded regardless. Taking her arm, he silently guided her into the treatment room. A nurse was sitting by the bed. At a meaningful look from Steven, she rose and quietly left the room.

As she approached the bed Izzie was distressed to see that Walter's face was swollen out of all proportion and covered with an array of cuts and bruises. She had expected to see him wired up to instruments, attached to tubes, but he wasn't. The medical profession really had given up all hope of his recovery. But she hadn't. She sank down on the chair the nurse had just vacated and took his hand in hers, stroking it tenderly.

She never heard Steven respectfully leave the room.

Choking back her own emotion and the threat of imminent tears, she said with forced lightness, 'Hello, Mr Waters, it's Izzie. I've got some great news for you. I went to see Suzy and Sally's mum tonight. You know, she's my sister-in-law? I just happened to tell her I was on the look out for lodgings for a very dear friend of mine. That's you, Mr Waters. You are my dear friend, you know that, don't you? All the residents at Westleigh are your family and will remain your family, whether you're living among them or not. It's not true that family has to be blood-related. Family is people who care about each other, and so many people care about you, Mr Waters.

'Anyway, would you believe that my sister-in-law . . . Pat her name is . . . well, she's got a spare room and is looking for a lodger. She really liked the sound of you when I told her about you. She doesn't need much in exchange for the lodgings, just a couple of bob which you could afford from your pension and a few light jobs doing . . . Well, I can tell you all the ins and outs when you get better. But you'll be happy with them, I know you will. Suzy and Sally are so excited about you maybe going to live with them. Can I tell them you might be interested?' She eyed him closely. 'Mr Waters, what do you think, eh?'

She spotted his eyelids flicker slightly and the ghost of a smile touch his lips. She felt a slight pressure on her hand. Then his eyes fell shut and he let out a slow exhalation of breath.

Izzie felt a hand on her shoulder and glanced up to see Steven looking down at her kindly. He had re-entered the room to check everything was all right, just in time to hear Walter Waters breathe his last.

'You want me to leave Mr Waters to rest for now, I suppose. Can I wait and come back in later?' she asked, gently releasing her hand from Walter's.

'Izzie, I'm sorry, but Mr Waters is . . .'

'No!' she uttered. 'No, please, he can't be?' Then her shoulders sagged and tears gushed unashamedly down her face.

Steven looked on helplessly. How he dearly would have loved to have offered Izzie the comfort of his arms, his shoulder as a place to cry, but she had made it clear to him that his attentions were repugnant to her and he had no choice but to accept that state of affairs. Regardless, his own feelings for her were growing stronger, the more he discovered about her and the qualities she possessed. How many women would shed tears of genuine sorrow and loss for an old man they had known only a few months? This woman had a capacity for love and compassion that was obvious to him. He was only sorry some of it could not be directed towards himself.

If ever Izzie had felt the need for a pair of comforting arms around her it was now, and she'd rather have Steven's than anyone else's. But his interest in her was purely business and she had no choice but to accept that.

Taking a clean handkerchief from his pocket, Steven held it out to her. 'Such a dreadful accident. He obviously didn't hear the bus coming.'

She knew that morally she ought to let Doctor Landers in on the fact that it was more than likely Walter Waters had staged his own death, but then an investigation would result and his son's swindling of him come to light, and if it was decided by the coroner at the inquest that Walter had committed suicide he'd be buried in unconsecrated ground. She couldn't bear the thought of that. Besides, she had not actually witnessed him walk in front of that bus . . . it could still have been an accident.

Gratefully accepting the handkerchief, she wiped her face and said stiltedly, 'Thank you. I'll make sure I return it to you washed and ironed.'

How he would dearly have loved to tell her to keep it. 'No rush,' he said quietly.

'I've not had any experience in such matters but I trust someone will be contacting Miss Johnson to inform her what to do about the funeral arrangements, Doctor Landers?'

'*Miss* Johnson?' he queried.

'Oh, you wouldn't know yet that Mrs Johnson has gone to nurse a terminally ill relative and it's not certain when she'll return. Meanwhile Leonie Johnson is in charge. Well, thank you, Doctor Landers. I'd better get back and break the terrible news to them all at Westleigh Lodge.'

He wondered whether to offer her a lift or not, but before he could she had turned away from him and was hurrying off down the corridor.

CHAPTER TWENTY-ONE

Four days later, Alma gave a deep sigh and said to Izzie, 'Don't seem right, decorating a Christmas tree on the same day we attended Mr Waters' funeral.'

Izzie sighed also. 'No, I agree, it doesn't.'

Her mind went back over the events of the last few days. The rest of the residents were deeply shocked and upset to learn of the accidental death of Walter, and Westleigh Lodge had taken on an air of deep mourning for the loss of a well-liked member of their community. Thankfully, though, amongst his private papers an insurance policy to cover funeral costs had been found so Izzie's fear of his having a pauper's funeral did not come about.

Pat was stunned when Izzie went around to tell her of Walter's demise straight after she had informed Westleigh Lodge. Suzy and Sally had shed floods of tears when their mother explained to them the next morning why they would no longer be having him to live with them. Like all children, though, they were resilient. Very soon other matters came to the fore, helping them quickly to come to terms with the loss of their friend.

Izzie had been surprised to see Steven Landers at the funeral. Doctors regularly dealt with the deaths of patients, it being one of the hazards of their job, but Izzie wouldn't have thought many would take the trouble to pay their last respects. Steven really was proving to be a very caring and thoughtful man, the sort who would make a wonderful husband for some lucky woman – not her, though, regrettably. She had caught him a couple of times looking over at her during the proceedings, a look on his face that she could only describe as regretful. She assumed it was because he regretted the fact he had not been able to recruit her, leaving him with the trouble of finding someone else.

Izzie hadn't been surprised to see Joyce and Beattie at the funeral. As soon as the graveside service was over they both approached her.

'Thought Walter had a son?' Joyce queried.

'He has, Joyce, but he's moved house and the police haven't located a new address for him yet. We've had to parcel up Walter's belongings and store them in the cellar meantime.'

'Bit of a queer state of affairs that, the son not telling his dad where he's moved to,' Beattie mused. 'The usual reason someone moves and doesn't tell family or friends where is 'cos they don't want to be found. Knowing Walter Waters as I did, I can't imagine his son would be anything other than an upright man like his father. Walter never struck me as being forgetful but the son must have written his new address down and Walter lost it, it's the only explanation. Oh, dear, going to be a shock for him when he does find out his dad has died, and not only that but he's missed the funeral too. Anyway, how's it all going at the Lodge, Izzie?'

'Busy, Beattie, as you can imagine. Alma and I feel we're running around like headless chickens, but we're just about managing. We do miss you both, and not just to handle the work. Alma will be sorry to have missed you now but one of us had to stay behind with the few residents who decided not to come. She asked me to tell you that she's missing having her two adopted mothers chewing her ear off.'

They both laughed.

'We both miss you and all, don't we, Beattie?' Joyce said.

Beattie nodded forlornly.

'Have you managed to find work yet?' Izzie asked.

They both nodded and told her they were starting at the Infirmary on Monday, on different wards for different departments, and Izzie got the distinct impression neither of them was particularly looking forward to it.

'I miss Mr Waters' chirpy little face,' Alma was saying to her now, back at the Lodge, a sad look on her face. 'He was a lovely old chap, Izzie. I do wonder where he was going at that time of night. It was bloody freezing and no shops were open, and he wasn't one for going off down the pub.'

Alma wasn't the only one who had queried this. Izzie responded in the same way to Alma as she had to everyone else who had raised the subject. 'We'll never know.'

'No, I s'pose not,' mused Alma. 'The new resident who's moving into his room on Friday seems a nice old dear. Chuffed to bits to be finally getting a place here, that was obvious when her daughter brought her to view yesterday. Been on the waiting list over two years apparently and the place she's in at the moment is nice enough but not a patch on here, so I overheard the daughter telling Miss Johnson when I accompanied them round.'

A discreet cough was heard and both of them turned to see an elderly gentleman looking at them expectantly. It was George Adams who had taken over Mr Granger's room.

Izzie smiled warmly at him. 'Can I help you, Mr Adams?'

'I'm very sorry to bother you, my dears, as I can see you're both busy with the Christmas tree but I was looking on the notice board in the lounge and I cannot seem to locate the list showing forthcoming entertainment. I understand there's going to be a film show on transport through the ages either this week or next and I'm a real tram buff. Such a shame the city decided to abandon its tram system for petrol-driven buses eight years back . . . anyway, I'm keen to check the date and time so I don't miss it but the list is definitely not there.'

Izzie looked puzzled, then a thought struck her. 'Oh, Miss Johnson has probably taken it down to make some adjustments to it. We do get occasions when something has been arranged then the person doing the demonstration has a problem on that date and has to rearrange. I'll mention it to her the next time I see her.'

'Thank you, dear. I appreciate that. I am also looking forward to the whist drive this afternoon. That takes place in the lounge, I understand, at three?'

'Yes, that's right, Mr Adams. Two ladies from the WVS come in and run it every Thursday.'

He beamed with delight. 'The last home I was in was perfectly adequate and the staff very pleasant but it did not compare with being here. They never laid on any entertainment for the residents for a start, and nor was there a beautiful conservatory to sit in or . . . well, I could go on. Mrs Johnson really does go that extra mile for her residents, doesn't she? I am very fortunate to have got in here, very fortunate indeed. I did understand, though, that she employed lots of staff to take care of us but I must have been mistaken there as you two certainly have your work cut out, looking after all twenty of us.'

As he moved away, out of the corner of her eye Izzie saw Steven coming through the entrance door. Immediately she hardened her heart and tried to ignore the attraction she still felt for him.

Little did she realise that Steven in his turn was doing exactly the same.

He had been surprised the previous Tuesday when he had arrived in the late-morning to discover Joyce and Beattie were no longer employed at Westleigh Lodge, but the way Mrs Johnson staffed her establishment was none of his business nor something he should get involved in unless the health of the residents was affected, which at the moment didn't appear to be the case. He suspected that the two remaining members of staff were run off their feet coping with the extra workload, though. But Izzie, being the person she was, was doing her damnedest to make sure the residents didn't suffer from it.

'Good morning, Doctor Landers,' Izzie greeted him in business-like fashion as he approached. Fishing in her uniform pocket, she pulled out a list which she handed to him. 'That's a note of residents' prescriptions that are running low, and we also need a top up of Mogadons as we had a run on them last week for some reason. Alma did a check amongst the residents to find out those who wish to see you this morning besides the ones you prearranged yourself when you were here on Tuesday.'

Alma rooted in her uniform pocket and pulled out a scrap of paper. 'Just Mr Danvers and Mrs Philpots today, Doctor. They're waiting for you in their rooms.'

He smiled at her appreciatively. 'Thank you, Alma. There's only two other appointments here today so four altogether. That's good as I have a busy afternoon ahead of me. This bitter weather brings out the worst in people's health, especially the elderly. Well, I'll let you get on.'

As Steven headed off up the stairs, Izzie realised Alma was staring at her quizzically. 'What is it, Alma?' she asked.

'Eh? Oh, it's just that Joyce and Beattie swore blind Doc had a fancy for you and you him, but it doesn't seem that way to me. Not with how you was with each other just now.'

'A relationship between myself and Doctor Landers was just Joyce and Beattie's wishful thinking, Alma. Now, can you manage trimming up the tree alone while I go and help Winnie Mason in and out of the bath?'

'Yeah, 'course I can, Izzie, though I don't think much of this one. It's not half as good as the one we had last year.'

'Well, I expect Miss Johnson changed the order for a cheaper one in her effort to cut down on outgoings, and that's why we've only been given one and not the usual two.' Then another thought struck Izzie. She had been told that Jenny Johnson always bought all of the residents a present each, and the staff too. Izzie wondered if she had got around to doing that before she had been called abruptly away. If not, would Miss Johnson do the honours on her mother's behalf? It didn't seem likely, judging from the drastic action she had taken in cutting down on staff. But Jenny gave each resident a present to ensure that those who had no relatives were not left out. Izzie made a decision. She would buy all the residents a present out of her own money, on Jenny's behalf.

She was just about to take her leave when Leonie Johnson reached them. She had a pile of envelopes in her hand.

'Izzie, would you make sure these are put under the doors of all the residents, please? Doesn't matter which goes under which as the memo says exactly the same in each one.'

Izzie took them from her. 'Yes, of course, Miss Johnson. Oh, one of the residents was querying the missing lounge entertainments schedule on the notice board, and I wondered if you'd taken it down to add something or make an alteration to it?'

'Yes, I did take it down. With the way things are at the moment, I couldn't justify paying out fees for these people to come in. Some of them charge quite a lot for their demonstrations. The residents are still well catered for on the entertainment front. The WVS ladies come in once a week to oversee the whist drive, the librarian sees to their reading material and they have the television. For your information, I have also cancelled the order for the selection of daily papers we have delivered every morning. Over a year the bill comes to a substantial amount and by rights the residents should be buying their own papers should they wish to. Oh, and while I have you both here at the same time, in future I will be deducting ten shillings a week from your wages for the cost of your meals each day. I am sorry it has come to this but I have to look at every avenue I can to save costs. Please excuse me, I have a lot to do.'

Alma was gawping after her as she walked back inside her office, shutting the door behind her. 'Bloody hell, Izzie, getting me dinners here free was a perk! Ten bob a week is a lot out of my wages. Things must be worse than we realised. Well, why don't Miss Johnson put the residents' fees up if that's the case?'

Izzie looked down at the pile of envelopes in her hand. She had a feeling that was exactly what Leonie had done.

'Better get on, Winnie Mason will be waiting for me,' she told Alma.

A while later, having seen Winnie safely back to her room to ready herself for dinner, Izzie was making her way back down the corridor towards the stairs when a pensive-looking Elinor Stringer came out of her room and almost collided with Izzie.

'Oh, I'm so sorry, Miss Stringer,' she automatically apologised to the older woman.

'No need for you to apologise, Izzie, it was my fault, I wasn't looking where I was going,' she responded.

'You all right, Miss Stringer?' Izzie asked her.

'My health is fine, Izzie, thank you, and in respect of what I know you are referring to, well, I will never forget my loss, but thanks to you I'm still living among friends and that is what keeps me going. But all the same, I am a little worried. I appreciate that costs rise all the time and fees have to rise commensurately. We have been very lucky since I have been here in that Mrs Johnson hasn't put up her fees once, but two pounds rise a week now is an awful lot more to have to find. I have a good pension from my years of teaching but have no idea how long I'm going to live for and consequently how long my money has to last. I'm not sure whether I can actually afford to stay on here. I shall have to make an appointment with my bank manager and ask his advice on what I should do.

'I appreciate that there are people who can afford to pay the fees here so filling my vacancy will not be a problem. Oh, but I'm so settled here. I've made friends and . . .' Her voice lowered for fear of being overheard, a fleeting look of sadness crossed her face. 'I still feel Frederick's presence so strongly, that he's watching over me, and it's such a comfort. If I left, I would feel I was leaving him behind.

'Anyway, I'm not the only one who'll be affected. Mrs Wilks is very worried as her daughter pays her fees and she's not sure how much more can be afforded. Mrs Wilks fears she'll end up having to move into a cheaper place which is nowhere near as nice as this or the staff so friendly and obliging. I understand there isn't to be any more entertainment laid on in the lounge on a Wednesday afternoon in future. Most of it wasn't to my taste, I have to say, and I chose to read in my room or go out for a walk during those times, but most of the other residents attended and looked forward to it.' She paused and looked at Izzie quizzically. 'I might be getting on in years but I am not stupid. Neither are many of the other residents here. What with the subtle cut backs that are taking place and now this rise in fees we are beginning to wonder if Westleigh Lodge is in financial trouble? I would never dream of putting you in a compromising position so I don't expect you to furnish me with any information you are privy to as an employee, but I should warn you that some of the other residents might not be so sensitive towards your position and you might start to be quizzed.'

She appreciated Elinor's respect for her position and was just about to thank her for her warning when Katherine Philpots reached them.

She addressed Elinor Stringer. 'Excuse this intrusion into your conversation, Elinor, but I need to give this to Izzie for her to deal with urgently.' She then focused her attention on Izzie. 'I've just discovered that Doctor Landers left this behind in my room after his visit to me this morning.' She held out a stethoscope to Izzie. 'He always checks he's not forgotten anything before he leaves but I spotted this under the table when I bent to pick up a pen I'd dropped. It must have got knocked off the table somehow when he was rooting around in his bag for a sample of the new ointment he suggested I try. If it works better than my old stuff, he'll write me out a prescription for it. Anyway, it's my guess he won't realise he's missing his stethoscope until he goes to use it next. I trust you will make sure he gets it as a matter of urgency?'

Izzie took it from her. 'Of course I will, Mrs Philpots. I'll run it around to his surgery now and give it to his receptionist.'

'Oh, well, before you rush off, I just wanted to ask you if you knew anything about this sudden rise in . . .'

'Now come along, Katherine,' Elinor cut in. 'Izzie needs to get Doctor Landers' instrument returned to him urgently. Let's not delay her any longer.'

Izzie looked gratefully at her for her intervention before she hurried off.

Unexpected occurrences and emergencies had been quite easy to accommodate when there had been four of them on duty, but now there were only two it was like knocking out the support column on one side of a pack bridge and expecting the middle span not to collapse. Therefore having promised Alma she would be as quick as she could, Izzie kicked up her heels and rushed off to do her errand as quick as she could.

Steven's surgery was housed in a two-roomed, single-storey building sandwiched between a long row of shops fronting the main Narborough Road. It had once been the store room for a seed merchants. It lay empty for years until the owner agreed to let Steven take over the rental of it when he was searching around for premises.

Izzie arrived panting and breathless at the surgery, having narrowly escaped slipping on the icy pavements, only to find the premises locked up.

A middle-aged woman weighed down by the weight of the clothes she was wearing in her attempt to keep out the bitter weather, and also by the weight of the shopping she was lugging in the brown carrier bags she was holding, noticed Izzie looking dismayed before the closed door and said to her, 'Yer too late for morning surgery, ducky, it finished at ten-thirty. Evening one starts at six.'

Izzie blew out her cheeks in exasperation and before she could check herself exclaimed, loudly and frustratedly, 'Oh, blast! Sorry, I do apologise, it's just that I was hoping to catch Doctor Landers as I've got his stethoscope. Well, actually he left it behind.'

'Oh, dear, he'll need that 'saf'noon on his home visits. What time is it?' she asked Izzie.

'Oh, er . . .' She flipped back the sleeve of her coat and looked at her watch. 'It's just coming up for one o'clock.' Time she was back at the Lodge taking advantage of all the residents being occupied with dinner so she could catch up with a few duties that hadn't been tackled by herself or Alma that morning and couldn't be left undone. No doubt she'd be pestered by several of the residents to accompany them into town for a spot of Christmas shopping that afternoon. The women who'd requested her company were all able-bodied residents who could well manage on their own, but they felt safer when a member of staff came along and it was nice to have someone to advise them over purchases and, even better, help carry their shopping.

'Well, everyone knows that about now Doctor Landers will be at his mam's, having his dinner,' the woman announced. 'Twenty-six Wilmington Street.'

Izzie thanked her and rushed off in the direction of Wilmington Street.

She knocked purposefully on the door of number twenty-six. Presently it was opened by a small rotund man with a kindly face.

He smiled at her in greeting. 'Hello, lovey. If it's me wife yer

253

want, well, you've just missed her. She's rushed off to meet up with a couple of her friends, they're all going into town Christmas shopping.'

Izzie looked at him in surprise. She'd understood Steven's mother to be dependent, possibly an invalid, yet she'd just been told the woman of this house had rushed off to meet friends for a trip up to town. She must have the wrong house.

She smiled politely at the man. 'I apologise, I must have the wrong address. It's Doctor Landers I'm looking for.'

'Oh, you've got the right address, lovey. Well, you have and you haven't. You see, Steven has his own house, has done for eight years, on Upperton Road, but his mother insists he comes in every day for his dinner so at least she knows he's had one square meal a day. Steven tries to stop her fussing over him, but she keeps telling him that the day she stops fussing is the day he finds himself a lovely woman and *she* takes over the responsibility for his welfare. My poor wife is giving up hope of ever becoming a doting grandma.

'Anyway, normally you would have caught our Steven here at this time but today he asked his mother if she'd mind dishing up earlier as he had a busy afternoon ahead of him. He wanted to get a move on with it or he feared he'd be late starting his evening surgery, and he doesn't like to keep people waiting unless he can help it. Well, that suited Dorothy as she had a busy afternoon planned for herself.' He looked quizzically at Izzie, noticing the puzzled look on her face. 'Have I said summat wrong, lovey?'

'Sorry! Oh, no, it's . . . well, it's just that I understood Mrs Landers was infirm and needed constant care and Doctor Landers was looking at employing a companion for her.'

He looked stunned. 'What! My Dorothy infirm? She suffers from diabetes but that's controlled by medication. It doesn't stop her from doing anything she's always done. Like a whirlwind is my Dorothy, always rushing around here or there. Tek more than a medical condition to have my wife take to her bed. She's the sort that'd have to be drawing her last breath before she did. You must be mistaking her for someone else, lovey. Anyway, you'll have to excuse me, I have to get meself back off to work shortly. You'll catch our Steven at his evening surgery tonight. It starts at six.'

Now Izzie was looking stunned. If Steven hadn't after all taken her out for a meal to discuss her becoming his mother's companion, then the only other reason for asking her out was because he liked her and wanted her company. It was obvious to her now that he had babbled on about his mother because it was the first topic that had come to mind in his nervousness. What a complete and utter idiot she had been to assume a man like Steven was just another Lawrence, out to use her.

Linus Landers was still looking at her quizzically. 'You all right, lovey? You look . . . well . . . like you've suddenly lost something precious.'

Oh, but she had. Something precious like Steven. And through her own bad judgement. She had scuppered any chance of putting her mistake right by her cool manner towards him since that night, leaving him in no doubt she was not at all interested in him personally when in fact the exact opposite was true.

'Er . . . yes, Mr Landers, I'm fine,' she fibbed. She had no choice but to be fine. Time didn't travel back, allowing people to put wrongs right, unfortunately for Izzie. 'Look, I didn't want to see Doctor Landers personally, it was to give him this,' she said, thrusting a carrier bag at him. 'Doctor Landers left it behind at Westleigh Lodge this morning. We were worried he would need it this afternoon on his round.'

Linus Landers took the bag from her and took a peek inside. 'Oh, how kind of you to drop it round but you needn't have put yourself out, he keeps a spare in his car. I'll make sure he gets this back when he calls in for his dinner tomorrow.'

Wishing her good day, he went back inside.

It was a very subdued Izzie who hurried back to Westleigh Lodge.

CHAPTER TWENTY-TWO

She was just about to turn into the driveway when she heard her name being called out. She knew instantly who the voices belonged to and spun round to greet them with a beam of delight.

As they all hugged each other, she said to her nieces, 'This is not the way back to school, young ladies. Anyway, isn't it a little early for you to be going back after your dinner?'

'We ain't going back to school, Aunty Izzie,' Suzy told her. 'We all got sent home this morning 'cos the boiler's broke. Bloomin' freezing it was an' all.'

'And Mam's got Mrs Fisher coming around this afternoon to perm her hair. She doesn't want us mithering her so she sent us to mither you instead,' Sally piped up.

Regardless of how down and dejected Izzie's mood might be, the presence of her nieces always managed to lighten it. Today was no exception. 'You can both mither me anytime,' she laughed. 'Well, actually . . . assuming nothing crops up to stop it . . . I'm escorting four of our ladies to town this afternoon, for them to do their Christmas shopping. You can come too, if you like, otherwise I'm sure the other residents will be pleased to see your happy little faces in the lounge. I think I heard Mr Swann say yesterday that he was looking for someone to play a game of chess with him, Suzy. And, Sally, a couple of the ladies need a hand winding their wool which neither me nor Alma have found time to do. I know they'd be grateful for your help.'

In all seriousness Sally said to Suzy, 'I think we should help Aunty Izzie take the ladies up the town.' She then addressed her aunt. 'Well, you'll need help watching 'em like me and our Suzy did when we all went to the circus, Aunty Izzie.'

'Yeah, you will,' said Suzy, equally as serious.

Izzie hid a smile. 'Oh, good, because I was wondering how I was going to manage to cope with them by myself. My good fortune the boiler broke at school today, isn't it? Right, well, I've a few chores that need doing first so you can give me a hand with those.'

At just after two o'clock, Izzie having satisfied herself that Alma could cope on her own for a couple of hours, she and the girls, Nora Hopgood, Winnie Mason and Katherine Philpots were waiting for Amelia Austin to join them so they could set off.

'What on earth is keeping her?' Katherine Philpots grumbled. 'She went up at the same time as I did after dinner to get herself ready and I've been down over twenty minutes. Oh, she does dither, that woman.'

'Shall I go and see what Mrs Austin is dilly and dallying about, Aunty Izzie?' Suzy offered.

'I'll go, dear. You stay here with Sally and make sure none of the other three wanders off.'

'Count on me, Aunty Izzie,' she responded, puffing out her chest importantly.

'Yeah, me too.' Her sister immediately began to walk in a circle around the three women, like a sheepdog circling sheep.

Izzie tapped purposefully on Amelia's door and called out, 'It's Izzie, Mrs Austin. We're all downstairs waiting for you.' Receiving no response she tapped and called out again. 'Mrs Austin, it's Izzie. Are you struggling with your coat and need a hand?' Again she received no response.

She glanced over in the direction of the bathroom. The door was open so it wasn't occupied. Izzie had definitely not passed Amelia on the way up so she must still be in her room.

Tapping on the door again, she opened it and popped her head in. She frowned to see Amelia sitting in the chair by the window, her outerwear lying on the bed. She looked deeply distracted, worried even.

Entering the room and shutting the door behind her, Izzie walked over to her. 'Is anything the matter?'

The older woman turned her head and looked at her. 'Oh, it's you, dear. I didn't hear you come in.'

'Well, it's obvious you've got something on your mind so I'm not surprised you didn't. Are you worried about something, Mrs Austin? You do look worried.'

She nodded. 'Yes, I am rather, Izzie dear. Something I completely forgot to do is what is worrying me. I know I do forget things sometimes, but to forget to do this . . . well, it is so dreadful of me, it really is. I do need to put it right, though. It was the rain that jolted my memory.'

'The rain, Mrs Austin?'

'Yes, dear. On the window. I happened to notice it just as I was about to put my coat on for our trip into town. Noticing the rain brought back to mind the dream I had last night.' It was actually ice, having been melted by the weak December sun, that was trickling down the window pane, but Izzie didn't correct her. 'It was raining in my dream, you see, dear. Tibbles was soaking wet and I was trying to coax her inside only she wouldn't come. The rain was pouring down on her and she was just staring over at me, as if she was trying to tell me something. Well, of course, I realise what now. She's long dead now, the real Tibbles, I mean. Mr Austin adored that cat . . . He found her one night, sheltering from the rain in a bombed out house during the war when he was a blackout warden. The poor cat . . . well, kitten she was then . . . was near dead from starvation. He tucked her inside his coat and brought her home with him. Between us we nursed her back to health and called her Tibbles and she was with us for twelve years before she died. Mr Austin wasn't one for showing his emotions but he did shed tears the night Tibbles left us . . .'

Izzie hadn't a clue where this story was heading but experience with the older generation, especially females, had taught her that they tended to go around the houses with a story before the gist of it became clear.

'Mr Austin liked to keep our affairs in order. He was a real stickler for paying bills promptly. When Tibbles died he'd already had our will drawn up and lodged it with our solicitor. Whichever of us died first, our estate automatically passed to the other. The one remaining would then have a new will drawn up which would incorporate any bequests the deceased had expressed to the other before their death. Neither Mr Austin nor myself had any family, not even distant that we knew of, so whatever was left in our estate after we were both departed was to be divided between charitable organisations that were dear to both our hearts, apart from a small bequest to the WVS and local children's home on my behalf, and the Leicester Horticultural Society and Aylestone Twitchers' Group on behalf of Mr Austin. My husband was a keen bird watcher, you know, Izzie dear, out every Sunday morning at the crack of dawn with his binoculars, documenting in his notebook what he spotted that morning to discuss with the group later.

'We both loved Tibbles but poor Mr Austin was so grieved by her death he wanted to make a bequest of a hundred pounds to the local cats' home, our way of doing something for just a few of the abandoned animals that weren't fortunate enough to find good new homes like Tibbles had with us. But you see, Izzie dear, when I had my will rewritten a couple of weeks ago, I was in such a tizzy at the time, trying to remember all the bequests, that it completely slipped my mind about Mr Austin's bequest to the cats' home. It was the rain on the window that brought back a memory of my dream of Tibbles last night, and that reminded me I hadn't observed my husband's express wish. Do you know, dear, I'm convinced Tibbles instigated that dream from the hereafter, by way of prompting me to remember.'

Izzie reassuringly patted her hand. 'Well, all you have to do is make an appointment with your solicitor and add that bequest to the list of others.'

'Oh, but I could never trust another solicitor after what I'd discovered about my old one! He was up to no good, Izzie. Thankfully he was caught and is now paying for what he did. That is how I came to have my will redone, so I could be absolutely sure no one had tampered with mine, as my solicitor was caught doing with someone else's. You don't need a solicitor, you know, to make out your will and hold it for you. You can do it yourself so long as your signature is witnessed by two people. My new will is in a sealed envelope in a box along with my other private papers in the drawer of the writing desk.'

'Oh, I see. Well, in that case you can add the bequest to your will yourself, Mrs Austin.'

Amelia looked quizzically at her. 'Is it as simple as that, dear, just to add it in, or does the whole will need rewriting? You see, that's what is worrying me.'

Izzie gave a helpless shrug. 'I've never had any need to write my will. I've nothing of any great value to leave at this moment in time except for a couple of pieces of jewellery that were my mother's and a few of her ornaments.' She gave a laugh. 'My nieces have decided for themselves what bits of mine they're having when the time comes.' She gave a frown. 'I'm just thinking who I could ask for you who would know about wills, Mrs Austin.'

'Oh, I don't wish to put you to any trouble, dear. I'll ask Mr Knowles.'

Izzie frowned quizzically at her. 'Mr Knowles? Brian Knowles? But he's a carpenter, I don't think he would know anything about making wills.'

'Oh, but you're wrong, Izzie, he does. All there is to know, in fact.' A guilty look crossed her face then and her hand went to her mouth. 'Oh, dear, oh, dear,' she uttered remorsefully. 'I gave my solemn promise to Mr Knowles I wouldn't tell anyone about the help he's given me just in case people might think he's becoming too familiar with the residents and he loses his work here. He has a wife and three children to support, you know. Oh, but it's you, Izzie, and I know I can trust you not to repeat anything I tell you in confidence. Do you happen to know when Mr Knowles will be here again? I can look out for him then and ask him the question. If it does transpire that my whole will needs writing out, then I'm sure he'll be good enough to oblige me again but this time I must make sure I recompense him for his trouble. He wouldn't take a penny from me for what he did before, you know. Such a nice, kind man he is.'

So Brian Knowles rewrote Mrs Austin's will for her? Izzie

wondered why Mrs Austin had asked him to help her with it and not one of the regular staff? 'I don't think we have any repairs of the sort Mr Knowles handles for us outstanding at the moment, Mrs Austin, so I don't know when he'll next be in.'

'Oh! But what if it's weeks before he next comes and I die meantime? Then my husband's wish will never be fulfilled, will it?' A look of distress filled her face. 'I shall not sleep for worry until it's done.'

'Oh, Mrs Austin, you have years in front of you yet,' Izzie reassured her.

'I'd like to think I had, dear, but no one knows when or where their time will be up, do they?'

She had a point, thought Izzie. 'Well, maybe to be on the safe side it would be best if you rewrote your whole will and then your mind will be put at rest.'

'You're right, dear. Can you do it for me, now please?'

'Me, Mrs Austin?'

'Well, I can't hold a pen properly with my arthritis, and besides, I might have won prizes for my handwriting when I was young, but these days even I have a job to read back what I have written. After what I discovered about my solicitor, well, I couldn't keep him on as executor so instead I have designated my bank manager. He's a good man who will make sure that my wishes and my dear late husband's are carried out, but he won't be able to do that if he can't decipher my handwriting, will he? I didn't need to explain about my arthritis affecting my handwriting to Mr Knowles because he'd already kindly offered to write it out for me anyway. He's the helpful sort. It seems anyone can write a person's will out for them as long as the person doing the writing is not a beneficiary and the witnesses aren't either, then it's all legal and above board. Mr Knowles told me that.'

Brian Knowles certainly was very knowledgeable on the subject of wills, Izzie thought. 'Oh, well, in that case of course I'll do it for you. As soon as I get a chance after we return from town.'

'Oh, I can't go to town, dear, not until I've had my will

rewritten. What if I was accidentally knocked over by a bus, just like poor Mr Waters was? I really would like you to help me with it now. I'd be much obliged to you, Izzie.'

Putting an old lady's mind at rest that her affairs were all in order was more important than a trip to town which could be rearranged for another time. The other ladies would be disappointed but it wouldn't be enough to stop them sleeping that night. Her nieces would be disappointed, too, but they would soon get over it as they became embroiled in another activity with the residents here.

'I'll just pop down and inform the others an emergency has cropped up and I can no longer accompany them into town.'

'All right, dear. I'll sort out my writing implements meantime.'

As Izzie arrived at the top of the staircase, she had a clear view of the entrance hall below and could see no sign of the three ladies or her nieces waiting where she had left them. The three women must have got fed up and gone off by themselves or else decided to shop locally. Suzy and Sally would be in the lounge, being amused by or else amusing other residents in there. There was no need for Izzie to inform Alma where she was as her colleague was under the impression she was managing on her own for the couple of hours Izzie accompanied the ladies into town. Izzie would tell her later what had transpired.

She returned to Amelia's room. Sitting at the writing desk, pen in hand and sheet of paper before her, she said, 'You tell me what you wish me to write then, Mrs Austin.'

Amelia looked down at the previous will Brian Knowles had written out for her and said, 'Oh, I'll need my reading glasses.' While Izzie waited patiently she searched around for them. Finding no trace, she retook her seat, handing Izzie the copy of the will. 'I can't find them. Can't even remember where I had them on last . . . I think it was in the lounge or was it the television room? They could be anywhere, dear. Why don't you copy across from my old will on to the new one, and when you have done all that I will tell you how I'd like the bequest to the cats' home worded.'

Made common sense and would be quicker that way, Izzie thought. Laying the old will on the desk to the side of her, in her best handwriting she began her task. Having completed the introduction she began listing the actual bequests. As she wrote out the name of each beneficiary she repeated it to Amelia with the relevant bequest to check that this was exactly as she wanted it.

She had just finished transferring the details of the last but one bequest when her eyes took in the details of the final one. They widened in surprise. Brian Knowles might not have accepted payment for his help to Amelia Austin in writing out her will for her, but he was going to get a nice surprise in the future when he discovered she had repaid his kindness by leaving him a nice little nest egg. The last bequest in the will stated: 'For Brian Alfred Knowles, a trusted friend. In appreciation of the help and guidance he has given me, I bequeath the sum of two hundred pounds.'

'Well, if my memory serves me correctly all the beneficiaries are accounted for, so now I'll tell you how I wish the wording of the bequest to the cats' home to be,' Amelia was saying to her.

'Oh, but what about the one for Brian Knowles, Mrs Austin? I haven't done that one yet.'

Amelia frowned at her quizzically. 'What one for Brian Knowles? Why would I leave Mr Knowles a bequest in my will? Admittedly, he's been very kind to me over this will business but many people have shown me kindness over the years, Izzie, and I wouldn't consider that a good enough reason to include them in my will.'

Izzie looked puzzled. Brian Knowles was definitely a bene-ficiary of Amelia's will, the evidence was clearly written before her. Mrs Austin was though, at times, very forgetful. Had she simply forgotten she had repaid his kindness in this way? Then a memory stirred. On three occasions she had witnessed Brian Knowles handing white envelopes over to residents, one of them Amelia Austin herself. Izzie couldn't work out at the time what they could possibly have contained. Had they in fact been rewritten wills? If so then Mrs Austin's case was not an isolated one. Brian Knowles must be in the habit of helping old ladies rewrite their wills. Was he hoping his efforts would be rewarded in the way Amelia had done? But what if Izzie was completely wrong and those other envelopes had contained something else entirely. The rewriting of Amelia's will could indeed be an act of pure kindness on Brian Knowles' part, and an isolated incident.

A niggle of concern began to gnaw away in the pit of her stomach, nevertheless. Was something not right here? Was everything above board? She wasn't sure. Izzie felt she needed to delve into what lay behind all this and find out, one way or the other.

She turned in her seat to give Amelia her full attention. 'As a matter of interest, Mrs Austin, how exactly did Brian Knowles come to help you rewrite your will? It's just my curiosity getting the better of me, you understand. But people's wills are normally private, aren't they, and not the topic of general conversation. I am intrigued to know how come Mr Knowles knew it was your solicitor who had been caught acting fraudulently.'

'Oh, well, Mr Knowles had read it in the newspaper, dear. Splashed across the front page of the *Leicester Mercury* in bold headlines, and being a reader of that paper that's how Mr Knowles instantly knew the name when I told him who my solicitor was.'

'Oh, I see. But exactly how did the conversation about wills and fraudulent solicitors come about in the first place, Mrs Austin?'

'Oh, well, you see, dear, Mr Knowles came here to fix my faulty window catch. He came to find me, I was in the conservatory at the time having elevenses with . . . oh, dear, who was it now . . . oh, yes, Katherine Philpots and Walter Waters. Oh, dear, poor Walter, such a gentleman. I do miss him, dear. But we all have to go sometime, don't we? No one can escape death. Anyway, Mr Knowles came and asked my permission to go into my room to fix the catch. Of course, I gave him it. Mrs Johnson only employs trustworthy people so I trusted him in my room without me being present. Besides, I'd come to know him during the chats we've had when he's been doing other jobs in my room so I knew he could be trusted on his own He then told me he would prefer I was present in order to ascertain if I was able to manoeuvre the catch backwards and forwards after he'd fixed it. He was very mindful, you see, dear, that old fingers can be stiff, and what you youngsters find easy to do can prove difficult for us older ones. Such a thoughtful man!

'While he was taking the broken catch off the window and replacing it with the new one . . .' She paused and looked thoughtful. 'Quite strange that, because the catch worked perfectly for me before . . . still, Mr Knowles knows what he's talking about, and if he said it was broken then it must have been. Anyway, he was standing on the stool he carries around with him as he wanted to check none of the sash ropes were frayed while he was at it, and I was telling him . . . what was I telling him? . . . oh, yes, about how much my husband loved gardening. Have I ever told you, dear, that Mr Austin was a very keen gardener? He was a member of the Leicester Horticultural Society and regularly won prizes for his sweet peas. He was a twitcher too you know, Izzie dear. Very keen on birds. Used to be out every Sunday morning at the crack of dawn and . . .'

'You were telling me about the faulty window catch, Mrs Austin,' Izzie prompted her, to steer her back on track with her narrative.

'Sorry? Oh, yes, so I was. Well, Mr Knowles was happy the window was now all right and went to step down from the stool when he seemed to lose his balance and tumbled off. Oh, he went down with such a crash, hitting his head on the carpet, and he was so very still that for a moment I thought the worst had happened and that he was . . . well, dead. I was so relieved when he sat up and rubbed his head and told me he was none the worse for his ordeal. He even joked that if the worst had happened then it was all right as his will was all in order. "I trust yours is too, Duchess," he said to me.' Amelia gave a coy smile. 'Mr Knowles always refers to me as Duchess because he says I remind him of the Queen Mother – very regal. I told him my affairs most certainly were in order and lodged with my solicitor. He told me he didn't trust solicitors for things like wills himself, not after he'd read about one who'd been caught adding in a bequest in his own favour to a will he'd made out for a client after they had signed it. It would have proved a nice little nest egg for him sometime in the future, should he have got away with it. When the person who'd supposedly left the money to the solicitor was dead and buried, their relatives weren't likely to query a couple of hundred pounds bequeathed to an obliging family solicitor. Mr Knowles then joked to me that he hoped I didn't use the same firm. That wouldn't be our firm, I told him, as my husband only used the best. He asked me who our firm were, and I told him Mr Marker of Marker, Wilson and Rightman. That's them, he said, that's the firm that crooked solicitor worked for. Well, I couldn't believe it, but Mr Knowles was adamant that was definitely the name of the firm he'd read about in the newspaper.

'Well, of course, I was most upset. Said I'd make an appointment to see them and demand they take my will out of the firm's vault for me to inspect that all was in order. Mr Knowles said it could take a few days for me to get in to see the solicitors and in the meantime I'd be having sleepless nights worrying over it. Plus I'd be billed for the appointment so it would cost me to see my own will. He said, why didn't I just write my own will out? It wouldn't cost me anything and would revoke all previous ones. That way I would know all was in order and it could never be tampered with as it would be here safe with me. He said he'd dealt with his own will and his mother's and some of the neighbours' too, so he knew what he was doing, and offered to help me with mine. That's when he told me all the ins and outs of will-making. It was obvious he knew what he was talking about. He said if I wanted his help then we could do it there and then. He had over an hour before he was due at his next job and that way I wouldn't lose any sleep over it. The only thing he asked was that we kept this to ourselves in case the management thought he was being too familiar with the residents and he lost his job because of it. Of course, I agreed.

'We set to immediately. I was very upset to think that the solicitor we had trusted had turned out to be so untrustworthy and got myself into a tizzy, trying to recall exactly how my old will was worded, but Mr Knowles was very patient with me. When it was done he said we would need another person to witness my signature as well as him, so he kindly went off to find someone. The cleaner was hoovering the corridor outside and she obliged. Mr Knowles respectfully waited outside while she did the deed and then when she'd left he returned and signed it himself, folded it up and sealed it inside an envelope so I could put it away for sake-keeping.'

This still seemed above board to Izzie. Amelia had obviously made Brian Knowles a beneficiary of her will and then forgotten it. But something struck her. Amelia had said that Brian Knowles had told her by law a beneficiary of a will could not also act as a witness to it. Yet Knowles must have known he was a beneficiary because he'd written it down in the will. Why offer to sign it when he knew it wasn't legal and would void his own bequest? She took a look at the witnesses' signatures on the bottom. Sadie Vines the cleaner's signature was there but the other signatory was the resident of the room next-door to Amelia's. Brian Knowles himself hadn't signed it. Yet Mrs Austin had just told Izzie she had seen Brian Knowles sign the will. Something very strange was going on here.

'Er . . . Mrs Austin, did you actually *see* Mr Knowles witness your signature on the will?'

'Yes . . . well . . . I wasn't actually standing over him when he did it because he asked me for an envelope to put the will in so I was getting one out of my writing case as he was signing it. Only the envelope I gave him was no good as it was a small letter type and wills need to be put in a proper long white one, for official purposes. He said Mrs Johnson was bound to have one as she would need them to post out business letters and he would go and ask her for one to save me the journey down.'

Izzie's mind was whirling. She didn't at all like what she feared she had uncovered here. 'Mrs Austin, when Mr Knowles went off to fetch an envelope, was he away for long and did he take the will with him?'

'Why are you asking all these questions, Izzie? I feel as if you are interrogating me.'

'Oh, er . . . I'm sorry. I didn't mean to make you feel I was probing. As I said, I'm just interested, that's all.'

Amelia patted her hand. 'It's nice to know people are interested in me, dear. When you're on your own you have no one to look out for you. I am so lucky to be living here. To answer your question, Mr Knowles was gone longer than I would have thought but I assumed Mrs Johnson was busy at the time and he had to wait. Come to think of it now, he must have taken the will with him as he brought it back already sealed inside the envelope, ready for me to put safely away. Now can we get back to finishing this off, please? I really want to get it over with now so I can put the whole thing to the back of my mind. It's all been very upsetting, very upsetting indeed.'

So while Brian had supposedly been collecting an envelope he had in fact been adding to the will his own bequest and had somehow fooled the resident next door into acting as the other witness, obviously giving them a plausible excuse for wanting their signature, perhaps folding the will in such a way they hadn't known what it was they were signing. Amelia Austin was not the only one who was upset. Izzie was too, very much so. If she was right, then Brian Knowles was doing exactly what he had told Amelia Austin her fraudulent solicitor had been caught doing, though in fact Izzie suspected the solicitor had never been caught doing any such thing. It was all a fabrication by Brian Knowles so that he could cajole a vulnerable old lady into letting him rewrite her will when he would be in a position to add a bequest to himself. He'd never quite be sure when he was going to come into such a bequest but depending on how many times he'd actually done this, and she suspected he had at least three times at Westleigh Lodge, then at least three tidy sums were coming his way sometime in the future. If Amelia hadn't forgotten her husband's bequest to the cats' home what Brian Knowles was doing might never have come to light. But Izzie couldn't prove he had done what she suspected. If she accused him he would no doubt deny it, saying he had just obeyed

Amelia's wishes to include himself in the will he was writing out for her, only she had forgotten about it. How could Izzie prove otherwise?

She felt sick. She wanted to be wrong. But the evidence was telling her she wasn't. She needed to find out whether this was an isolated incident or whether he was doing this on a wider scale. To do that, though, she'd need to question residents, particularly the two she had seen him handing envelopes to. But it wasn't a nursing assistant's place to probe into residents' private affairs without invitation. It was the head of Westleigh Lodge's place to, if she felt there was a need. She needed to involve Leonie Johnson.

Quickly completing Amelia's will for her, Izzie then witnessed her signature and, having procured the services of another resident to be the second witness, she sealed the will firmly inside an envelope and left Amelia's room. She made her way immediately to Leonie's office and knocked on her door.

Leonie was dressed for outdoors. 'You've come to tell me my taxi's here?'

'Er . . . no. I would like a word with you though, please, Miss Johnson.'

She picked up two ledger-type books and put them securely under her arm, then hooked her handbag over the other. 'Well, as you can see, I'm on my way out. Look, I really have a lot on my mind at the moment, I can't deal with anything else just now. Everything is running smoothly, isn't it?' Her tone left Izzie in no doubt what she expected to hear.

Leonie seemed very anxious to Izzie, even nervous. Wherever it was she was going, she was taking the ledgers with her so Izzie assumed it was to see the accountant. Maybe Leonie was worried that her efforts to improve the business were not enough and was dreading what he might recommend next.

'We're doing our best to make sure it does, Miss Johnson,' Izzie assured her.

'Good. Well, I'm sure whatever it is you want to speak to me about, you can deal with yourself. As long as it doesn't involve spending any money?'

'Well, no, it doesn't.'

She looked relieved. 'I'll leave you to it then. I'll wait outside for my taxi. I do hope it's not going to be late, I cannot miss this appointment.' She looked meaningfully at Izzie. 'I need to lock my office up now.'

It was a hint for her to leave.

'Oh, yes, of course, Miss Johnson.'

As she walked out of the office Alma, who was coming out of the lounge, spotted Izzie and came across to join her. 'Oh, yer back then. I was just on me way to grab a cuppa while I could. Do you want one while I'm mashing one? Izzie, are you listening to me?'

Her mind was whirling, filled with solving the problem now Leonie was out of the equation. 'Pardon? Oh, sorry, Alma, what did you say?'

'I asked if you wanted a cuppa while I was mashing?'

'Oh, I'd love one, thanks.'

'Trip up town go okay?' Alma asked her.

'We never actually went. Something urgent came up that I needed to help Mrs Austin with so the ladies must have gone by themselves. I hope Suzy and Sally have been behaving themselves?'

'Last time I saw them was when they was waiting with you for Amelia Austin to come down so you could all go into town. I haven't seen them since, Izzie.'

'But you've just come out of the lounge haven't you, and that's where they would normally be.'

'Well, I wasn't actually in the lounge but had just popped me head inside to see everyone in there was all right before I popped off to the kitchen to mash a cuppa. For the last hour I've actually been up in Mrs Peters' room cutting her toe nails for her, she can't manage herself. Oh, Izzie, I didn't *want* to do it but now Joyce and Beattie ain't here to do things like that for the residents I'd no choice, had I, unless I wanted to upset the old duck, and I didn't want to do that so I agreed. While I was up there she took advantage of me and had me helping her write out her Christmas shopping list. I kept telling her I had to get back downstairs 'cos there was only me on duty but she kept saying she'd nearly finished and wouldn't keep me much longer. I feel awful we can't spend the time with the residents we used to, Izzie, now we're so busy with all the stuff Joyce and Beattie used to do as well as our own duties. All we do now is rush round, don't we? All I want to do when I get home is go to bed I'm that exhausted, and I know you are too. If I didn't like me job here so much I'd start looking for summat else. But then, I ain't exactly enjoying it at the moment. I might look round after Christmas if there's no sign of Mrs Johnson coming back or we at least get another assistant to help us. Anyway, I didn't see Suzy or Sally in the lounge when I had a check in there just now.'

'Oh, they must have taken themselves off home then. Look, you go in the lounge and have a chat to the residents. Use that as an excuse to have a sit down for five minutes while I go and mash us a cuppa.'

'Did I hear the mention of a cup of tea?' a reedy voice enquired. 'If so I'd love one. And you would too, wouldn't you, Doreen?'

Izzie and Alma turned their head to see two old ladies coming out of the lift behind them. They looked at each other and gave helpless shrugs.

At a quarter to five Izzie was crossing the lounge on her way to the dining room to make sure everything was in order for the residents' tea when she heard the outer door open and glanced across to see Pat entering. Izzie went to greet her.

'Hello, Pat. Your hair looks nice,' she commented on the newly permed hair.

She gave it a pat. 'Oh, do yer think so? Ta. We tried a Richard Hudnut perm this time instead of me usual Twink and it seems to have took better. Pity I wasn't blessed with a few of your curls, Izzie, then I wouldn't have to keep forking out for some. Anyway, I've come to collect the kids as Santa's parade is coming down the Hinckley Road on its way into town at about quarter-past five so I'm going to take them to watch it.'

'Oh, but the girls aren't here. I thought they'd returned home a couple of hours ago.'

Pat's face paled. 'They haven't, Izzie. Where can they be?'

Izzie's face paled too. She had no idea.

As a surge of panic rose within both women the outer door opened and to their surprise Suzy and Sally, along with Katherine Philpots, Nora Hopgood and Winnie Mason trooped in. They were all carrying shopping bags.

Suzy and Sally beamed in delight to see their mother and Izzie and galloped across to them. 'We've had a great time, Mam, Aunty Izzie. We held the ladies' hands to make sure they got safely across the road and made 'em stay all together so we didn't lose any of 'em.'

'Your nieces have been so helpful,' Katherine Philpots said to Izzie as the three women arrived. 'We couldn't have managed without them, could we, ladies?'

'No, indeed not.' said Winnie Mason. 'I couldn't have carried all my shopping by myself, and we would certainly not have managed to catch that bus if the girls hadn't raced ahead and asked it to wait for us. Such dears, they are.'

'When you never came back down after going up to see what was keeping Amelia, we assumed you had forgotten about us, Izzie, and gone off to do something else,' Nora Hopgood said to her. 'We thought we'd have to forget about our trip as we'd no one to accompany us, until Suzy and Sally kindly offered to come with us.' Putting her hand in her pocket, she pulled out two sixpences which she held out to them. 'My way of saying thank you, dears.'

The other two women did likewise, holding out their own offerings to the girls.

'Oh, we don't want no money,' said Sally.

'No, we don't,' said Suzy. 'We was just trying to help Aunty Izzie out 'cos we know she's busy.'

'Oh, well, very commendable of you both,' said Katherine Philpots, putting her money back in her pocket, the other two women doing likewise. 'Your mother must be very proud of you. Well, we'd better get a move on, ladies, or we'll be late for tea.'

The three women retrieved the bags of shopping that Suzy and Sally had been carrying for them then they all moved off in the direction of the lift.

Pat looked down at her daughters, her face blank. 'Well, this proud mother will expect you to show yourselves as willing to accompany me up the town next time I go, and not complain when I ask you to carry some shopping for me. I trust neither of you is too tired to go and watch Santa's parade?'

They both yelped in delight at the thought.

Izzie patted both their heads, smiling fondly at them. 'Thanks, girls. You've saved me having to try and fit the trip in for them tomorrow.' She looked at Pat. 'See you soon . . .' Then her own problem came to mind. Maybe her brother or Pat could give her their thoughts on what she felt was a shocking discovery and be able to advise her what to do about it. 'Oh, Pat, is it all right if I pop around later? I need your help over something.'

'You know you never need to ask, Izzie. See you later.'

Pat looked at her in concern when Izzie arrived just after seven-thirty that night.

'You looked bushed, gel. That Miss Johnson might be trying to up the business's fortunes, but cutting down on the staff is taking advantage of the ones left behind, in my opinion. Sit down and I'll mash you a cuppa. Have you eaten?'

Hanging up her coat on the back of the door, Izzie smiled appreciatively over at her sister-in-law. 'Yes, thanks, Pat.' She knew she was making Pat believe she had eaten a full evening meal, not the two leftover sandwiches she had gobbled down quickly as she had been rushing around clearing up the dining room after the residents' evening meal.

'So what's this something you need help with?' Pat asked her, intrigued, as she lit the gas under the kettle.

Izzie took a breath and related her findings of that afternoon.

When she had finished Pat looked stunned. 'So you think this carpenter chap has manipulated at least three of your old dears into making new wills and put himself in as a beneficiary? Bloody hell, Izzie, you can't keep this to yourself. You have to take this to Mrs Johnson's daughter for her to deal with.'

'I did approach Miss Johnson but I never got the chance to tell her as she was just on her way out to an important appointment.

She told me whatever I wanted to speak to her about, just to deal with it myself. But I can't deal with something like this myself, Pat, I'm only a nursing assistant. I have no authority to probe into residents' private affairs.'

Pat stared at her thoughtfully. 'Well, you can't go to the police with this until you have firm evidence. Hang on, I'll ask Arnold what he thinks you should do.'

She rose and went into the back room, returning almost immediately. 'We're out of luck. He's sound asleep and ain't gonna be happy when he wakes up and finds out he's slept through his favourite programme.' She sat back down again and stared thoughtfully at Izzie for a moment, then she exclaimed, 'Oh, Doctor Landers is yer answer! He's the official doctor for Westleigh Lodge and the residents won't think someone in authority like him is out of order, asking them their private business. They'll just think he's looking out for their welfare. With Mrs Johnson being away and her daughter too busy, the Doc's the only one you can go to.'

'Oh, you've a point but . . .'

'But what?'

'Well . . . I don't think I could face him, Pat, not after what I realised today.'

'And just what did you realise today?'

Izzie gave a heavy sigh. 'That I'd totally misjudged him.'

'Oh, in what way?'

Izzie told her how she had come to discover that she had been totally mistaken in her belief Steven had taken her out purely by way of interviewing her for the position of companion to his mother.

When she had finished Pat shook her head at her. 'So the poor chap had taken you out on a date after all? I asked you at the time if you could have been mistaken and you were adamant you hadn't been. So he just wittered on about his mother because of nerves then. Oh, Izzie, you idiot! Well, you need to put the man straight.'

Izzie looked aghast. 'Pat, I can't. I've been so rude to him since that night and can't imagine what he thinks of me now.'

'Well, he's probably wondering what he did to suddenly make you go from being all nice with him, to treating him like someone who's got a highly infectious disease. Now you know you came to the wrong conclusion about him, the least he deserves from you is an explanation for your behaviour towards him. And an apology.'

Izzie smiled weakly at her. 'Yes, you're right, Pat. What he'll think of me then, I have no idea, but I suppose it can't be any worse than it must be now?'

Pat smiled mischievously at her. 'Yer never know, once he hears why you acted as you did he might ask you out again.'

Izzie doubted that very much. He'd more than likely be grateful for the lucky escape he had had from her.

'As for this other matter, Izzie, well, I think you should deal with it straight away. If it does turn out that your suspicions are correct, that man's little game needs putting a stop to before one of his victims dies and he reaps the benefit.' Pat cast a glance at the kitchen clock. 'It's not too late to go and see Doctor Landers now. Do you know where he lives?'

Izzie nodded. 'Not the number but I do the road as his father mentioned it today.'

'Well, someone on that road will know. Make sure you call in on me on the way back and let me know how you got on.'

Izzie wasn't looking forward to an encounter with Steven. She was feeling actuely stupid and embarrassed but she needed his help and so she had no choice.

Promising Pat she'd call back, she took her leave.

Steven was most surprised to see who his caller was. 'Why, Izzie. Er . . . how nice to see you.'

Despite feeling awkward, she managed to smile warmly at him. 'I'm so very sorry to bother you at this time of night, Doctor Landers, but is it possible for me to have a word with you? That is, of course, if I'm not disturbing you?'

He smiled warmly back at her. 'You're not disturbing me at all. I was just catching up with the news in the evening paper Please, come in.'

She followed him down a brightly lit, carpeted passageway and on into the lounge. It was obvious no woman lived here as there were no feminine touches, but regardless the room had a very welcoming feel to it. The furniture looked to be of good quality, possibly not new when bought by him but extremely comfortable. The radio was playing pleasant background music.

As Izzie was taking in her surroundings she was unaware that Steven's eyes were on her. He was wondering what could possibly have brought her to his door at this hour. She had made her feelings towards him on a personal level very clear so it was obviously nothing of that nature.

'Please sit down and make yourself at home, Izzie,' he said, indicating a large brown leather Chesterfield. 'Can I get you a cup of tea or anything?'

'Oh, no, Doctor Landers, thank you.' She just wanted to get this over with so she could make her escape.

Sitting down opposite in a matching armchair, he looked keenly at her and said, 'Well, Izzie, what is it I can do for you?'

She took a deep breath. 'Well, Doctor Landers, it's like this . . .'

He listened to her in respectful silence, his face betraying no emotion as she related her findings. When she had finished he said evenly, 'In the circumstances you were right to come to me with this, Izzie. No disrespect to your position but some of the residents would not look kindly on a nursing assistant poking her nose into their private affairs, whereas I can do it in a subtle way and they will be under the impression my interest is purely a doctor's.' He smiled. 'Patients will tell their doctors everything. You have my promise I will find out if Mrs Austin's case is an isolated one or not. If I suspect a crime is being committed by this man, I will take it to the police for investigation. In the meantime, should you cross paths with Brian Knowles just act towards him like you normally would. I appreciate that could be a tall order but if he suspects we're investigating, well, he might resort to breaking into residents' rooms and stealing back the wills he's tampered with. Then we'd not be able to bring him to book and he'd still be at liberty to carry on his activities elsewhere.'

Izzie smiled gratefully at him. 'Thank you, Doctor Landers.' She made to rise and take her leave but hesitated. She owed this man an apology and there was no better time than now to give it to him, while she had his undivided attention. There was no telling when she would get another chance like this. But how did she begin?

Steven could see Izzie was deliberating over something. 'Have you discovered something else about this man you think I should know?'

'Oh, no, Er . . .' She took a deep breath. 'Doctor Landers, I . . . well, I owe you an . . .'

Just then the telephone rang in the hallway.

He jumped up from his chair. 'Excuse me, Izzie, but I need to answer it in case it's an emergency.'

'Oh, yes, of course.'

She heard the murmur of his voice, then the telephone being replaced in its cradle and his footsteps making their way back. Taking a deep breath, she prepared to take up where she'd left off only to be thwarted as he entered the room, pulling on his overcoat.

'I do apologise, Izzie, I have to dash off to see a patient who's having a suspected heart attack.'

'Oh, no need to apologise, Doctor Landers, I'd finished anyway.'

'But you were about to tell me something, and I was going to ask if you'd tell me tomorrow when I come to Westleigh Lodge.'

It was too late, the moment had gone along with her nerve. 'Oh, it was nothing important. I can't remember what it was now anyway. You need to rush off so I'll leave you to it. Thank you again, Doctor Landers. I'll see myself out.'

'Well, at least Doctor Landers has taken the situation out of your hands and you can rest easy the matter is being looked into,' Pat said to her a short while later. 'So how did he react to your apology?' She saw the look on Izzie's face. 'Don't tell me you bottled out?'

'No, I didn't. I made an attempt but the telephone rang and he had to rush out on an emergency. There's no telling when I'll get him on his own like that again, and I'm not doing it when there's a risk of anyone overhearing me. It's embarrassing enough admitting to him I got the wrong end of the stick and behaved very badly to him without all the world knowing.'

Pat sighed despondently. She hadn't had the privilege of meeting Doctor Landers but from what Izzie had told her of him, he sounded a very decent man. She did know Izzie, probably better than anyone, and Pat knew without a doubt that she was lovely. It seemed to her that two wonderful people were being kept apart through a silly misunderstanding on Izzie's part. Pat felt positive that once Steven Landers was aware of it he would be just the sort to be understanding, to forgive Izzie and want them to start again. She hoped her sister-in-law found it within herself to put the wrong right and then those two lovely people could find out if they had a future together. The sooner the better, as far as Pat was concerned.

CHAPTER
TWENTY-THREE

As Izzie tackled her duties the next morning she wondered how and when Steven would go about finding out the truth. She got her answer at just after eleven-thirty.

She was systematically visiting all the residents' rooms, collecting soiled towels left outside their doors and replacing them with clean ones. She was in the linen cupboard picking up another batch of clean towels when Alma, who happened to be passing, stopped and poked her head inside.

'Oi, Izzie!' Doc's took up residency in the nurses' room for a couple of hours, and again tomorrow and the next day. He's holding special clinics so he can have a chat with all the residents, make sure he's up to speed with all of them health-wise. He's a good doc, ain't he, Izzie? And he apologised for putting extra work on me. Said he knew I already had enough to do. Weren't that nice of him, Izzie? Anyway, he's gave me a list of the old dears he wants to see today. Most are in the lounge, having just finished their elevenses, but a couple of them are in their rooms so I'm just off to tell them what time Doc's got them down on his list.' She gave a disdainful tut. 'Can't remember the last time me and you had time to stop for elevenses, can you? Anyway, best get on. I'll catch up with you later.'

So Steven wasn't wasting any time, Izzie thought. She hoped that his efforts today resolved this matter one way or the other and then this worrying situation could be put behind her. She had enough to concentrate her efforts on keeping Westleigh Lodge running smoothly without worrying whether outsiders were coming in and taking advantage of the residents.

Her arms piled with towels, she walked out of the cupboard just as Brian Knowles was passing by.

He stopped and grinned at her. 'Hello, Izzie,' he said jocularly.

He had caught her off guard. She stared at him for a moment before Steven's advice to her to act normally with him came to mind and she quickly pulled herself together. Planting a smile on her face, she said with forced breeziness, 'Hello, Brian. Come to do a repair job, have you?'

'A floorboard in the bathroom at the end of this corridor needs replacing so I've popped in to measure up.'

Well, at least he wasn't attending to anything in a resident's room, giving him an opportunity to size up his next victim, if indeed her suspicions of his activities were correct.

'Best get these towels delivered and the dirties down to the laundry, the girls are waiting to wash them,' she said.

'Yeah, and I'd best get measuring up that board before I'm labelled a slacker. See you, Izzie.'

'Yes, see you, Brian.'

She looked after him as he sauntered on his way towards the bathroom. He came across as such a nice man, had an honest air about him. But was that just a persona he adopted to fool innocent old people? She hoped not.

Two days later, at just after midday, Alma sought Izzie out to tell her Doctor Landers wished for a word and was waiting for her in the nurses' room.

Having been on tenterhooks for this summons from him, Izzie immediately dropped what she was doing and rushed off to respond to it.

She knew immediately she entered the room and saw the grave expression on his face that his questioning of the residents had not reaped the result she had been hoping for.

'Brian Knowles has duped at least three other residents into rewriting their will, using the same story about the fraudulent solicitor that he gave Amelia Austin,' Steven told her. 'They are all in the same mould as Mrs Austin, easily taken in. I will be referring this matter to the police for them to investigate further.'

She looked equally as grave. 'I was so hoping I was wrong about all this. The ladies involved are going to be very distressed when they find out they've been conned. Oh, dear, they will have to appear in court, won't they? How are they going to cope with that?'

He smiled. 'Better than you think. I admit, this will come as a shock to them initially, but after that I suspect they will be more worried about what to wear in court. It'll be a day out for them and they'll all revel in being the centre of attention.'

'Oh, I never thought of it like that.'

'You deserve a pat on the back for not turning a blind eye to this situation, Izzie. I shall make sure Mrs Johnson knows when she returns how lucky she is to have such a conscientious person as her employee.'

'Oh, I don't want any praise, Doctor Landers. I'm just glad Brian Knowles will not benefit from his lies. Anyway, thank you for not thinking I was letting my imagination run riot when I came to ask for your help.'

'I wouldn't take you for that sort of person, Izzie.'

She wasn't normally but she certainly had displayed those traits when it came to misconstruing his reason for taking her out. She was reminded again that she owed him an apology. She ought to do it now and get it over with. Taking a deep breath, she opened her mouth and simultaneously the door opened and Nora Hopgood bustled in.

'Oh, I'm glad I've caught you, Doctor Landers. When I left after my consultation with you, I never properly thanked you for taking such an interest in me, not just my health but personal issues too. I just want to say what a wonderful doctor I think you are. All the residents think so, in fact. I've never had one before who's been so thorough. Anyway, after I left I remembered something I'd forgotten to mention when we were discussing any health problems I might have that you didn't know about.' She suddenly stopped, realising that Izzie was present while she was about to discuss a personal matter with her doctor. 'You will excuse us, dear, won't you?'

It seemed to Izzie that she was never going to get a chance to apologise to Steven. 'Yes, of course I will.'

Steven was right. Amelia Austin and the three other elderly ladies Brian Knowles had conned at Westleigh Lodge were deeply shaken when the next day a police inspector and constable turned up to interview them all. It was quickly ascertained by an inspection of the other three wills that Brian Knowles had indeed included himself as a beneficiary which none of the ladies recalled authorising him to do. But the shock of all this was indeed quickly replaced by feelings of excitement that their testimonies in court were going to put paid to Brian Knowles' criminal activities and a request was made to Izzie to accompany them all into town before the trial date so they could choose new outfits.

It quickly came to light that Brian Knowles had no wife or children to support so what he was doing was not to provide a better living for his family, but just for his own greed.

CHAPTER
TWENTY-FOUR

A week before Christmas Izzie was in the kitchen fetching a glass of water for Muriel Peters who had a dry throat after practising songs for her recital in the lounge after tea the following Sunday afternoon. Izzie was perturbed to notice that the normally very good-humoured and chatty Hilda Williams was unsually quiet and looking preoccupied. But then so was Rita her assistant.

'This time of year I guess is your busiest, Cook?' Izzie said to her as she was making her way back out of the kitchen.

Scooping up a piece of suet dough, she began forming it into a small ball in her palms to add to a pile of dumplings for the stew that was bubbling merrily away on the stove and smelled delicious. 'Usually, ducky, it would be, but this year . . . well, don't look like it's gonna be to me. I was as shocked as all us staff were when Miss Johnson explained how fickle the profits on this business were due to Mrs Johnson's over-generous ways.

'I've being doing me damnedest to stick inside the tight budget Miss Johnson set me, something I never had to do under Mrs Johnson who gave me free rein to produce the meals using the best quality foods. I'm glad to say that up to now the residents don't seem to have noticed the cheaper foods and meats I'm using as I've received no complaints so far, but I thought I'd have me budget upped to cater for some extras at Christmas. It seems not, though. When I approached Miss Johnson about it, she just said she'd already stretched the food budget as far as she could.

'Well, I'm a good cook if I say it meself, and the residents will get a proper dinner like I always give them, but nothing more special than a normal Sunday roast and sandwiches for tea. 'Cos miracle worker I ain't! I can't stretch a ten bob note to make a pound, much as I'd like to. So there'll be no salmon in aspic, homemade pork pies, ham off the bone... nothing like that. Thank goodness the cake and puds were made before Mrs Johnson went off so at least there'll be something marking the day.

'But that's not all I'm in a quandary about. I've always done as much preparation as I can beforehand. Mrs Johnson has done the honours on the day itself and given me the day off to spend with my family. But with no sign of her returning and it being just over two weeks away, I brought this matter up with Miss Johnson and all she said to me was she'd let me know. Well, that's no good to me. I always have all the family over on Christmas Day, all twenty-four of them, and if I have to work then that's fair enough, but I need to let them know one way or the other so they have time to make their own arrangements.'

Izzie appreciated it wasn't possible for Leonie Johnson to confirm one way or another whether she would require Hilda Williams' services on Christmas Day as she had no idea herself whether her mother would have returned by then. It all depended on the health of her aunt. She wished she could resolve Hilda's problem by offering to cover the kitchen duties on Christmas Day, but that would leave Alma on her own to cope with the needs of twenty residents, something two of them were only just managing as it was.

But there was something she could do to ensure the residents were provided with festive fare on Christmas Day to make their day a special one.

As soon as it was safe for Izzie to leave Alma by herself for ten minutes – actually she wasn't entirely on her own as Suzy and Sally had come along after school, the boiler now having been fixed, and were entertaining several residents in the lounge and vice versa – she donned her coat and ran across to the Post Office where she drew sixty pounds out of her savings. Fifty pounds to pay for festive fare for the residents and ten which she hoped would be enough to cover the cost of a small gift each for them that they would believe was from Mrs Johnson. Along with her own Christmas shopping she still had to find time to do this. The withdrawal was making a large dent in her savings but she felt what she had taken out was for an excellent cause. Writing a note which stated, 'Hope this helps provide a good Christmas for the residents of Westleigh Lodge. Best wishes, a well wisher', she sealed the fifty pounds and note inside an envelope which she addressed to Hilda Williams, intending to leave it unobserved in the kitchen after Hilda and her assistant had finished for the day.

At just after four o'clock Izzie thought she might get a chance and was on her way down the corridor that led to the kitchen when the door opened and her nieces came out. They were both giggling and acting like they were sharing a secret.

'And just what has tickled both your fancies?' she called down to them.

They both froze in their tracks, staring back at her guiltily.

'Er . . . nothing, Aunty Izzie,' stammered Suzy.

'No, nothing,' her sister joined in.

Izzie had reached them by now. 'So you're both laughing at nothing, are you? So why are you looking guilty? Were you up to something in the kitchen that you shouldn't have been?'

'No, we weren't,' insisted Suzy.

'No, honest,' Sally added. 'We were getting a drink of water, weren't we, our Suzy?'

'Yeah, 'cos we was both thirsty.'

Just then Alma's voice was heard from the other end of the corridor. 'Oh, there you are, gels. I was wondering where you'd got to as you went to get a drink ages ago. The ladies you were helping wind their wool are asking where you are.'

'We're just coming,' Suzy shouted to her.

Both girls then ran off down the corridor to join Alma.

Izzie turned and looked quizzically after them. They had both been up to something, she felt sure of it. She continued on her way to the kitchen and once inside cast a look around. It was as neat and tidy as Cook and her assistant always left it. The sandwiches for the residents' tea didn't look as though they had been tampered with, nor the cakes, so the girls hadn't been helping themselves, not that Izzie would believe they would even consider doing such a thing. The only thing she could see amiss was that she and Alma had not yet got around to washing up the afternoon tea cups which were stacked on the draining board and would be needed for the evening meal. She might as well do them while she was here.

Propping her gift for the residents on the kitchen table, she rolled up her sleeves and set to.

Hilda Williams couldn't believe her eyes when she opened the envelope the next morning to find inside the means to pay for all the extra ingredients she required to produce special Christmas fare for the residents. Try as they might, neither she or Rita could work out who the mystery benefactor was and it never was discovered.

The same evening that Izzie had left her gift to the residents for Hilda Williams to find, she flopped down in Pat's armchair and gave a weary sigh. Handing her a mug of tea, her sister-in-law looked worriedly down at her. 'You can't carry on working as hard as you do, Izzie. Look how tired you are. You haven't had a full day off since Miss Johnson made the staff cutbacks. Look, you have to tell her that her cuts are too severe. She has to take one of the nurses back on or at least hire another nursing assistant. You're doing more than Alma is, staying on much longer after yer shift finishes to help out the night staff, and the weekend ones too. I'm worried about you, Izzie.'

Before she could respond a voice piped up, 'Maybe Aunty Izzie won't have to work so hard when Mrs Pain takes over.' It was Suzy who along with her sister was sitting at the dining table, colouring pictures and painstakingly cutting out paper dolls from the latest copy of *Bunty*.

'Will Mrs Pain still let us come in after school and do things with our friends like Mrs Johnson does, Aunty Izzie?' Sally asked her, looking bothered.

Izzie sat up and looked quizzically at them both. 'Who's Mrs Pain?'

'Oh, she's the lady who's buying the place from Mrs Johnson,' Suzy replied matter-of-factly.

Izzie frowned. 'And what makes you think that?'

''Cos we heard them talking about it, didn't we, our Sally?'

'Yeah, we did,' Sally responded, her tongue sticking out of the side of her mouth as she carefully cut around a difficult bit of her paper doll's fingers.

'Them?' queried Izzie.

'Miss Johnson and Mrs Pain,' Suzy told her, searching through her colouring pencils for the particular blue she wanted for the sky.

'And where was this?' Izzie asked them.

'Oh, in Mrs Johnson's . . .' Sally began.

'Office,' Suzy blurted loudly. 'In Miss Johnson's office. We were just passing, weren't we, Sally, and overheard 'em?'

'Eh? Yeah, that's right, we did.'

'What have I told you two about eavesdropping?' snapped Pat at them both.

Izzie was staring in disbelief. Mrs Johnson was selling up! But Westleigh Lodge was her pride and joy. This couldn't possibly be true. The girls must have misconstrued what they had overheard. 'Look, you know what I think about you listening behind doors, the same as your mother does, but . . . well, just what did you hear Miss Johnson and Mrs Pain saying?'

'Can't remember all of what we heard,' said Suzy, frowning thoughtfully, and chewing on the end of her pencil. 'Something about signing . . . things . . . er . . . er . . . contracts,' she said, smiling triumphantly when she had remembered the right word.

'And Miss Johnson told Mrs Pain she was getting a good price and so wanted it all done before Christmas,' said Sally. 'Then we scarpered before we was caught,' she added.

'Yeah, we did,' said Suzy. 'Because we didn't know that the door led in there, did we, Suzy?'

'No, we didn't,' she responded as she carefully laid the finished doll on the table and began on the dress next.

Both Pat and Izzie were staring at them, confused.

'What door led where?' Izzie asked them.

'Eh?' they both exclaimed.

'Er . . . I'm tired so I'm going up to bed,' Suzy said hurriedly, grabbing her colouring pencils and book together. 'You're tired too, ain't yer, Sally?' She was eyeing her sister meaningfully.

'Eh? Oh, yes, I am.' Dropping the pair of scissors she was holding, Sally leapt off her chair and rushed upstairs, calling out behind her, 'Good night, Mam, Aunty Izzie.'

Her sister followed right behind her, calling out the same.

Izzie and Pat both looked bemused.

'My kids are scarpering before they get it in the neck for earwigging again,' said Pat. 'They think I'll have forgotten all about it come morning, but they're wrong 'cos I won't have. Interesting what they overheard, though,' she said, sitting down on the settee.

'What was interesting?' asked Arnold as he came into the room, rubbing his hands together. 'Hello, Izzie. You look bushed, gel.' He sat down in the armchair opposite his sister, stretching his feet out on the hearth. 'It's like an ice box in that privy tonight. I fear a few people are going to have burst pipes in the morning. Hopefully, not us, eh, Pat?' He pulled down his braces and undid the top button of his trousers, breathing out a grateful sigh. 'Oh, that's better. I think these have shrunk 'cos they ain't half getting tight round me middle.'

'Couldn't be that you're just getting fatter,' said Pat to him dryly.

'If I am it's your puddings that are doing it. They're so delicious I can't resist seconds. Anyway, what was it that was interesting?' He repeated his question, looking keenly at them both.

'Summat your daughters did. You're going to have to have a strong word with them, Arnold, 'cos they don't take any notice of me and one of these days they're going to cause a lot of trouble for someone when they innocently repeat something they shouldn't have been earwigging over.'

'I will, Pat. A strong word, believe me.'

She gave him a look as though to say, And pigs might fly. 'Huh!' she snorted. 'Well, anyway, your daughters seem to have overheard a conversation between Miss Johnson and a woman, discussing the sale of Westleigh Lodge.'

'Seems like it, Pat, but they could have been wrong,' said Izzie. 'Mrs Johnson told me she'd never sell Westleigh Lodge.'

'Well, she must be or the conversation the gels overheard don't make any sense.'

Izzie frowned as a thought struck her. The girls had said the woman Leonie was talking to was called Mrs Pain. Wasn't that the name of the woman Val the night nurse had overheard Leonie making an appointment with on the night of Walter Waters' death? And where had she heard that name in connection with old people's homes before? At the moment she couldn't recall. 'I still can't believe Mrs Johnson is selling up. The girls must have been confused about what they overheard.'

Pat tutted. 'They aren't usually. They usually repeat it word for word. Anyway, Suzy's eight and Sally's seven What do they know about signing contacts?'

She had a point, thought Izzie. 'Well, Miss Johnson has maybe managed to persuade her mother that she ought to sell up while she's still got something to sell. When I tried to talk to her the other day about Brian Knowles she was on her way out with the account books. Well, I assumed that's what they were. Maybe it was the accountant she was going to see and it's him who's advised her it's best to sell up now.'

'Well, if that is the case, I hope your new employer is as nice to work for as Mrs Johnson.'

'Mmm, so do I, Pat.'

Izzie lay in bed that night, tossing and turning, unable to sleep. She just couldn't comprehend why Jenny Johnson was selling up. But having gone over and over what Suzy and Sally had repeated, it seemed she must be, though Leonie had to be handling it for her since she could not leave her sick relative. She wondered when the staff were going to be told that Westleigh

Lodge was in the process of changing hands? Christmas was just over a week away and Suzy and Sally had said they had over-heard Leonie saying she was hoping it could be finalised by then.

Izzie dearly hoped that Mrs Pain was going to prove a good person to work for, but then no one would prove as good as Mrs Johnson had been. Her only fault was that she had been over-generous to the residents, to her own detriment. Oh, if only her daughter could have persuaded her to curtail her generous ways then maybe it wouldn't have had to come to the place being sold while it was still worth selling.

Izzie was deeply concerned to find out if Mrs Pain would honour her living arrangements when she took over, because if not then she would be faced with the difficult task of finding somewhere else that was affordable on her wages. A vision of a damp tiny bed-sitter rose up before her and she shuddered. She would put up with such conditions if it was all she could afford for the sake of staying in a job she so enjoyed, but she couldn't have her beloved nieces over to stay with her then as she wouldn't have the facilities to accommodate them and neither would she want to subject them to it. If Mrs Pain did not let her continue to live in the attic rooms Izzie would have to give serious thought to changing her job. She felt bereft at the thought. Westleigh Lodge had become like home to her and the people there her extended family.

Then suddenly she sat bolt upright as she remembered why the name Mrs Pain had rung a bell with her. On her first morning at Westleigh Lodge, Joyce had told her how she had gone to work for a Mrs Pain prior to securing her job with Jenny Johnson. She said she'd left because the way the residents in the home were treated was utterly appalling. They were drugged to keep them quiet, she remembered Joyce telling her, amongst other things. The owner was only in the business of caring for old people to gain as much money as she could.

Was the Mrs Pain who was buying Westleigh Lodge the very same Mrs Pain Joyce had worked for? Izzie couldn't believe that, regardless of how quick a sale Mrs Johnson was hoping for, she would ever consider handing over her establishment to someone who would treat her own residents like that.

Izzie's mind raced frantically. Leonie Johnson needed to be made aware that the woman she was in the process of selling to was known to have ill treated old people in her care. Then another thought struck. But what if this was a different Mrs Pain? She needed to find out.

But how did she do that?

She lay for an age, pondering this problem. There was only one answer. She had to ask Leonie Johnson direct.

At the first opportunity the next day Izzie tapped on Leonie Johnson's office door and waited for a summons.

Leonie was busy ringing orders through to suppliers and didn't look happy to be disturbed. 'What is it, Izzie?' she almost snapped. Then she said, 'Look, I'm sorry, it's just that I've a lot on my mind.'

Well, she would have if she was worried about the sale of Westleigh Lodge going through smoothly, thought Izzie, while in the meantime keeping up with all that needed doing to keep the business going. 'Well, Miss Johnson, I . . . well, you see, it's like this. I've heard a rumour that you're possibly selling this place to a Mrs Pain, and I wondered if that's the same Mrs Pain who owns . . .'

'Where did you hear that rumour?' she interjected, looking at Izzie sharply. 'From someone here?' she demanded.

Izzie hadn't thought she'd be quizzed on just where she had gained her information and hadn't prepared an answer. To be truthful would mean her getting her nieces into trouble for eaves-dropping and Leonie Johnson could take offence and put a stop to them coming on the premises. They would be so upset about that, and the residents too. She hated lying but to protect her nieces she would. 'Well, it's, . . . er . . . I have a friend, you see, who works for Mrs Pain and . . .'

'And this friend has been eavesdropping on Mrs Pain's conversations?' Leonie took a deep breath and fixed Izzie with her eyes. 'It's true, Westleigh Lodge is being sold to Mrs Pain, but my mother does not want this publicised until the deal is done. I expect you to respect her wishes. If I hear one word of this from anyone here, I will hold you responsible. Mrs Pain has made a success of her other home to the point where she's able to expand into buying another place, unlike my mother who's done the opposite. Mrs Pain has assured me that she has no intention of making any staff changes so you'll be all right.'

Izzie's heart sank. So the Mrs Pain who was buying Westleigh Lodge and the one Joyce had worked for were one and the same. Grave-faced, she blurted, 'Oh, but Miss Johnson, I really feel you need to know that Mrs Pain is successful in making money because of the way . . .'

'Izzie, Mrs Pain has the means to buy this place and that's all I need to know. Now you have work to do, don't you?'

Izzie sighed. 'Yes, Miss Johnson. I'm sorry to have disturbed you.'

'Miss Johnson never gave me chance to tell her how terribly Mrs Pain treats her residents, Pat,' Izzie told her sister-in-law later that night, having gone to see her as she knew Pat would be waiting to hear how she had got on. 'There's nothing else I can do. I did try, believe me. But I just know that Mrs Johnson would never knowingly turn her residents over to a woman like that, despite wanting a quick sale. I can't bear the thought that our residents will be treated like Joyce said Mrs Pain's were.'

'If you're that sure Mrs Johnson wouldn't, then she can't know what this Mrs Pain is like, Izzie. Maybe she has conned Mrs Johnson and her daughter into believing she's whiter than white and they believe they're putting the care of the old dears and you staff into safe hands. If Miss Johnson won't listen to you then you'll have to tell Mrs Johnson yourself what you know about this woman. At least then you'll know you've done all you can to put a stop to Mrs Pain buying Westleigh Lodge and the residents there ending their days in misery under her care.'

Izzie gave a helpless shrug. 'How can I warn Mrs Johnson when I don't know where she is? All I know is that she's nursing a terminally ill relative.'

'Her daughter will know.'

'And what excuse can I give Miss Johnson for asking for the telephone number or address where I can contact her mother? She'll want to know why I want to speak to her, which is natural.'

Pat frowned at her thoughtfully. 'Pity Arnold's out tonight playing darts. He might think of an excuse you could use, 'cos damned if I can.' Both women looked at each other blankly for several long moments before Pat suddenly exclaimed, 'Oh, just a thought, but this relative's address and telephone number, if she's on the telephone, would be written down in Mrs Johnson's address book, surely? Under the name of something Johnson I would have thought. It'll be in Mrs Johnson's flat.'

'And how am I supposed to get into her flat to have a look in her address book? Apart from the fact I'd be trespassing, I haven't a key.'

'We know how to get into Mrs Johnson's flat without a key!' Suzy dashed into the room.

Sally simultaneously launched herself after her sister, wailing, 'Oh, yer can't let that horrid woman be nasty to our old ladies and gentlemen. You've got to stop her, Aunty Izzie. You've got to tell Mrs Johnson not to sell it to her.'

Both women looked askance at the girls for a moment before Pat erupted.

'I bloody tucked you two up in bed half an hour before yer Aunty Izzie came. You were both obviously earwigging when I told your dad I was hoping she would call tonight. Oh, my God, how many times do you need to be told? Will a thrashing maybe do the trick?' She then frowned quizzically. 'Hang on, what do you mean by saying you can get into Mrs Johnson's flat without a key, our Suzy?'

She looked proud. 'Well, yer can, by going up in the moving cupboard.'

Pat and Izzie looked at each other. 'Moving cupboard?' they both mouthed to each other, completely baffled.

'What moving cupboard?' her mother asked.

'The one in the kitchen that moves up and down when you

295

pull on the ropes, *that* moving cupboard,' Sally told them. 'The door at the top goes into Mrs Johnson's kitchen.'

Izzie twigged what they were referring to then. 'Oh, you mean the dumb waiter. *That's* what you were both giggling over when I saw you coming out of the kitchen the other day. Alma came to find you because you'd been gone a long time. You'd both been playing in it, hadn't you?'

Neither had the grace to look ashamed but both nodded.

'I found it ages ago, Aunty Izzie, when I was in the kitchen for a drink of water. I was looking for a glass,' Sally told her. 'It's been our secret, ain't it, Suzy? We play on it when we can. We both squeeze inside and pull ourselves up and down by the ropes. It's such fun.'

'Yeah, it's great, but we didn't know 'til yesterday that the door at the top went into Mrs Johnson's kitchen,' said Suzy. 'We didn't know it even was a door 'til our Sally got fidgety 'cos she got cramp in her foot and when she was trying to wiggle her toes to stop it, her foot caught the door and it opened. That's when we heard Miss Johnson and that Mrs Pain talking.' Her eyes lit up eagerly. 'But, Aunty Izzie, I could go up in the dumb thingy and get into Mrs Johnson's kitchen. I'd open the front door for you, and you could look for the book with the address in where Mrs Johnson is then tell her about Mrs Pain.' She paused long enough to draw breath before adding, 'She'll listen to you, Aunty Izzie, 'cos Mrs Johnson's lovely.'

'We can't do that,' Izzie said to her aghast. 'Why, it's breaking and entering and . . .'

'Ah, but hang on a minute, Izzie,' Pat cut in. 'I'm not saying what our Suzy's suggesting is right exactly but it seems the only way to me you're going to get hold of Mrs Johnson.' She then looked at her daughters, wagging a warning finger at them. 'This is our secret. Don't you dare breathe a word about this to your dad, are you listening?'

'We won't, Mam,' they both promised.

'So can I be the one to go up in the moving cupboard and open the door for Aunty Izzie?' demanded Suzy.

'But I wanna do it!' erupted Sally.

'Neither of you will,' said Izzie. 'I can't believe you're agreeing to your daughters doing something like this, Pat.'

'And I ain't lightly, Izzie. But it's not like we're using them to rob a bank. This is to try and save the old dears from a life of purgatory, not to mention you working for a dragon.'

'Yes, but all the same, I dread to think what would happen if one of the girls was caught.'

'How many times have you been up and down in the dumb waiter?' Pat asked her daughters.

'Loads,' said Suzy.

'Lots and lots,' said Sally.

'And has anyone ever caught you?'

They shook their heads.

'No one is in the kitchen when we play on it,' said Suzy.

'By the time Suzy and Sally come after school, Cook and her assistant have finished for the day and gone home,' Izzie told Pat.

Izzie stared thoughtfully into space. She couldn't bring herself to agree to her beloved nieces acting in a criminal manner, however much of a good cause it was in aid of. But how else could she get into the flat and get hold of Mrs Johnson's address book? Images of Amelia Austin, Muriel Peters, Peregrine Danvers and all the other residents she had grown so fond of flashed before her. She saw them sitting zombie-like in chairs in the lounge, sedated in order to give the staff an easy life. She shuddered. That could be their future if Mrs Pain took over. But not if *she* could help it. She knew that once Mrs Johnson heard what her intended buyer was really like she wouldn't go ahead with this sale but seek another buyer.

She looked earnestly at her sister-in-law. 'If I make sure that Miss Johnson is in her office while we do this, it would be just a matter of minutes before one of the girls is actually inside the flat. The chances of being caught by Miss Johnson are very slim for them. If I get caught by her looking for the book I will suffer the consequences, and if Suzy or Sally are caught I will say I made them do it.'

'Oh, great, that means we're going to do it,' erupted Suzy in glee. 'So can I be the one?' she begged.

'No, me?'

'Suzy's the eldest so it's her,' said their mother.

'Ahh, but that's not fair,' wailed Sally. 'Weren't my fault I was born second.'

'But I'll need a look out,' Izzie said to her. 'When Suzy goes off to the kitchen to get in the dumb waiter and I go upstairs to wait for her to open the flat door from the inside, I'll need you to keep a watch out for Miss Johnson coming out of her office. And as soon as you do, you race ahead of her up the stairs and come and warn me, okay?'

Sally puffed out her chest importantly. 'You can count on me, Aunty Izzie.'

Izzie gnawed her bottom lip anxiously. She just wanted to get this over and done with.

CHAPTER TWENTY-FIVE

At just before four the next afternoon everyone was in position, Izzy having first checked the residents were all occupied and commandeered Alma into helping them wrap up their Christmas presents. Leonie was working inside her office, observed by Sally from her stance by the Christmas tree. To any onlooker she was admiring the pretty ornaments adorning it. Hopefully by now Suzy was pulling herself up to the second floor inside the dumb waiter. A highly charged Izzie stood outside the Johnsons' flat, waiting for Suzy to open the door.

The seconds seemed to drag by. Inwardly she screamed, Come on, Suzy, hurry! Please hurry. Then she started to panic that the girl had somehow been discovered in the dumb waiter and was being questioned. But then, she reasoned with herself, none of the residents ventured into the kitchen. If they did need anything from it, they would ask either herself or Alma to oblige. Then another worry replaced that one. Her own heart was hammering so painfully, ringing so loudly in her own ears, she feared it could be heard all over Westleigh Lodge and everyone would start to investigate where the noise was coming from and find out it was her.

Suddenly, to her horror, one of her fears came to fruition as a door opening further down the corridor caught her attention and she froze rigid. Amelia Austin was coming out of her room. Hardly daring to breathe she watched frantically as the old lady, with slow deliberate movements, shut her door behind her and to Izzie's most grateful thanks turned in the direction of the stairs and slowly made her way down the corridor away from Izzie.

Just then a sound from inside the flat alerted her. It was the turning of the Yale lock. Then the door opened and Suzy's grinning face was looking back at her. Izzie immediately slipped inside, closing the door behind her.

'Oh, thank God you're all right, Suzy, I was beginning to think you'd been caught. Anyway, you get off back downstairs now and leave me to it.'

Suzy's angelic face puckered. 'Oh, but . . .'

'No buts, Suzy, please do as I tell you,' said Izzie sternly. 'Collect your sister and go and do what you normally do with the residents in the lounge. I don't want you two involved in this any more.'

Izzie then pulled open the flat door and tentatively poked out her head to check the coast was clear. Satisfied it was, she pushed Suzy outside. She headed towards the open door to the Johnsons' lounge. The doors to the other four rooms were closed. To Izzie's knowledge most people kept address books on their telephone table. That's where she was going to begin her search.

As she arrived inside the lounge the first thing she observed was that Leonie had already started packing for their intended move as the room was bare of adornments and several boxes were stacked against a wall by the radiogram cabinet. Then she spotted the telephone table she was seeking. As she made to go over to it, papers lying on a coffee table in the middle of the room, a tasteful three-piece suite surrounding it, caught Izzie's eye. They looked official. Despite the fact that she was conscious of her overwhelming need to find what she was seeking and get herself out of here unobserved, she couldn't help but take a look.

Picking up the document, she scanned her eyes over it. Not that she was conversant with matters of such a nature, but it appeared to be a document for the transfer of ownership of Westleigh Lodge from Jenny Johnson to her daughter. Izzie frowned quizzically. If the place was being sold, why would the deeds have to be transferred from Jenny Johnson to Leonie first before the property was transferred to Mrs Pain on her purchase of it? It didn't make sense to Izzie. But there was no time to think about it now. Replacing the document, she dashed over to the telephone table where to her relief, sitting by the black Bakelite telephone, was a small red leather-bound book. Picking up the red book, she opened it and from the alphabetical cut-outs running down the side of the pages selected the 'Js'. She couldn't believe her luck to see that the first entry in that section was for a Miss Lillian Johnson and beside it an address and telephone number in Nottinghamshire. Laying the book down on the telephone table, she quickly jotted both address and telephone number on the adjacent note pad, tearing off the page and putting it in her pocket. Then she shut the address book, making sure she replaced it in exactly the position she had found it.

Spinning on her heel, she retraced her steps back to the hallway where she was just about to reopen the front door and check the coast was clear to let herself out, when a sound coming from within the flat froze her. She strained her ears. It was a voice. Someone was calling out. It was coming from behind one of the closed doors off the hallway. The voice was laboured-sounding, dopey. 'Leonie,' it was saying. 'Leonie, is that you?'

Izzie's mouth fell open. Despite its contorted tones, she knew who that voice belonged to. But she must be mistaken. Jenny was in a village in Nottinghamshire caring for her sick relative, it couldn't belong to her. But, regardless, whoever the voice belonged to was in great distress and needed her help. The voice called out again and Izzie realised which room it was coming from. She tried to open the door but it wouldn't budge. It was stuck. No, it was locked. Why? No time to wonder, as the person inside was calling out again. 'I'm coming,' Izzie automatically called back. 'Hold on, I won't be a minute.' Thankfully the key was in the lock. She turned it and hurried inside.

The sight that met her eyes brought her to an immediate standstill. Against the wall stood a bed and in it was Jenny Johnson. Her usually immaculate hair was wildly tousled, night-wear crumpled, her whole appearance that of someone who'd been bedridden for a while. She was acting as if coming out of a drunken stupor, trying to raise herself into a sitting position but unable to find the strength to do it and falling back against the pillows.

'Leonie, is that you? Oh, I feel so dreadful,' she was saying. 'My head feels like I've a woolly cloud in it. My body feels so heavy. What's wrong with me, Leonie?'

Pulling herself together, Izzie shot over to the head of the bed and knelt down beside it, taking Jenny's hand in hers. 'It's me, Mrs Johnson, Izzie.'

Jenny looked at her. It was obvious she was fighting to focus her swimming vision. 'Izzie? Oh, it is you, Izzie. Could you get me a glass of water, please? I'm so thirsty.'

Izzie's thoughts were racing rapidly. Nothing about this situation was making sense to her. Why had Leonie lied to everyone, saying that her mother was nursing a sick aunt, when all the time she was in her flat – and, more disconcertingly, locked in her bedroom? Then a terrible thought struck her. Was it that it was Jenny Johnson herself who was terminally ill and Leonie was keeping this from everyone? That could be the only explanation. But Leonie locking her mother inside her bedroom still didn't make sense to Izzie.

'Oh, yes, of course I can, Mrs Johnson.'

On the other side of the bed, Izzie spotted a glass and water decanter. Quickly, she filled the glass from the decanter. As she began to aid Mrs Johnson into a sitting position she caught sight of a small dish almost hidden behind a box of Kleenex. The dish held small white pills, about half a dozen or so. If this was Mrs Johnson's medication, why wasn't it in a proper bottle? She looked more closely at the pills and the 'M' stamped in the middle of them told her what they were: Mogadon. But they were sleeping aids, not medication for a terminal illness. Then Jenny's symptoms registered with Izzie. She was showing all the classic signs of someone coming out of a drug-induced sleep, the sort a couple of Mogadons would produce. These must be the pills that had mysteriously disappeared from the full bottle in the nurses' room. The residents hadn't suffered from mass insomnia after all. But why was Jenny dosing herself up with sleeping tablets so assiduously she hardly seemed to know where she was?

Then Izzie remembered the transfer of ownership document

from Jenny Johnson to her daughter. And all the secrecy surrounding the sale of Westleigh Lodge. As though someone had flicked a switch in her brain, Izzie knew exactly what was going on.

Leonie was in the process of robbing her mother. By rendering her unconscious with sleeping pills, Leonie was free to negotiate the sale of the business unhindered. Fuddled from the pills, Jenny Johnson could be duped by her daughter into transferring the deeds of Westleigh Lodge over to Leonie so she was then legally at liberty to sign the sale contract. Was her plan to abscond with the proceeds then, leaving her own mother stripped of everything she owned? Faced with the facts before her that was the only conclusion Izzie could draw. She couldn't believe that beneath Leonie's pretty façade lurked such a calculating monster. How could a lovely woman like Jenny Johnson have given birth to such a monster?

'Izzie, the water, please,' Jenny was saying thickly to her.

Jolted from her thoughts she said, 'Oh, yes, Mrs Johnson. Let me help ease you up first.' Gently she guided Jenny into a slumped position and put the glass of water to her lips.

Once she had sipped from it, Jenny looked at Izzie. 'What's happening to me?' she asked. 'I can't remember anything really, just bits and pieces and they're so hazy. Leonie was giving me drinks and telling me I needed to take pills to make me better. Then she was there again, telling me the same thing. Over and over, Izzie. Just what illness do I have?'

Izzie needed to tell her exactly what was going on but first Jenny needed to be compos mertis in order to be able to take it in. After that the police needed to be involved. How Jenny was going to take that, Izzie couldn't imagine. Nothing could be worse than finding out that the daughter you cherished was in the process of committing a heinous crime against you.

A strong cup of tea would help clear her mind a little. No, strong black coffee would be better.

'I'm just going to get you a hot drink. After you've drunk it and you're thinking clearer, I'll explain what's happened to you, Mrs Johnson.'

In the kitchen, Izzie lit the gas under the kettle on the stove and spooned a heap of coffee powder into a mug. As she waited for the kettle to boil, dreading what she had to divulge to Jenny, her eyes fell on a packet of Complan, a food supplement given to sick people unable to stomach solid food. So that was what Leonie had been feeding her mother on since she had started carrying out her diabolical plan. Well, at least Izzie knew the young woman hadn't been planning to starve her mother to death.

Having added cold water to the scalding liquid in order not to burn Jenny's lips, Izzie took it through to her.

After she had obediently sipped the coffee she said, 'My brain doesn't feel quite so fuzzy now, dear. I'm thinking a little clearer. You're going to tell me something terrible, Izzie, I know you are. I'm dying, aren't I?'

The time had come for Jenny to hear just what Izzie had happened upon. Taking a deep breath, she opened her mouth to speak. Before she could utter a word, a voice challenged her.

'What's going on? What are you doing in here?'

Izzie looked over to the doorway to see Leonie glaring at her. It was obvious she was shocked to find someone with her mother.

'Oh, Leonie dear, please don't shout at Izzie. She's . . .'

'Leave my mother alone and get out!' Leonie commanded, cutting her mother off. 'You've no right to be in here,' she cried. 'Can't you see my mother's ill? If I'd wanted your help nursing her, I would have asked for it. Now she needs her medication . . .'

'Oh, yes? More sleeping pills to knock her out,' Izzie shouted out, jumping off the bed to glare at her accusingly.

'Sleeping pills? What is Izzie saying?' a baffled Jenny asked.

'Tell her, Miss Johnson. Tell her what I'm talking about,' Izzie demanded. Then: 'I know what you're up to.'

'Up to? What does she mean, Leonie?' Jenny asked, confused.

'Nothing, Mother,' she cried, eyes darting wildly. 'I'm not up to anything.'

'Yes, you are,' Izzie shouted back at her. 'Well, if you won't come clean to your mother then I will.' There was no easy way of telling her employer this, but she had to be truthful. 'Miss

Johnson has been drugging you with sleeping pills so she can be free to arrange the sale of Westleigh Lodge.' She then turned back to face Leonie. 'I've seen the document transferring ownership from Mrs Johnson to you. I know you were going to trick your mother into signing it. It's my guess you were then going to run off with the proceeds once the sale had gone through.'

Jenny was staring at her daughter aghast. 'Oh, Leonie, is this true?'

'No!' she cried. Then her shoulders sagged in defeat. 'Yes, it is,' she admitted. 'Oh, but, Mother, it's not like Izzie is saying. You gave me no choice! I tried so often to make you see sense! Your squandering was ruining us financially, but you just would not listen to me. I was so worried, I didn't know what to do to make you see reason.'

Jenny was staring at her, horrified. 'But you know I never intended to make money when I set up this establishment. My aim was to provide the best standard of care I could for the number of people I could comfortably manage. I'd pay decent wages to enough qualified staff to care for them properly and do my best to ensure they enjoyed what years were left to them. If there was enough money left in the kitty to give my residents extra treats, then I was happy to spend it. I had everything I needed, made sure you were paid decently for your work, so what better use for the rest of the proceeds than making the lives of old people brighter? You're worried about your financial future, aren't you? You think I haven't been properly mindful of that in my own need to fulfil my dreams. Leonie, I intended to tell you of our true financial situation on your twenty-fifth birthday, when I felt you'd be old enough to cope with the responsibility, adult enough to use it wisely.

'I never needed a penny of your father's money to fund this place, I had enough of my own left to me by my mother. Half of it I put safely away to have something to fall back on should I need it, and the rest I ploughed into buying this place and refurbishing it. All the money your father left when he passed away, including the settlement from the insurance company, I put in trust for you. It's a substantial amount, Leonie, enough for you to set up your own business if you wish and to buy yourself a decent house. I kept telling you not to worry about your future but you wouldn't listen to me.'

Leonie was totally flabbergasted by the news. 'Then all this was for nothing. I could have let you carry on doing exactly what you were, knowing I would be financially able in my own right to take good care of you when Westleigh Lodge went bankrupt, as I feared it would.' She shook her head. 'You're so very wrong, Mother. It wasn't my own future I was worried for when I resorted to this, it was yours. I could always work for my living, but you're not getting any younger. All I could see was you ending up in rented rooms, having to return to the grind of nursing – that was, if you were still young enough to work – and me only able to help you out a little with the wage I earned. I couldn't bear that for you, Mother, I love you so much! You run this place the way you do because you want the best for the old people who live here under your care. Well, I resorted to what I did because I wanted to make sure my own mother, who didn't seem to care about her own future, only other people's, was as well looked after in her old age.

'I hated having to do what I did to you, Mother, so I could carry out my plan. I hated getting rid of our loyal staff and all the other things I had to do to make this place an attractive proposition to a buyer. I thought I'd crack under the strain of it all so I did my best to push it through quickly. I wasn't going to abscond with the proceeds, like Izzie's accused me of, nothing could be further from the truth. I was going to take control of it and buy you a nice house, the type we lived in with Father, and with what was left over give you an income to live on each month. I would get a job and live on my own wage. That's the truth of it, Mother, you have to believe me! I can prove what I'm saying. I've booked us both rooms at a nice hotel while you choose a house you'd like to live in. I have the details of several properties I thought you might like to look at. I've also paid a deposit on a storage place where we can leave our belongings in the meantime.' Tears brimming in her eyes, she begged, 'Oh, Mother, please say you understand why I did this?'

Jenny had her hands clasped to her ashen face. 'Oh, Leonie, this is all my fault. I've been so wrapped up in making sure I was doing the best for my old people, I never stopped to look at what was going on with my own daughter. At the time I bought this place I should have told you how I was funding it and why I felt at liberty to be as generous as I was with its profits. But I thought it was enough that I'd told you you had no worries for the future, and that as your mother you would just trust me on that. You see, I worried that if you did know your financial future was secure, you might not feel the need to equip yourself to handle it wisely but just squander it away when it became yours. It never crossed my mind for a minute it was *my* future you'd be worried about Oh, Leonie, when you kept on at me to curb my spending habits, I should at least have explained to you that we weren't just dependent on the Lodge's profits, that I had enough put by in an investment account to provide very well for us if it came to it. I realise now I should have done.'

Her arms went out to Leonie then and her daughter needed no persuasion to take advantage of this.

Izzie took it as her cue to leave mother and daughter alone. She no longer had any fears that Leonie Johnson had ever had criminal intentions towards Jenny. What she had done, terrible as it was, was purely from love for the woman who had given birth to her. Izzie herself had impinged far enough on their private matters.

Just before Izzie finished her shift that night and went to visit Pat to inform her and her daughters what had transpired, Leonie sought her out to request her presence in the flat as her mother wished to speak to her. Izzie arrived and was thankful to find Jenny dressed and sitting in an armchair, if looking very tired. She asked Izzie to explain to her why she had taken it upon herself to enter the flat in the first place. After Izzie had – leaving out the Brian Knowles affair and the sad death of Walter Waters during her absence, feeling Jenny had enough to cope with and these were things she could be informed of later – Jenny thanked her profusely for her brave and loyal actions and for acting over and above the way most other people would have attempted to do. As soon as she was back at the helm all the changes Leonie had instigated would be repealed, she told Izzie. It was then Leonie's turn to speak. She said she could not express how eternally grateful she was that Izzie had put a stop to her own misguided actions and had averted the dire consequences.

Izzie appreciated their generosity. The most important thing to her, though, was that Westleigh Lodge would not now be sold to anyone, let alone the likes of Mrs Pain. All the residents were saved from a terrible fate at her hands.

CHAPTER TWENTY-SIX

From her stance just inside the lounge doorway, Izzie surveyed the scene before her.

Colourful paper trimmings hung from the ceiling, bunches of balloons were tied about, garlands of berried holly placed around the walls. In the dining room, tables had been cleared of debris after the most sumptuous Christmas dinner, to make way for an equally sumptuous buffet tea. There were enough bottles of quality sherry and whisky, port and beer, to afford the whole gathering an air of good cheer.

It was the people here, though, who were responsible for creating the true spirit of Christmas. At Westleigh Lodge the old, not so old, young and very young, found joy in each other's company.

'What are you standing on your own here for?' asked Pat, coming to join her.

'Oh, I'm just savouring the atmosphere, Pat.'

Pat leaned back against the wall and scanned her eyes around the room. 'Jenny Johnson sure knows how to hold a Christmas party. Best Christmas Day I've ever had, Izzie. Arnold was saying as much when I asked him a minute ago if he was enjoying himself. I don't need to ask the girls. You only have to look at them to see they are.'

Izzie's eyes settled on her beloved nieces, pretty in their best frocks, the centre of attention amongst a circle of their dear elderly friends. They were all showing each other their gifts from Santa – the girls' ones extra-special by way of a thank you from both Jenny and Leonie.

'Do you regret not extending Mrs Johnson's invitation to your mother? She might have enjoyed herself,' Izzie said.

Pat looked astonished. 'Do I hell as like! I appreciated Mrs Johnson's offer very much but my mother is only happy when she knows she's been the cause of making someone else miserable. She wouldn't have enjoyed herself here. Even an expert like her in creating misery couldn't have managed to upset anyone here today. Look at them all, Izzie. Everyone has a smile on their face. They all look like the Christmas Fairy has granted their wishes.'

Just then Izzie saw Jenny and Leonie Johnson give each other affectionate pecks on the cheek before they parted to continue their duties as joint hostess. Izzie was happy to see that recent events had not damaged their relationship, but if anything strengthened the bond between mother and daughter.

Pat then asked her sister-in-law, now her dearest friend, 'Has the Christmas Fairy granted your wish, Izzie?'

'Oh, most definitely. I've everyone I love and care for around me right now. What more could I wish for?' She caught sight of Steven then, disrobed of the Santa suit he'd worn to dish out the sack of presents Jenny Johnson had given him for distribution amongst the throng, and was back comfortably dressed in a smart pair of slacks and white shirt under a blue jumper. He held a glass of port in his hand, talking to Joyce and Beattie and their respective husbands. Izzie was in no doubt he was welcoming them back to the staff at Westleigh Lodge. Well, there was something else she could wish for though she doubted it would ever be granted. 'Has the fairy granted your Christmas wish for you?' she asked.

Pat had not missed the wistful glance Izzie had given Steven just now. Neither had she missed the look of regret on his face a short while ago when he had witnessed Peregrine Danvers giving Izzie a peck on her cheek under the mistletoe. She shook her head. 'It's not been granted yet, but there's still time,' she said optimistically.

Izzie cast a look at her. She couldn't think what Pat's wish could be. She had not mentioned anything she was hankering after.

Pat meanwhile was wishing her special Christmas wish would

hurry up and be granted. Trouble was, the two people who could bring it about didn't look like they were ever going to. Maybe this particular wish of hers needed a little help. And she was just the person to give it. Well, it was *her* wish after all.

After a moment of pondering her plan, she turned to Izzie and asked her, 'Would you fetch me a glass of lemonade from the dining room, please?'

The ever-obliging Izzie automatically responded, 'Yes, of course.'

Immediately she had gone towards the dining room, Pat hurried over to Steven Landers. Excusing herself to Beattie, Joyce and their respective husbands for interrupting the conversation, she pulled Steven aside and said to him, 'I'm Izzie's sister-in-law, Patricia Jenkins. She's asked me to ask if you could spare her a couple of minutes in the nurses' room. She needs to talk to you.'

'Is Izzie ill?' he asked worriedly.

'No, she's fine.'

'Oh. Then what does she want to talk to me about in private?'

She gave a shrug. 'No idea, Doctor Landers.'

'Oh, well, I'd better go and find out for myself then.'

As soon as he had gone off in the direction of the nurses' room, Pat hurried across to the dining room where she met Izzie coming out armed with the glass of lemonade she had gone to fetch.

Taking the glass from her, Pat said, 'Thanks for that. Oh, Doctor Landers has asked me to ask you if you could spare him a couple of minutes in the nurses' room? He wants a private word.'

Izzie looked puzzled. 'With me? What about?'

Pat gave a shrug. 'He didn't say.'

'Oh! Well, I'd better go and see what he wants me for.'

As Izzie departed for the nurses' room Pat called after her, 'Just a thought, but maybe while you have him on his own you ought to give him that apology you owe him for the way you treated him? It's the least he deserves. And you know, Izzie, good will at Christmas and all that.'

Yes, Pat was right, she thought. If she got a chance, she would.

Izzie found Steven perched on the edge of the table in the nurses' room, waiting for her. He smiled at her welcomingly when she entered the room. 'You wanted a word, Izzie?'

She looked at him, taken aback. 'Oh, but Pat told me *you* wanted a word with me?'

They both looked at each other quizzically.

'It seems to me your sister-in-law has had a little too much Christmas cheer,' said Steven, grinning good-naturedly.

Pat hadn't seemed drunk in the slightest. Regardless, though, Izzie said, 'Yes, it does. I apologise for her, Doctor Landers, and for wasting your time.'

She made to leave the room when she remembered Pat's words about the apology she still owed him. Taking a deep breath, and hoping she would be able once and for all to get it over and done with, she said, 'There's another apology you deserve, Doctor Landers.'

'There is?' he asked, bemused.

'Yes. From me.'

He looked surprised. 'You? Whatever do you owe me an apology for?'

'Well, I was very rude to you the night you kindly took me for a meal, and for a while afterwards. It was unforgivable of me and I am so sorry for my behaviour. Anyway, I hope you will accept my sincere apology.'

She turned to depart but he stopped her by saying, 'Just a minute, Izzie.' He waited until she had turned back to face him and he had her attention. 'Knowing what I do of you, I can only imagine you must have had your reasons. Was it something I did? If it was then it is I who owe you an apology, Izzie.'

'Oh, no, it was nothing you did at all.'

'Oh! Then something I said?'

'Well, not exactly.'

He frowned at her. 'I don't understand?'

She sighed. 'Doctor Landers, I got the wrong end of the stick over something you were talking about.'

His confusion deepened. 'Something I was talking about? We were discussing the menu . . . what to choose, weren't we?'

'Yes, we were, but you were also talking about your mother. How she likes to make sure you have a good dinner every day, and telling me how wonderful she is. I thought . . . well, you see, because of the way you were singing her praises, I thought you were interviewing me to work for you as her companion.'

He looked stunned. 'What! Why on earth would you think that?'

She gulped and shuffled her feet awkwardly. 'This is very embarrassing for me to admit but . . . well . . . you see, for fifteen years I was stupid enough to let myself be conned by a man into thinking he loved me and wanted to marry me once he was free from his dependent mother. But all the time he was just using me as an unpaid companion for her only I was too gullible to see that. As soon as his mother died, he married someone else.'

Steven was totally stunned by her confession. 'Oh! Oh, I see.' He slapped his hand to his forehead. 'Oh, goodness, now it all makes sense to me. Why you insisted on telling me you weren't looking for another job or part-time work either.' His eyes then bored into hers and he said with conviction, 'That man was the stupid one, Izzie, if he was blind enough not to see what he had in you. Well, his stupidity is someone else's good fortune.'

'Very nice of you to say that in an effort to try and make me feel better, Doctor Landers. Anyway, I've told you now and hopefully you won't think too badly of me.'

She was about to depart but he stopped her by grabbing her arm.

'I'm so glad you've told me this, Izzie. I really did think at the time that you'd suddenly developed a headache that night and were off-hand with me afterwards because you didn't enjoy being with me.'

That was the last thing she wanted him to think. Before she could stop herself, she blurted, 'Oh, no, I did enjoy being with you, very much.'

His face lit up. 'You did! Oh, I enjoyed being with you too. You're a very special lady, Izzie, and I'd really like the chance to get to know you a lot better, if you'll let me? Well, now you know it's you I'm interested in and that I'm definitely not interviewing you for a job as minder to my mother . . .' He paused to look at her intently. 'If I were to ask you out for dinner again, would you accept, Izzie?'

Suddenly she knew what Pat's Christmas wish was. And that she had given it a nudge along its way in an effort to get it fulfilled. It looked like she had succeeded. A surge of excitement swelled up inside her. 'Oh, yes, most definitely, Doctor Landers.'

'Oh, that's wonderful. That's great.' His face bore the look of someone who had just been granted their every wish. 'Would tomorrow night be too soon?'

Most definitely not, she thought. For her it was the sooner the better, and she knew without doubt that he felt the same.